THE
DECEPTION

Book **Five** in the
Munro Family Series

CHRIS TAYLOR

LCT Productions Pty Ltd
18364 Kamilaroi Highway, Narrabri NSW 2390

ISBN. 978-1-925119-09-1 (Print)

The Deception is a work of fiction. Names, characters, places, brands, media and incidents either are the product of the author's imagination or are used fictitiously. Any resemblance to actual persons, living or dead, events, or locales, is entirely coincidental.

Published in the United States of America

Ambitious newspaper journalist **Savannah O'Neill** will do anything for a story, even if it means pretending to be a prostitute in Sydney's most exclusive brothel. She's there on a tip-off that underage girls are being held illegally and kept compliant with illicit drugs. What's more, unidentified bodies of young women have turned up in Sydney Harbour and at least one of them is linked to the brothel.

Detective Will Rutledge has vowed to destroy the man he holds responsible for his brother's suicide. Vince Maranoa is the kingpin of Sydney's illegal drug industry: He's also the owner of the city's most exclusive brothel. Working undercover with the New South Wales Drug Enforcement Agency, Will is determined to put Maranoa behind bars.

When Savannah and Will cross paths at the brothel, there's an instant attraction, despite the fact she presumes he's a cohort of the crime boss and Will assumes she's a prostitute under Maranoa's employ.

With both of them determined to pursue their personal agendas to infiltrate the covert life of Maranoa, they will both be left gasping when the brothel's secrets are finally revealed...

THE MUNRO FAMILY SERIES

THE PROFILER
(Book One—Clayton and Ellie)

THE INVESTIGATOR
(Book Two—Riley and Kate)

THE PREDATOR
(Book Three—Brandon and Alex)

THE BETRAYAL
(Book Four—Declan and Chloe)

THE DECEPTION
(Book Five—Will and Savannah)

THE NEGOTIATOR
(Book Six—Andy and Cally)

THE RANSOM
(Book Seven—Lane and Zara)

THE DEFENDANT
(Book Eight—Chase and Josie)

THE SHOOTING
(Book Nine—Tom and Lily)

THE MAKER
(Book Ten—Bryce and Chanel)

DEDICATION

This book is dedicated to my children who have given up asking when dinner will be ready and as always, to the love of my life, my husband, Linden.

ACKNOWLEDGEMENTS

As usual, no book comes into being without a lot of help and support by my friends and family. A world of thanks must go to my friend and fellow author Angela Bissell, critique partner extraordinaire, and a girl who loves the Munro family as much as I do.

To Pat Thomas, the best editor in the world. To Alisha and Damon Za, thank you for yet another fantastic cover. To my sister, Nicole Guihot, thank you for your excellent editorial comments and suggestions. Nic, I hope you like the final result.

To Amy Atwell and her dedicated staff at Author EMS who are so much more than book formatters. Amy, once again, thank you for your magic.

To the fantastic writer organizations such as Romance Writers of Australia, Romance Writers of America and Romance Writers of New Zealand for all the help, support and encouragement they offer new and aspiring writers, including me.

To my readers, thank you for your support and love for the Munro family. Your encouragement and enjoyment make this journey all worthwhile.

And lastly, to my friends and family, especially my husband and children. Thank you for putting up with late dinners and even later conversations as I've emerged day after day from the sometimes scary but always enthralling world I've created on my computer.

Prologue

Billy hefted the dead weight of the girl's slight body over his shoulder and strode toward the water. Her head lolled to one side. Her arms hung lifelessly down his back. He was glad it was too dark to see the mask of terror that had frozen on her face. He'd seen it earlier, of course, while Vince tortured her. He'd seen it again, right before he'd killed her.

She'd stared at him through eyes that had been almost swollen shut from Vince's beating. Her breath had rattled through broken teeth and even more broken insides. It was probably a relief when Billy snuffed out what was left of her life with a pillow jammed hard against her face. She'd barely even struggled...

"Hurry up, Kid. We don't have all fuckin' night."

The impatient command was issued from somewhere behind him. He glanced over his shoulder. The glow from a cigarette briefly illuminated the narrow-eyed features of his boss.

Vince Maranoa blew out a mouthful of smoke and then hawked up a glob of phlegm. The sound of it turned Billy's stomach, but he knew better than to complain.

Turning away, he plowed through the low, coarse bushes clinging to the cliff top that surrounded part of Sydney's eastern shoreline. His boots sunk into valleys of soft sand and scraped across the rocks. Slight she might be, but the dead woman was a cement pylon across his shoulders.

"You could give me a hand here, you know," he grunted half heartedly.

"You're weak as piss, Billy. I knew I should have let Georgie do the job. Just fuckin' throw her over and stop your fuckin' whingin'."

Billy bit back an angry retort. If he didn't want to be the next corpse tossed into Sydney Harbour, he'd best watch his mouth. Just like the girl in his arms, Mia had learned the hard way: You didn't fuck with Vince Maranoa.

Getting as close to the cliff's edge as he dared, Billy swung the body off his shoulders. With a soft thud she landed on the ground at his feet in a tangle of arms and legs. *Rigor mortis* had yet to set in.

Taking a few moments to catch his breath, he stood back with his hands on his hips. His chest heaved. He sure as hell now knew why they called it a dead weight.

"What are you waitin' for? Someone could drive by any minute. Throw her over the fuckin' edge and let's get out of here."

Without even a twinge of guilt or another thought for the girl on the sand at his feet, Billy bent forward and toed her with his boot. Leaning over, he rolled her to the edge. He glanced over his shoulder and met Vince's hard stare. Turning back, he gave one last heave and let her go...

CHAPTER 1

Saturday night

Detective Will Rutledge took care to conceal the anger that burned just below the surface. Plastering a pleasant smile on his face, he adjusted his tie and sauntered into the subtly lit, inner-Sydney brothel. The sweet, pungent aroma of incense, cigars and expensive cologne thickened the air. Smoke curled around the crowd of designer-suited men. Most were seated at round tables set close to a sunken stage that dominated the center of the room.

Will strode over to the bar, his black-on-black Armani blending in with ease. Sliding onto a red velvet-covered stool, he glanced at his watch.

Eleven-thirty. Half an hour to go.

Facing the stage, he scanned the scene, noting everything. *Patrons. Bouncers. Exits.* A door on the other side of the bar was marked with a sign that read: Staff Only.

Restless anticipation hovered over the men. Laughter and conversation grew louder, in line with the increased frequency of orders from the bar.

"What'll it be?"

Will swung around and eyed the tuxedo-clad bartender.

"I'll have a scotch, thanks."

Within moments, a drink was placed in front of him. He

fished a few bills from his wallet and placed them on the bar. "So, what's on tonight?"

The man offered a leering smile. "If you're into tight-assed, dark-haired girls with nice tits, you won't be disappointed."

Will eyed him calmly over the rim of his glass. "And if you're not?"

The man bristled. "Then you're in the wrong place, mate. This is a brothel, not a gay bar."

Will narrowed his eyes, but his voice remained mild. "You've got me all wrong, *mate*. I'm not adverse to a nice piece of ass, but I like a little something else with it, a bit of extra fizz. You get my drift?"

The man's expression relaxed. He leaned over the bar. Thick muscles bunched beneath his black suit coat. "You should have said so. I'm sure we have something you might be interested in."

"What are you offering?"

The bartender bent closer and lowered his voice. "We call it the *Room of Dreams*. We stock whatever turns you on: Grass, coke, pills, ice... You name it, we've got it. Everyone knows Vince has the best gear in town and you can enjoy all of it from the privacy and comfort of your own cubicle."

Will's expression remained indifferent. "Keep talking."

"I'll need to get the okay from Vince, first. He has to approve anyone who wants to buy extras like that. What's your name?"

"Rutledge. William Rutledge."

The bartender's face creased into a smile. "Rutledge? You're not Robert's son?"

Will tensed and then forced himself to relax. He was used to people recognizing his surname. His father was a big player in the advertising world. He'd expected his oldest son to follow in his footsteps. The fact that Will had chosen to go into law enforcement was still a source of aggravation between them. There was no way his father would breathe a word about his career choice—to anyone—let alone an employee of a brothel. Besides, it was ludicrous to consider his father would fraternize in the Black Opal, no matter how exclusive.

Aware that the barman still eyed him with frank interest, Will eased out his breath and nodded. "Yeah, that would be me."

"Well, what do you know? I'll run it by Vince, but I'm sure he'll be more than willing to give the nod of approval to the son of Robert Rutledge."

"How long will it take? When can I sample the wares?"

"Vince is busy right now, but if you stop by in a day or so, I'm sure I'll be able to give you the nod. We can take it from there."

Taking care to hide his frustration, Will slid off the stool. "Hey, I'm here now and I have a wad of cash burning a hole in my pocket. Once Vince finds out who my father is, he'll bust his balls putting me on his list of approved customers. You said so yourself. How about you just tell me where this dream room is?"

As soon as the words were out of his mouth, he realized he'd blundered. All signs of friendliness left the bartender's face. He leaned over the bar, a menacing glint in his small, black eyes.

"Hey, you listen to me. Nobody, and I mean *nobody*, gets access to the gear without Vince's approval. I don't care who you are; you'll wait like everybody else. If you don't like the rules, you take it up with Vince." With another hard look, the bartender moved away and turned his attention to a noisy group at the other end of the bar.

Damn! Will cursed under his breath. He should have known it wouldn't be that easy. It'd been worth a shot, though. And at the worst, it had only put him back a day or so. This time Monday night, he'd be that much closer to blowing the lid on the dark secrets concealed behind the velvet-clad doors. From the intelligence they'd already gathered on Vince Maranoa, it was clear the brothel's notorious owner wouldn't give them up without a fight.

A commotion at the end of the bar snagged his

attention. An argument had broken out between two men. The bartender stepped forward to intervene.

Seizing the moment, Will stepped away from the bar and pushed through the press of bodies. He headed toward the door marked with the sign. With a last glance over his shoulder, he opened it and slipped through.

Finding himself in a poorly lit corridor, he gave his eyes a moment to adjust to the sudden darkness. Shadows revealed closed doors on either side. Small lamps glowed dully above each one, casting just enough light so that the room numbers were visible.

Grateful for the thick carpet that swallowed the sound of his footsteps, he moved to the first door and listened. Silence greeted him. Alert to the slightest noise, he turned the door handle.

It opened smoothly.

He held his breath and inched inside. A pair of antique lamps set on low nightstands on either side of a king-sized bed emitted a soft glow, illuminating most of the room. It was empty. Relief soughed through him.

He scanned the room. A pile of condoms and tubes of lubricant sat on the nightstand nearest to him. Dildos and other sex toys were laid out on the opposite one. Bondage equipment was scattered throughout, some of it hanging from hooks on the walls. Fantasies limited only by imagination could be bought and had here, but it wasn't the room he was looking for.

Drawing the door closed, he moved to the next and put his ear to the wooden panel. Faint voices came from behind it. He prayed the hinges were as well-oiled as the previous ones and eased the door open.

Light poured through the crack. A half-filled suitcase lay open on an unmade bed and an Asian woman stood nearby with a pile of clothes in her arms. She spoke in heavily accented English.

"It will work, trust me. No one will know." Tossing the clothing into the suitcase, she moved out of his line of vision.

The reply was hesitant. "I don't know, Malee."

Another woman came into view. His gut clenched. A mane of red hair fell across her shoulders in long, messy waves. Green eyes, full lips and pert breasts barely concealed beneath a black lace bodysuit crowded his mind. He cursed under his breath and redirected his attention to their conversation.

"What if he suspects something? What if we're caught? Are you sure there isn't an easier way?"

"No." The woman identified as Malee walked back into his range of vision and dumped toiletries into the suitcase. She spun around to face the redhead, gesticulating with her finger. "Listen to me. I got you in here. I gave you what you wanted. Now, it's *my* turn."

The redheaded woman remained silent. Some of the bravado left the woman called Malee and her shoulders slumped. Her voice dropped lower and Will had to strain to hear her.

"Mia managed to escape a couple of nights ago. We were close. Like sisters. Vince knows that. I'm the first one he's going to question when he discovers she's gone. If I don't get out of here, I'm dead. I'm *dead!* Don't you understand *anything?*"

The reply was quick and full of contrition. "Malee, I'm sorry. I know I promised to help you any way I could, I just didn't expect... I mean, that I'd have to go out there and—"

"Put a wig on. There's one in the cupboard. No one will notice. Vince won't notice. Billy won't notice. They're busy tonight. That's why we have to do it now."

"Who's Billy? What do you mean, busy?"

"I mean—"

A noise from somewhere behind him muffled the reply and drew a silent curse from Will. Belatedly, he realized the sound was coming closer and cast around for somewhere to hide.

Darting back to the empty room, he wrestled with the door handle.

Come on!

He lunged through the doorway just as the burly bartender

came into view. With no time to pull the door shut behind him, he prayed silently the man wouldn't notice anything amiss. The bartender's movements slowed. Plastered against the wall, Will held his breath.

Just walk on by, mate. Just walk on by. The thought echoed in Will's head. To his relief, the man continued down the corridor and disappeared. Across the hall, the women had also fallen silent. A prickle of curiosity tingled down his spine.

What were they trying to hide?

With his close shave uppermost in his mind, he drew in a breath, straightened his clothing and ducked out into the corridor. With a cautious glance left and right, he strode back the way he'd come. The search for the *Room of Dreams* would have to wait.

The crowd in the main reception room had swelled and the noise and laughter had taken on a harsher edge. Will blended into the throng lining the bar. What the hell had the woman meant—*busy*? Was Maranoa meeting with his suppliers tonight? Were the women involved? Who the hell was Billy?

Without warning, loud music pulsed from the stage's sound system. A roar of approval went up from the crowd. Will shouldered his way through the horde of men until he'd reached the front, ignoring the mutters of displeasure his actions provoked. If the women he'd overheard were dancing, he was sure he'd recognize them. Then he'd get them alone again and this time, he'd be the one asking the questions.

The throbbing house music increased to almost deafening levels, and all eyes were drawn to the stage. At least half a dozen dark-haired, scantily clad women entered from a set of stairs at one end of the platform. As far as Will could tell, they were all Asian.

Dressed in similar attire to the redhead—with the addition of brightly colored feather boas and black fishnet stockings—their painted faces held a look of dazed sensuality. Their lithe bodies began to gyrate to the sexual beat. Fixed smiles failed to reach their glassy-eyed stares.

The girls were high. No big surprises there. As they danced before him, he scanned their faces closely. He recognized the redhead and his gut tightened. She now wore a long black wig, but there was no mistaking her green-eyed gaze. He turned and tried to catch the eye of one of the bouncers. Anticipation coiled inside him.

The music swelled. Hips ground to the beat. The men surged forward, jostling each other in an effort to get closer. A solid *whumph* almost knocked the wind out of him as he took a shoulder to the kidneys. Stumbling forward, his boot caught on the wooden edge of the stage and he lost his balance.

"Fuck!" He toppled down toward the sunken platform and braced himself for a fall. He came down hard upon one of the dancers, pinning her to the floor beneath him. She shrieked in alarm and then struggled against him.

"Just hold still, damn it, so I can get up." Will raised himself on one elbow and stared into a pair of angry green eyes.

"Get off me, you clumsy jerk." The woman tried to move again.

With a curse, he rolled away and got to his feet. He mumbled an apology and his hand came out automatically to assist her.

Pointedly ignoring his outstretched hand, the woman got to her feet unaided and shakily resumed the dance. The other girls remained oblivious and continued to move their bodies to the beat.

Will climbed out and shouldered himself back into a spot at the front. He pinned the woman with his gaze. Watching her dance to the music, he tamped down his body's instinctive reaction. She twisted and turned and her lace-clad breasts dipped and swayed. Any minute, he expected them to fall out of their flimsy covering. Despite his best efforts to remain aloof, his cock hardened.

———————

Savannah O'Neill did her best to ignore the man in the front row who watched her with a flinty-eyed gaze. It wasn't easy. He towered over the other men. With his sable hair, fine physique and aura of refined sophistication, he looked like James Bond.

An image of her lying, cheating ex-fiancé flashed before her. She forced her gaze away, disgusted that one good-looking man—okay, one *exceptionally* good-looking man— had made her forget for even a moment her vow never to have her head turned by a male again.

A sweaty hand connected with her almost-bare thigh, startling her from her thoughts. She deftly side-stepped the drunken patron. The sea of desire-hardened faces blurred in front of her. Panic threatened.

What the hell had she gotten herself into this time?

She concentrated with narrow-eyed determination on her goal—a story. And not just any story. After interviewing Malee, she had a sensational one. Max O'Connor, her editor, would be thrilled. It might even mean a raise in pay, which would be more than welcome. Her brother's rehab bills were adding up.

Not that Vince Maranoa would know anything about that. She flicked her gaze around the smoky room. A rough calculation of the net worth of the men in front of her was mind boggling. She recognized a television executive, a high-profile lawyer and a well-known heart surgeon.

Without conscious thought, she sought out the man who'd fallen onto the stage. As her gaze connected with his for the second time that night, she felt lightheaded from the impact.

Blue steel stared back at her. Her heart pounded again, this time with nervous excitement. His eyes dipped to her mouth and then moved lower. She drew in a quick breath. A cool smile of appreciation tugged at the corners of his sensuous mouth. Finally, his gaze returned to her face.

She flushed under his appraisal, her face burning with embarrassment. He was staring at her like she was a delicious treat he was about to enjoy, nibble by nibble. And why wouldn't he? The man thought she was a prostitute. She was just thankful there'd been no sign of Vince Maranoa. Avoiding the notorious brothel owner was at the top of her list.

Savannah's face was stiff from smiling. The unaccustomed odors that thickened the air made her head spin. *Had Malee managed to escape?*

In desperation, she fought against a wave of dizziness, unable to believe the lengths she'd gone to for her story.

The music finally came to an end. She stumbled toward the staircase and staggered past the groping hands of the men who lined the stage. She almost tripped in her borrowed platform heels.

She shuddered with revulsion and genuine fear. A grip of steel tightened around her wrist. She squealed in panic. Spinning around, she came face to face with James Bond.

She gasped. Her heart pounded. The heat of the room enclosed her in its suffocating grip. Seconds later, blackness descended...

CHAPTER 2

A dim circle of light penetrated Savannah's closed eyelids. She struggled against an encroaching headache. Cracking open her eyes, she located the source of illumination. A lamp beside the bed where she lay had been switched on, bathing the room in a golden glow. Another quick peek confirmed she was in the room she'd recently vacated. She was relieved to note that Malee had disappeared, along with her suitcase.

How had she gotten there? All she could remember was the blur of noise, grasping men and semi-naked women... And *him*.

With a slight motion, she turned her head and realized the black wig had been lost somewhere along the way. Her hair spilled over the pillow in a tangled mess.

She must have fainted. If only she could remember, but her mind stayed stubbornly blank—aside from remembering the handsome stranger. She had way too many thoughts about him and every one of them was unwelcome.

She frowned in consternation. She'd rubbed shoulders with powerful men before. It wasn't like being close to a man who exuded an unmistakeable air of authority should have been enough to weaken her knees and yet she couldn't deny his effect on her...

As if she'd conjured him up, the man in question materialized beside the bed. Half of his face was in shadow, but there was no mistaking his broad-shouldered form or the mesmerizing gleam in his cobalt eyes.

She gasped, startled. "W-what are you doing here?" Wrenching herself into an upright position, she caught sight of her scanty attire and flushed with renewed embarrassment.

Grappling awkwardly with the bedspread, she did her best to cover herself. It was one thing to dance among a group of girls all similarly clothed. It was another thing entirely to be sprawled on a bed in a brothel with a man who presumed she was available.

"I wouldn't worry about that if I were you, sweetheart. I've already seen it, along with about seventy or eighty other men out there. Don't you think it's a little late for modesty?"

His deep drawl sent a shiver of awareness down her spine. Her cheeks burned. He was right, of course. Thank goodness he didn't know who she *really* was. She had to get out of there. Fast.

Hoping to maintain the charade with a show of confidence, she threw off the covering and climbed off the bed.

"Listen, I-I'm due back out on the floor in a little while and I-I have to freshen up. If you don't mind, I'd like you to leave." She marched to the door, ready to usher him out. His eyes narrowed—from suspicion or annoyance, she couldn't tell.

"Don't bother, Red. I locked it when I brought you in. I would have thought you were used to clients doing that."

Savannah gritted her teeth. She stared at the door and refused to answer him. The less he knew about her, the better. She'd bluff it and get rid of him so she could make good her escape.

Knowing she had no choice, she turned to face him.

He leaned against the dresser as if he belonged there. His legs were crossed at the ankles and a smile tugged at his lips. He looked like he'd stepped out of the pages of GQ magazine.

A shaft of light caught on the door key he twirled between his fingers. She cursed under her breath. This was going to be harder than she thought. Her mind worked furiously. She inched toward the chair where she'd draped the clothing she'd arrived in. It felt like a lifetime ago. He pushed away from the dresser and came toward her.

"Why don't you sit down so we can have a chat? I've wanted to..." He paused, a glint of amusement in his eyes. *"Chat...from the moment I saw you."*

He sauntered closer. So close, he could probably see the pulse that pounded in the side of her neck. Savannah's alarm ratcheted up another notch. She looked longingly at her clothes, still out of reach. Swallowing a sigh, her gaze returned to his. She found him frowning at her.

"Surely you've known worse clients than me? I can assure you, I shower every day and I've been told on more than one occasion that I'm passably attractive."

He was certainly right about the latter. In other circumstances, his sinfully good looks could be enough to tempt her to break her vow of eternal singledom, but charming or not, she had to get her clothes and get out of there before things got out of hand. Already the situation was slipping out of her control.

"Look, um, I think it might be best if we call it a night. I'm sure you can find another girl to...ah..."

He moved even closer and it took all her courage to hold her ground. "As I said, I'm a little busy right now," she added in a rush and gave in to the urge to move away from him.

"For Christ's sake, woman, relax. I'm not going to force myself upon you. You're not that irresistible." He brushed past her. In two long strides, he'd made it to the chair. Throwing himself into its cushioned depths, he dragged a hand through his thick hair.

Savannah couldn't prevent a groan of disbelief. Her clothes were now trapped beneath his butt. Mistaking her panicked reaction for loathing, he cursed long and loudly.

"For fuck's sake, lady. If I repulse you that much, I'll give you my word. I promise I won't touch you. I told you before I don't force myself upon women, even ones that can be bought and paid for. I only want to talk."

She remained silent, watching him, wondering if she could trust him. As if he could read her thoughts, his glare eased and his face smoothed into an almost amiable expression. A smile widened his mouth.

"So, how long have you known Vince?" he asked, his tone now conversational.

Her heart skipped a beat, but she hid it behind a wall of bravado. "Vince who?"

"Vince Maranoa. Don't tell me you don't know the man who pays your wages? How long have you worked here?"

"Oh, you mean *that* Vince. I-I guess I've known him long enough. How about you? How long have *you* known him?"

Her question caught him by surprise. His eyes widened and a kaleidoscope of emotions passed over his expressive face. Anger, frustration, pain—even bitterness—before he managed to suppress them. He barked a laugh, his eyes now cold. "Vince and I go a *long* way back."

Savannah stared at him. Her mind raced.

What was going on? Was James Bond involved with Maranoa's drug ring? But, if so, why would he find that association painful? She blinked and tried to clear her head. *Had* it been pain she'd seen?

By his own admission, he knew Maranoa well. The man could be a valuable source of information, especially if he thought she was a woman in Maranoa's employ. He'd said he wouldn't touch her. If she kept her head about her and borrowed some courage, she could use his misunderstanding to her advantage. That raise could be coming her way yet.

Savannah sauntered over, closing the gap between them. Coming to a stop between his thighs, she drew in a surreptitious breath and did her best to slow her pulse.

"Sounds like you've known Vince for much longer than I have." She fluttered her eyelids at him and scraped a languid fingernail down his shadowed cheek, hardly able to believe her daring. "Tell me, are you the man we have to thank for keeping Vince in drugs?"

Surprise flashed across his face. Judging from the quality

of his clothes, he probably wasn't used to being questioned by a prostitute—or anyone, for that matter. Then again, she couldn't imagine he'd advertise the fact he was in the drug trade.

A lazy smile played around his mouth. "I bet you enjoy getting high. Tell me, what's your poison? Pills? Coke? Ice? Or maybe it's good old-fashioned weed that gets you going? Vince must have a pretty decent supply stored here if he manages to keep all of you satisfied. What happens when he runs out? Have you ever escorted him on a buying trip?"

His persistent questions, as ludicrous as they were, hammered into her already-foggy brain and she wondered dazedly how he'd so easily turned the tables. *She* was the one asking the questions, wasn't she? So much for her prowess as an investigative journalist. Did she learn nothing during her years walking the halls of Parliament House?

"Cat got your tongue, Red?" His eyes taunted her. "Perhaps I could help you find it again?"

Savannah's heart thudded, this time in nervous anticipation. He unfolded his long, lean body from the chair and stretched to his full height, the wicked glint in his cool blue eyes pinning her where she stood.

Breaking the spellbinding contact, she wrenched her gaze away and stared blindly toward the curtain that covered the window on the other side of the room. Her mind spun.

What the hell was she thinking? She was way out of her league. It was time to leave. At least now she could make a grab for her clothes.

She took a step away from him. He moved closer. Too close. She could almost feel the heat of him through his shirt. Expensive cologne teased her nostrils. Her pulse skittered. His gaze wandered over her again, leaving a trail of fire.

Renewed panic surged through her. Her information-gathering would have to wait. Getting out of there unscathed had just become her top priority. She only hoped Malee had left the back door unlocked, as she'd promised.

Despite the fact armed security guards regularly traversed the perimeter of the building, the girl had come through on her earlier promise to get Savannah into the place. She only hoped she was as reliable when it came to getting her out. She refused to dwell on the fact that, if things had gone to plan, Malee would now be long gone and that meant Savannah's departure or otherwise from the brothel would be the last thing on the girl's mind.

The man who stood much too close for comfort smiled at her with a lazy confidence. Her gaze was drawn once again to his lips—full, yet masculine. Despite the seriousness of her situation, desire sparked along her nerve endings.

As if sensing her response, he drew her hard against him. She tensed and silently cursed her wayward libido. Before she knew what was happening, his mouth found hers. They both gasped at the impact. Trying to ignore the waves of pleasure that coursed through her, she braced her hands against his chest and pushed him away.

"You promised! You promised you wouldn't touch me!"

He shrugged. "So, I lied." With practiced ease, he slid the strap of her bodysuit down her arm and freed one of her breasts, cupping it in a strong, warm hand. Despite the danger of her situation, desire shivered through her.

With one quick movement, he lifted her in his arms and tossed her onto the bed. Seconds later, he joined her. Seizing both of her hands in his, he pinned them above her head. His mouth hovered inches away from hers. He gazed into her eyes, his expression unreadable.

"How about we forget about our questions for a while and get to know each other a little better?" he murmured. His lips found hers again.

Everywhere his mouth touched, left her wanting more. She moved against him, aware only of a need to get closer and satisfy the liquid fire that had ignited inside her.

"I knew I could get you to relax, Red." An entirely masculine laugh tickled her ear.

His words penetrated her passion-dulled mind. Savannah gasped in outrage, her anger directed not only at his arrogance, but at herself for so completely forgetting her precarious situation.

Knowing she'd never best him by force, with concentrated effort, she relaxed in his arms, grateful when his hold loosened. She looked up at him through lowered lashes and teased her fingers along his strong jawline. Her voice dropped to a husky whisper.

"You're sure good at making a lady forget where she is, all right."

At his answering chuckle, she twisted sharply beneath him. Bringing her knee up, she caught him squarely in the groin.

"Fuck!" He yelped in pain and surprise. His arms dropped away, giving her the crucial seconds she needed.

Scrambling off the bed, she wrenched up the straps of her bodysuit and stumbled to the chair. Making a grab for her clothes, she bundled them under her arm and ran toward the door. Suddenly remembering it was locked, she pulled up short.

Shit.

Slowly, she turned around to face him. James Bond leaned forward on the bed, pain, shock and confusion clouding his handsome features. "What the hell...?"

Savannah didn't dare waste another second. She raced across the room to the single window. Wrenching open the heavy velvet drapes, she sagged in disbelief at the sight of the thick steel bars that blocked the opening.

Stifling a groan, she sent a desperate glance around the room and spied the key on the nightstand. Relief surged through her, but she ignored it; she wasn't safe yet. Resisting the urge to look at the man on the bed, she dashed over to the nightstand and palmed the key. The heat of anger from his gaze only feet away singed her.

She tightened her hold on the bundle of clothing and strode to the door. With a deep breath, she managed to steady her hand long enough to fit the key into the lock. Seconds later, she swung it open.

Unable to help herself, she threw a glance over her

shoulder. She gasped at the emotion that burned in the stranger's eyes: anger, confusion, uncertainty and the tiniest hint of admiration flitted across his face. He rolled to the edge of the bed and sat up. Adrenaline surged through her.

Not willing to risk being detained by him further, she checked that the corridor was clear of guards. She slipped out of the room, all the while praying silently that Malee had left the back door unlocked.

CHAPTER 3

Monday morning

Will parked his unmarked police vehicle in its usual spot and proceeded into the station. The strident calls of a newspaper boy slowly penetrated the tangle of thoughts that vied for his attention. Though it hadn't been long since the sun had poked its face over the horizon, it already promised to be another fine summer day.

He nodded a greeting to the cleaner who stood with a mop and bucket in the foyer and then picked up a copy of the *Daily Mirror* from a pile that lay on the front counter. It was still too early for the administrative staff and Will was grateful for the solitude. Taking the stairs two at a time, he pushed open the door to the squad room that housed the detectives. With a murmured greeting to the officers who were winding down after their nightshift, he made his way over to his desk.

It looked the way it always did, spilling over with paperwork and files. A tattered copy of the *New South Wales Crimes Act 1900* stood at one end. Yellow post-it notes were stuck to his computer monitor, detailing reminders of things to be done. Some of the notes had turned up at the corners.

After making his usual brew of straight black coffee in the tea room, he carried his mug back to his desk and sat down.

The vinyl chair squeaked in protest. Ignoring it, he reached for the newspaper.

The phone on his desk rang, the noise of it loud in the quiet office. He silenced the racket by answering it.

"Yep?"

"What's up, Will? You sound like shit."

"Gee, thanks, mate. I'm so glad you called."

Andy Warwick laughed. "Let me guess, big weekend? Who was it this time? Susie? Or maybe it was Candi? Oh, I know. *Maxine*." His voice was full of innuendo.

Will took the teasing from his best friend in stride and grinned into the phone. "Jealousy's a curse, mate. Didn't anyone ever tell you that?"

Andy pounced. "So, I was right. It *was* Maxine. The marvellous, magical Maxine."

"No, smart ass, it wasn't Maxine." His mind skittered over images of the redhead. "It was nobody. I was on a job."

Andy turned serious. "Any luck?"

Will groaned, not bothering to hide his frustration. "Not yet, but we're getting close. I put in a late one on Saturday night and then made the mistake of poring over the file yesterday. The hours slipped away. I couldn't switch off. The answers are in there somewhere, I know it."

"Don't be too hard on yourself. You'll find them. It's what you do best."

Will picked up his coffee cup. Taking a grateful sip from the strong, black brew, he waited for the caffeine to work its magic. "So, how are you going with your course?"

There was silence on the other end of the phone. When Andy finally answered, his voice was heavy with disappointment.

"Not so good. I failed. Now I'll have to reapply and hope they give me another chance."

Will briefly closed his eyes. Memories of the stories Andy had shared about his fucked-up childhood crowded Will's mind. He knew how much his mate wanted to be a police negotiator and he knew the reasons why. A decade as a detective in the New South Wales Police Service wasn't enough. Andy wanted to prevent people from suffering the agony he did as a child when communications between the police and the perpetrator broke down and there was nothing left to lose.

Desperate men did desperate things. Andy wanted to get into their heads, to get between them and the blackness that consumed them; to give them hope when all else had failed.

And now *he'd* failed. The negotiators' course was a tough one. It weeded out those officers not mentally strong enough to withstand the stresses they would experience during high pressure situations when a single wrong word could mean the difference between life and death.

Will felt Andy's failure as he would his own and his gut clenched in response, but as much as he wished it were otherwise, there wasn't a damned thing he could do to change it. His mate would simply have to try again.

Switching subjects, he tried to lift the mood. "I know it's only Monday, but what are you doing next weekend? Maybe we could take the yacht out? The weather should be good for it."

Andy's voice hitched. "Thanks, mate. Sounds perfect."

After assuring him he would call him later in the week to firm up the details, Will ended the call. Sinking further into his chair, he took another mouthful of coffee and picked up the newspaper. His gaze flicked idly over the headline…and he choked in disbelief.

Hot black coffee sprayed across his desk. Staring incredulously, he shook his head and read the headline again.

'DARK DEALINGS DISCOVERED IN EXCLUSIVE SYDNEY BROTHEL'

The story was remarkably accurate: the million dollar crowd; the live show; the drugged girls. A further surprise was that the article went on to allege the prostitutes were illegally tenured.

"What the *hell?*" He searched for a byline and frowned when he didn't find one. The journo must have been inside the brothel, or at the very least, his source had been an insider. It wasn't easy to gain entrance to The Black Opal. The man either had an extremely valuable contact or was already a member of the elite circle of gentlemen who frequented the place. Either way, the story didn't bode well for Will's investigation.

"Fuck." He was getting so close and now some damned fool of a journalist was also nosing around. It could ruin everything. And for what? Some blasted story that would get the bloke's name on the front page of the paper.

Except it hadn't. The name wasn't there. A technical glitch? Or had it been something else? Everyone knew how much a byline meant to a newspaper journalist.

Of course, if the journo was a member of the club, it would explain the need for secrecy. Maybe he knew how nasty the repercussions would be if Vince Maranoa discovered his identity?

At least Will's presence had gone undetected. It was bad enough to have some idiot messing around with the investigation. The last thing he needed was to have a journalist recognize him. It was one of the reasons he stayed well clear of his father's multi-million dollar business empire. Will preferred anonymity and it sure as hell made his job doing undercover work a lot easier.

Frustration surged through him. His Saturday night stakeout had left him with too many questions and no answers. Most of the prostitutes he'd seen were using. He could only assume they were being supplied by Maranoa. He frowned and took another sip of his coffee.

Why would a man like Maranoa, a man who would sell his mother if the price was right, bother supplying his employees with drugs when he could make a lot more money selling them to other dealers? And why did he only employ women of Asian appearance—apart from the redhead? Will's frown deepened. Where the hell did *she* fit in?

It was obvious she hadn't been high. Those green eyes had been clear and bright and she'd been more than articulate. At the time, it had almost felt like she was probing *him* for information. It didn't make sense. Why would a prostitute care where her next fix came from?

And then there was the way she'd fainted during the stage show and the even stranger way she'd acted on the bed. If he didn't know better, he'd have guessed it was her first time. She'd told him she'd known Vince long enough, but that could mean anything.

His thoughts centered on the scene he'd stumbled across earlier in the night. He hadn't forgotten the snatches of conversation he'd caught between her and the girl named Malee. It was obvious Malee intended to leave the brothel and it was just as obvious the redhead had been aiding her escape. Were the girls illegally tenured, as the article suggested? It wouldn't be the first time.

He recalled the way the redhead had panicked when she'd discovered the bars across the window. Surely she should have already been aware of them? Her hasty departure from the room was also odd. Okay, she'd woken from a faint to find herself in a room with a strange man who had locked the door and taken the key, but surely that action hadn't warranted such a drastic reaction? She'd looked genuinely frightened.

As soon as he'd been able to stand without wincing, he'd stumbled to the door she'd departed through and had peered out into the dim corridor, but there had been nothing to see. A moment later, a security guard had appeared via the staff entry and Will had reluctantly withdrawn. Locating the mysterious redhead hadn't been worth blowing his cover, no matter how tempting.

Unbidden, her lush body now filled his mind. Like it had when he'd first spotted her, his body reacted. Blood rushed to his cock.

He should never have touched her. He'd been on duty, for Christ's sake. Prostitute or not, he knew better. Not once in the ten years since he'd joined the force had he put himself in a position where his professionalism could be brought into question. And yet, a pair of come-hither eyes, legs that went on forever and a more than bountiful chest had almost done him in.

While he'd been potentially putting his career on the line by letting his cock lead the way, he hadn't bothered to wonder why a prostitute would be so flighty when it came to finding a man in her room. Then there was the final insult when she'd kneed him in the balls right when things were getting interesting.

He gritted his teeth at the reminder. Something didn't add up.

A handful of hours later and a scant half dozen blocks away, Savannah O'Neill relaxed into her office chair and opened the newspaper she'd collected from the stand on her way in. There it was in bold, black type.

After much internal deliberation, she'd decided to leave the presence of the mystery man out of it until she had more evidence, but she'd still managed to score her first front page story since her arrival at the *Daily Mirror*. She smiled at the *zing* of satisfaction and skimmed over the headline.

"*Max!*" Her shriek of outrage could be heard halfway across the room. Her editor poked his head out of his office, a frown darkening his face. A moment later, he waddled toward her, hitching his suit pants up as they strained around his formidable belly. He closed the distance between.

"Savannah, you're here. Good. I've been waiting for you. I wish you'd told me beforehand you were going to the Black Opal. I would have talked you out of it."

Coming out of her chair, she flung her arms wide in confusion. "Talked me out of it? Are you *kidding*?"

Heat rose from her chest, along her neck and spread across her cheeks. Even her forehead was hot. She took a breath and fought against her agitation.

"Max, you told me to go and find something sensational. So I did. You can't get more sensational than this! I've heard it's already sold out on the newspaper stands."

"What I mean is…" Max paused and appeared to consider his words. "You don't know anything about the people behind this thing. Vince Maranoa is a career criminal. Blowing the lid on his operation isn't the smartest thing you've done, regardless of the newspaper sales."

"But, Max, it's a great story! People want to know about—"

"Enough! The bean counters are going to have a conniption when they realize the risks you took. If you'd been injured on the job… Next time you want to go off on a jaunt fraught with such danger, you come to me first. Understand?"

Gritting her teeth, she made another effort to control her temper. "You left off the byline."

Max wet his lips and glanced away. "Savannah, something as big as this could have repercussions, nasty repercussions. You've raised a lot of serious allegations. I don't want some hit man running you down in the street over this."

"Don't be ridiculous, Max. This is Sydney, not New York."

His ears quivered, like they always did when he was irritated. She heaved a huge sigh of disappointment and turned away. The only reason she'd gone to such lengths was to gain recognition. She'd hoped a few scandalous articles would raise her profile in Sydney. She might have been a well-respected journalist among the political circles in Canberra, but that meant little on a paper like the *Daily Mirror*, where the toughest political questions were generally asked by the resident cartoonist.

If it hadn't been for her brother, she'd never have given up her lucrative job as a political reporter and headed north to Sydney. Dylan's drug addiction had demanded a change of scenery and Sydney boasted the best rehabilitation centers in Australia.

By lifting her profile and gaining a local readership, not only could she ask Max for a raise, but she'd reach an even greater audience when she eventually wrote about what was really close to her heart—serious social issues that affected people every day: the breakdown of the family unit, the rise of unemployment, domestic violence, homelessness, drug abuse. They were issues that affected everyone. People needed to be informed; people needed to be educated.

And now what? The entire escapade had been for nothing. Without the byline, nobody would even know the story was hers.

Knowing further argument would be useless, she threw herself back into her chair. Her gaze lit on the faded picture of her mother where it sat on the shelf above Savannah's computer. It was the last picture she had of her, taken right before her death. Savannah couldn't believe it had been six years.

Her anger folded. Another sigh escaped—this one heavy with sadness and regret.

What would you have done, Mom? You always knew how to get what you wanted.

Savannah's mother had been the most determined person she'd ever known. Even now, she couldn't help the sharp pang of regret at the thought that she'd never told her how much she'd admired her. And now it was too late...

Tears burned behind her eyes. She stared at the woman with mischievous hazel eyes who smiled back at the photographer. Savannah's father had taken the photo. It had been shot right outside her apartment, only hours before her parents had embarked on their ill-fated holiday around outback Australia.

Her mother had been a university English professor and Savannah knew her love of writing had come from her. Along with the innate sense of social justice she attributed to her politically active father, it was no wonder she was upset at not receiving recognition for her article.

What started out as a bit of scandalous fluff to satisfy her editor had turned into a serious story with monumental implications. If everything Malee told her was true, there was enough criminal activity going on in the Black Opal to put the owners behind bars for a very long time.

"Is everything all right?"

Savannah turned. Barbara Layton propped her hip against Savannah's desk. Upon discovering Savannah was an orphan, her much older colleague had taken it upon herself to watch out for her. Now, Barbara's warm brown eyes were filled with kindness and concern.

"Yes, thanks, Barb." Savannah scrabbled for a tissue in her handbag and blew her nose. Turning to face her, she offered her a wry smile. "I guess you heard?"

Barbara pushed back her heavy gray bangs. Her smile was wide and genuine. "It's a great story. You did well, kid. And your first front page in the paper with the largest circulation in Sydney! Whoopee do!"

A small smile curved Savannah's lips. "Yeah, my first front page. Not bad, hey?"

"You betcha. The first of many—you mark my words. I've been here a long time, hon, and I know talent when I see it. And you've got talent, kid. Don't let anyone tell you different."

Barbara left her with a reassuring pat on her arm. Savannah's anger and disappointment faded. She was a good writer, dammit. There *would* be more front page stories and next time, her name would be right up there alongside it. She'd write the kind of stories nobody else had the courage to; the kind of stories her parents would be proud of.

Taking a deep calming breath, she squared her shoulders. Max may have gotten his way this time, but it wouldn't happen again. Danger, be damned. She wasn't a woman who frightened easily—not when it came to getting something she wanted.

Her thoughts strayed to the James Bond look-alike she'd met at the brothel. Well, not exactly *met*...

When he'd come onto her, it had taken her by surprise. Her adrenaline was already pumping... She was turned on by the rush of success but when he added himself to the mix... She recalled how easily she'd let her guard down, how wantonly she'd responded to him, and blushed. She couldn't believe how reckless she'd been. Her behavior had been so atypical. She barely recognized the woman she'd become in his arms.

She thought how easily he'd made her forget her recent vow of celibacy and a spark of annoyance shot through her.

Who was he? His clothes bespoke money and lots of it and his voice had hinted at an expensive private school education. The germ of a new story grew in her mind... She dragged her keyboard closer. She hadn't been in Sydney long enough to know the who's who of the social set, but her James Bond definitely looked like *someone*.

What if he was a judge or a doctor or a politician? No, not the last one. She'd spent the past few years warming a seat in the press gallery of Parliament House in Canberra. She'd have recognized him if he were one of those.

Besides, he seemed a little too...too... *Dangerous* was the only word that came to mind and she shivered as she recalled the sensual effect of his piercing blue eyes and the anger and disbelief that had filled them after she'd kneed him in the groin.

Not that it was likely she'd ever run into him again. Judging from his manner and bearing, to say nothing of his costly clothes, it was fair to say they didn't run in the same social circles.

Savannah typed in names of various local rags and surfed through endless photos and snippets from the social pages, hoping to catch a glimpse of the sexy stranger that had her tied up in knots. Surely, a man that looked like he'd stepped off the cover of a glossy fashion magazine would show up somewhere in the gossip columns with a starlet or two on his arm?

A new email notification appeared on her screen and she opened the message. It was from Lucy, a friend she'd known since high school. Scanning the words, she couldn't help but smile.

Don't forget the ball is on tonight. Don't even think about chickening out. We both know you need to get out. IT'S TIME!!

Lucy knew her too well. They'd talked about the black-tie charity event more than six months ago and Savannah had agreed it would be fun to attend, but that was before Jonathan—before she knew what it felt like to have her heart broken. Not just broken, but *mangled* and in the most humiliating way. There was nothing like walking in on the man you thought was the love of your life, to find him rolling around naked on the sofa with another woman, to cause a little long-term suffering.

Her jaw set with determination. She was over the lying, cheating jerk and she was glad she'd discovered the truth about his character before she married him. The ball was probably just what she needed. The thought of a night out on the town with a close girlfriend was enough to brighten anyone's day.

Images of the elusive James Bond flashed once again through her mind. Lucy was just the person to talk to about this. She should have thought about it earlier. Lucy had lived all of her life in Sydney and with her father a prominent orthopedic surgeon, her family had always run in the upper circles of Sydney society. Lucy might even be able to put a name to the face Savannah simply couldn't seem to get out of her mind.

CHAPTER 4

Detective Superintendent Peter Duncan, of the New South Wales Drug Enforcement Agency, or DEA as they were otherwise known, strode through the doorway of the squad room, his ever-present, battered leather briefcase in hand. Will pushed away from his desk.

"Pete, you got a minute?"

"What is it, Will? I have a meeting with the Director of Public Prosecutions in about five minutes. I only stopped in to pick up a file I left behind."

Will hesitated. The DPP didn't meet with police officers without a damned good reason. It was usually a prosecutor much lower down the food chain that did that. Something must be seriously wrong.

"Sorry, boss. It won't take long." Will picked up the newspaper and followed him into the cramped confines of his office. "Have you seen the story in today's paper?"

"Haven't had a chance. I've just come from the Police Minister's Office and now I have to front up to the DPP. No doubt there will be a meeting with the Attorney General before the day is out." He spared Will a glance as he searched distractedly under an avalanche of paperwork. "What's the problem?"

"A journalist at the *Daily Mirror* has decided to poke his nose into the city's brothels. The Black Opal, in particular."

"Shit." Pete groaned with irritation. "Just what we need."

He picked up a thick warrant book and looked underneath it. "How bad is it?"

"Yeah, pretty bad. There's a shitload of detail about the place—the girls, the live shows, the drugs. It must have been written by someone who was there—or else their source was. There's no other explanation."

"Which means we have a problem."

"I'm afraid it gets worse."

Pete stared at him, his face grim. "Let me get this straight: An overeager journalist without a clue what he's getting into is sniffing around a brothel owned by one of Sydney's most notorious drug dealers, smack in the middle of a year-long covert police operation we've only just started to make headway through. How could it get any *worse*?"

Will grimaced, but forged on. "The journo also alludes to a human trafficking scheme. According to the article, the girls at the brothel are being brought over here from Thailand under false pretenses."

"How would a journalist get information like that? Who the hell is it?"

"No idea. There's no byline, but if the story's true, we know two things: one, that the drug dealing isn't the only criminal activity going on in the place and two, the journalist has got some balls getting hold of information like that and printing it."

"Find out who that damn writer is and warn him off before he starts interfering with the investigation, or even worse, ends up in the harbor," Pete growled. "Just make sure you're discreet about it. The last thing we need is the media wising up to our investigation."

Will nodded. "I'll get onto it. Rutledge Advertising is about to run a considerable ad campaign in the *Daily Mirror*. I'm sure I can wangle a meeting with their editor."

Curiosity sparked in Pete's brown eyes. "I thought you didn't have anything to do with the day to day running of your father's company?"

"I don't, but if Dear Old Dad feels the need to spend twenty-five thousand dollars on newspaper ads, who else but his only son and heir should attend the meeting? Don't worry, that kind of money will bring the editor." His smile widened. "I'll ask him about the story."

Pete looked dubious. "Will your father go along with it?"

"Sure he will. He still hasn't given up hope I'll get over my desire to dabble in law enforcement and join him in the boardroom."

"Just don't let the editor get suspicious about your motives. We don't need him wondering about why we're so interested in the Black Opal. It's bad enough there's a Rambo-style journo on the loose."

"I'll be the epitome of discretion."

With a smile that turned into a triumphant yelp, Pete seized a slim file from beneath a pile of papers and brandished it in the air.

"Found it!" Stuffing the file into his briefcase, he made his way to the door. "Are you still going tonight?" He threw the question over his shoulder.

Will frowned, drawing a blank. "Tonight?"

"Yeah, the ball at the Hilton, remember?"

"Shit, that's right. I forgot all about it. What time does it start?"

"Seven, I think."

"Yeah, well, I guess so."

"No need to sound so enthusiastic. These nights are fun. Are you bringing a date?"

"Nope, I couldn't be bothered. If I ask someone I haven't dated before, she'll think I'm keen and if I ask someone I have dated before, she'll think I'm *really* keen. Sometimes it's easier to go solo. No hassles then, right?"

Pete chuckled. "You need to find yourself a nice girl and marry her, Will. That way, there's no decision to make. The expectations are neutralized and you have a date whenever you need one."

Shaking his head, Will sighed. "You might be right."

Will's dejected tone elicited another laugh. "You won't get any sympathy from me, mate. Most guys would kill to have the kind of attention you receive."

"It's not all it's cracked up to be—believe me."

"If you say so." Pete shook his head, his smile still lingering. "I'll catch up with you at the ball. My wife will be there. You'll get to meet her. I'm sure once Lucy finds out you're single, she'll do what she can to fix you up with someone, so prepare yourself. In fact, I think a high school friend of hers will also be there. Savannah's young and single. If you don't watch out, Lucy will have the two of you hooking up in no time."

Will swallowed a groan. The last thing he needed was a merry matchmaker. "Boss, I don't need—"

Pete smiled and waved his concerns away. "I'm joking. Lucy's seven months pregnant and counting down the weeks. Matchmaking is the last thing on her mind. Besides, a mate of mine from Canberra and his wife will also be coming. Declan Munro works for the Australian Federal Police now, along with a couple of his brothers, but before he abdicated to the AFP, he used to be one of us. I've known him for years. We even worked together for a while at the DEA. He and Chloe got married about six months ago. He's a good bloke and from all accounts, Chloe is a gem. She's also with the AFP. I'm sure you'll enjoy their company."

Pete opened the door to his office. "Anyway, I have to go. I'll talk to you later. Let me know how you get on with that editor."

"Yeah, sure thing."

"Have you lost your *mind*?" Lucy Duncan's words rose above the sound of the kettle whistling on the stove.

Suddenly regretting her impulse to confide in her best friend, Savannah leaped up from the table and reached for her handbag.

"Look, I'm sorry. I shouldn't have said anything. I'll just go, okay?" She slung her bag over her shoulder and headed toward the front door.

"Savannah O'Neill, stop right there!"

Savannah halted midstride and slowly turned around to face Lucy. Her friend looked only mildly contrite.

"I'm sorry, I shouldn't have yelled at you. I'm just in shock. You've done some pretty wild things before, but to spend a night in a brothel pretending to be a *prostitute*? How did you expect me to react?"

"I thought you'd understand," Savannah muttered.

Lucy plowed her fingers through her short dark cap of hair. "Understand? Do you have any idea of the danger you put yourself in? What if one of the men had tried to have sex with you?"

A vivid image of her James Bond look-alike with his mouth on hers flashed through Savannah's mind. A hot flush of embarrassment spread across her cheeks. "Th-they did," she stammered and glanced away.

"*What?* Are you saying you and some *stranger*—?"

"No, not quite." She attempted a strained laugh. "We didn't really *do* anything and he probably isn't a total stranger, I mean, *you* might even know him."

Lucy gaped, stumbling backwards. Her eyes were wide with confusion and disbelief. Mindful of her protruding belly, she collapsed awkwardly into a chair that matched the cedar dining room table.

"Someone *I* know? What are you talking about? Who was it?"

Savannah shrugged. "I'm not sure, but he definitely had the presence of a man who had standing in the community and his clothes were straight out of a fashion magazine. You and Pete socialize with people from that set." She shrugged again. "I thought you might know him."

Lucy shook her head. "Did you find out anything about him before you started making out? Like, maybe a *first* name even?"

Savannah's shoulders slumped. She crossed back to the table. Dropping her handbag on top of the dark, polished surface, she sank into a nearby chair. It would be a relief to talk about what had happened with someone she could trust. She'd tried to ring Chloe Munro, a close friend left over from her old life in Canberra, but her call had gone straight to Chloe's voicemail and she had yet to return Savannah's call.

What she'd seen and heard at the brothel had kept her sleepless all weekend. The thought of what was happening there appalled her. Then there was the mystery man who continued to hover in the forefront of her mind.

She drew in a deep breath and glanced over at her friend.

"I-I saw this guy at the front of the crowd. It was impossible not to notice him. He was so tall and broad and exuded an air of wealth and authority. I was drawn to him right away, even while I was doing my best to keep up with the other dancers."

Lucy looked shocked all over again. "You were *dancing* with the brothel workers? Please tell me you weren't doing lap dances."

Savannah grinned. "Of course not! What do you think I am?"

Lucy offered a reluctant smile. "Sometimes, I wonder. Now, are you going to tell me how you managed to get involved in being part of the live entertainment and why doing something like that would even *occur* to you?"

Remembering Malee's fear and desperation, Savannah sobered.

"One of the girls from the brothel contacted me. Don't ask me how she got hold of my number, but she called me at work late last week and told me about a string of criminal activities that were going on at the Black Opal in Darlinghurst. We agreed to meet. She told me she was unable to leave the brothel, so I agreed to talk to her there. She suggested we get together Saturday night."

Lucy stared at her, transfixed. "Keep going."

"When I got there, it was kind of scary. Malee, the girl I was to meet, had warned me to watch out for the security guards. Ostensibly, they're there to keep out uninvited guests, but Malee told me they're more about ensuring the girls don't escape."

"Escape? Surely, you don't mean they're being held there against their will?"

Savannah bit her lip and nodded. "I'm afraid so. I had to sneak down a side alley and come in through the back door. Malee told me she'd timed the departure of one of her regular clients with my arrival so that she could ensure the back door was unlocked." Savannah shrugged. "Apparently he prefers to leave that way. Thankfully, I didn't run into him on my way in." She shuddered at the memory.

"What happened next?" Lucy asked.

"Malee met me at the door and we talked in one of the empty bedrooms. She told me she'd been there two years, servicing men against her will."

"What do you mean "against her will"? This is Australia! Surely that's illegal?"

"Of course it is, but it still happens. Vince Maranoa has ten girls there and according to Malee, all of them are prisoners."

"Who's Vince Maranoa?"

Savannah drew in another deep breath. To an outsider, her story sounded unbelievable. She wouldn't believe it herself, if she hadn't been there.

"Vince Maranoa is the owner of the brothel. Apparently, he brings girls over from Thailand with false promises to the girls and their families and then forces the girls to work at the Black Opal. They're given drugs to keep them compliant. Of course, they have to pay for them. Maranoa takes it out of the money they earn. Before they know it, they're hooked and barely earning enough to cover their habit."

Her lips compressed. "Naturally, Maranoa charges a premium. Some of the girls have been there for years and don't have a dollar to their name. They're drug addicts selling their bodies to pay for their next fix."

Lucy frowned. "Thank God one of them had the courage to reach out to you. Now you can do something about it."

"Exactly! I knew you'd understand!"

"It still doesn't explain how you came to be posing as a prostitute."

Savannah averted her gaze and forged on. "After speaking with Malee, my heart was breaking. She's little more than a child—sixteen, seventeen—somewhere around there. She asked me to take her place on the dance floor so she could escape. The guards would be less likely to notice if everyone was accounted for. I guess she saw it as an opportunity too good to miss."

"But you don't look anything like a young Thai girl!"

"I wore a wig and Malee found me some clothes. There was nothing I could do about my height, but we thought amongst the crowd of girls on the dance floor, I might get away with it. By then, I was willing to do anything to help her get away."

Lucy shook her head in disbelief. "I still can't believe you did it." She pushed away from the table and headed back to the open-plan kitchen. Pulling the makings of coffee out of the cupboard, she went about filling two cups and handed one to Savannah who murmured her thanks and took a sip before continuing.

"This whole thing at the Black Opal—it's just so *wrong*. Maranoa gets these girls started on drugs the day they arrive. He woos them with promises of a good life, but it's all a lie. He has no intention of letting them go. Once they're hooked, they don't care about anything but their next fix!"

"You have to tell Pete."

"I don't want to get the police involved until I know a bit more about who's who."

"You mean, your mystery man."

A blush stole up Savannah's cheeks. "Well, yes—him for one. Once the police are involved, anyone with a public profile will be fodder for the tabloids. Who knows, maybe he has an innocent explanation for his presence?"

"But you think that's unlikely."

"Yes, I do. In fact, I think he's Maranoa's drug supplier."

"I thought you said he looked like he was from old money?"

"A lot of wealthy people lost serious money when the stock market crashed back in 2008. Okay, a few of them are recovering, but times have been tough. Maybe our high flier isn't flying quite so high, any more? Maybe it simply comes down to money?"

She shook her head. "Of course, I don't have any evidence yet and that's why I haven't printed anything about him. That, and the fact I'm giving James the benefit of the doubt."

"James?"

Savannah grinned. "Yeah, James. That's what I've taken to calling him. He's a living, breathing personification of James Bond. Pierce Brosnan, not Daniel Craig," she added. "Actually, I think he'd even give Hugh Jackman a run for his money."

"Wow, that's some serious good looks. No wonder you're keen to know more," Lucy joked.

Savannah's smile slowly faded. "I wish it was that easy."

"What makes you think he's a drug dealer?"

Savannah stood and leaned her hip against the pale granite island countertop which dominated the kitchen. Late afternoon sunlight glinted off the steel pots which hung galley-style above it. "I guess it was more what he said—"

"You mean he *told* you he was involved with this Maranoa guy?"

"Well, not exactly." She squirmed under Lucy's direct gaze. Heat crept up her neck. "He said he'd known Maranoa a long time. He said they went *way* back."

Lucy shook her head in exasperation. "For heaven's sake, that doesn't mean he's supplying the man with drugs."

"But it's possible."

Lucy shook her head. "I'm sorry, you're not convincing me."

"Well, what do *you* think he meant? When I woke up in the bed, I was alone with him. He must have carried me." Her eyes narrowed with suspicion. "How did he know where to go unless he was familiar with the place?"

Lucy gaped. "*Whoa!* Back up just a minute! What the hell are you talking about, when you woke up in the bed? What haven't you told me?"

Savannah's cheeks burned. She turned away and busied herself by taking another sip from her cup. Forcing a nonchalant tone she was far from feeling, she replied, "It's not as bad as it sounds, Luce. It was hot and smoky and crowded. The men were so close—"

Lucy looked aghast. "Savannah! I can't believe you'd put yourself in that situation. You're damned lucky you weren't hurt—or worse. What the hell were you thinking?"

Turning, Savannah held up her hands in an act of surrender. "Hey, don't go getting upset again, especially in your condition. Pete will have my head if your blood pressure is up at your next prenatal visit." With a sigh, she moved back to the table and lowered herself into her chair.

"I think I fainted from the heat. The next thing I knew, I woke up on a bed. James Bond was in the room."

Ignoring Lucy's disapproving frown, she hurried on. "It was a good opportunity to ask him a few questions, you know, find out why he was there." Her gaze dropped to the floor. "But somehow we ended up kissing and before I knew it, we were rolling around on the bed."

Lucy shook her head in disbelief, but amusement sparkled in her eyes.

"Savannah O'Neill, I don't believe it! What happened to your Y-chromosome ban? Don't tell me you finally decided to go for it? I've only been telling you since you split up with Jonathan to go out and enjoy some no-strings-attached sex. I never dreamed you'd take up my suggestion in the midst of such a seriously dangerous situation." A grin tugged at her lips. "I have to hand it to you. I'm impressed!"

Savannah offered a sheepish smile. "Hey, what can I say? Whatever else he may be, there's no denying this guy is hot."

"Don't think I don't know you're trying to deflect my attention from your little stunt with your oh-so-indifferent mention of a passionate encounter with a perfect stranger," Lucy admonished with a smile that slowly faded. "What if he hadn't been so trustworthy? You were in a *brothel*! Who would have listened to a lone voice calling rape from a bedroom?"

Savannah sobered. "I agree. It's not the smartest thing I've done. But now that I know what's going on, I can't just ignore it. It's like you said; we need to do something about it. Forget the story—those girls need help." She took another deep breath and looked her friend squarely in the eyes. "I have to go back."

"No, Savannah." Lucy's voice was firm. "What you have to do is get the police involved. Let me talk to Pete—"

"*No!* I've already told you, I don't want Pete to know anything about this. Not until I've asked a few more questions. James Bond is not the kind of man to go unnoticed. If he has anything to do with the illegal activities going on, one of the girls will know about it. Malee mentioned something about a man called Billy—maybe that's who he is?"

"Savannah, I get that you want to help, but you *can't* go back there. You've just finished telling me how dangerous it is. You were lucky you got out unscathed the first time."

Knowing there was no use in rehashing the argument, Savannah glanced at the clock on the kitchen wall and pushed away from the table.

"Goodness, look at the time. If you want me to attend this charity "do" with you and Pete tonight, I'd better get home and drag out some glad rags."

Lucy stared hard at her a moment longer and then sighed. "I'm sure you'll look fabulous and don't worry, I'm not going to try and set you up with anyone. I just thought you might like a night out, a chance to kick up your heels." A rueful smile crossed her face. "Little did I know you've been taking care of that just fine, all on your own."

Savannah laughed and collected her handbag off the dining room table. "What about a ticket?"

"You can pick it up at the door. It'll be fun. Trust me."

"Yeah, that's what you said about that trivia-night thing. I ended up seated next to a recently divorced father of five who spent most of the night sobbing on my shoulder. It was the best fun I'd *ever* had."

CHAPTER 5

Monday evening

Savannah's taxi joined the stream of traffic heading into the city over the Harbour Bridge. She gazed out over the impressive expanse of dark water and the usual magic imbued her spirits. Lights spilled out of the multi-million dollar houses and ritzy restaurants perched along the waterfront and sparkled onto the waves below.

The colorful city skyline looked beautiful with the iconic Centrepoint Tower and the Opera House dominating the view. A warm breeze drifted off the ocean and in through the car's open windows, gently lifting strands of her unbound hair.

Less than fifteen minutes later, the cab turned into the sweeping entryway of the Hilton Hotel. She paid the driver and climbed out of the car. On her way inside, she was met by a smartly dressed hotel ambassador.

"Good evening, madam. Do you require any assistance?"

Excitement and anticipation jiggled around in her belly. It had been much too long since she'd dressed up and gone out for a night on the town. She vowed to make the most of it.

"Thank you. I'm here for the Emergency Services Charity Ball."

"Of course. That's being held in the Grand Ballroom on level three. The elevators are right over there." He pointed and Savannah nodded her thanks.

Walking through the grand lobby, she couldn't help but be impressed. The Hilton was one of Sydney's oldest hotels, but in recent years, it had undergone an extensive refurbishment and the results were nothing short of breathtaking.

An enormous glass atrium stretched up to the fourth floor. She could imagine how it would flood the lobby with natural light in the daytime. A scattering of people patronized the café that lay off to her right and the soft murmur of their conversation drifted toward her.

She took the elevator to the third floor and gave her name to the doorman. Within minutes, she'd been ushered inside the ballroom. The sheer size of the room and the crowd already within was overwhelming. The rich patterned carpet of gold and maroon and sage was complemented by walls the color of wheat, right before harvest. Despite the vastness of the room, a myriad of down lights created an intimate ambience. The room vibrated with the sounds of conversation, laughter and the tinkle of crystal.

Savannah made her way through the press of people, scanning faces as she went and eventually spied the back of Pete's head. His prematurely gray hair was cut military short. The style might have looked austere on some men, but on Pete, it only enhanced his appeal. It also helped that the stark hairstyle was relieved by a pair of sparkling brown eyes and a mouth that barked laughter as often as it barked orders. Lucy was a lucky girl.

Speaking of Lucy, where was she? Savannah craned her neck, but couldn't see her friend anywhere in the vicinity. As she got closer, she realized Pete was speaking with someone. She caught a glimpse of black tuxedo and crisp white shirt before Pete moved and blocked her view.

A low, familiar drawl registered only seconds before Pete turned and caught sight of her. Almost simultaneously, she was offered a view of his companion. Her heart stopped and then took off at a gallop.

It was him.

James Bond. Her mystery man. The man she'd allowed to put his hands and lips all over her—until she'd kneed him in the groin. Her chest tightened with apprehension.

"Savannah! It's good to see you again. Lucy told me you were coming."

Pete greeted her with a friendly smile and drew her close for a hug. She buried her face in his jacket and clung to him in desperation. Her heart continued to pound. She tried with increasing panic to get her brain to work.

Maybe he wouldn't recognize her? After all, she'd been decidedly underdressed the last time they'd met. And he'd thought she was a prostitute. He'd hardly be expecting to see a working girl in the Grand Ballroom of the Hilton Hotel.

Much too soon, Pete pulled away and she had no choice but to lift her head and greet the man who'd haunted her thoughts. Fixing a polite smile on her face, she strove to keep her expression neutral. At least she'd find out who he was.

"Savannah, I'd like you to meet Will Rutledge. He's—"

"In advertising." Will interrupted and held out his hand.

"Savannah O'Neill." Returning his firm handshake, she battled to bring her heart under control.

Will Rutledge? Had Pete really said Will *Rutledge*?

"Savannah's a friend of my wife's. They were at school together."

Pete's words forced her frenzied thoughts back to the men. She kept the smile in place with a sheer act of will and hoped she didn't look as stunned as she felt. James Bond was Will Rutledge, presumably of Rutledge Advertising.

Surely, there couldn't be another one? He'd said he was in advertising. She chanced a glance at him. His curious gaze was still assessing her closely.

"Nice to meet you, Savannah."

She eased her breath out on a shaky smile, relieved to find no hint of recognition in his eyes.

She could get through this. He hadn't recognized her. It was fine. It was good. She could do this.

"Nice to meet you too, Will." Her gaze landed somewhere

near his perfectly executed bow tie and stayed there. He extricated his hand and she blushed, unaware until then that she'd still been holding it. The butterflies in her stomach multiplied and were now making it hard to breathe. Despite her silent reassurances, she didn't know how long she could sustain her charade of nonchalance. She turned to Pete with a tight smile. "Where's Lucy?"

"Where do you think? We've barely been here half an hour and already she's headed off to the bathroom." He grinned and rolled his eyes at Will. "Pregnant women. This baby can't come soon enough."

Forcing another tense smile, Savannah stared unseeingly into the crowd. Her palms were sweaty and she felt lightheaded. She hadn't taken a full breath since the moment she'd recognized Will.

She could still feel his gaze upon her. The longer she stood there, the greater the chance he might recognize her. She stole a look around the crowd for another familiar face...and found one.

Savannah smiled in surprised delight when she spied her friend.

"Chloe Sabattini! I mean, Chloe *Munro!* What on earth are you doing here?"

Chloe was just as pleased to see her. She enveloped Savannah in a warm hug, made a little awkward by the fact that Savannah towered over her.

"Savannah! How fantastic to see you! I'm so sorry I haven't returned your call. I've been flat out at work and—"

Savannah waved off her explanations good naturedly. "It's fine. Don't worry about it. It's so great to see you! You didn't even tell me you were coming!"

Chloe smiled. "Well, we didn't know we *were* coming until the last minute. Pete spoke to Declan about it a few months ago, but we've both been so snowed under. I didn't dare mention it to you in case we didn't make it. Fortunately, Declan managed to wangle some time off work and we jumped in the car and hightailed it to Sydney. And here we are."

Chloe twirled around in her sapphire-blue cocktail dress that fitted her curvy, petite frame like she'd been sewn into it. Chloe often bemoaned the fact she barely came up to Savannah's armpits, but another truth was, Savannah often felt tall and awkward around her more delicately proportioned friend.

Savannah shook her head and grinned. "You look wonderful. I didn't even know you knew Pete! How's that for coincidence? Talk about six degrees of separation. We live in a very small world."

Chloe nodded in agreement. "You're absolutely right. It's amazing, isn't it? Pete used to work with Declan, when he was still a New South Wales detective. Declan spent a number of years living in Sydney. When Pete invited us to come, I was more than keen. It gave me an excuse to catch up with you."

"Well I'm certainly not complaining. It's wonderful to see you! Where are you staying?"

"Two of Declan's brothers are also in Sydney. We're staying with his older brother, Tom, and his wife, Lily. You might remember them from the wedding?"

Savannah nodded and smiled at the memory. "Of course. There was a tribe of them. They filled the first few pews to bursting. Huge, broad shouldered Goliaths. Not one of them was less than six feet."

Chloe laughed. "You're right. They're all fine strapping men. Too bad they're all married. I could have put in a good word for you."

Savannah grinned and wagged a finger in front of Chloe's face. "Oh no, you don't. Have you forgotten about Jonathan? I'm not going to give my heart away again. It hurts too darn much when it's trampled and tossed by the wayside."

Chloe's expression sobered. "I'm sorry, I didn't mean to make light of it. What happened to you was absolutely horrible and I hope you never have to experience something like that again."

"You and me both, Sabattini." She grinned. "Sorry, *Munro*. I keep forgetting."

"Well, it's only been six months. I forgive you for forgetting. I forget myself sometimes."

"Well, one thing's for sure: it suits you, this thing they call marriage. I've never seen you looking so happy."

A blush stole across Chloe's cheeks. "You're right. I'm more than happy. I'm ecstatic. And I'm so glad I ran into you here. Now I get to tell you our special news in person." Chloe's hand drifted to her stomach.

Seconds later, comprehension dawned. "You're *pregnant?*" she squealed. Are you *really?*"

At Chloe's delighted nod, Savannah laughed. "Chloe, that's fantastic! No wonder you look over the moon. You're simply glowing."

"Thank you, Savannah. "We're both thrilled."

"How far along are you?"

"We're just through the first trimester. Still a long way to go, unfortunately."

"It will be here before you know it."

"Yes, that's what the nurse told me at the prenatal visit. I guess I'm just impatient for it to arrive. We both are."

Savannah smiled and stifled the tiny burst of envy. "Do you know what you're having?"

Chloe shook her head. "No, we thought we'd leave it a surprise."

A moment later, Declan joined them and gave Savannah a friendly greeting. Savannah offered him her congratulations. She noticed Will's eyes narrow when Declan drew her close for an enthusiastic hug.

Having almost forgotten him amidst the surprise of running into Chloe and Declan and the excitement at hearing their news, when Will's gaze clashed with hers, Savannah's heart somersaulted. With slow deliberation, his gaze dropped lower and leisurely and ran over her body.

She had dressed in a long halter-neck dress. The slit up the side of the black crepe outfit ran from ankle to mid-thigh and displayed a fair amount of smooth, tanned skin. She recalled how she'd looked at herself in the mirror and had been pleased with the stylish and sexy image reflected back at her. She'd even welcomed the idea of flirting with someone at the ball.

The crowd receded. A fresh wave of nervousness surged through her. What would she do if he recognized her? How would she explain she wasn't a prostitute, but was actually a well-respected journalist? How would she explain it to Pete? He'd be as upset as Lucy had been that she'd put herself in so much danger. Her dilemma resolved itself when Will offered to go to the bar for fresh drinks.

"Savannah, can I get you something?"

She forced herself to look up at him. His gaze challenged hers.

"A beer? A glass of champagne? An orgasm?"

Her face flamed, despite the fact she was sure he was merely referring to a popular Kahlua-and-Baileys-based cocktail.

"No, no, I'm fine, thanks." *Just go.* She needed to get away from him so she could breathe properly.

"How about you, Pete? Declan? Chloe? Are you guys right for drinks?"

Just say yes! Just say yes! The thought reverberated inside Savannah's head. She didn't want Will Rutledge to have a reason to come back to their party. Surely, a man of his social stature would know plenty of people in the room? There must have been nearly a thousand of Sydney's wealthy and influential there. What were the odds she'd run into him again? She refused to even consider that he might be sharing their table.

"Yeah, another beer would be great, thanks," Pete replied. "And I guess you'd better get Lucy a glass of orange juice." He turned to Chloe and Declan. "What are you two drinking?"

"I'll have a beer, too," Declan replied and then looked at Chloe. "How about you, sweetheart?"

Declan gazed at his wife with tender adoration and Savannah's heart clenched. She swallowed a sigh and forced away another flash of jealousy. How would it feel to have a man look at her like that? Like she was the most important person in the world? Jonathan had never looked at her like that, not even after they became engaged.

"No thanks, I'm good," Chloe replied. "Why don't you guys go ahead? I'll stay here and keep Savannah company."

"Sounds like a plan," Pete agreed. "That way Lucy will be able to find you when she comes out of the bathroom."

"Are you sure there's nothing you want, Savannah?" Will murmured.

He'd moved closer. His voice glided over her, low and intimate and her belly clenched with remembered desire. She cleared her throat.

"Actually, I-I might have a glass of champagne, thank you." If there was even the slightest possibility she was going to share a table with him, she sure as hell needed something to take the edge off her panic.

He eyed her boldly. "Coming right up," he murmured.

Her cheeks flamed at the double *entendre*. Once again, his gaze slid down her body, leaving a trail of fire. She held her breath and turned her face away, refusing to acknowledge his comment. He moved even closer. So close, if she leaned in just a little, she could touch him.

A hot blush stole across her face and spread lower to her neck. Every part of her burned. Unable to help it, she breathed in the fresh, woodsy aroma of his expensive cologne. Memories of their encounter in the brothel assailed her. Her pulse accelerated. He was way too close.

A knowing smile turned up his sensuous lips. The same lips she remembered driving her crazy. As if he could see the pulse that beat frantically against her neck, a glint of pure male satisfaction gleamed in his eyes. Moments later, he turned and shouldered his way toward the bar, Pete and Declan following in his wake.

She took a deep breath and worked on trying to relax, glad that the man who'd haunted her thoughts since Saturday night had finally moved away. Chloe sidled up beside her, a shrewd look in her eyes.

"What was that all about?"

Savannah blushed again and averted her gaze, deciding to play it cool. "What was what all about?"

Her friend grinned and nudged Savannah with her elbow. "Don't play coy with me, Savannah O'Neill. I know you too well. I can't believe you haven't told me about Will Rutledge. He's *gorgeous*! And here you were not more than five minutes ago trying to get me to believe you were still heartbroken."

Savannah shook her head. "No, no, you have it all wrong. I might not still be suffering from a broken heart, but that doesn't mean I'm looking for a replacement. I-I don't even know the man. We-we only just met. Just now. Like…a minute ago. Right before you showed up."

"*Mm*, no wonder you haven't mentioned him. I'm sure I'll be hearing a lot more about him in the future, though. I saw the way he looked at you. He couldn't drag his eyes away."

Savannah's heart thumped. Excitement mixed with more than a little nervousness flooded her veins. Maybe she'd overreacted? After all, nothing had been said about Will recognizing her. Apart from his parting comment—and that could have been simply a quip from a man who found a woman attractive—his behavior had been nothing out of the ordinary. Maybe she was worrying about nothing?

She looked at Chloe and smiled. She'd been gifted a few hours with a friend she hadn't seen since she'd moved to Sydney. It might have only been six months ago, but when they'd been used to catching up every few days, it felt like a lifetime.

She recalled her earlier vow to let her hair down and enjoy herself. There was no reason it couldn't still happen. Having Chloe along for company was an added bonus. Will looked good enough to eat in his tuxedo and he was obviously not immune to her.

What could it hurt if she flirted with him? He didn't know anything about her and after tonight, she was unlikely to see him again. It wasn't as though they ran in the same social circles. He was clearly known to the Duncans and yet she'd never crossed paths with him before.

She frowned and wondered why Lucy had never mentioned him. Perhaps he was married? She couldn't recall reading anywhere about a wife, but it wasn't like Lucy to pass over an opportunity for matchmaking. Speaking of Lucy, where *was* she?

The queue at the bar extended at least three men deep. Will breathed a surreptitious sigh of relief. It meant he'd have a decent length of time before he had to return to Savannah and keep up the façade that he hadn't recognized her, a chore he was finding more and more difficult.

She looked breathtaking in the long black gown that clung to her curves like a second skin. Her hair fell in a mass of auburn ringlets, loose and unfettered down her back. He wanted nothing more than to bury his hands in it and breathe in her exotic scent.

But he couldn't do any of that. To do so, would mean he would have to acknowledge he'd already met her—in a brothel, no less. She was a friend of Pete and his wife. There was no way Will was going to be the one to make them aware of her occupation. He could only assume they didn't know—after all, it wasn't something one would necessarily choose to advertise.

The fact that Savannah hadn't recognized *him* caused a moment's consternation. It wasn't as if he'd been in disguise. In fact, he'd been dressed just as formally then as he was tonight, minus the bow tie.

Then again, it had been dark and she'd been taken unawares. It was possible she truly didn't realize he was the man she'd encountered in the brothel. Either way, there was no denying his body had reacted to her as strongly tonight as it had the first time they'd met and he was having a hard time keeping his interest under wraps. Not that she seemed to mind over much. He was sure he hadn't mistaken the way her chest rose and fell just a little bit faster after his quip about the drinks.

"So, Declan, how's it going down in Canberra?"

Pete's question interrupted Will's reverie and he forced himself to concentrate on the men who stood beside him.

"It's been a good move, Pete. You can't beat the weather down south in the summer and as much as I enjoyed working as a state copper, there's nothing like doing it for the Feds."

Pete snorted. "It sounds like you've gone all snotty on us, Declan. Don't tell me you're going to turn into one of those Feds who look down their nose at lowly state coppers like Will and I?"

Declan encompassed Will with his smile. "Not at all. Some of my fondest memories are of the times we nailed drug-dealing crime bosses up and down the coast."

"Yeah, well, there are still plenty of them left," Will stated. "In fact, we're in the middle of a complex investigation right now."

Declan sobered. "Who is it?"

Will's voice turned grim. "Vince Maranoa."

"That's a familiar name."

"Yeah, it's amazing the number of investigations his name's cropped up in over the years," Pete answered. "We've never had enough evidence to pin anything substantial on him, despite the rumors. About four years ago, he bought the Black Opal and the gossip mill went into overdrive. Will's been hanging out there undercover for the last few weeks."

Declan grinned at Will and wiggled his eyebrows suggestively. "How's that been working out for you?"

Will grinned back at him, liking Declan more and more. "It's been tough on occasions. I'm glad I haven't had to explain myself to a wife or girlfriend after a night out there. I usually come home reeking of cigar smoke and cheap perfume." He shrugged. "It's a tough job, but someone has to do it."

"Ah, but are you making any progress?" Declan chuckled. "That's the real question."

"You're absolutely right," Will agreed, his mirth slowly receding. "A taskforce conducted a raid late last year, but they came up empty handed. That asshole knew they were coming. There's no other explanation." Will shook his head. "They didn't find so much as an ounce of evidence and yet anyone in Sydney can tell you he's a big-time dealer."

Determination tightened in Will's gut. He stared at Declan. "We're going to nail the shithead this time, once and for all."

Declan held Will's gaze. After a moment or two, he nodded, as if satisfied with what he saw. "I wish you all the best with it, Will. Drug dealers of Maranoa's caliber are some of the most cunning operators in the system; they know exactly what to do to fly under the radar and always have a patsy or two to sacrifice if the heat gets too much.

"But, that's what makes them the most satisfying to put away. Every single member of the local law enforcement knows how hard you've worked to get them there."

Will nodded, relieved that Declan got it. It's what came from swapping shop talk with a fellow DEA officer, even if the man had turned traitor and transferred to the Feds.

A moment later, Declan spied another former colleague a little distance away. After putting in a request with Pete for a beer, he excused himself and turned and headed toward his friend. The line at the bar moved forward and Will and Pete finally got close enough to lean against the bar while they waited for service.

Pete shot Will a quizzical look. "What was with that comment you made to Savannah about being in advertising? I didn't realize you were so picky about who you told about your occupation in law enforcement."

Will cast around for a suitable response. "Yeah, um...sorry about that. I just..." He shrugged and looked away.

He should just come right out and tell Pete the woman was a prostitute. But he couldn't. The words kept getting stuck in his throat.

Pete's eyebrows rose. Feeling the pressure, Will latched onto the first explanation that fell into his mind.

"The thing is, I really like her, but she's just not into coppers." He kept his eyes lowered and prayed Pete would leave it at that. He should have known better.

"Since when? I've known Savannah for years. I've never heard her say anything remotely like that. In fact, I'm sure she went out with a bloke from the Fraud Squad a few years ago." His gaze narrowed on Will's face. "I didn't realize you'd met her before."

Will fidgeted and prayed for the bartender to appear. He schooled his expression into one of mild curiosity. "I've only met her once, about a week ago. It was late. We were at a club. I doubt she'd remember me." He gave him a quick grin. "But I'd appreciate it if you can keep the cop thing quiet. I'd like to give it the best shot that I can."

Pete's face relaxed. "Yeah, well, I guess so. It doesn't matter to me what you call yourself. Just don't go breaking her heart, will you?" he warned. "You've said yourself how much you hate commitment. Savannah's like a kid sister to me."

Will choked, hiding his surprise behind a bout of coughing.

Thank Christ he'd kept his mouth shut. He *so* didn't want to be around when his boss discovered what the redhead beauty with the pair of very fine green eyes did for a living.

Thankfully, Pete didn't seem to notice anything amiss. He glanced over his shoulder and peered through the crowd to where the women were waiting. "It looks like Lucy's made it back."

Will breathed a surreptitious sigh of relief and clutched at the opportunity to bring an end to the questions.

"Why don't you head back and keep the ladies company?" Will nodded down the length of the bar. "From the line-up around here, it looks like we're going to be waiting awhile longer. I'll bring the drinks as soon as I can."

"Yeah, thanks. I might do that," Pete replied. A moment later, he disappeared into the crowd.

CHAPTER 6

From out of the throng of people, Lucy appeared, looking radiant in a satin evening dress of deep crimson, her pregnancy belly well pronounced against the stretchy fabric.

"Savannah! Hi, you're here. I *finally* got out of the bathroom. I hope I don't have to go back there in a hurry. It took me *forever* to reach the front of the queue. What is it with women and the bathroom? I know I should have gone before we left home, but you know, we were running late and the taxi was waiting and..." She shrugged her shoulders and grinned.

"Don't you mean *you* were running late?" Pete materialized behind her. "I was ready *hours* before. I don't know why it takes you women so long to get prepared."

"Well, aren't you happy with the results? If you want me to look like *this*, you have to expect it's going to take some time." She twirled around a little awkwardly in front of him, the long narrow skirt shifting slightly with the movement. The sleeveless bodice complemented her light tan and emphasized her pregnancy-inspired cleavage. Three-inch heels in matching crimson patent leather helped to elevate her five-foot nothing frame.

"Of course, you're absolutely right, darling." Pete pulled her into his side. "And it was *definitely* worth the wait." He bent and kissed her lightly on the nose. "Oh, by the way, have you met Chloe Munro? Her husband Declan and I used to work together. They've come up from Canberra. I invited them and Will Rutledge to share our table."

Savannah bit back a groan as her worst imaginings were confirmed. She was going to have to share a table with him. For hours.

Oblivious to her distress, Lucy held out her hand to Chloe. "Hi, I'm Lucy. It's lovely to meet you."

Chloe returned her smile. "You, too. Declan's often mentioned his time working in Sydney and he's talked about you and Pete more than once. It's nice to finally be able to meet you both."

Lucy acknowledged Chloe's reply with another warm smile and then turned to her husband. "Do I know Will Rutledge? The name sounds familiar, but I can't place him. Have I met him before?"

"Probably not," Pete replied. "I only met him about five months ago. He's...the son of Robert Rutledge. As in, Rutledge Advertising. Maybe that's why he sounds familiar? I hope you don't mind that I invited him?"

Savannah's breath left her mouth in a rush. At least she knew now why Lucy had never mentioned the man.

Lucy grinned. "No, not at all. Is he cute?" She winked up at her husband.

"You'd have to ask Savannah. She's already met him." Pete's gaze turned in her direction, glinting with humor. "What would you say, Savannah? Is he cute?"

Three pairs of eyes stared at her with various degrees of interest. Savannah's mouth went dry and she struggled for something to say.

"If-if you like that type, I guess you'd say he was cute." She looked at Lucy meaningfully. "You know, the *James Bond* look-alike type. I'm thinking Pierce Brosnan meets Hugh Jackman."

Hoping desperately that Lucy would take the hint, Savannah almost gasped with relief when her friend's eyes went wide with comprehension. She turned abruptly to her husband.

"Pete, honey, could you go and get me something to drink from the bar?"

"Actually, Will's at the bar now with our order." He grinned back at her. "He's a pretty handy man to have around."

Savannah could almost see Lucy's brain constrict with panic as she scrambled for another excuse. "Um...What did you order for me?"

"A glass of orange juice."

"Oh, thank you, honey, that's great. But, you know, I would *really* like some iced water right now." She fanned herself a little frantically with her hand. "It's so hot in here with all these people. I'm feeling a little lightheaded. Would you mind?" Her smile was pure innocence.

Pete looked down at her and frowned, but then sighed and shook his head, mumbling something about pregnant women as he walked away.

As soon as he'd moved out of earshot, Lucy flashed a look of apology toward Chloe and grabbed Savannah by the arm and pulled her a short distance away.

"Oh my *God*, Savannah! What are you trying to *tell* me? Is Will Rutledge your *mystery* man?"

Several people turned their heads to look in their direction. Panic burned low in Savannah's belly.

"*Shh!* Keep your voice down!" she whispered harshly. "I don't want the whole room to know." She glanced over at Chloe and beckoned her closer. "It's okay," she explained to Lucy. "Chloe's an old friend from Canberra."

Lucy looked vaguely interested in Savannah's announcement, but seconds later, returned to the more urgent matter at hand.

"So, it's *true!* He *is* your mystery man!" Lucy's mouth suddenly dropped open as another thought occurred to her. "Please tell me he didn't recognize you?"

"No, I don't think so." Savannah glanced around to make sure the man in question hadn't returned. With the way still clear, she bent her head close to her friends, pitching her voice just above a whisper.

For Chloe's sake, she quickly offered a few brief words of

explanation about how this wasn't *quite* the first time she'd met Will, like she'd said and then added, "When Pete introduced us, I pretended not to know him. He said hello in a perfectly normal way, gave me a once-over, and that was it."

"Are you *sure*?" Lucy whispered. "Pete's going to be furious if he finds out about all of this. Apart from the danger you've put yourself in, keeping it from him is not going to go down well." Her voice held a dire warning.

"I agree," Chloe said. "And I could tell right away there was more between you and that hottie than what you were saying."

Savannah drew in a deep breath. "Look, if Will Rutledge recognized me, don't you think he would have said something?"

Lucy's bark of laughter was strained. "What would he say—*haven't I seen you somewhere before*? Savannah, he can hardly own up to knowing you without admitting he was also in the brothel—probably not something a man of his social stature would like to admit in public. The fact that he didn't say anything is hardly reason to believe he didn't recognize you. And now you're going to spend the rest of the evening *sitting* together. Can't you beg off with a headache or something?" Lucy's eyes pleaded with hers. "I don't think I can cope with the *stress*!"

Savannah chuckled. "Luce, I'm certain he didn't recognize me. I would have been able to tell. I would have seen something in his eyes. I would have noticed *something*."

She turned to Chloe. "Despite what you *think* you might have seen," she added before offering Lucy a reassuring smile.

The truth was, despite her earlier concerns, now that she had Lucy and Chloe watching her back, she'd suddenly become very intrigued at the thought of spending a few hours with Will over dinner. He was undeniably the most attractive man she'd ever met and she couldn't forget how he'd made her feel when his magical hands and mouth had roamed over her body.

He'd been able to make her completely forget her disillusionment with the male of her species and her adamant vow to steer clear of them. After what Jonathan did to her, this was a feat in itself.

As for her suspicions about Will's possible connection to Vince Maranoa, right here and now, with the anticipation building low in her stomach, her libido didn't much care what he might be involved in. Besides, he was a friend of Pete's. The man couldn't be all bad.

Even better, she was sure her interest was reciprocated. She hadn't imagined the heat of his gaze upon her or the desire that had darkened his eyes. And she *certainly* hadn't misheard his little pun as he'd left to order their drinks.

Her heart raced at the thought she might end the night in his bed. Was she really ready to get close to a man again? Not that having a one night stand qualified as getting close. The very definition of a one night stand precluded any emotional involvement.

Besides, she wasn't an awkward teenager. In fact, she was more than confident with twenty-eight years of life experience behind her, she'd be able to keep her emotions well and truly separate from the overwhelming physical attraction she felt for him. Maybe, sex with Will was just what she needed to get him off her mind? Kind of a reverse therapy?

Lucy tugged on her arm. Savannah looked around and spied the man in question coming toward them, carrying a tray laden with drinks.

"Oh my, Savannah... You were right," Lucy murmured under her breath. "*Definitely* Hugh Jackman. And he's heading our way."

"It's going to be okay, Lucy. I promise." She gave her friend's arm a reassuring squeeze. "Relax. You're the one always telling me how I need to get back on the horse." She winked at Chloe and then turned back to Lucy, offering her a wide-eyed gaze brimming with innocence. "*Isn't* that what you've been telling me?"

At Lucy's reluctant nod, Savannah smiled and shrugged

with studied nonchalance. "Well, that's exactly what I intend to do."

"But, Savannah—" Lucy broke off her urgent whisper as Will reached them. Chloe merely grinned.

Savannah gave him a slow, seductive smile. Coming up close beside him, she leaned forward to take the glass of champagne off the tray, making sure the side of her breast brushed against his arm.

"Thank you." She took a small sip of the sparkling wine, savoring its sharp bite. "Mm, delicious." Holding his gaze, she ran her tongue slowly across her top lip and gathered up the small droplets of wine.

Will watched her, transfixed. His blue eyes darkened to almost black. She made a show of taking another sip of champagne and saw him snatch a quick breath.

"Ahh hmm." Lucy cleared her throat, breaking the silent, heated exchange. As one, they turned toward her. Will looked slightly dazed and it was a few moments before he took the hand Lucy had extended in his direction.

"I'm Lucy Duncan. You must be Will. My husband told me you were here. I understand you're joining us for dinner?"

Will smiled. "It's nice to meet you, Mrs Duncan. May I say, you're looking lovely this evening. Your husband's a lucky man."

"You bet he is and don't worry, I tell him every opportunity I get."

Pete arrived back with the bottle of water, Declan not far behind him. "What do you tell me every opportunity you get?"

Lucy grinned up at him. "Will was just saying what a lucky man you are, darling." She moved closer to him and took the bottle of water out of his hand. "I was merely agreeing with him."

An announcement that dinner was about to be served came from the master of ceremonies who stood behind a microphone on a makeshift stage at the far end of the room. People began to disperse, heading toward their tables.

"We're over this way. Table thirty-six." Pete gestured in the direction adjacent to the bar. With his arm around Lucy, he shepherded his wife through the crowd. Declan reached for Chloe and followed suit. Savannah darted a look in Will's direction. His gaze remained steady on hers. A smile tugged at one corner of his mouth.

"Ladies first," he murmured and made a sweeping gesture with his arm, inviting her to proceed ahead of him.

Savannah offered him a brilliant smile and hoped it concealed her nervousness. With her glass in one hand, she picked up the skirt of her long dress and made her way through the crowd to their table. The others were already seated. The remaining two vacant chairs were beside Lucy. When Savannah realized what close proximity she would be to Will, her heart hitched in excitement and low grade panic.

Determined to ignore her misgivings, she set her glass on the table and pulled out the seat closest to her friend. Will stepped forward to assist her and his hand brushed over hers. Her skin tingled from his touch. Ignoring the butterflies that swarmed in her belly, she took her seat.

Will sat beside her. His thigh brushed against hers beneath the table. She tensed and her heart skipped a beat. Heat from his body traveled up her leg and pooled in her core. She couldn't be more aware of him. Oblivious to her plight, Lucy's gaze drifted around the room.

"There's a good turnout here," she said.

"Yes, it bodes well for the auction to be held later tonight," Pete replied.

"Is it always this well attended?" Chloe asked, directing her question to Will.

"I'm not sure," he replied.

Acutely aware of his presence, Savannah struggled to keep up with the conversation. She picked up her glass and emptied the contents in a couple of swallows, feeling the need for something to settle her nerves. Lucy threw her a startled look, but remained silent. With a burst of renewed courage, Savannah turned to Will and smiled.

"I take it you haven't attended one of these before?"

He smiled back at her and shook his head. "No, this is a first. And you?"

With a boost of alcohol-inspired confidence, Savannah flipped back her hair and laughed. "Oh no, it's the highlight of my social calendar. Where else can you get good food, fine wine and enjoy the company of friends, new *and* old, all in the same place? And then there's the dancing... I just *love* dancing."

Her eyes meshed with his. He gazed at her, amusement glinting in their depths.

"Is that right?" he murmured.

Savannah bit her lip and cursed under her breath.

Darn it, how could she have been so stupid? What was she trying to do—*make* him remember? She scampered for something else to say. "Do you dance?"

The words fell out of her mouth. Heat flooded her face.

What the hell was she doing?

Lucy's stiletto found her instep. "Ouch," she said.

Will frowned. "Is something the matter?"

Savannah plastered a smile on her face and replied through gritted teeth. "No, no of course not. I'm fine. I think it must have been a-a pin or something that dug into me."

"A pin? As in a *dressmaker's* pin? You dance *and* sew?" His eyes now twinkled with laughter.

Savannah averted her gaze. In desperation, she prayed for the floor to open up and swallow her.

What the hell was wrong with her? Was she a complete nincompoop?

"So, Will, tell us about yourself? How long have you been in advertising?" Chloe asked, coming to Savannah's rescue.

The distraction appeared to work. Will leaned back in his chair and prepared to answer. Savannah breathed a surreptitious sigh of relief.

"My family has been in advertising for as long as I can remember. My father inherited Rutledge Advertising from his father who'd inherited from his father before him. I grew up with ink running through my veins."

Lucy smiled and joined in the conversation. "So you'll take over when he retires?"

Will gave a derisive laugh. "Who knows? Dad's not going anywhere in a hurry. He might be carrying a few extra pounds, but he's as fit as Michael Phelps. He still swims at least twenty laps a day, rain, hail or shine. He'll live forever."

With her wayward tongue now firmly back under her control, Savannah risked another question. "What's your role in Rutledge Advertising at the moment?"

Will lifted his glass and took a mouthful of beer before replying. Savannah watched the movement of his throat as he swallowed. His tongue snuck out to swipe at a tiny piece of froth on his lip.

Her belly clenched with nerves and something else. Heat rushed through her. She did her best to stem the blush that blossomed in her cheeks.

Will eyed her knowingly, almost as if he could see the desire that held her body in its grip. She dragged her gaze away and reached blindly for her glass, forgetting that she'd already drained it.

The first course of their meal appeared. Savannah murmured her thanks to the waiter who set a plate before her. She waited for the rest of their party to be served. Using that time to regain control of herself, she snuck quiet breaths until she was sure her equilibrium had once again been restored.

Glancing down at her plate, she smiled in appreciation. "*Mm*, oysters Kilpatrick. My favorite."

Will leaned in close and just like that, her senses were once again knocked askew.

"Some people say oysters are an aphrodisiac," he murmured against her ear.

Savannah's pulse spiked from his nearness and the intoxicating scent of his cologne. "Really?" she managed. "How interesting."

Will popped an oyster into his mouth, chewed briefly and swallowed, his gaze still on hers. "Isn't it just?"

Savannah forced herself to concentrate on the meal in

front of her. Her hands were less than steady when she took an oyster off her plate and lifted it to her mouth.

The heat of Will's gaze scorched her and sent nerves dancing through her belly. She did her best to ignore him and began to eat.

The oysters were delicious. It was a shame having Will seated so close beside her distracted her from fully enjoying them. With her tight budget, it was rare for her to have the luxury of eating such a delicacy.

She lifted the final oyster off her plate and carefully brought it up to her mouth. Despite her best efforts, a drop of Worcestershire sauce dribbled down her chin and onto her dress. She gasped in surprise and embarrassment.

Will leaned over with his napkin and dabbed at the soiled fabric. His hand pressed against her chest, mere inches from her breast. Her heart stopped and then galloped away. His long fingers continued to work away at the stain.

"It's fine; it's okay," she squeaked. He licked the napkin and dabbed again.

"Please," she gasped, unable to take any more. She pushed at his hand and he slowly withdrew, taking his time as his fingers slid across the soft fabric of her dress. A knowing grin tugged at his lips.

Her body was on fire and not just from embarrassment. Her nipples had hardened beneath his ministrations and her breasts ached to be touched. Her backless dress hadn't allowed for a bra and with her breasts soft and unfettered, they hung full and needy.

Desire ignited inside her, heavy and hot. She groaned under her breath and squirmed on the seat. Lucy darted a questioning look in her direction. Savannah averted her gaze.

"Are you all right, Savannah?" Chloe asked, her eyes clouded with concern.

Savannah managed a nod and a strained smile. "Of course. I-I spilled a little sauce on my dress. I-I might take a moment and head to the bathroom."

Without waiting for a response, she pushed back her chair

and stood. Will stood with her and Savannah was once again reminded of his impeccable manners.

Chloe nodded her understanding. "Would you like me to come with you?"

"No, no. I'll be fine. Really." She encompassed both women in her glance. "Please, stay and enjoy your meal." She turned and hurried in the direction of the restrooms, her face in flames.

She reached the bathroom without further mishap and went to a sink at the far end. Mindful of her dress, she carefully splashed cold water on her face. Lifting her head, she stared at her reflection in the mirror and gasped.

Her eyes were wild with need. Her color was so high, it looked like she had a fever. Her pulse still hammered madly in the side of her neck. She drew in a deep breath and held it, determined to get herself back under control.

It had been much too long since she'd been with a man—that's all it was. She was reacting to Will as if he were the first man she'd ever set eyes on. It was ridiculous. He was a man, albeit an incredibly sexy one, but a man, nonetheless. Her strong reaction to him was completely unwarranted. For heaven's sake, if they'd been alone, she probably would have propositioned him.

As ludicrous as the idea was, she couldn't discount its appeal. She was sure he was interested and she'd never desired a man so much. Her body was taut with the thought of his hands on her skin, this time without the barrier of clothing. To feel his mouth on her breasts, his hands kneading their fullness, his hard body pressed to hers.

Her clit throbbed and tingled. A renewed wave of heat scorched her cheeks. She wanted him, plain and simple. So, what was she going to do about it?

Nothing. Of course she wasn't going to do anything about it. She wasn't the kind of girl that went around sleeping with "almost strangers," even if he did look good enough to eat. It didn't happen. Not in her world. Besides, it was always possible he might remember her and then she'd be in all sorts of trouble.

Determined to leave the ball before things got complicated, she patted her face dry, refreshed her makeup and ran a brush through her hair.

She would return to the table and plead a headache, like Lucy had suggested. As much as she wanted to spend more time with Chloe, it would be best to leave before her libido ran completely wild and she did something she'd later regret. It was the most sensible thing to do, despite what her hormones urged. With her mind made up, Savannah left the bathroom and headed back toward their table.

Although Chloe expressed her disappointment that their time together had been cut short, both of the women seated at the table nodded their understanding when Savannah offered her excuses and prepared to depart. Lucy couldn't hide her relief. Will stood and waited while Savannah said her farewells.

"I'll walk you out," he said.

Grappling for a reasonable excuse to turn him down and coming up empty, she collected her evening bag and turned toward the exit, leaving him to follow her. They were barely halfway across the room when his arm came around her shoulders and pulled her up tightly against his side. She turned her head in surprise.

"Wh-what are you doing?"

He didn't break stride. As they neared the empty doorway, he shot her a heated glance.

"Headache, be damned. You and I both know we're burning to fuck each other. Why waste any more time?"

She gasped at his bluntness. At the same time, a jolt of excitement went through her. The sound of his voice close to her ear evoked memories of them together in the brothel. Her nipples contracted.

He chuckled knowingly and reached for her hand, pressing it against his thick erection. "See, I feel it, too."

Savannah gasped again. Her face flamed with shock and desire, but she didn't move her hand away. Instead, she stunned herself by tightening her fingers around his hardness. At his sharp intake of breath, she smiled. Two could play at this game. Despite her earlier resolve, she suddenly discovered it was a game she was eager to partake.

His eyes were almost black with desire. He surged against her hand. A few yards away, another couple approached them, engaged in conversation. The reality of the situation reasserted itself in an instant and Savannah tore her hand away.

"W-what are you doing? We're in *public*!"

"Not for long."

He dragged her through the exit. Her stomach clenched with nerves. "Where are we going?"

"To find a room. This is a hotel, right?" His eyebrow lifted in sardonic amusement. Seconds later, he steered her toward the elevators.

Savannah realized his intention and shock zinged its way down her spine. Never before had she slept with a guy she barely knew and she'd never done it just for the hell of it, despite her earlier cavalier attitude.

She had to admit, though, there was something deliciously naughty about having sex with a man who was almost a stranger. It was so basic, so raw, so…*exciting*: sheer physical attraction and nothing else. She'd probably be appalled by her behavior in the morning, but right at that moment, she felt nothing but liberated…and intensely aroused.

In what seemed like just a few minutes, the elevator arrived and returned them to the lobby. Will strode over to the reception desk, leaving Savannah to contemplate the wisdom of her decision. Before she had time to change her mind, he returned, waggling a key card between his fingers. He guided her back the way they had come.

Keeping his arm around her, he pressed the up button for the elevator and then pulled her in close to his side while they waited. Everywhere they touched, his body burned into hers. She drew in a breath and tried to slow her racing heart. The elevator chime sounded distantly in her head. Moments later, she was drawn inside the empty elevator chamber.

The doors hadn't even fully closed when Will pinned her up against one wall. His arms remained by his side, holding her in place with nothing but the strength of his body. It was the most erotic thing that had ever happened to her.

His mouth found hers, crushing her lips beneath his. His skillful tongue slid through her open lips and delved inside. Then he lifted her. Gasping, she grabbed his arms for support. With the aid of the thigh-high split in her skirt, her legs automatically went around his waist and tightened around his hips. Her mind reeled from the explosiveness of his passion. She sensed he'd simply die if he couldn't have her.

The thought was exhilarating and banished any misgivings. She returned his kiss with a hunger that matched his own. His tongue swirled in and around her mouth and she moaned with desire.

Struggling for breath, she pulled away and buried her face in the side of his neck, her mouth hot against his skin. Her clit throbbed with need. She fought hard against the urge to beg him to take her right there and then.

The chime of the elevator as it reached its destination finally registered in her passion-fogged mind. The doors slid open. They pulled apart with surprise and reluctance. With a sheepish look, Will took her hand and tugged her into the corridor. He took in her disheveled state and grinned.

"I think I was wrong about the room. It looks to me like we might not have needed it."

Savannah burned with embarrassment, unable to meet his eyes. God, what was she *doing*? What must he *think* of her? What would Lucy and Chloe say?

Her friends would be thrilled. They'd be over the moon to discover she'd at last consigned her trampled feelings to the past, where they belonged. As if sensing her sudden misgivings, Will drew her up against him.

"Did I say something wrong? I was only teasing. It's so refreshing to find a woman who's honest about her sexual needs. I want you; you want me. It's that simple. Two people who find each other damnably attractive and aren't afraid to admit it. There's nothing wrong with that. In fact, it turns me on even more to know you're confident enough to go after what you want."

Oh, she wanted him all right. And he wanted her. It was just like he'd said. They were adults. There was nothing wrong in giving each other the satisfaction they both sought.

Pushing any lingering doubts aside, she reached up and pulled his head down to hers, giving him a long and thorough kiss. "*Mm*, you sure taste good."

He growled low in his throat and bent to scoop her up in his arms. Finding their room, he slipped the key card into the slot and pushed it open with his foot. He carried her inside and then slid her slowly down the length of his body until her feet touched the floor. The solid feel of his erection pressed against her belly and she shivered with need. Releasing her, Will switched on a lamp that stood on the nightstand before turning back to face her, his eyelids heavy with desire.

Holding his gaze, Savannah lifted her arms and untied the slinky fabric knotted at the back of her neck. She let the dress fall low, exposing her naked breasts to his heated gaze.

"You're even more beautiful than I remembered," he murmured and bent his head to take a hard, rosy nipple between his teeth.

Savannah frowned at his comment, but within moments, all thoughts but the feel of his body pressed against hers dissolved into nothingness. His lips continued their assault on her nipples, swirling back and forth across the hard nubs with his tongue. There was nothing and no one but Will and the heavy, pulsing need that consumed her. She pressed against his erection and moaned at the pressure against her swollen clit.

He eased her dress down over her hips. It skimmed along her legs and pooled at her feet. Lifting her in his arms, he strode over to the king-sized bed and gently laid her down. He kneeled and slipped off her stilettos, dropping them to the floor. With his gaze fixed on the scrap of black lace between her legs, he stood and hurriedly tugged off his jacket and tie. His shirt quickly followed.

Within moments, he was sitting on the side of the bed, his

bare chest illuminated in the soft light. Leaning over, he ran his hand with languid ease up the inside of her thigh, pausing when he got to her center. A finger pressed against the dampened lace which covered her opening and then slipped underneath.

Savannah gasped. When he finally pulled his finger away, she was almost mesmerized with need. With his gaze intent upon hers, he brought it to his mouth and licked it. "*Mm*, you taste good, too."

The heat from his gaze seared her. With quick movements, he tugged off his shoes and socks and tossed them to the floor. She sat up and pressed her breasts against his back, reaching around to run her hands over the bronzed muscles of his chest. Her fingers brushed across his nipples and found them hard.

He sucked in a breath and turned to kiss her. His lips moved over her mouth, tasting, sipping, licking, sucking, driving her wild.

Her hands wandered lower. Taking hold of his belt, she freed it from his trousers. His stomach muscles tensed. Undeterred, she undid the button and slid the zipper down slowly over his erection.

Sliding her hand inside his suit pants, she caressed his cock through his boxer shorts. The satiny fabric of his underwear slid easily over his hardened flesh. The tip of his cock peeked out above the waistband. It was shiny with fluid.

With her finger, she touched it, spreading the moisture over the head of his cock. Holding his gaze, she leaned back against the pillows and brought her finger up to her mouth. Her tongue stole out and licked it.

Will swore and threw off his trousers and underwear. He pressed her down into the bed, his weight fully upon her.

"You really know how to turn me on." His voice was rough with need. Lowering his head, he took her mouth in another mind-numbing kiss.

She kissed him back with a passion that consumed her. His cock pressed between her legs and she moved restlessly against him.

"I want you to fuck me." The words fell out of her mouth, shocking her in their crudity.

"Oh, I'm going to fuck you all right, sweetheart. I've wanted to fuck you from the first moment I saw you."

Leaning over the side of the bed, he grabbed his trousers off the floor and fished inside the pocket. Taking a condom out of his wallet, he tore it open with his teeth and quickly sheathed his cock.

He pushed her thighs open and settled himself between them. His cock pressed against her entrance. She pushed her bottom upwards, silently urging him to enter her.

Needing no further encouragement, Will plunged into her, gasping as he was fully sheathed within her warmth. Savannah grabbed hold of his shoulders and pulled him down hard on top of her. Meeting the drive of his hips with fierce thrusts of her own, she clung to him, her arms and legs taut around him as she urged him even closer.

Within minutes, she was on the edge of an orgasm and squeezed him tight. "Don't stop." Her voice was a ragged whisper of need. "I'm going to come."

His thrusts increased. She reached the pinnacle and cried out. Her orgasm washed over her. She moaned and clung to him while he continued to plunge into her. Moments later, he tensed above her. His face stilled in the dim light and then, he too, reached fulfilment.

Collapsing on top of her, his breath came in harsh pants. A few moments later, he moved his weight off her and shifted to lie onto his back.

Savannah stared up at the ceiling and heaved a sigh. She'd never before experienced such *ravishment*. And ravished was the only way to describe what had just happened. One night stands had suddenly gone a long way up in her estimation.

Stealing a glance at Will, she caught her breath in surprise at the intensity of his gaze. His expression was unreadable. Unsure of the etiquette of their situation and totally out of her depth, she blushed furiously at the thought of her wantonness.

At least he hadn't recognized her. With a little bit of luck, she'd be able to escape his hotel room with a casual "fare thee well" and be on her way. Steeling herself to come up with a suitable exit line, she took a deep breath and turned on her side to face him.

"So tell me, are you just a prostitute on the weekends, or is it a full time job?" His casual tone belied the steel in his eyes.

The air *whooshed* out of her lungs in an avalanche of shock. Coughing and wheezing, she tried desperately to catch her breath.

Oh, God! When had he recognized her?

She couldn't believe it. She had to get out of there—just as soon as she could breathe.

With a muttered oath, he bent her forward and gave her a hearty thump on the back. Coughing loudly now, Savannah drew some much-needed air into her lungs. Frantically, she tried to think of a suitable response.

She couldn't tell him the truth. What if he *was* involved in the illegal activities going on at the brothel?

"Cat got your tongue, Red?"

Her gaze shot up and caught the wicked glint of humor in his eyes. Swallowing hard, she returned his grin with reluctance. It was clear she couldn't deny he'd met her at the brothel, but how was she going to explain her presence there?

She took another breath. "Look, you don't understand. I-I'm not... It's not what you think."

"And what do I think, Red?" Taking her chin in his hand, he looked directly into her eyes. "Is it that I think you're a hot-looking woman, a fantastic fuck and a girl who takes money for sex? I tell you what, even though I'm not usually into fucking prostitutes, I'd damn well be happy to pay for what we just shared."

Savannah gasped in shock and outrage, her face burning with fury and embarrassment. She pushed away from him.

"How *dare* you? Who the hell do you think you are, speaking to me like that? I'm not some common trollop—"

"Whoa, there! Calm down, Red." He offered an unapologetic smile. "I'm sorry if I was too vulgar. You didn't seem to mind a few moments ago."

Another wave of heat seared her cheeks. She needed no reminder of her uninhibited behavior. He reached out for her again, but she moved away, dragging the sheet with her as she tried to gather her thoughts.

Maybe she should just tell him? "The truth is," she hesitated. "I'm actually a journalist doing research for a story."

"Bullshit!" Will bounded up out of the bed and turned to face her, his expression now hard. "There's no way any sane, normal girl would put herself in the situation you were in on Saturday night for the sake of a story. You might be a good fuck, sweetheart, but you sure as hell need some work on telling lies."

Savannah was aghast. *How could he not believe her?* But then again, why should he? After all, the few things he knew about her hardly reflected well on her character.

Dancing nearly naked in a brothel and then having fast and furious sex with an almost stranger were not exactly things that sparkled on the resume of a decent, upstanding young woman. She tried again.

"Look, I don't know what I can say to convince you I'm telling the truth. I'm not a prostitute or-or anything like that. I'd never even been *inside* a brothel until last Saturday night."

Will paced the floor in front of her, seemingly oblivious to his nakedness. "Do you honestly expect me to believe you went into a brothel, danced half-naked in front of a group of drunk and disorderly men who were all looking for a bit of ass and took the risk that none of them would want to fuck you—all for the sake of a story?"

"But it's *true*." Her protest sounded weak, even to her ears.

"You might've just tried to bonk my brains out, Red, but believe me, they're still working just fine. You'd better come up with something a bit more believable than that."

Savannah sat up higher in the bed, yanking the sheet up around her neck. She wished she was confident enough to get up and pull her clothes back on, but she wasn't used to parading naked in front of men she barely knew—or any man, for that matter—despite what Will thought.

From the closed look on his face, nothing she said right now was going to change his mind. "You know what? I don't care if you believe me. It's the truth and I don't have to explain myself any further to you. But if I were you, I'd be careful about fraternizing in one of the city's most notorious brothels. You never know who might see you." Anger made her reckless. "I bet there would be plenty of tabloids that would pay good money to hear about a story like that, a man of your social standing and all."

He halted abruptly beside the bed and stared at her, his eyes widening in shock. "You little bitch. Now I get it. You planned this all along, didn't you?" Snatching his trousers off the floor, he jerked them up around his hips, fury radiating off every taut line of his body.

"*Fuck!* How could I have been so *stupid?* Of course you knew who I was. You've known right from the start. Right from the first moment you saw me near the stage. You recognized me and saw a meal ticket. I don't know what game you were playing the other night, but I can see it clearly now. You're trying to blackmail me, aren't you?"

He leaned down and shoved his face close to hers, a menacing glint in his eyes. "You've lucked out, sweetheart. I don't know how the fuck you managed to find out I'd be here tonight, but somehow you did and you made damn sure I noticed you."

He sneered. "Well, congratulations. I noticed you all right. And I was happy to fuck you like you wanted. But I'm not going to fall for the little scam you've cooked up in that pretty little head of yours. Too bad for you, I couldn't care less what the tabloids print about me—the juicier the better, as far as I'm concerned."

He bent and picked up his shirt off the floor and yanked it on. "I'm afraid your little extortion scheme is about to fall apart. Take your story wherever you like, I couldn't give a fuck. You sure as hell won't see a dollar out of me."

In stunned silence, Savannah watched as he finished dressing, shoving his boxer shorts and bow tie into the pocket of his jacket. She felt sick to her stomach.

When he reached the door, he turned back to the bed and raked his scathing gaze over her body.

"Thanks for the evening, Red. It was real fun for a while, especially since you managed to get over your inclination to knee me in the balls. Too bad you know how to use your body better than your brains."

Savannah reeled back against the pillows as if he'd struck her. Shock and disbelief paralyzed her. The door to the hotel room closed behind him. The sound of the quiet click echoed long after he'd gone.

CHAPTER 7

Tuesday morning

Savannah pushed the hair off her face and stared at her reflection in the bathroom mirror. Her eyes were puffy and red. In contrast, her skin looked deathly pale. With her mouth as dry as sandpaper and a lingering headache pressing behind her eyes, the last thing she wanted to do was head into work, but she had no choice. If she didn't turn up, she didn't get paid.

Unless she called in sick. It didn't seem like half a bad idea, except she tried to save her sick days for the times when Dylan needed her. Lately, that had been more times than she cared to admit. She only hoped that this time around, her brother would stick with his rehab program and finally get on top of his addiction.

A soft, silky body slid between her ankles. She looked down and spied Milo. The cat's long golden hair felt like warmed custard against her skin. Bending down, she gave him a quick scratch between his ears. He meowed in protest when she stopped and a slight smile tugged at her lips. It was already seven-thirty. If she didn't get her butt moving, she'd be late for work.

Of their own volition, her thoughts flew back to the night before. She couldn't believe she'd been so-so... *Loose* was the only word that came to mind.

It was one thing to toy with the idea of picking a guy up and spending the night with him, but to actually go ahead and *do* it! And she couldn't just pick up *any* guy. Oh no, she had to pick up *Will Rutledge*, the multi-millionaire advertising tycoon who frequented brothels and no doubt had scores of conquests. Now she could add herself to his list.

Turning on the shower, she stepped into the glass cubicle and let the hot water pound onto her head and shoulders. Squeezing shampoo into her palm, she lathered her hair briskly, wishing she could wash away her memories from last night as easily.

After Will left the hotel room, it had taken her nearly an hour to get herself together enough to dress and leave. She'd never *dreamed* he wouldn't believe her—or that he would jump to such a wild conclusion. The mere thought of her trying to blackmail him was beyond ludicrous.

The thought of returning to the ball had been abhorrent, so she'd gone straight down to the lobby and had slipped out unnoticed through the double glass doors. Her friends thought she'd headed home earlier, anyway. The night had still been relatively young when she'd collapsed into her bed, but she'd been completely drained.

As tired as she'd been, her mind had refused to shut down and she'd spent the night tossing and turning, replaying the last few scenes with Will over and over in her head.

Turning off the shower, she stepped out and briskly toweled herself dry. Wrapping a second towel around her head, she padded into her bedroom and opened the doors to her built-in closet.

It was a luxury she appreciated every time she swung open the doors. She and her brother had previously rented a tiny bed-sit on the edge of Bondi, where the only available closet space had consisted of a miniscule cupboard with no more than a foot of hanging space. The majority of her clothes and all of Dylan's had spent most of their time lying in open suitcases on the floor, where she'd cursed every time she'd stubbed her toe on them.

Her mother and father, for all their impressive achievements in the academic world, hadn't seen fit to ensure adequate provision for their offspring in the event of their untimely deaths. Savannah could still hear the somber voice of the family's lawyer, a day after her parents had been interned at the North Sydney Crematorium, informing her that after the debts had been paid, there would only be a very modest amount left over for her and Dylan.

She'd been all of twenty-two. Her brother had just turned thirteen.

With an impatient shake of her head, Savannah pushed those memories away. It didn't ever do any good to think about "what ifs" and she didn't have the time or energy to indulge in a bout of self pity.

With quick efficiency, she selected a black-and-white striped cotton sleeveless slip dress and pulled it off its hanger. Formal enough for work, it was also cool enough to get her through what promised to be another hot day. Already, she felt the heat of the sun where it shone through her bedroom window.

Foregoing pantyhose, she slipped her feet into her favorite pair of yellow patent leather high-heel sandals. Although they weren't Manolo Blahniks—she was still saving up for those— they were comfortable and stylish and added another three inches to her five-foot-ten-and-a-half. Carrie Bradshaw she wasn't, but she was still pleased with the overall look.

Walking back into the bathroom, she pulled the hair dryer out of the vanity and plugged it in. Combing her fingers through her long hair, she couldn't help but remember the feel of Will's hands as he'd massaged her scalp while he'd pressed kisses all over her lips and cheeks and nose and eyelids, moaning about how beautiful she was and how he wanted to taste her all over.

Her pulse leaped in response to the memory. Whatever else he might be, there was no doubt Will Rutledge was a damned fine lover and she was kidding herself if she thought she'd be able to forget about him. It infuriated her that, despite his hurtful accusations, if he called and suggested another night of scorching sex, she'd be all but dragging him to the nearest bed.

The fact that he'd left believing the worst of her was unfortunate, but what could she do? She could hardly telephone Rutledge Advertising and ask to speak with him. He probably wouldn't even take her call. Besides, she still didn't know where he fit in as far as the illegal activities at the brothel were concerned. He was a friend of Pete's, but that didn't necessarily prove him innocent. It hadn't seemed to matter while she'd been in the throes of the best sex she'd ever experienced, but now, in the harsh and unforgiving light of day, she couldn't deny the possibility of his criminality, however slight, concerned her.

Pushing the thoughts aside, Savannah applied her makeup with the speed of an expert. A few dabs of concealer and some foundation went a long way to covering up the dark circles under her eyes. After applying blusher to her pale cheeks, a touch of mascara to her eyelashes and a slash of chocolaty-brown lipstick, she felt confident no one would be any the wiser about her sleepless night.

She left the bedroom and walked into the compact kitchen. With no time for breakfast, she picked up her second hand black leather Oroton handbag off the table—a lucky eBay find—and slung it over her shoulder. Pulling open the front door, she closed it firmly behind her.

With a silent vow to put into action her plan to return to the Black Opal as soon as possible, she headed toward the train station. She owed it to herself to get to the bottom of what was happening at the brothel before she allowed herself to get any more familiar with the delectable William Rutledge.

Max O'Connor had heartburn. Pain twisted in his chest and burned with white-hot heat. He groaned in agony.

Despite his pleasantly cool, temperature-controlled office, sweat gathered on his upper lip and pooled under his arms. Another groan escaped his clenched lips. Oblivious to Max's suffering, the man on the other end of the phone continued his tirade.

"What the fuck is goin' on Max? I pick up the paper and find a front page story about my own fuckin' brothel. How the fuck did that happen, Max?"

Max wheezed and tried to breathe through another attack. "I know, Vince. I know. Mate, what can I say? I told the little twit to give me something sensational and she came back with this. I was talking about finding one of those soapy stars with their pants down, not this kind of shit. I had no idea—"

"Bullshit, Max! Don't try that shit with me. I know how it works. You're the fuckin' editor! Nothin' in that paper gets printed without your say-so."

Max did his best to placate him. He forced himself to appear unaffected by Vince's anger, despite the fact that his insides were quailing.

"You're right, Vince. I'm sorry."

"Of course I'm fuckin' right." Vince's voice was even louder. "That's why I'm so fuckin' pissed. My own *mate* goes and does this to me. What the *fuck*!"

Max cleared his throat. "The girl who wrote it only passed it by me on Sunday afternoon—a few hours before we were due to go to print. We'd reserved the space for her. I could hardly refuse to run it. It would have raised suspicion. She's a smart girl. Used to be part of the press gallery in Canberra."

"I don't give a fuck who she is and where she worked! She could be Oprah fuckin' Winfrey for all I care. It better not happen again, you understand?" Vince's voice dropped lower. "Have you forgotten what I did for you, Max?"

Fear clutched at his belly. The implied threat was unmistakable. His knees turned to jelly. Stumbling, he fell into his chair as another bout of pain seized him in its fiery grip. In desperation, he reached for the packet of Rennie again and forced a nervous laugh.

"Shit, Vince. You know I haven't forgotten."

"I fuckin' hope not."

"Mate, I'm sorry. I don't know what else to say. I didn't have a clue she was writing about it until it was too late."

"I've got enough fuckin' problems around here at the moment. Another one of my girls tried to run on Saturday night. I had to deal with it."

Max feigned interest. Anything to take the heat off him. "Which one?"

"Malee. She'd been with me for two fuckin' years. She was one of my best girls. She really knew how to get 'em in."

Max forced another laugh. "I hope you taught her a lesson. I hope you made her suck cock until she gagged."

"She won't be suckin' any more cock. I can tell you that for sure," Vince chuckled.

The sound of his mirth made Max shiver. His answering chuckle was anything but natural. "That's what you get for being ungrateful. It sounds like she deserved everything she got."

"Oh yeah, she deserved it all right. No one fucks with Vince Maranoa."

The line went dead in his ear and Max dropped all pretense of humor. Another attack seized him. He clutched at his gut and groaned. From fear or pain—he could no longer tell.

Making her way along the carpeted corridor of the *Daily Mirror's* offices, Savannah nodded greetings to various work colleagues before heading toward her cubicle. Stowing her handbag in its customary place beneath her desk, she logged onto her computer and checked her emails.

As she suspected, there was a new message from Lucy and another one from Chloe. She swallowed a groan.

What was she going to tell them?

She and Will had just disappeared. She hadn't even

called her friends later to let them know she was okay. No doubt they were frantic.

Opening the email from Lucy, she read the message.

What the hell happened to you last night? I know that headache was nothing more than an excuse. Believe me, I was pleased when you decided to get out of there. Knowing WR could recognize you at any moment was giving me indigestion. But then he left with you AND DIDN'T COME BACK! Don't even think about not spilling all. Call me AS SOON AS YOU GET IN!!

Okay, so her best friend since high school wasn't as concerned about her as she'd thought. Clearly, she assumed she'd left with Will Rutledge. There wasn't even a *hint* of alarm in her email.

Savannah was miffed. For all Lucy knew, he could have drugged her and forced himself upon her. Did she really think the man was so far above reproach she didn't even express the slightest hint of worry that her best friend had last been seen in his company and no one had heard from her since? Obviously, she did.

After reading a similarly themed email from Chloe, Savannah drafted a reply to both of them. She wasn't ready to talk to Lucy or Chloe about what had happened. She hadn't yet sorted it out herself.

Got home safe and sound. Alone. Thanks for your concern, but no need to worry. Talk soon. S xx

She clicked on "send" and sank down low in her chair. Until she'd determined how Will was involved with Maranoa, she wouldn't spend another second thinking about what had happened between them.

An image of his gloriously naked body flashed through her mind. Her lips twisted into a wry smile. Okay, forgetting about their night together might be easier said than done. It didn't mean she couldn't give it her best shot.

Glancing up, she noticed her editor striding toward her, his sizeable belly leading the way. His face was flushed and his gaze glinted with determination. She swallowed a groan and logged out of her email account. As short on niceties as he was on height, Max got straight to the point.

"Savannah, I want you to do a follow-up on yesterday's story. We've received hundreds of emails about it. People are outraged and they're dying to know more. You have to strike while they're still salivating."

She blinked in surprise. "I thought you said it was too dangerous for me to go poking around in places like that? Who'd have thought a jump in sales was more important than my safety?" Her voice was as dry as Milo's kitty litter. She still hadn't forgiven her editor for refusing her byline. Not even having the grace to look embarrassed, he plowed on.

"Forget about what I said. That was yesterday. The only thing is, I'd rather you have a look at some of the other brothels in the city. Widen the scope a bit, you know? I'm sure the Black Opal's not the only one involved in shady dealings. You could do a whole series."

"But, Max I can't just—" Her protest was cut short.

"You're not listening to me, Savannah."

He spoke to her like one would speak to a preschooler. It was all she could do not to roll her eyes.

"Go onto Google and do a little research," he continued. "Widen the net. I want to expose every last one of these places for what they are. You're a good writer. I'm sure you're up for the challenge and I'm also sure I don't have to remind you how good another sellout story will look to the people responsible for paying your wages. With all the cutbacks around here, it will help shore up your position if you manage another sellout. You never know when the bean counters will turn their gaze on you."

He stared at her meaningfully. Savannah lowered her gaze. Max knew that she couldn't afford to lose her job. Besides, what he said made sense. There probably were other brothels in the city carrying on illegal activities. The thought of other poor girls being subjected to what was happening at the Black Opal made her blood boil. It was only right that they be exposed.

Apparently satisfied by her lack of response, Max

nodded. "Good, I'm glad that's settled. Get onto your sources and see what you can find out. I want something on my desk by Thursday." He turned and stalked away, ending the conversation as abruptly as he'd started it.

Savannah's mouth dropped open in astonishment. Finding her feet and her tongue, she pushed away from her chair and shouted, "Max, that's only two days away! I can't make contact with the girls working in other brothels in that time. It's impossible."

Max stopped and turned, his face dark with a frown she knew from experience was not to be taken lightly.

"Savannah, I don't want to hear excuses. You managed it the first time around. I'm sure you'll manage it again. We have to strike now, while the public are still outraged over our expose´. Next week it might be something else that has them all hot and bothered and we'll miss our opportunity. Now, get on with it." He stalked away, hauling his bulk in the direction from where he'd come.

Her thoughts turned sour. *Yeah, right. Just get on with it.* Like it was that simple.

There was no way in the world two days was enough time to allow for fresh sources to be contacted and persuaded to talk. She didn't know what planet he was on, but the women she'd spoken to at the Black Opal were extremely wary about coming forward with information. She couldn't simply waltz into another brothel, snap her fingers and get people to talk to her. Even last Saturday night, it had taken a good couple of hours of gentle persuasion to finally get Malee talking and it had been Malee who had made the initial contact.

She couldn't possibly achieve that kind of trust and openness from an unfamiliar sex worker who might or might not appreciate the media looking into their livelihood. It was beyond ridiculous to suggest otherwise.

Chances were zero to none that she'd come up with the kind of story Max was angling for in the time frame he'd allotted. The only brothel she had a hope of cajoling further information out of its employees by Thursday was the one she'd already visited. Max may have asked her to 'widen the net,' but if he wanted a story that week, he'd have to accept it would be on the Black Opal.

Besides, he was in the business of selling newspapers. Hers wasn't the only job that depended upon sales figures. She was sure once they'd managed two sellouts in one week, he'd forget all about his request to investigate other establishments. At least, she hoped so.

With a sigh of resignation, she took out her cell and scrolled through her list of contacts, stopping when she found Malee's number. Pressing the send button, she prayed silently that the girl would answer. The phone rang for what seemed an eon of time before it was finally directed to voicemail. Malee's message had obviously been recorded for clients as her voice, even with its broken English, came through low and sultry.

"It's Malee. If you're after good time with very sexy girl, please leave message. I fit you in—all of you—just how you like it."

Savannah spoke quietly into the phone. "Malee, it's Savannah O'Neill from the *Daily Mirror*. I really need to get back into the brothel tonight. Please, call me." After leaving her number, she ended the call. All she could do now was wait.

———————————

Dylan listened to the voicemail message for a third time and reluctantly accepted the truth.

It was her. It was Savannah who had written the story.

How much she knew, was anyone's guess, but from the accuracy of her article, it was clear she'd spoken to at least someone inside the brothel with firsthand information.

Dread tightened his gut. She had no idea the danger she faced. No one fucked with Vince. If he found out, she'd wish she were dead already.

Did he risk warning her away? Would she even listen?

He'd be forced to tell her how he'd come upon his knowledge. Was he ready to do that? Was he ready to have her look at him with eyes full of sadness and disappointment, yet again? But what choice did he have? A warning from him might be enough to keep her away, keep her safe. After all, she was his sister.

Quiet panic gripped his insides. He'd already eradicated two of Vince's "problems" in the space of less than a week and that didn't count the first time. What if Vince ordered him to get rid of her? His own sister?

He shook his head in despair and confusion. When had his life spiraled so far out of control?

It had seemed so easy in the beginning. He'd first met Vince through his nephew. Tony Maranoa was only a few years older than Dylan and was also on a stint of court-ordered rehab. Meeting Tony in the rehab facility had been a stroke of luck. Not only that, it had changed Dylan's life.

Tony had made the introductions during a family visit. Vince had come to the facility to replenish his nephew's supplies. He had a thriving business in rehab. Demand inevitably outstripped supply and Tony named his price.

Dylan had been immediately drawn to the air of authority and power surrounding Vince. His Rolex had glinted impressively in the sun, as did the heavy gold chain around his neck. His suit was custom made and his leather shoes were so shiny they almost reflected the sky. Dylan wanted in and he was prepared to do anything it took to make it happen.

After consulting closely with Tony about Dylan's suitability, Vince finally agreed to take him on as a runner. He'd work with Georgie to hustle up business in the alleyways and in the darkened corners of the nightclubs that lined the streets of Kings Cross. It was Vince's main stomping ground. Dylan was young, good looking and charismatic. People would be drawn to him. People would trust him. It was a win-win situation.

Dylan had signed out of rehab a month early, eager to commence his new career. But first, to prove his loyalty to his new boss, Dylan was asked to take care of a little "problem."

Sam Fenton was a drug addict way past his "best before" date. The debt he owed to Vince was so out of control, it would take him three lifetimes to pay it back. The solution was simple: Vince would make Sam an example. It was important Vince's other customers realized what would happen if they didn't pay off their debts.

Though Dylan had nearly shit himself when the bum had opened his eyes right before Dylan had pulled the trigger, he'd done it anyway and Vince had been pleased. He nicknamed him "Billy the Kid." Life became a whole lot more pleasant.

It wasn't long before "Billy" was invited into the world behind the plain wooden doors that housed the Black Opal. The drugs were plentiful, the girls were friendly, the money poured in. But recently, he'd sensed a change. Vince was feeling the pressure—from what, Dylan didn't know.

What he did know was that Vince had turned meaner and with it came a nastiness Dylan had never contemplated. For the first time since he'd met his boss, he was scared. The usual caustic banter had been replaced by dark scowls and barked orders and after the week Dylan had just had, he was in no doubt that Vince meant business: Obey orders or disappear. No one was indispensable. It was as simple as that.

With an effort, Dylan shrugged off the dread that had weighed him down for the last twenty minutes, ever since he'd listened to Malee's voicemail. Taking care to delete the final message and wipe the phone clean of his prints, he tossed it into the harbor and watched while it slowly sank out of sight.

Savannah stared at her phone and willed it to ring. It had been more than half an hour since she'd left the message for Malee. With a sigh, she pushed away from her desk and collected her coffee mug. She walked to the tea room and filled the kettle.

Leaning against the counter while she waited for it to boil, she picked up a copy of the newspaper. Despite her best efforts, she'd arrived late and hadn't had time for her usual routine of coffee and a quick scan over the headlines before she started work.

A grainy picture on the front page snagged her attention. She read the short article. Almost immediately, fear tightened her belly.

The body of a female had been dragged out of the harbor the night before. The girl had been naked and so far, no one had come forward to identify her. Savannah stared at the photo and her blood ran cold.

It was Malee. She was sure of it.

The story went on to say the girl was thought to be between thirteen and eighteen-years-old. She'd been badly beaten and had suffered multiple fractures prior to her death. It was believed she'd been in the water for several days. An autopsy was underway. The homicide detectives were appealing to anyone with information to come forward.

Nausea swirled in Savannah's stomach. She felt sick at the thought she might have had something to do with the young girl's death. Malee had assured her she had somewhere to go—a trusted client who had promised to look after her. Savannah didn't want to begin to imagine what had gone wrong...

The gravity of the situation hit her hard. Her chest tightened, making it difficult to breathe. This wasn't just a sleazy brothel story. This was now a murder investigation, a matter of life and death. A woman who'd shared her secrets about the Black Opal and its owner had been killed. The coroner was yet to confirm the cause, but Savannah was prepared to wager her next month's pay that it hadn't been accidental.

Malee had been a strong, vibrant young woman,

determined to escape the hellhole that was her life and start again. There was no way she would have committed suicide if her escape had been successful... And the paper said she'd been badly beaten. Had she told the perpetrator she'd spoken to a reporter?

Savannah swiped at the perspiration that beaded her brow. She bit her lip in indecision, knowing she should contact the homicide squad immediately and tell them what she knew.

But what about Will? Was he somehow involved? He'd been at the brothel the same night as Malee's failed escape attempt. Could he have something to do with her murder?

She shook her head, refusing to consider it. No, there had to be some other explanation for his presence, some other reason why he and Maranoa went "way back." There had to be. She just hadn't found it yet.

If she went to homicide and shared what she knew, matters would be taken out of her hands. She would lose all control of the situation and there was a chance Will would be caught up in something he was totally innocent of. It would ruin his life. Even if he proved any potential allegations false, a man with such a high profile would never clear his name. He'd never be free of the whispers behind closed doors, the surreptitious glances, the people who would always question, always wonder.

She knew firsthand how it felt to be the brunt of cruel gossip and innuendo. When her parents had died, there were many in the academic world who had rejoiced just a little too loudly over their passing; people who had dropped sly comments that the bizarre accident that had claimed the lives of her mother and father had been no less than what they deserved; people who lived their lives within the sheltered walls of a university had no business trying to be outback adventurers.

Matters got even worse when Dylan went off the rails. First, it was shoplifting. Little things—a soft drink, a packet of gum—but it quickly escalated to electrical goods, alcohol and worse.

Savannah had been beside herself. She'd moved down to Canberra a year after the funeral to take up a job offer with the *Canberra Times* and had relocated Dylan with her. She'd hoped a new environment would help him through his troubles, but he'd found it difficult to fit into his new school, often complaining he had no friends and his teachers were dumb. She'd lost count of the number of suspensions.

It was almost inevitable that he'd turn to drugs. She was horrified when she'd discovered he was using. He was sixteen and smoking pot. He'd laughed off her concern, telling her she was old fashioned, shouting at her that she wasn't his mother, and she had no right to tell him what to do.

Their relationship deteriorated. No matter what she tried to say and do, he refused to listen. His drug use escalated. He was moody and unpredictable; there were times when she barely recognized him.

Despite the turmoil in her personal life, her career had been slowly flourishing. She'd quickly climbed the ladder from a junior journalist on the *Canberra Times* to rubbing shoulders with senior staff members who more often than not found themselves walking the corridors of Parliament House.

The thought of covering the often-animated discussions that occurred in the most powerful building in the country excited her. She worked even harder and stayed back even longer, prepared to do whatever it took. Looking back, she couldn't believe she'd existed for so long on sparse meals and snatched periods of sleep and through it all, she'd borne the stress of living with a drug addict.

But her efforts had paid off, at least where her career was concerned. Six months before her last birthday, she'd landed her dream job. That night, she'd gone by Jonathan's condominium to celebrate and had found him getting naked with another girl. Two hours later, Dylan had landed in jail.

The reality of her brother's situation had hit her hard and went a considerable way to distracting her from her heartbreak over her fiancé. Dylan was at crisis point and it was up to her to do something. He was now over eighteen. There would be no gentle raps across the knuckles from the courts. He would be dealt with by the full force of the law.

The judge said as much when he'd sentenced Dylan for being in possession of marijuana. Because it was his first conviction, he'd been given a choice: Go to a court-sanctioned rehabilitation center or do time in jail.

For Savannah, there had been no choice. The day after she'd walked down the aisle as Chloe Munro's bridesmaid, she'd packed up her home. With her car loaded to the roof with their luggage, she and Dylan had returned to their hometown of Sydney where she'd immediately enrolled him in a rehabilitation program. Within a few weeks, she'd been fortunate to pick up a job at the *Daily Mirror*.

Six months down the track, she was beginning to question her decision. Despite the enormous bills she paid every month to the rehab center for his treatment, she had yet to see any proof that Dylan had reformed. On top of that, her job was getting her down.

It was a far cry from the excitement and action of Parliament House. Until she'd broken the story on the Black Opal, the majority of her stories had covered nothing more exciting than the occasional break and enter or a pile-up on the freeway. Not that those items weren't newsworthy, but writing about them wasn't quite the same as the make-and-break stories she'd covered in the parliamentary press gallery.

Once again, her thoughts returned to Will. She still couldn't believe how quickly she'd become entangled with him. She'd hoped that by dumping Jonathan and moving to Sydney, the complications in her life would drift away. But Will had become "complication" personified. Was she mad to even contemplate trying to sort out what was going on with him? And did she really care?

She did. That was the problem.

There was nothing for it. She'd go back to the Black Opal. Only this time, she was going to have to do it without Malee's help.

Determination surged through her. She wouldn't rest until she had all the proof she needed to expose Maranoa for the criminal that he was. The stories Malee had told her hurt her head and her heart.

She vowed to see an end to it. She would make sure Malee's brave escape attempt that had ended so tragically hadn't been in vain and while she was at it, she'd determine once and for all the level of Will's involvement.

Chapter 8

Will leaned back against his chair and enjoyed his first cup of coffee that morning. A few other uniforms and a couple of plain clothes detectives mingled in the tea room, trading idle chitchat and the usual off-color jokes as they prepared for the day ahead.

Pete strode into the squad room and the hum of conversation lowered momentarily, amongst casual morning greetings. Setting his cup back onto his desk, Will stood and followed Pete into his office, closing the door behind them.

Pete glanced at him and then turned to hang his jacket in the locker which stood in the corner of the room. His desk held the usual clutter of papers, files, photographs and endless piles of police statements. Will could relate to the mess.

"Will, how's it going? What happened to you last night?

Heat flooded Will's face and his gut churned with sudden nerves. "I-I was wondering if I could ask you a question?"

Pete nodded and took a seat. "Fire away."

Now that the moment was upon him, Will wasn't sure what to say. The truth was, he wanted to ask Pete about Savannah. Ever since he'd left her at the hotel, he hadn't been able to get her off his mind. It was so unlike him. He'd been happily playing the field for years. Not once had he met a woman he'd wanted to spend more than a night or two with.

But with Savannah it was different. He wanted to know

everything about her and at the top of the list was why she worked as a prostitute.

He didn't believe her claim she was a journalist, but there was something not quite right about the picture of her as a call girl, either. Not that she hadn't been sensational in bed, but there were times when she'd seemed a little shy and uncertain—almost surprised—by her responses. Not to mention her predilection for a number of very intriguing blushes. They weren't the kind of things he expected from a woman who made a living taking money for sex.

"Come on, Will. Spit it out." Pete's brusque order jarred him out of his reverie. Swallowing hard against sudden nerves, he chose his words with care.

"The-the other night, when I was at the Black Opal, I saw a girl there."

"Surely that's not unusual."

Heat stole up his neck. He briefly closed his eyes to avoid the other man's sardonic gaze.

"What I mean is…um… I-I saw Savannah there."

Pete frowned. "Savannah? You can't mean Savannah O'Neill?"

Will glanced away. This was going to be more difficult than he'd imagined. He gritted his teeth and forced himself to continue. "Yeah, Savannah O'Neill. Of course, I didn't know it was her at the time, but when you introduced us at the ball last night, I recognized her straight away. After I left with her, we got to ah—" He stopped abruptly, his face burning.

"Talking," Pete supplied, deadpan.

"Talking, yeah… That's right." He cleared his throat noisily. "We got to talking about…*things* and she told me she was a journalist. Of course, I know that's a load of shit."

"Really?" A smile played around Pete's lips. "What makes you say that?"

Will's entire face was now on fire. He squirmed under Pete's steady regard. If only the man hadn't told him he regarded Savannah like a kid sister. Knowing he had to get it over with, he took a deep breath and met the other man's amused gaze head-on. "How well do you know Savannah?"

Pete picked up the Styrofoam coffee cup he'd brought in with him and took a sip. "Better than you, I'd say. She's been a friend of Lucy's since high school. I've known her almost as long as I've known my wife. I think we clocked over five years last anniversary. Of course, Savannah's only been back in Sydney six months, but the girls have always kept in touch."

"So, you know she's a prostitute?" Will blurted.

Pete almost choked on his laughter. "A *prostitute?* You're kidding, right? That's the most ridiculous thing I've ever heard."

Will's anger stirred. "Have you forgotten what I told you? This girl, the one who's been your wife's best friend for like, forever, was in the Black Opal on Saturday night."

Pete waved his hand dismissively. "You must be mistaken, Will. Savannah wouldn't even know how to find her way to the door of one of those establishments. It must have been someone else who looked a little like her."

Will clenched his jaw. "I know what I saw. I was there doing *surveillance*, remember? I noticed everything. Believe me or not, but she was there."

Pete sobered. His eyes drilled into Will's. "Do you mean to tell me Savannah O'Neill, my wife's best friend, was *working* in a city brothel? You can't be serious!"

Refusing to mince words any longer, Will stepped closer. "She was working there, all right. She even performed in the live stage act."

"What?" Pete exclaimed. "She was *performing* on stage? In a *brothel?*"

"Yeah. The Black Opal's the only brothel in town that offers nightly live entertainment—kind of like a cabaret thing, but there's no singing and a hell of a lot less clothing. I guess it's supposed to draw the crowds in—which it does, by the way.

"Anyway, like I said, Savannah danced half naked on the stage with a group of other girls who were equally scantily clad, in front of an almost capacity crowd of blokes in

Sydney's most exclusive brothel." He glared. "Any part of that you didn't get?"

Pete appeared momentarily lost for words. Seconds later, he exploded. "*Christ!* I'm going to kill her! What the *hell* was she doing?"

"Earning a living, I guess."

"Would you stop *saying* that? You don't honestly think she's a *prostitute?*" Pete's face reflected his incredulity.

Will shrugged. Pete laughed in disbelief.

"She's a journalist, you idiot! Just like she told you. If you'd been thinking with your head instead of your cock, you might have actually believed her."

Comprehension slowly dawned, leaving Will speechless. He suddenly recalled the words he'd thrown at her, offensive, nasty words that he'd used with the intention of drawing blood, hurled in retaliation for the hurt and disappointment he'd felt at what he thought was her deception. She'd kneed him in the balls, after all... *Fuck.*

"I take it she's a girl who goes to extreme measures for a front page," Will muttered. "Very convincing measures. *I* certainly fell for it."

Pete shook his head. "Are you telling me when I introduced you to her last night, you thought she was a prostitute?"

Will nodded, unable to meet his eyes.

"I don't believe it! You thought I would introduce you to Lucy's best friend, who, by the way, happens to be a prostitute?"

He flushed under Pete's sarcasm. "I thought perhaps she was an escort or something and that maybe the Saturday night gig was a one-off."

"Hell, this gets better and better." Pete growled, running his hands through his hair in exasperation. "I guess that explains why you disappeared with her less than an hour after you met? You thought, what the hell, she takes money for sex, why not avail myself of her serv—"

"*No.*" Will's cold retort stopped Pete short. "That's *not* the reason I slept with her less than an hour after we met."

"So you're not denying you slept with her." Pete glared at him, breathing heavily.

Will fought to bring his temper back under control. He understood why Pete was upset, but he refused to wear the tag his boss was trying to pin on him. When he spoke again, his voice was quiet but brooked no argument.

"The reason I went upstairs with her was because she had me so hard, I couldn't think of anything else. Yes, at the time, I thought she was a prostitute, but that's not why I slept with her." His eyes drilled into Pete's, almost defiantly. "I slept with her because I wanted to. And she wanted it, too."

"Bloody hell!" Pete ran both of his hands through the short bristles of his hair. "How did it come to this? I send you in there to get information about the drug ring we're trying to close down and you come out with *this!* What am I supposed to tell Lucy? Who, by the way, did not fail to notice your very conspicuous absence at our table. Couldn't you have at least kept it in your pants until after the ball was over?"

Will grinned, shrugging unapologetically. "Apparently not. Besides, why do you need to tell Lucy anything?"

"Spoken like a man who's never been married."

"Tell her you couldn't get a thing out of me." Will grinned again. "Let her go and ask her best *friend* all about it. Isn't that what girls do?"

"Yeah, you're right. I'm going to stay well away from this one." Pete glanced at him over the rim of his coffee cup. "By the way, what was that bullshit you fed me last night all about?"

"What do you mean?"

"At the bar, when you told me Savannah didn't like coppers."

Will shrugged, embarrassed now to reveal how off-base his assumptions had been.

Pete's eyes narrowed. "She does know you're a cop, doesn't she?"

He shrugged again. "I'm not sure. I haven't said anything to her."

"What's the big secret?"

Another flush warmed Will's cheeks. "No big secret. It's just... I just..." He stared at the certificates on Pete's wall and scrounged around for the courage to tell his boss exactly what he'd thought.

"Come on, Will. Spit it out." Pete's voice held a tinge of impatience as he began sorting through the mess of papers on his desk.

Will took a deep breath and eyed his commander. "You have to remember I first met her at the brothel. At the time and even last night, I thought she might be involved in Maranoa's operation."

Pete's head snapped up in surprise. "How the hell would you come up with an idea like that?" He shook his head slowly. "Will, I know you're a good investigator. I read your file from top to bottom when you applied for the transfer out of homicide. I saw all the citations, your success rate, the letters of appreciation. I read it all." He paused.

"But you're starting to worry me. You've been putting in a lot of hours on this Maranoa thing and it hasn't even been six months since your brother died. Something's got to give, mate." Pete's gaze was steady on Will's face. "You refused to take leave after Cole's funeral, but I think you should reconsider. As much as I hate to suggest it, given how short staffed we are, you could do with a bit of time off."

Will bit off an instinctive protest and forced himself to remain calm. "I'm fine, boss; I'm fine. You're right, I have been working hard. I want to nail this bastard so badly I can taste it. And you're right about Cole. I'm still struggling to come to terms with his suicide."

He drew in a deep breath and appealed to Pete for understanding. "But I don't need any time off. I need to be here, boss. I need to stay on the job. I need to stay on this investigation. We're getting close; I'm sure of it."

Pete's nodded, but he continued to look troubled. "Okay, I'll give you the benefit of the doubt, for now, but as soon as we've nailed this case, you're taking leave. At least a month. No arguments."

Will's shoulders slumped in relief. "Absolutely. You have my word on it. As soon as we have Maranoa behind bars, I'll hang up my boots—for a week or so."

Pete offered a grudging smile and nodded his acceptance. Will smiled back.

"You know, whoever wrote that story might have done us a favor," Will mused.

"What do you mean?"

"Well, to begin with, I was pissed that it might jeopardize the investigation. But now, I think it's probably just what we need. Maranoa must be hopping mad to know someone's infiltrated his domain. He's bound to react in some way. He might get sloppy. This could be our chance."

"Do we know who wrote it, yet?"

"No, but I'm meeting with the editor this afternoon."

"Could the story have been written by Savannah?"

Will frowned and for the first time gave genuine consideration to the possibility. "I guess so. That would explain why she was there and the article contained far too much detail to have been written by someone without intimate knowledge of the place."

"I guess I could phone her and ask?"

"I'd rather you didn't." Will fidgeted under Pete's scrutiny. "I probably need to apologize to her before she finds out we've been talking. I wasn't exactly flattering when I told her I didn't believe she had journalistic qualifications. Besides, I'm sure her editor will clarify it for us. As far as he knows, I'm merely a curious advertising executive. Whatever his initial reasons for withholding the byline, my casual enquiry as to the journalist's identity will hardly rouse his suspicions."

Pete frowned back at him. "Just you be careful with her— you understand? I'm sure you're a love 'em and leave 'em kind of guy." He shrugged. "That's your choice. But Savannah's not like that. She's a nice girl, a *really* nice girl. I don't want you breaking her heart. She's been down that road before."

Will nodded, but remained silent. He couldn't deny the

relief he'd felt when Pete told him she wasn't a prostitute, but he wasn't ready to think of her as a "nice" girl or analyze his feelings for her yet.

"I won't hurt her. I promise."

Pete stared at him for a moment or two and then looked away. "Let me know how you go with the editor. If it *is* Savannah who wrote that story, she has some explaining to do." Pete's face darkened and he shook his head. "What am I saying? Story or no story, she already has some explaining to do and I'm just in the mood to get some answers."

CHAPTER 9

Tuesday afternoon

"Savannah? Got a minute?" Max's head appeared over the top of the partition that divided Savannah's desk from her colleagues.

"Sure." Savannah glanced up at the editor and then continued to type on her keyboard. "If it's about the story, I haven't—"

"In my office." He heaved his bulk around and lumbered away.

She frowned. Usually, Max was only too happy to broadcast any conversation, personal or not, to anyone who happened to be listening. To be summoned to his private domain, and in such a brusque manner, left her feeling nervous, especially after their earlier confrontation.

What could he possibly want to say to her that required the privacy of his office? Her mind raced over various possibilities. Maybe he was giving her news of a promotion? *Hardly.* Hadn't he mentioned cutbacks?

Maybe he'd found out how she'd pretended to be a prostitute? He hadn't actually asked her how she'd come by her information. He'd already pointed out how the newspaper was responsible for her safety while she was on a job. Maybe he was going to fire her?

Knowing there was only one way to find out, Savannah

pushed away from her desk. A moment later she stood outside Max's office.

"Close the door." Max was reclined in his enormous leather chair, his hands stacked behind his head. His tie was askew and his shirt had pulled away from his suit pants. His beady eyes glittered with something she couldn't define. Her nervousness ratcheted up another notch.

"A little while ago, I had a very interesting conversation with Will Rutledge. I'm sure you've heard of Rutledge Advertising?"

Her mouth fell open in surprise. *He* was the last reason she'd expected. She hurriedly cleared her throat. "Yes, I've…I've heard of them."

"It appears he's interested in yesterday's story."

She frowned in confusion, but remained silent.

"See," Max continued, "the thing is, I met with him about a substantial advertising feature his father's company is running in the paper. Curiously, he asked who wrote the brothel story. In fact, he seemed more interested in that than he was with the ad campaign."

Savannah's heart skipped a beat. Was Will reconsidering his abrupt dismissal of her claim she was a journalist?

Trying her best to look disinterested, she shrugged. "Did you tell him it was me?"

Max smiled with glee. "Oh, I sure did."

With a sheer act of will, and despite the sudden tightness in her chest, Savannah remained unmoved. Will now knew she'd been telling the truth. He hadn't bothered to call her and apologize. Perhaps he didn't think an apology was warranted? Anger simmered just below the surface.

Max eyeballed her. "Why would a man like that be interested in your story?"

She scrambled for something to say. "Um, I'm not sure. Unless, of course—" Savannah stopped abruptly, unsure she wanted to share her suspicions with her editor.

"Unless what?" he pounced.

Knowing she had no choice but to continue, she took a deep breath. Her words came out in a rush. "Unless he's involved, somehow."

Max snorted with laughter. "Is that the best you can do? Surely, you know who Rutledge *is*?"

Savannah flushed in annoyance. "Of course I know who he is! But so what? It wouldn't be the first time someone rich and influential has broken the law and it would certainly explain his interest in the story."

"True, but we're talking about Will Rutledge here. He's hardly your ordinary rich guy. He's involved in a host of charitable projects around the city, donates thousands of dollars each year to drug rehabilitation centers and halfway houses... You do know his brother died of a drug overdose, don't you?"

Surprise surged through her accompanied by a twinge of sympathy. Pushing them aside, she shook her head.

"No, I didn't, but that doesn't mean he's not involved in the illegal drug trade on some other level. I'm not suggesting he's a drug *user*, but—"

"Whoa, Savannah! My, you do have an active little imagination."

Savannah gritted her teeth at his condescending tone and forced herself to remain silent.

"You didn't make mention of this in the article. I take it you don't have any proof?" Max asked.

She hesitated. If she was honest, she didn't really know what she had. Yes, she'd seen Will at the brothel, and yes, he'd made a pretty damning remark about having a history with the owner, but none of that could be called evidence.

"No, but I-I saw him there..."

Max leaned forward in his chair and pinned her with his gaze. "You *saw* him at the Black Opal? When?"

"L-last Saturday night. The night I spoke to the women."

"What was he doing?"

Savannah shrugged and did her best to back-pedal. She really had no idea what she'd seen or what Will had meant.

"I-I don't know. He was just *there*."

Max turned his head and stared at the wall near his desk. A long moment later, he drew in a deep breath and turned back to her.

"Savannah, I suggest you listen and listen well. Rutledge Advertising is one of this paper's biggest clients. The money they spend on advertising every year is enough to pay the annual salaries of at least a quarter of your colleagues. I'm not going to have that jeopardized by some half-cocked theory about what Will Rutledge may or may not do in his spare time. Do you understand what I'm saying?"

Savannah gaped in shock. "Are-are you telling me you want me to drop a story because it might offend Will Rutledge?"

Menace glimmered in Max's eyes. A shiver of unease ran down her spine. A moment later, his face was wreathed in smiles and she wondered if she'd imagined it.

"Savannah, Savannah, Savannah. You're taking this much too seriously. It's like I've already told you. There are a lot of other brothels in this city. Go and investigate one of them. The fact is, it appears young Rutledge likes the Black Opal. It *is* the city's most exclusive establishment. It makes sense it's where a man of his social standing would choose to go to...*relax*."

His expression was full of innuendo. Savannah suppressed a shudder of distaste. Max continued, undeterred.

"It's not a crime for a man to frequent a brothel. I've been in one or two myself. That hardly makes me a criminal, or a drug dealer, or whatever other fanciful ideas you have running around in that pretty little head of yours."

Swift anger heated her blood. She'd had enough of Max's insults. If he wasn't the editor of the city's largest paper and if she didn't need the money quite so badly, she'd tell him where to stick his attitude. And his job. She could almost hear her mother's voice in her ear, encouraging her to do just that.

As if sensing he might have pushed her too far, Max offered a conciliatory smile. "From what you've said, you don't have time to discuss the whys and wherefores of these men and their secret pleasures. Why don't you get back to work and make sure you have something ready for me by Thursday?"

Savannah bit down on her anger and turned away. Fumbling with the doorknob, she finally managed to open it. She stumbled, dazed, toward her desk.

What the hell was that all about?

Granted, the newspaper would lose a great deal of money if Rutledge Advertising pulled their campaign, but surely a man in Max's position couldn't be bought? Not running another story on the Black Opal in order to appease a favored client was tantamount to bribery.

Savannah's temper flared again. It wasn't right for Max to make such a request. So what if he was the editor? Surely they had a responsibility to inform the public about these kinds of things? If Will was involved in criminal activities, it was only right that he be exposed. If he had nothing to hide, then he had nothing to fear.

What Max had said about the other brothels in the city was probably true, but she'd promised Malee she'd do all she could to get the Black Opal shut down. The girls were sex slaves and people like Vince Maranoa, and maybe even Will Rutledge, were getting rich from it. She wasn't going to stand by and let it keep happening. Job be damned, she was more determined than ever to return.

Her mother would be proud.

With fingers that were far from steady, Max reached for his phone and dialed Vince's number. Max would never admit it, but Vince scared the shit out of him. Always had.

Savannah's revelation that Will Rutledge had been at the Black Opal on top of the man's obvious interest in yesterday's story weighed heavily on his mind. It could be simply a coincidence, but what if it wasn't?

The young Rutledge was known as a man about town, a playboy with access to more money than sense. It was ludicrous to suggest he could be involved in a police sting, but still, it paid to be sure. Max hadn't come this far without being careful.

Vince answered with his customary brusqueness. "Yeah?"

"It's-it's me. I-I was wondering what you knew about Will Rutledge?"

"Robert's son?"

"Yeah. I met with him a little while ago about an advertising package and he expressed more than a little interest in the story we ran on the brothel. I've just discovered he was at the Black Opal last weekend."

"How good's your information?"

"Reliable."

Vince puffed out his breath on the other end of the phone. "Robert's been a member of the club for years. He's a regular who's more than happy to pay generously for the services we provide. I don't know much about his young whelp. Let's just say the boy's never come to my attention."

Max's shoulders slumped in relief. "That's good to hear. I-I just wondered. You know, with him being so curious and all..."

"I'll ask around. See what I can find out. You never can be too careful."

"My thoughts exactly."

The afternoon sun reflected off the tall glassed buildings that surrounded the offices of Rutledge Advertising in sparkles of white light so bright it hurt Will's eyes. Grateful for the protection of his Ray Bans, he strode to the parking station where he'd left his unmarked police vehicle. Along the way, he tugged out his phone and dialed Pete's number.

"Will, how did it go with the editor? I take it you got a name?"

"Yes, as a matter of fact, I did." Will paused, still a little hesitant to tell him.

"So, who is it?" Exasperation tinged Pete's voice.

Biting the bullet, he laid it on the line. "It was Savannah."

"I'm going to kill her."

"Max O'Connor seemed only too pleased to tell me." Will frowned. "Not that I think he was lying, but there's something about him I don't trust."

"What do you mean?"

"I thought it would be more difficult to get the information out of him. It could have been the money talking, but that doesn't explain the rest of it."

"What do you mean?"

Will drew in a breath and let it out slowly. "This guy's the editor of the city's largest newspaper, right? What do you think he'd be earning?"

"Oh, I don't know, a hundred grand a year, something like that, I guess."

"Yeah, that's what I figured, but he came into my office wearing a five thousand dollar suit. His briefcase probably cost another couple of grand and he wouldn't have gotten change out of a thousand bucks for his shoes. How does an editor, on a hundred grand a year, afford to dress like that?"

"It does sound a little odd. I guess, he could have married into money, or inherited it. What's your take on it?"

"I don't know, but it got my antennae up. I've learned to pay attention when that happens."

"I'll get one of the general duties boys to look into it, see what they can dig up. It would be nice to know there's an innocent explanation."

"Yeah." Will arrived at his destination and unlocked his car. "Oh, speaking of digging up, I'm returning to the Black Opal tonight to do a little more reconnaissance. With a bit of luck, I might run into Maranoa. I should be cleared to visit the *Room of Dreams* by now."

Pete murmured his assent. "Just watch your back. You never know when your cover might be blown. All it will take is for someone who knows you're a cop to recognize you and you're going to be in a world of hurt. Even with your backup, there's no guarantee they would get to you in time."

"Who's rostered on with me?"

"I'll arrange for Baines and Michaels to be there. They can pose as out-of-town businessmen. Provided they can get past security, I'll have them situated somewhere in the main bar. If they're turned away at the door, they'll be outside in the nearby vicinity."

"Good. Let's hope our luck holds."

"What about this sex slave thing Savannah mentioned? Do you have any information about that?"

"No, I didn't get a chance to speak to any of the girls there, other than Savannah. I noticed that all the rest were Asian, though. That's a little strange in itself, although that doesn't mean they're being held illegally."

"I'll find out if anyone in Central Division is looking into it. Maybe there's a taskforce already working on it. If Savannah's found out about it, I'd like to think someone in law enforcement knows."

Will smiled into the phone. "You'd hope so. If I get a chance, I'll speak to some of the girls tonight. Savannah must have obtained her information from someone."

Pete's voice filled with disbelief. "I still can't believe she did it."

"You and me both."

"I meant what I said, Will. You be careful tonight, okay?"

He laughed. "I'm always careful, boss. I might not be good, but I'm *always* careful."

Vince pinched his chin in thought and then pushed away from his desk. Opening the door to his office, he stuck his head out into the corridor.

"Billy, get your ass in here now," he yelled. "I want to talk to you."

The Kid sauntered into the room and flung himself down in the only other available chair. If anyone else had approached Vince with such a cavalier attitude, he'd have had their balls, but he liked the Kid and the boy had proved useful on more than one occasion.

"What is it, boss?"

"I've got a job for you."

"Yeah?"

"I want you to pay particular attention to one of our patrons. As far as I know, he's not a regular, so I can't tell you when he might show up again, but when he does, I want you to take notice."

Billy showed only slightly more interest. "Who is it?"

"His name's Will Rutledge. He's Robert's son."

"The advertising bloke?"

"Yeah, the one who comes in every Friday night and asks for Polly. He's a handsome tipper." Vince's lips twisted wryly. "I'm sure you know him."

Billy nodded. "Yeah, big old guy, white hair. Always has a Cuban with his scotch."

"That's the one. I've got no issue with him, so leave him out of it. It's his son who's caught my interest."

Billy sat forward, curiosity now plain on his face. "Why's that?"

"Never you mind. What I want you to do is keep an eye on him. He was here on Saturday night. He asked Georgie to get him approved for the *Room of Dreams*. I've given him the go ahead. If he gets on the gear, or even if he just wants a fuck, I want you to be there watching, you understand?"

"Yeah, sure. I can do that. How will I know what he looks like?"

Vince pulled open the drawer of his desk and handed Billy a sheaf of papers. "Here. I got these off the Internet. Lucky for you, our boy's popular with the paparazzi. Take a good look at 'em."

Billy leaned over the desk and studied the photographs and then shook his head in annoyance.

"Fuck, Vince. He looks just like all the other rich assholes that frequent this place. How the fuck am I supposed to know it's him?"

Vince narrowed his gaze on Billy. "Those rich assholes

keep you and me in business, Billy. Don't forget it. And you'll fuckin' memorize those pictures until you can pick him out of a fifty-man lineup. Understand?"

Billy nodded.

"Good. You'll work it out, Kid. You can never be too careful. It's as simple as that. I like to call it insurance. You just don't know when you're gonna need it."

CHAPTER 10

Tuesday evening

Savannah applied a thick coat of black mascara to her eyelashes. Her hand shook from barely contained nerves. Her eyelids were already heavily made up with a blend of brown and green and purple eye shadow. It was way overdone, but it wouldn't look out of place in the muted lighting of the brothel.

She glanced at the clock on her iPod dock where it sat on her nightstand.

Nine o'clock.

She had half an hour to psych herself up about returning to the Black Opal. Despite her earlier determination, her courage had diminished with every passing hour and she was at the point where she wondered whether she'd be able to risk it all again.

Thoughts of Malee and her broken body were fresh in her mind. Vince wasn't a man to be messed with. If he even suspected something wasn't right, she'd be fish bait. Did she really want to take the chance?

And then there was Max. He'd be livid. Her only hope was that he'd see it her way if she managed to get the scoop on the entire story of the shocking dealings at the brothel. Max was a numbers man and nothing sold newspapers better than a story on sex, drugs and celebrities.

With another nervous glance at the clock, she quickly applied a second coat of chocolate-brown lipstick. Slipping on five-inch, black high-heels, the same ones she'd worn to the ball, she checked her appearance in the mirror.

The tight, black leather skirt rode high on her thighs and she blushed at the thought people were actually going to see her in it. She'd bought it on eBay last year and it wasn't until it had arrived and she'd put it on, that she realized how short it was. It hadn't looked that short on the website. One of the problems with buying things online.

Still, it had been a bargain at fifteen dollars, including postage, and it had fit her perfectly. Until now, she'd never imagined actually wearing it, but she hadn't given it away, either. Now, she was glad she'd kept it.

Teamed with a short and clingy, low cut, black midriff top and black fishnet stockings, she was sure she'd pass inspection, if it came to that. While she was hopeful it wouldn't, she didn't want to draw attention to herself by looking out of place.

In the likely event that she found the back door locked, her plan was to prevail upon one of the security guards to let her inside. She was relying on the fact they'd never imagine a woman, other than one of the working girls, would want to get in and so they wouldn't question her story. Once inside, she planned to locate at least one of the girls and talk to them.

Taking a deep breath, she did her best to calm the anxious fluttering in her stomach. She considered the list of questions she hoped would be answered tonight. Adrenaline pulsed through her at the thought of what was to come.

A sharp rap at the front door sent her nerves into a frenzy. She took a peek through the peephole and breathed a sigh of relief at the familiar face on the other side. With quick movements, she opened the deadbolt and swung the door inwards.

"Dylan! What are you doing here?"

Her brother stepped over the threshold, a disarming smile

stretching his mouth wide. Sweeping her into his arms, he squeezed her tightly.

"Hey, sis. Thought I'd drop around for a visit. It's good to see you."

Taking in his appearance, she frowned. He was in dire need of a haircut with his reddish-brown hair wild and unruly. In direct contrast, his shirt and pants sported designer labels. "You should be at Dexter House, Dylan. What are you doing here?"

He shrugged and his gaze skipped away. "I had to get out of there, sis. I couldn't stand another minute of their bullshit. Meditation, quiet solitude, counseling sessions, group therapy—it's all such a load of shit."

Her lips tightened with barely suppressed frustration. She looked up at him. She was older by nine years, but it had been a long time since she'd seen the top of his head.

"Dylan, they're trying to help you. You promised your lawyer you'd stick it out this time. What's going to happen if you have to front the judge again?"

He thrust his bottom lip out in a familiar display of petulance. "Don't worry about it, Sav. It'll be cool. You'll see. I'm clean." He stepped away from her and spread his arms wide. "I haven't used for months."

Wanting to believe him, but not sure if she could, Savannah led him into the kitchen. "Can I get you a cup of coffee?"

"Yeah, that'd be great." He glanced around the tidy room. "So, how've you been?"

Filling the electric jug with water, she glanced back at him. "Not too bad. Busy at work. Actually, I was on my way out." She plugged the jug in and switched it on, then turned to face him.

As if noticing her appearance for the first time, Dylan's eyes widened. "You're all dressed up. Hitting the nightclubs?"

Now it was her turn to avoid his gaze. She forced a smile. "S-something like that. I'm youngish and single. Thought I'd go and have a good time."

He grinned back at her. "Good on you. I thought you'd never get back on the scene after all that shit you went through with that asshole you were engaged to." His gaze moved over her. "You're looking good. I might even join you."

Savannah thought fast. "Um, look, normally I'd love to hang out with you, but it's just that—um, it's kind of a girl's night." The lie burned in her throat. She looked away, hoping he wouldn't discern the guilt in her eyes.

She needn't have worried. His lips tugged upwards in a grin. "Way to go, Sav. Good for you." He came forward and rested his hands on her shoulders. "I wouldn't dream of cramping your style." His eyes twinkled down at her. "Besides, those girls are all way too old for me."

"Hey!" She punched him playfully in the arm. "Easy on the age thing, little brother. None of us have hit thirty, yet."

Dylan held his arms up in surrender. "Okay, okay. I was joking. I think it's great that you're getting out again." He smiled broadly and she was reminded how good-looking he was. She sent a silent prayer that he was off the drugs for good. So much wasted potential. If only...

"I promise I won't wait up for you."

Savannah blinked and focused her attention back on him. "You're staying?"

His eyes skittered away from hers. "Yeah, if it's all right. It will only be for a night. Maybe two."

"What about Dexter House? You still have a month to go on your program."

"I've learned all I'm going to there."

"But, the judge—"

"Will only find out if I break my bond, which I'm not going to do. I promise." He shot her a beguiling smile. "I'm good, Sav. I'm great. I'm clean and I feel on top of the world. I went to rehab kicking and screaming and all their carrying on about therapy and crap annoyed the shit out of me, but I'm happy to admit it was for the best. It worked and I'm glad, but I'm finished. What can I learn in another month that I haven't already?"

Savannah suppressed a sigh and headed into the hall. She pulled out a blanket from the linen cupboard. "Here." She tossed it to him. "You can sleep on the couch."

"Thanks, sis. I knew I could rely on you."

"Just as long as you know it's only temporary," she warned.

His face was a picture of innocence. "Of course."

"If you're feeling so good, you need to start looking for a job and an apartment of your own."

"Absolutely. It's time I stood on my own two feet. You've done more than enough for me over the years."

Savannah searched for signs of insincerity and found none. Her heart filled with love. Stepping closer, she put her arms around his waist and hugged him.

"I'm so glad you're better," she whispered against his shirt front. "I didn't know if I'd ever get my brother back again."

Dylan squirmed out of her embrace and moved away. "Yeah, yeah, yeah. No need to go all soppy on me. I thought you had somewhere to go?"

Glancing at her watch, she noted the time. "You're right." She picked up her keys and wallet off the top of the TV cabinet and turned to face him.

"I have to go. The..." Savannah hesitated. "The girls are waiting for me." She gave him another quick hug. "Help yourself to the kitchen. I'm sure you'll find something to eat, if you're hungry."

"Thanks, Sav." He caught her eye and held it. "I really appreciate it."

She shrugged and looked away. "Hey, that's what family's for, right?"

Leaving him in the living room, she picked up the dark-colored canvas bag she'd left on the kitchen table and checked to make sure the long black wig she'd replaced earlier was in it. She still had no idea where the other one had ended up. Somewhere in the brothel, no doubt.

She stowed her wallet in another pocket and picked up her phone. Dread settled heavily in her stomach at the thought of what lay ahead. Only Lucy knew she intended to return to the brothel, but Savannah hadn't apprised her friend of her recent plans. If anything happened to her at the Black Opal, no one would even know where to start looking for her. She called out to Dylan.

"Hey, do you still have your phone?"

"Yeah, of course. Why?"

"I-I just wanted to check. Is it the same number?"

"Yeah." Dylan sauntered back into the kitchen. "What's going on?"

"Nothing," she said hurriedly. "I just wanted to make sure I could contact you, just in case…"

"Just in case what?"

"Just in case I need to. I'm…meeting the girls at a club in Darlinghurst. Just so you know."

Dylan frowned. "Darlinghurst? That's a little out of the way for you, isn't it? Why not just go into the city?"

Flustered, Savannah thrust around for a response. "One of the girls knows the owner of a club there. She…she invited us for drinks." Waving a casual hand in his direction, she forced a smile. "I'll be fine. I'm nearly thirty, remember? Way old enough to look after myself. If I need you, I'll call. I promise."

Hurrying forward, Savannah switched on the small lamp which sat on the side table in the hall and then kissed her brother good-bye. Closing the front door behind her, she made her way down to the darkened car park.

———————

Dylan watched his sister's compact Mazda pull away from the curb and cursed aloud. He'd had her alone, completely unaware. His hands had been on her shoulders. With the tiniest movement they would have been around her neck. Within minutes, he could have squeezed the life out of her.

And yet, he hadn't.

"Fuck," he cursed again, his fists clenched tight. He should have done it. He'd come here to do it. She should have been dead right now, not blithely driving away for a night on the town with her girlfriends—or so she said. After she'd thrown in that bit about Darlinghurst, he had to wonder. What if she was going back to the Black Opal?

The thought made him swear again. Why the fuck hadn't he killed her? He hadn't hesitated when Vince had ordered him to get rid of the other girls. He'd barely blinked when their surprise had turned to fear and then to terror as he'd come at them with the pillow that eventually snuffed out their lives. It was quick and it was clean, much better than his first kill with the gun. He hated the sight of blood.

Even when he was a kid, he'd bawled like a baby when he'd grazed his knee or elbow or shoulder enough to draw blood. He'd relied on Savannah to clean him up and cover his wounds with a bandage. Only when the blood was safely concealed by the white wadding had he dared to turn back around and survey her workmanship.

The memory sent a surge of tenderness through him. She'd been such a good big sister. He hadn't made it easy for her.

It was too damn bad she'd gotten mixed up in Vince's affairs. Writing that story had been just plain stupid. Didn't she have any idea who she was dealing with? Vince wasn't about to let something like that pass. Any day now Dylan expected to receive the order to get rid of her.

It was why he'd decided to preempt it. Vince was known for his voracious appetite with women. If it was simply straight sex, Dylan could live with that, but he'd seen firsthand the effects of Vince's lovemaking. Bite marks and burns that left scars. Bottles and other items being forced into orifices they had no business being. No one left Vince's bed without permanent memories of their time with him— that's if they left at all.

Vince would take one look at Savannah and would want her. There was nothing surer. She was like some rare, exotic plant. Masses of wild red hair and alabaster skin and a body to die for. Dylan may have been her brother, but he wasn't blind.

Vince would still order her death—after he'd used and abused her—that was a *fait accompli*. It was the agony of the moments beforehand Dylan fretted over. That and the inevitable beating she'd endure.

He'd had the opportunity to kill her with his own hands, to end it before she even conceived of the kind of sick horror Vince could inflict upon her... Yet he'd let it slide. His courage had failed him at the moment when he'd needed it most. And now she could be headed back there...

Bile rose in his throat. He dashed toward the bathroom, but it was too late. Hot, acidic vomit filled his mouth and spewed out. It sprayed up the walls and across the carpet. He sank to his knees in the hall, his head bent forward and he retched until there was nothing left.

Savannah pulled her car into the curb a block away from the brothel and switched off the engine. The streets of Darlinghurst were quiet and only pale illumination from the intermittent streetlights and the muted light from windows of the residential houses lining the street broke the darkness.

Locking her wallet in the glove box, she unzipped her gym bag and pulled out the wig. Quickly tying her hair back into a ponytail, she leaned forward and awkwardly drew the wig over her head.

Tucking in the strands of her hair around her ears, she switched on the small flashlight she'd brought with her and checked her appearance in the rearview mirror. She straightened the wig and smoothed the dark strands down until they hung neatly. Then she drew in a deep, nervous breath and steeled herself to climb out of the car.

The clock on the dashboard showed it was a little after ten. According to Malee, the security guards should have started their routine patrol around the building.

It was time to go inside.

Fear surged through her, rooting her to the spot. The last

girl she'd come into contact with had been savagely murdered. What if someone discovered she was not what she appeared? She would vanish, just like Malee. Did she really want to risk her life for a story?

But it wasn't just the story. Okay, she needed to keep Max happy and she sure as hell needed the job, but it was her need to find out the dirt on Will and to honor her promise to Malee that drove her.

It would be easier to go to the police, or at the very least, to Pete, and the more she thought about it, the more the idea appealed. Especially now, sitting outside the brothel in the darkness, praying that she'd live to see the morning.

But getting the police involved would mean she'd lose the opportunity to discover Will's connection to the place. It was possible he was nothing more than a wealthy patron seeking out all the brothel had to offer, just as Max had suggested. The thought made her frown, but it was an infinitely better option than what she'd conjured up earlier. She'd be devastated to discover he was involved in something more sinister...

Knowing the only way she'd find out was to question those inside, she opened her car door, stepped out and closed it quietly behind her before she could change her mind. Having nowhere to stow her keys, she squatted beside her car and fitted them carefully onto the inside ledge of the vehicle, just above the back tire. It wasn't the cleverest hiding place, but it would have to do.

Coming upright, she picked her way along the sidewalk. Her high heels made walking difficult on the uneven surface and the dim glow from the streetlights provided very little assistance. The last thing she needed was to twist her ankle and be forced to abort her plan. She'd never find the courage to repeat it.

Her breath came in short, choppy pants and her heart pumped hard. She struggled to calm down. She assumed the back door would be locked. The thought of what might happen if the guard didn't believe her excuse for being outside filled her with dread. Now that she had intimate knowledge of the dark and evil underbelly of the brothel and the punishments it could inflict, she was a hundred times more nervous about entering the building than she'd been the first time.

When Malee had initially contacted her and told her about Vince, she'd been somewhat sceptical about the accuracy of the girl's reports. But Max had wanted a story and she'd had nothing else in the pipeline. The first time, sheer bravado and a fair splash of naivety had carried her right to the door of the brothel and beyond. But could she do it again?

The first time, she'd been met by Malee and had been hurried into a nearby bedroom. She'd been nervous, but had felt equal parts excitement and adrenaline at the adventure she was on—and her mind had been firmly fixed on getting a story. She hadn't allowed herself to dwell on the danger and hadn't given any thought to the possibility that she could have been caught. Or worse, that Malee would be floating in the river soon after.

It wasn't until she'd taken part in the stage show that she'd felt any misgivings. Even then, it wasn't anything she thought she couldn't handle, even when Will fell on her.

But this time, it was different. Malee had been telling the truth. The knowledge Savannah now had about the brothel owner's criminal activities, not to mention his proclivity for violence, left her feeling a whole lot less brave and all of the excitement had evaporated. If the thought of leaving the girls to the mercy of Vince Maranoa didn't almost nauseate her, she'd very nearly pull off her heels and bolt straight back to the safety of her car.

The fact was, she couldn't do it. She owed it to Malee's memory and she owed it to the other girls who were still living a hell they could never have imagined. Then, there was Will. She owed it to herself to find out once and for all whether he was part of it.

Holding onto that thought, Savannah took another deep breath of the still-warm air, squared her shoulders and turned into the narrow alleyway that ran between the brothel and the adjoining building. The security guards were nowhere in sight. The only sound was muted music coming from somewhere inside the brothel.

Peering intently at the ground before her, she took care not to trip on the loose stones and gravel which comprised the walkway. Praying the guards were still on the opposite side of the building, she continued forward, not even daring to breathe as she strained to hear over the sound of the gravel and stones that crunched beneath her feet.

A sudden bark of laughter not far behind her forced the air from her lungs in a rush and she gasped in fright.

Had the guards completed their circuit already? She risked a glance behind her, but saw nothing in the darkness.

Chancing a twisted ankle, she picked up her pace and walked as quickly as she dared along the rough path until she came to the end of the building. A bright glow came from a light above the closed wooden door halfway along the back of the building. She made out a couple of concrete steps that led up to the door and sent up a silent, frantic prayer that it was unlocked.

The crunching of footsteps sounded on the gravel behind her. Her heart jumped into her throat. She half ran, half stumbled toward the door. Scrambling up the steps, she turned the brass doorknob and put her shoulder to the wood.

The door didn't budge. Panic tore through her, leaving her lightheaded. She tried the knob again, but knew it was useless. It was locked.

She could now hear the sound of muffled conversation. Thinking fast, she spied a bag of trash resting against the concrete steps. Picking it up and praying the trash can was somewhere toward rear of the yard, she headed in that direction.

"Hey, you! What the hell are you doing?"

Savannah froze. The question had been shouted at her from close behind her. Slowly, she turned and squinted into the light. Two guards stood near the back door. Dropping the bag of trash, she plastered a smile on her face and sauntered toward them.

"I'm just takin' out the trash." She closed the distance between them and sidled up to one of the men. Running a teasing finger down his chest, she winked at him. "What are you doin'?"

The man stared at her, his eyes dark with suspicion. "You shouldn't be out here. You know that. Who sent you outside?"

Savannah shrugged and thought fast. "I dunno. Maybe I just wanted a bit of fresh air. It gets awfully…*hot* in there." She pressed herself against him and splayed her hand across his cheek.

"Wanna kiss?" she murmured, her lips brushing against his ear.

"Fuck off, slut. You know we're not allowed to fraternize with you. Vince will have our hides. Now, get back inside where you belong."

Savannah moved away and stumbled up the steps. She tried the door and then turned around and shrugged, a helpless expression on her face.

"Oops, it must have locked behind me."

With a muttered oath, the other guard stormed up the steps and pulled a set of keys from his belt. Moments later, the door opened. Smiling sweetly, Savannah made her entrance.

She was in.

CHAPTER 11

Savannah closed the door to the brothel behind her and leaned against it. She pressed a hand to her chest in an effort to slow her racing heart. For all her outward show of bravado, the run-in with the security guards had left her shaken. She didn't want to spend another moment longer than was necessary to achieve what she was there for.

A few steps down the hall, a door to one of the bedrooms stood ajar. Faint light seeped through the gap. With a deep breath, she squared her shoulders and walked toward it, hoping to find a girl who might be willing to talk.

She had to assume the girls knew about Malee. Someone like Vince would make sure they knew she'd died while attempting to escape and that it had been a slow and painful death. It was sure to terrify them and an even surer way to deter them. It wouldn't be easy to overcome their fear and gain their confidence, especially in the short time she had. And she didn't want to endanger any other lives.

Savannah eased the door fully open. A petite Asian girl who looked younger than Dylan lay semi-naked on the bed. Savannah drew closer. The girl gasped and drew herself up into a ball.

The lamps that glowed on either side of the bed had been turned down low and the room had an air of intimacy that was more than a little disconcerting. *Was the girl expecting a client?*

Once again, Savannah was reminded of how tenuous her position was. Vowing silently to get out as quickly as possible, she approached the bed with tentative steps.

"Wh-who are you?" the girl stuttered in broken English, surprise widening her almond-shaped eyes.

"I'm Savannah O'Neill. I'm a newspaper reporter. It's okay. I'm not going to hurt you. I only want to ask you some questions."

The girl's eyes breathing hitched. Fear darkened the depths of her eyes. "I not talk to you. Billy not like it."

There was that name again. *Billy.* Savannah was determined to find out once and for all who he was. She stepped closer.

"I want to help you get out of here. I'm not going to tell anyone you spoke to me, I promise."

The girl looked unconvinced. Savannah tried again. "What's your name? A beautiful girl like you must have a beautiful name."

The girl's lip wobbled. A tiny smile tugged at her lips. "Angel," she whispered.

Savannah reached the bed and eased herself onto it. Angel pulled her knees up to her chest and held onto them. She stared at a spot on the floor, distrust still plain on her young face.

"Angel. That's a lovely name. It suits you." Savannah paused. "I meant what I said, Angel. I want to help you. I want to help all of you."

With obvious reluctance, the girl lifted her gaze. Savannah's heart ached at the fear and hopelessness in Angel's dark eyes.

Clenching her jaw in anger, she vowed to see whoever was responsible for exploiting the young girl put away for a long, long time.

Savannah squeezed the girl's hand, trying to impart a reassurance she didn't feel. "How old are you, Angel?"

"Fourteen."

The reply was so low, Savannah was uncertain whether she'd heard correctly. Had she really just said *fourteen?* She shook her head, aghast. She wanted to rant and rave against the injustice of it. She wanted to hit something or someone. But she didn't have the liberty of doing any of those things at that moment. She hid her distress by doing what she did best.

"Angel, I want to ask you some questions and I need you to tell me the truth. It's very important. I can't help you unless I know what's going on here. Do you understand?"

The girl kept her gaze lowered, but nodded.

"Okay." Savannah took a deep breath and glanced at her watch.

Ten-thirty. She didn't want the girl to feel hurried, but the sooner Savannah got out of there, the better. Any minute she could be discovered and she didn't even want to think about what might happen to her then.

Leaning over, she brushed the long, black, shiny hair off Angel's face. Angel turned to look at her.

"Angel, how long have you been here?"

The girl shrugged. Her dark gaze slid away.

"Please talk to me, Angel. The only way I can help is if I know what's going on. I need something definite to take to the police."

"Police?" The girl reared back in horror. "No! No police! Please." Tears welled up in her eyes. Her shoulders shook. Savannah moved closer and put her arms around her.

"Angel, it's all right. In Australia, the police are good. They help people like you and they put men like Vince Maranoa in jail."

"B-but Vince say—" Angel hiccupped on a sob. "Vince say police throw us in prison if girls ever tell. No one know where girls go. Vince say...girls rot here forever. Never see family again."

A fresh wave of tears erupted and Savannah hugged her again and waited for them to subside.

"It's okay; it's okay," she murmured, rubbing the girl's back with her hand. After awhile, Angel quietened and her tears subsided to the occasional sniffle. Savannah released her. Swallowing a sigh, she tried again.

"Honey, how long have you been here?"

Angel shook her head slowly before raising her tear-stained face to Savannah's.

"Don't know how long. No TV. No radio." She shrugged, her expression pitiful. "Don't know what day it is. Vince take me from Bangkok one week before I turn fourteen. He tell father he get me job. He say I have good life. Vince tell father I send money home. Father pay Vince five thousand dollar to take to Australia."

Savannah gasped, appalled. Not only was Maranoa using the women illegally, he was also taking money from their families under false pretenses. She was shocked at how far his evil exploitation extended. Tamping down her anger, she reached for Angel's hand again and gave it a reassuring squeeze.

"Sweetheart, when's your birthday? If you tell me, I'll be able to work out how long you've been here. It's January twentieth today."

"My birthday July second."

"Oh my God, Angel, you've been here over *six* months! I'm so, so sorry, honey. We need to get you out of here! You need to tell me everything so I can help you!"

Angel nodded slowly. "I understand. Not sure how long until Billy come with needle."

Savannah's heart thumped at the mention of Billy, but she frowned in confusion. "The needle?"

"Yes, needle. Vince make girl take drug with needle. I hate needle! Make me sick. Vomit everywhere. Billy go away, leave me alone. Give needle to other girl."

Savannah was horrified. Never in her wildest dreams had she imagined such depravity. When Malee told her Maranoa kept the girls drugged, she hadn't had time to hear what that entailed, but hearing a firsthand account made her feel sick to her stomach.

"Most girl take needle," Angel continued, interrupting Savannah's furious thoughts. "Feel sick at first, but then they like. They want needle. Make them happy. Make Billy happy." She shook her head. "Not me."

Savannah struggled to keep her anger in check. With an effort, she kept her voice calm and asked the question that weighed heavily on her mind.

"Angel, who's Billy?"

Angel stared at the floor. "Billy work for Vince. Billy make me scared."

"Do you know his last name? What does Vince call him?"

"Billy, Billy the Kid."

Suppressing her frustration, Savannah tried again. "What does he look like? Young, like you? Or is he old, like Vince?"

The girl shrugged. "Not old like Vince. Young, I guess, but not young like me."

"What color hair does he have?"

Another shrug. "Dark. Only see him night time. Light not so good in here."

Savannah bit her lip. It *could* be Will. But then again, it could be anyone. She had to get the police involved. She had no choice. It had gone way beyond her limited resources. She could hardly waltz out the door with Angel in tow. *Could* she? The thought accelerated her heart beat. *Did she dare?*

But what about the other girls? Malee had said there were ten of them altogether. Counting Mia, the girl who'd escaped before Malee, and Angel, that left at least another seven who were at Maranoa's mercy.

"Girl who take needle don't care about men," Angel murmured, drawing Savannah's attention back to her. "They happy to dance when Vince say. Me not happy. Vince say I must. Vince say I cost lot of money. Must pay back bill. Must see men. Must be nice. When bill all paid, I go home."

Tears once again filled the young girl's eyes and slid down her cheeks. Savannah's heart broke at the shame and desolation on Angel's face. She drew her back into her arms and held her. When the girl finally quieted down, Savannah pulled gently away.

"Angel, none of this is your fault. Don't ever think that. You're being held here illegally by some very evil men and

I'm going to make sure they never do it to any other girls again, okay?"

With quiet desperation, she tilted Angel's chin up with her finger until the girl finally met her eyes. "I want to help you, honey, but I can't do it on my own. I need to get the police involved. The police will help us, okay?" She tried to inject as much confidence into her voice as she could.

Angel nodded, the fear back in her eyes, but she held Savannah's gaze and even offered her a small smile. Her voice was a ragged whisper when she spoke again.

"Thank you."

A loud banging on the door next to their room startled both of them. A moment later, the knock sounded on their door.

"Girls, get your asses out here now! Vince wants a show. I want two of you out here *now!*"

Savannah gasped. That voice… It was familiar… It sounded like…*her brother.* She shook her head at the absurdity of even thinking Dylan could be at the Black Opal. It was totally ludicrous.

Angel clawed at her arm and Savannah's chaotic thoughts scattered like confetti on the wind. The girl looked like she'd seen a ghost.

"My turn!" she choked, her eyes wide with terror. "My turn to dance."

Savannah's heart clenched with dread. She couldn't sit there and let the poor girl perform in front of a roomful of excited men. Angel was little more than a child! It didn't matter that she'd been doing it for six months. She wasn't going to go out there again. Not on Savannah's watch.

"They only need two girls. That's what the man said. Maybe one of the other girls—"

Angel shook her head violently back and forth. "No! No! No! My turn! Must dance!"

Cold fear settled like molasses in her stomach. As much as she shrank from the idea, another look at the crying, pitifully young girl on the bed decided it for her. She knew what she had to do.

With a sigh, she stood and walked over to the full-length mirror that was fixed to the wall opposite the bed. Tugging down her skirt as far as it would go, she adjusted her wig and pulled down the hem of her midriff top. She was now decidedly uneasy at the scantness of it. Recalling the crowd of girls on stage the previous Saturday night, she silently hoped she could take refuge behind some of the others.

She turned to Angel. "What kind of dance are you supposed to do?"

"Pole dance, two girl together."

Savannah gasped. A *pole* dance? The girl was freaking *kidding*, wasn't she? Savannah didn't know squat about pole dancing and there was no way she could pull it off in a tight leather skirt! Hell, she could barely *move* in the outfit, let alone shimmy up and down a pole in it!

But she had no choice. It was as simple as that. She made her way back to where Angel continued to sniffle quietly on the bed.

"It's okay, honey. I'm going to dance in your place tonight and when I leave, I'll bring back the police as soon as I can. It's going to be all right. You need to stay very brave and not say anything to any of the other girls. It's very important, okay?"

Angel nodded. Her eyes swam with gratitude. "You dance for me?"

Nerves warred with dread in Savannah's belly, but she forced them away. "Yes."

Angel smiled. The simple action lit up her young face. "Thank you, thank you, thank you. You very kind. Me stay very quiet. Promise."

Just like the last time Will had been at the brothel, the air was smoky and pungent with the scent of incense and cigars. It was a little after ten-thirty and he was on his second glass of scotch. He swirled the drink in his hand. The golden liquid slid over the ice cubes. He'd been there for almost an hour and so far hadn't noticed anything out of the ordinary. Impatience ate into him.

The place was quiet, with only twenty or so patrons scattered around the room, mostly drinking and murmuring amongst themselves. He spotted Baines and Michaels, his undercover backup, seated at a table in the far corner and was relieved that they'd passed inspection from the guards.

Conrad Birmingham, the owner of a rival advertising firm, sat a couple of tables over. Will gave him a slight nod of acknowledgement. He wasn't concerned the man would identify him as a cop. Robert Rutledge had gone to great pains to conceal the fact that his only surviving son and heir had turned his back on the family company. Conrad raised his glass in tacit response before his attention was captured by a new arrival.

Curious, Will swung around on his bar stool. He immediately recognized Vince Maranoa and tensed. Surrounded by security, the drug lord strode through the entryway exuding authority and power. His designer suit was custom made and his longish, dyed-black hair was combed to a neatness that was almost disconcerting.

A moment later, the brothel owner pulled out a bar stool and seated himself beside Will, shooting him a look filled with frank curiosity. Will steadied his pulse rate by taking another sip of his drink and tugged out his cell phone. Faking interest in composing a text message, he surreptitiously watched Maranoa from the corner of his eye.

The dark hair belied the crow's feet around the man's eyes and the deep lines engrained across his forehead. Will knew from the three-inch thick police file that Maranoa was scraping sixty.

Vincent Michael Maranoa. The only son of George and Christina Maranoa, born and raised in the inner Sydney suburb of Marrickville. Graduated with a leaving certificate from Marrickville High School in 1970. There were no significant achievements mentioned in the high school yearbooks, but neither were there any other indicators of the life of crime the young Maranoa would eventually embrace.

Who really knew what made someone choose the path they did? Fate was a slippery thing. Will didn't think anyone felt completely confident their choices in life were the right ones. Surely the most anyone could do was conduct the research and then hope for the best? Even then, things didn't always turn out as planned. The twists and turns in his life were proof of that.

He wondered at what point Maranoa's life had deviated off course. According to the file, his first arrest was for an assault occasioning actual bodily harm. It was a serious charge. He'd been all of eighteen.

Will hadn't been able to access any juvenile file, but he'd bet his father's company a file existed. The kind of scum like Maranoa, who'd turned crime into a career, didn't start out when they turned eighteen.

He had no information on Maranoa's early life, apart from the names of his parents, but regardless of how shitty his childhood might have been, no misfortune could ever excuse the way he now chose to live his life. Will was as determined as ever to see him put behind bars.

"Will? What the hell are *you* doing here?"

The familiar voice brought Will's thoughts to an abrupt halt. Directly behind Vince's entourage stood Robert Rutledge.

CHAPTER 12

Will's jaw dropped open. His heart thudded. His throat was so tight he could barely breathe. How could his *father* be standing less than two feet away from him in a notorious city brothel? Shock followed quickly by panic rendered him speechless. He stared hard at his father and hoped like hell the man wouldn't break his cover.

He glanced over at Maranoa. Despite Will's training, his heart rate refused to slow. With a concerted effort, he feigned disinterest and casually returned his phone to his coat pocket before turning to acknowledge the question from the man who looked just as surprised as he was.

"Dad! Fancy seeing you here."

Vince chuckled. "You're Robert's young whippersnapper? How about that? I should have guessed. You're the spittin' image of him, apart from the fact you're hair's still dark and you're carryin' a few less pounds, of course." He grinned. "Your old man loves this place. It's where he comes to relax, you know, a few drinks, a girl or two." Vince turned to face Will's father. "Isn't that right, mate? You told me once you do some of your best thinkin' in here."

Robert offered the brothel owner a tight smile. "That's right, Vince. I-I'm just a little surprised to see my boy here. I wasn't expecting him."

Will thought frantically. "Well, you know, Dad. You were talking so much about the place the other week, I thought I might come along and see for myself what all the fuss was about."

Vince chuckled again, delighted, and turned back to Will. "Georgie told me you were lookin' for a session in the *Room of Dreams*. At least I know you're not like your old man in *every* way. I can't get him interested in the shit, but don't worry, I'm sure we have whatever you need." Vince winked and let out a loud guffaw. One of his bodyguards grinned.

Will offered a tight smile and glanced back toward his father. Robert's eyes were wide with shock.

"Will, how could you? After what happened to—"

Will silenced him with a glare. "Leave him out of it. I've come along to relax and enjoy myself, unwind after a hard day's work, just like you were telling me." He stared hard at his father, willing him to understand. All the while, Will grappled with images of his father being a patron of the city's most exclusive brothel—and not only a patron, but a somewhat favored customer, if the fondness in Maranoa's voice was any indication.

The discovery, coming so soon after the drug-induced suicide of his little brother—something else he hadn't seen coming—shook him to the core. He didn't know what his father had told Maranoa about him, but it was obvious he hadn't shared his disgust at Will's career choice. Maranoa couldn't have appeared more at ease. Provided Will could trust his father's discretion, it was the perfect opportunity to get him to talk. Will couldn't afford to let the chance slide.

"I can see why Dad likes to hang out here." He indicated the luxurious surroundings with a tilt of his chin and turned back to Maranoa. "You've got a nice place here. What are you drinking?"

"You wanna buy me a drink?" Vince shook his head, chuckling again. "Mate, don't you know, I'm Vince fuckin' Maranoa. I *own* this joint!"

Will's expression didn't change. "So? You want a drink, or not?"

"This is fan-fuckin'-tastic!" Vince grinned and moved his

stool closer. "Do you know how many times someone has bought me a drink in this fuckin' place?"

Not waiting for Will to respond, Vince continued. "I'll tell you. None, zero. Not one, ever! Not even your old man has offered to buy me a drink."

Will kept his gaze trained on Vince. "Well, I guess I'm not my old man," he quipped and turned back to the bar. "Bring my mate a scotch," he said to the barman who hovered nearby. Winking at Vince, he added, "And put it on my tab."

Vince grinned back, looking like he'd suddenly won the lottery.

That'a boy, Vince. Come to Papa.

Robert shouldered his way to the bar. "I'll have one, too, son." He glanced down at Will's half-empty glass and raised his eyebrow in silent query.

"I guess that makes three," Will said.

A few moments later, the barman placed three scotches before the men. They each took a sip in silence.

"So, Will, tell me, how long you been comin' to my place?" Vince asked, his eyes full of curiosity.

Will shrugged. "After Dad kept raving about it, I decided to check it out. I've been here a few times. Your barman only thought to mention the *Room of Dreams* to me the other night. It sounds more like something I'd be interested in. Dad never mentioned anything about getting gear here. I'd have been by sooner, if I knew."

Maranoa chuckled. "Well, you're always welcome. We got some real nice ladies here too, if you're interested in that kind of thing."

Will forced a smile and swirled the scotch in his glass. "Thanks for the offer, Vince. I appreciate it. I must admit, I don't mind getting a bit of attention from a nice-looking girl." He leaned in closer and lowered his voice. "But it's the sizzle and pop that really gets me going."

Vince nodded in understanding and gave him another friendly pat on the shoulder. "Mate, you've come to the right place. I can get you anythin' you want. Top quality, the lot. It'll cost you, of course."

Will spread his arms wide. "Money's no option, Vince. I'm sure you know that. I've got no complaints about my old man in that regard." He smiled at his father and winked.

Vince nodded. "All you gotta do is name it, and I'll get it. We don't call it the *Room of Dreams* for nothin'."

Will's eyes widened in false surprise. "Really? How come the cops haven't caught onto it?"

Robert choked on a mouthful of scotch, but Vince didn't appear to notice.

"Don't you worry about that, mate," he chuckled. "I got a good set-up and I got good men on my team, if you get my drift? No one crosses Vince Maranoa. Well, not if they want to see their next birthday!" Vince laughed uproariously and slapped his hand on his thigh.

Will stretched his lips into what he hoped would pass for a grin and snatched a look at his father. Robert stared at him, unease shadowing his eyes.

Will glanced away. He had to keep Vince talking. The man seemed to be in the mood for sharing confidences. Before he could question him further, Vince thumped his hand on the bar and yelled at the barman.

"Georgie, where are the girls? I want some girls out here!" He turned back to Will and his father and gave both of them a wink. "I'll get some tits out here for you. How's that sound?"

Will nodded. "Sounds good to me. Bring it on."

Georgie gestured to one of the bouncers. After speaking with him briefly, the man disappeared through the door restricted to staff.

Minutes later, spotlights shone on a couple of round, raised platforms, each three or four feet in diameter. Protruding from both of them were shiny, stainless-steel poles which were fixed to the ceiling. The platforms were raised about three feet off the floor and were situated on either side of the large stage where Will had watched Savannah perform the previous Saturday night.

He shook his head at the memory. He owed her an apology. With all that had been going on, he still hadn't found the time—or the words.

The dimness of the room was in stark contrast to the bright spots of light that surrounded the platforms. A buzz of excitement ran through the small crowd. Will studiously ignored his father and took another sip of his scotch. Maranoa sat beside him, eyeing him expectantly.

Music burst from speakers near the stage. Two dark-haired women materialized and climbed onto the platforms. They were clad in black, gauzy camisole tops which left nothing to the imagination. Fishnet stockings, stilettos and black thongs added to the look.

Aware of Vince's scrutiny, Will did his best to look enthralled with the show, following the girls' moves as they gyrated around the poles.

"See anything you like?" Vince's low murmur was close to Will's ear. "You just give me a nod and she's yours."

Will chuckled and gave Vince a conspiratorial wink. "Thanks."

The music changed. He looked back toward the stage. The first two dancers were replaced by another couple of dark-haired women. He leaned over. "Where are all the blondes?"

Vince scowled. "Too much trouble, mate and way too expensive. The Asian stuff's much better, trust me."

Will mulled over the response, wondering again if there was any truth to Savannah's allegations regarding the illegal sex slave trade. He made a mental note to follow it up with Pete in the morning.

Returning his attention to the dancers, he couldn't help but notice one of the girls looked decidedly amateurish. She was doing her best to slide up and down the pole, but the tight, black leather skirt she wore kept getting in the way. The leather kept gripping the pole, making her descent less than elegant. In fact, the moves looked more like a bunny hop than provocative dancing.

Trying to restrain a genuine grin of amusement, he glanced at Vince, but the man's attention had been drawn to a bouncer who was speaking to a security guard at the far end of the bar. It was the same one the barman had spoken to a few moments earlier.

Will turned back to the show and kept his comments to himself. The girl was clearly new to the scene or she would have known not to wear something so inappropriate. A leather skirt and pole-dancing was never going to work. Even he knew that.

The girl continued to battle with the stainless steel. Will felt almost sorry for her. Lifting his glass, he took another sip and his gaze swept over her face.

The ice cube in his mouth got caught in his airway. He choked and coughed and sputtered.

"Are you all right, Will?" his father asked, looking concerned.

Trying desperately to catch his breath, Will nodded a little frantically and watched in disbelief as Savannah hitched her leather skirt up to an indecent level and hoisted herself back onto the pole. Even though she wore a black wig, he had no doubt it was her.

What the hell was she doing here again? Surely she wasn't stupid enough to try her luck a second time? She'd been damned lucky it had been him who'd tried it on with her the last time and not some over-eager jock who refused to take no for an answer. Even with her ability to land a well-aimed kick to his balls, there was no guarantee her tactic would work a second time.

Anger erupted inside him at her foolishness. His father be damned, he had to do something to save her from herself. Leaning toward Vince, he tapped him lightly on the shoulder.

Vince spun around, his face visibly relaxing as he remembered Will beside him.

"That girl over there, the one in the leather?" Will pointed in Savannah's direction. "I'd like to get to know her a little better." He winked. Vince's face broke into a broad grin.

"No worries, mate. I'll have one of the boys bring her over. You wanna room?"

Will's gaze roamed over Savannah from head to toe with unmistakable intent. "Oh yeah, I'm going to need a room all right."

———————

Savannah knew the exact moment Will recognized her. She watched with a kind of morbid fascination as shock and disbelief registered on his handsome face. An involuntary thrum of nervous excitement shivered down her spine.

His narrow-eyed gaze followed her scantily clad form. Even from a distance, his anger was palpable. Her traitorous heart kicked into overdrive.

She'd spied him lounging by the bar right before her dance had started. She'd actually been shocked to see him and it wasn't until that moment she realized she'd almost convinced herself that his earlier visit to the brothel had been nothing but a coincidence.

But there he was, larger than life, this time, sitting very companionably with none other than the despicable Vince Maranoa.

She was glad she'd taken the time to Google the drug baron. Her search had hit on a picture of him taken by a rival newspaper at a court appearance a couple of years earlier. It made recognizing him easy.

The two of them looked more than cozy. She snatched quick glances in their direction while she continued to do her best to swing around the slippery steel pole without looking utterly ridiculous. Spinning around once again, she turned and caught Will and Maranoa laughing together.

Movement at the far end of the bar snagged her attention. She stared at the man who had caught her eye. It was a security guard from the *Daily Mirror*. She swallowed a gasp of surprise and fear.

Carlo something or other was usually found standing guard in the foyer of their building. She passed him every morning on her way over to the bank of elevators. She'd never paid him much attention before, except to say good morning or remark on the weather or toss some other inane conversational titbit, but she was certain it was him talking to another staff member who had his back to her.

Perhaps he had a second job and doubled as security for the brothel? She didn't know what the pay was like for a security guard, but she couldn't imagine it was too generous. Most people living in Sydney needed a second income if they had a mortgage to pay and he certainly appeared well known to the man he was speaking to.

Her gaze shifted to Carlo's companion. Something about him was familiar. His height, the way he stood, the color of his hair...

Savannah gasped. *It couldn't be...*

The man turned and her belly dropped to her feet with nauseating speed. Blood pounded in her ears.

It was Dylan.

The thought no sooner formed when Dylan ended his conversation and disappeared through the doorway that led to the bedrooms. Shock held her momentarily immobilized. She didn't notice the bouncer who stood near the platform until he grabbed her around the waist and lifted her effortlessly down to the floor. Before she could utter a word, he leaned down and mumbled something about a patron requesting her presence. He nodded briefly in Will's direction. Her heart plummeted.

Will glared at Savannah with barely controlled anger. She stared back at him, her green eyes blazing with shock. From the moment he realized it was her, his heart had pounded a rapid staccato against his chest. Now, as his gaze traveled over her skimpy ensemble, he struggled to remain calm.

Braless beneath the lacy black top, the shape and size of her rounded breasts was clearly visible. As she moved closer, he even made out her rosy nipples. Remembering the taste and feel of them, blood rushed to his groin. The bouncer stopped and pushed Savannah toward Will. She held his gaze. Her eyes burned with defiance.

A reluctant surge of admiration diluted his anger. Foolhardy or not, she was braver than most of the men he worked with. Turning to Maranoa, he tugged out his wallet and peeled off a couple of hundred-dollar bills, resolutely ignoring his father's gaze.

"Put your money away," Vince chuckled. "This one's on the house." When Will went to protest, Vince moved closer and put his arm around him. "What are mates for?"

Will returned the money to his wallet and turned to face Savannah. Fury reddened her cheeks. Her eyes spat fire. She stared at him with tightly compressed lips. He could tell it took all of her self-control not to snap at him, but he was grateful she still had enough sense to play along.

His admiration for her grew. It was possible she didn't yet know he knew the truth about her occupation and he'd just been offered her services by the brothel owner himself. Will was going to enjoy watching her try and get out of this one.

Turning back to Vince, he offered him a smile of thanks. "Which room's mine?"

"Go with—Hey, what's your name?" Vince yelled at Savannah.

"S-Sally." Savannah's voice was strained. Bright red patches suffused her cheeks. She kept her eyes cast down.

Vince frowned. "Sally? You sure? I don't—"

Will's heart pounded. He thought fast. "I don't give a fuck what her name is, Vince. Sally, Susie, Sonja? Who cares?"

Vince continued to eye Savannah distrustfully. Will held his breath. At last, Vince appeared satisfied.

"Yeah, well whatever your name is, take my friend here to your room and show him a good time. You understand?" Vince barked at her. He grabbed her roughly by the chin and forced it up.

Savannah gasped. She stared up at him in fear. Maranoa's eyes narrowed with menace.

"Sally, where are you from? When did you get here?" Vince demanded. "I don't remember seein' you before."

From almost beating out of his chest, Will's heart now stopped cold. If Vince realized Savannah wasn't one of his girls, who knew what he'd do? The situation could quickly get out of control.

Standing abruptly, Will turned to face Vince. The movement brought him face to face with his father, but it effectively blocked Savannah from Maranoa's view.

"Vince…" He smiled lazily. "Like I said, I couldn't care less about her name or where's she's from. All I want to do is fuck her. You with me?"

Vince stepped back and after a moment, his smile reappeared. "Yeah, mate, I'm with you. In fact, I might even have a go at her myself after you're finished. Let me know when you're through, okay?" He winked and turned back toward the bar.

Will's stomach clenched. He felt his father's stare all the way to his bones, but he forced himself to smile benignly at both of them before turning away to face Savannah. Her face was crimson and her eyes shot fire. To Will, she'd never looked more beautiful.

"Come on, *Sally*." Taking her by the arm, he led her away from the bar toward the door that led to the bedrooms. "Let's go find that room."

CHAPTER 13

Savannah gritted her teeth and did her best to remain upright in her high heels as Will dragged her along behind him down the dimly lit corridor that led to the bedrooms. It was fair to say her night had taken a decided turn for the worse.

When had things gotten so out of control? One minute, she'd been trying her best to shimmy up a goddamned slippery pole wearing a skirt that had never been made for that purpose and the next she was being manhandled by a bear and dumped unceremoniously before the man who now held her arm in a vice-like grip.

She still wasn't sure how it had happened.

Will pulled on her arm and she cried out. "Ouch! You're hurting me!"

He glanced back at her, a feral glint in his eye. "I'm eager to get you on your back, Red. You can't blame a man for that, surely? You ought to take it as a compliment." His grin was wicked.

She clenched her jaw in response and her mind worked furiously to come up with an escape plan. A door with the number eight in brass lettering suddenly appeared before them. Will shouldered it open.

Funny how he'd chosen the same room they'd been in before. He must have remembered. She didn't know whether that was a good thing or a bad thing. She didn't know anything any more.

Her mind still reeled from her sighting of Dylan and her near-certainty that Will and perhaps even her brother were involved in the brothel's criminal activities. She didn't know to what extent, but there could be no mistaking how comfortable Will had appeared with Maranoa, nor the fact that her brother had left via a staff exit.

Pulling her in roughly behind him, Will closed and locked the door with a flick of his wrist before releasing her. His arrogant gaze raked over her. He started at her black wig, which had twisted so that the thick bangs now hung somewhere near her left ear. His gaze moved painstakingly over her heavily made up face, across her chest, pausing noticeably on her barely covered breasts, before continuing past the tight leather skirt that still rode ridiculously high on her thighs.

He continued his meticulous inspection. As much as she tried to will it away, a slow, painful heat spread across her cheeks. His gaze rested on her stocking-clad legs and then slid lower to the black stilettos. Despite her suspicions, she couldn't help the traitorous reaction of her body. Liquid heat stole into her core.

He stepped closer and tilted her chin up with his index finger, forcing her to meet his molten gaze. "So, Red. We meet again." His gaze raked over her again. "How delightful."

Savannah took a step back, moving away from his touch. Taking a quick breath, she tried to slow the staccato beat of her heart and replied through gritted teeth.

"No, it's not delightful and once I've exposed you as Vince Maranoa's side kick, I doubt you'll find it delightful either."

He barked a mocking laugh. His eyes glinted blue steel. "I see you've spoken to your editor."

She narrowed her eyes at him. "Yes, Max informed me about your little conversation. You owe me an apology. I'm here for a story and you damn well know it and from what I just saw out there, I have a doozie. The public will eat it up. It's got all the elements—sex, drugs and celebrities. It'll make my career and there's not a damn thing you can do about it."

All signs of humor disappeared from Will's face. "You don't know what you saw and for a girl who claims to be a respectable journalist, you sure as hell spend a lot of time in disreputable places. What was I supposed to think?"

"You were supposed to *believe* me!" Savannah threw her hands up in the air in exasperation. She turned and moved away from him. "I *told* you I wasn't a prostitute. It should have been enough."

Will followed her. It wasn't until she turned back to face him she realized he was right behind her. Her breasts brushed against his hard chest. She gasped with awareness and stumbled back in surprise...and came up short against the bed.

Her heart thumped. She was alone in a room with Will Rutledge.

A room with a bed.

Again.

With a groan of frustration, she pushed hard against the solid wall of his chest. "Go away! Just leave me alone! I know who you are. I know that behind that charming veneer, you're a slime ball of the highest order. You're a black-hearted criminal taking advantage of innocent *children*, feeding them drugs, forcing them into prostitution—"

"Whoa! Wait a second!" Will held up a hand to halt her tirade. "Your story sounds like something from a bad B grade movie. What the hell are you talking about?"

Fury steamed through her veins. She wanted to scream and shout at him, but mindful of their need to remain undetected, she was forced to keep her voice low.

"You know darn well what I'm talking about, *Billy*! You and Vince Maranoa are thick as thieves! I saw the two of you out there near the bar—all chummy, sharing a drink together, behaving like best buddies. It nearly made me sick!

"I've just left the side of a fourteen-year-old girl who's being held here against her will, forced to prostitute her body, fed drugs to keep her compliant—she's *fourteen*! I come out and find *you*, William Rutledge, pillar of society, philanthropic man about town—you're *part* of it all!"

Too upset to continue, she turned away. With tears blurring her vision, she walked dazedly to the opposite side of the room. She took a few deep, shaky breaths in a desperate attempt to get herself under control.

She hadn't even told him the worst of it—that her brother was also involved. That knowledge hurt worse than anything else. She'd get over the stupid feelings she'd mistakenly thought she had for Will, but her brother was her brother forever. The thought that he was mixed up with Maranoa was beyond devastating.

Will remained silent, staring at her. Shock and anger were etched upon his face. After several long minutes, he broke the silence.

"How do you know all of this?"

Savannah's heart dropped like a stone. The weight of her disappointment almost suffocated her. She'd hoped he would deny her accusations; provide a plausible explanation for his behavior; protest his innocence.

But he hadn't.

All he wanted to know was how credible her information was. Probably so he could determine how strong his potential defamation case might be against her newspaper.

She fought against an overwhelming urge to cry. First her brother, now Will. The traumatic couple of hours she'd spent in the brothel were taking their toll and she struggled against the torrent of emotion that fought to be unleashed.

Despite her best efforts, her body betrayed her. The sob she'd tried desperately to suppress escaped her tight control. Before she knew it, hot, salty tears poured down her cheeks.

She turned away and leaned against the wall. Resting her head on the cold plaster, she cried like her heart was broken. She cried for the young girls like Angel who were living a hell on earth. She cried for Malee who had tried to get away from it all and had paid with her life. She cried for her parents who'd passed long before they should have.

She cried for her brother who had lost his way. She cried for the death of her secret hope that Will Rutledge was the man of her dreams. She cried and cried and cried...

Strong arms encircled her from behind and gently forced her around and into the warm haven of Will's chest. He cradled her head with his hand. His arms tightened around her.

Tugging at the disheveled wig, he tossed it to the floor. He pulled gently at the hair band in her hair and released the ponytail from its confines. His fingers worked their way through the long strands, massaging her scalp. Savannah tried not to think about how good it felt.

"*Shh*." His voice was a whisper of murmured comfort. His other hand caressed her back. "*Shh*, sweetheart, *shh*. Please don't cry. It's okay."

Savannah drew back, little sobs hiccupping from her mouth. "N-no, it's n-not okay! N-nothing's okay. It's all s-so damned wrong! W-why, oh why d-did it have to b-be *you*?"

Will frowned, but remained silent. When a fresh wave of sobs shook her, he pulled her back into his arms. She cried softly against the expensive fabric of his suit jacket. Her heart ached.

Eventually, the sobs subsided and cold reality surfaced. She had to know the truth. She had to know who he really was and what he was doing at the Black Opal. Again.

Pulling out of his arms, she moved away from him. With her arms crossed defensively over her chest, she tilted her head back and stared up at him. His eyes were dark with a tumult of emotion.

"Who are you?" she demanded.

CHAPTER 14

Will's gut clenched.

He had to tell her.

It was killing him knowing Savannah thought the worst of him. His heart ached over the sadness and devastation in her red-rimmed eyes and guilt and frustration burned through him for putting it there. He couldn't stand the subterfuge another instant. He swore under his breath. For better or worse, he was coming clean.

Needing to put a little distance between them, he stepped away from her and drew in a deep breath.

"Six months ago, my brother, Cole, died of a drug overdose. He was nineteen."

Savannah nodded and he realized his brother's death didn't come as a surprise. It had made the news, of course, but his father had friends in high places and after the initial report of Cole's death, the media had let the story die a quick death.

He compressed his lips and continued. "I'm not sure if you know that he took his own life."

She gasped. Her expression flooded with shock.

"Oh, my goodness! I had no *idea!* How absolutely awful for you—for all of you."

That her first thoughts would be for him and his family warmed him through. He nodded sadly. "Yeah, it was tough, especially on Dad." Renewed shock at the recent discovery of his father's connection to the Black Opal ran through him.

He shuddered. Now wasn't the time to dwell on it.

She stared up at him. "What about you?"

The question was whispered, but he felt the words all the way down to the bottom of his soul. His fists clenched. With every fiber of his being, he didn't want to resurrect the memories of his brother—the brother he'd loved and adored. He dragged his gaze away. "We all deal with life's challenges in our own way."

"Challenges?" You call your brother's suicide a challenge? You must be made of stone."

He closed his eyes against the anger that sparked in her eyes. He should have known she'd be way too perceptive to buy his casual dismissal. He shrugged, hoping to keep her questions and concerns at bay.

"It was his decision. Even if I'd had any idea what he was planning, I doubt I would have talked him out of it."

"You think it was your fault."

Her raw statement, said so matter-of-factly, shredded the carefully constructed wall of indifference that had helped him survive the months since Cole's death. Pain seared his heart. He almost gasped at the agony of it. He couldn't utter another word.

She closed the distance between them and put her arms around his waist. "It wasn't your fault, Will. It could never have been your fault."

He shook his head. "You don't understand. He was my little brother. He idolized me. I should have known he was struggling. I should have seen it. We lived under the same roof, for Christ's sake. *I should have seen it coming."* On the last words, his voice lifted to a harsh murmur.

Her gaze burned into his. "No, Will. *No.* That's not fair. For whatever reasons, your brother opted out. He didn't reach out for help—help you would have freely given. Don't blame yourself for his choices. Don't *ever* blame yourself."

Her fierceness surprised and comforted him. It had been more than two decades since he could remember having someone around who cared about *him*, how *he* felt, how *he* was coping. The feelings were overwhelming. He wanted to draw her close, to take comfort from her presence, her warmth, but his arms stayed resolutely by his sides. Until she knew the truth, knew *everything*, he had to keep his distance. It was only fair.

She was looking at him like she wanted nothing more than to hold him close and offer him all the things he'd missed out on during the many lonely years of his youth. She couldn't know how his mother had died right after Cole's birth; she couldn't know how his father had doted on his baby son to the exclusion of his first born, almost as if he could replace the hole his wife's death had left in his heart by giving all of his love to the baby who had lived. And yet, the way Savannah stared at him, imploring him to open up to her, it was as if she could see everything, all the way through to his tortured soul.

"Savannah." His eyes burned with emotion. His gut clenched tight. He hoped like hell he was doing the right thing. "It's time I told you the truth."

CHAPTER 15

Savannah stared at him. Her belly somersaulted with jagged nerves. She had no idea what he was about to say and suddenly she didn't know if she was ready to hear it. It had been difficult enough to listen to him talk about his brother's suicide.

"Will, you don't have to—"

"Yes, Savannah, I do."

He took another deep breath, his eyes dark and unfathomable. "The thing is," he began, "when Cole overdosed on heroin, I-I went a little crazy. All I could think of was finding the scumbag responsible for supplying him with the stuff. I wanted blood. I was going to kill the asshole."

Her heart thumped hard at his admission and at the fierce anger in his eyes, but she held her ground and refused to look away. "Are you trying to tell me Vince Maranoa was your brother's supplier?"

Will made an impatient sound in the back of his throat. "I don't know for sure if it was Maranoa, but his drug turf extends across the eastern suburbs. At the time, Cole and I lived with Dad in Point Piper, which is—"

"In the eastern suburbs," she finished.

Will's expression hardened. "It's not too much of a stretch to imagine Maranoa, or one of his cohorts, supplying Cole."

Understanding dawned. Savannah couldn't help the relief that surged through her. "So, you're here on a personal mission of revenge? Is that what you're trying to tell me?

That rather than being in cahoots with Maranoa, you're actually trying to do away with him. Have I got it right?"

Will's cheeks flushed and he averted his gaze. Savannah frowned, assuming he was embarrassed by his admission of the degree of violence he was prepared to inflict on the drug dealer.

As far as she was concerned, he had nothing to be embarrassed about. She understood exactly where he was coming from. She felt just as angry about the scum-of-the earth dealers who got her brother hooked.

"It's okay," she reassured him. "I understand. I'm not condoning murder, but I understand how you feel."

Will turned to face her, shaking his head. "No, no you don't. I mean... That is, I don't mean that you don't understand how I feel. What I mean is that you don't have it right. Not all of it."

The intensity of his gaze as it burned into hers set her pulse galloping once again. She swallowed. "What are you trying to tell me?"

Will stared at her. For a long moment, he said nothing. Nerves swirled in Savannah's belly. She held her breath.

His shoulders slumped on a heavy sigh. "The thing is, I do have a personal vendetta against Maranoa and I've vowed to fight with everything I have at my disposal to put him away, but I'm not a vigilante. I-I'm a detective with the DEA. At the moment, I'm—"

"Working undercover at the Black Opal," she finished. Shock and disbelief strangled her voice. She stumbled away from him, not even knowing which direction she'd taken until the hard, cold surface of the wall pressed in on her.

"Why didn't you *tell* me?" she whispered harshly, mindful of their location. "After all the things I said to you, accused you of—you never once tried to defend yourself. I feel like such an *idiot!*" Her voice hitched. "You must have been laughing yourself silly."

"Savannah, don't be ridiculous, of course I wasn't. You forget that earlier, when we first met, I thought you were a hooker."

She frowned in consternation. "But, why would you think *I* was part of it? Okay, you thought I was a-a prostitute, but that didn't mean I was involved in the drug business."

"You're right. What you don't know is that I overheard you talking to one of the other girls the night we met. You talked about Vince and about Billy... To me, it sounded like you had intimate information about the goings on here. It was only after I asked Pete about you that I discovered the truth."

His voice was low and calm, a voice of reason.

Reason, be damned. She was shocked. And bewildered. And still angry. It was too darn bad their surroundings prevented her from shouting at him.

"Do you know what would have happened if I'd written about how I'd seen you fraternizing in a brothel? Do you have any idea what would have happened to your life, your father's business? Did you even *care?*" she whispered fiercely.

Will moved closer, effectively trapping her between his hard body and the wall.

"So why didn't you?" he challenged her.

She looked at him and then just as quickly looked away. Breathing rapidly, she tried to sort through the myriad of thoughts surging through her confused brain.

He wasn't a criminal. He wasn't Billy. He was a cop. He wasn't a drug dealer. He was a good guy...

But where did that leave her? Somewhere deep inside, she was relieved and elated her suspicions about him had proven false and there was also a tiny sliver of hope that maybe, just maybe she'd also been mistaken about her brother.

Will was a police officer, a good bloke. But could she trust him not to break her heart, like Jonathan had?

It was unfair to compare him to her ex-fiancé. Will was nothing like Jonathan, but she couldn't forget how Will had deliberately misled her. Never once had he even hinted she was getting it all wrong.

"I assume Pete knows?"

His body tensed. "Of course, he's my commanding officer."

"Right, of course he is. Who else?"

He shrugged. "It's not really a secret. I've been a copper for more than a decade. I don't go out of my way to advertise it, because it suits me better to remain incognito."

He grimaced. "Naturally, my father's appalled at my choice of career. I doubt he's told a single soul that his oldest, and now only son, prefers to work for a living as a lowly police officer rather than take over the old man's business empire."

She sighed at the enormity of their misunderstanding. Then another thought occurred to her. "You make the social pages on a fairly frequent basis. How come some enterprising journalist hasn't made the connection?"

Will shrugged. "I keep a low profile at work. I'm involved in a lot of undercover operations—especially ones that require me to be...well, myself: A young, wealthy entrepreneur enjoying life in the city. I have an office at Rutledge Enterprises. Most people assume I work for Dad." He laughed without humor. "Lucky for me, Dad's only too happy to keep up the subterfuge."

She stared at him for long moments. It was all too much to take in, particularly right there and then, in one of the bedrooms of the Black Opal. She needed to get away from him and from the possibility she might run into her brother again. She needed time to think and to come to terms with all that had happened and what she'd learned.

She bent low and collected the wig from where Will had tossed it to the floor. With a heavy sigh, she turned away from him and walked over to the door and unlocked it.

"Where are you going?" he asked.

"Home."

"You can't just walk out of here. Vince might still be—"

"I don't care. I need to go home. I managed to get out of here undetected the first time, I'm sure I can do it again."

"But—"

"Goodnight, Will." Opening the door quietly, Savannah

snuck a glance left and right. The corridor was clear. With relief, she slipped into the darkened hall and left without a backward glance.

It was well after midnight when Savannah arrived back at her condominium. She opened her front door and the stench of vomit hit her like a physical force. Her heart pounded in sudden fear. The only person she'd let into her condo was Dylan. Surely he hadn't been sick in the moments he'd been there? For her to have spied him at the Black Opal, he would have had to leave shortly after she had.

With a trembling hand, she switched on the lamp that stood on a side table in the hall and spied a large wet patch on the carpet a little further down. Stains marked the wall above it.

Cautiously, she stepped into the darkened living room and made out the sleeping figure of her brother spread-eagled across the couch. Her breath rushed out on a gasp of relief.

She must have been mistaken. He wasn't at the brothel. He was at home. Asleep. And he'd been sick.

She moved closer to him and put her hand on his forehead. It was warm, but not hot. His breathing was deep and even. Whatever had made him ill seemed to have passed. At least he'd had the decency to clean it up. She'd deal with the smell in the morning.

With a sigh that was equal parts relief and confusion, she left the room and headed toward her bedroom. Tossing the wig onto her dresser, she kicked off her shoes and went into the bathroom to remove her makeup. She switched on the light over the mirror and stared at her reflection.

Eyes wide with uncertainty stared back at her. Smudged mascara made her look as if she'd gone a few rounds with Mike Tyson.

During her drive home, she'd replayed the events of the night over and over in her mind, but still hadn't come to terms with it. She'd learned Will wasn't a criminal, but had almost convinced herself that maybe her brother was. Now those concerns seemed ludicrous. Dylan was asleep on her couch. There was no way he could have made it home before her. *Could he?*

She frowned. She'd spent time in the main bar and then later, with Will, long after she'd seen the man she believed was her brother. But what if she'd been wrong? What if it hadn't been Dylan at all, but someone who merely looked like him?

And sounded like him. She suddenly recalled the voice she'd heard outside the bedroom shouting for the girls. Had it been her brother, or was she mistaken on both counts? It wasn't the first time…

She couldn't deny the knowledge that Will wasn't a criminal lightened her heart. What weighed her down now was how long it had taken him to tell her. She accepted his explanation, but the fact was, there had been more than ample opportunity for him to call her and not only apologize for not believing her, but to tell her he was in law enforcement.

Pulling off her clothes, she dropped them onto the floor and stepped into the shower. Setting the water to as hot as she could stand it, she scrubbed her body clean of the night's events.

Long moments later, she shut off the faucets and briskly toweled dry. Slipping on a short nightgown, she turned off the light and climbed into bed, grateful for the cool cotton sheets that enveloped her in their softness. Despite her best efforts, her thoughts returned once again to the quandary of her brother.

Almost immediately, the tension returned to her body. She wondered briefly if Will had made it out and was confident he had. It was easy for a man like him to pass himself off as a patron of the exclusive brothel. He was exactly the kind of clientele they catered to.

She glanced at the clock. It was past one. In a few short hours, she'd be back behind her desk, doing her best to convince Max to run another story on the Black Opal. One thing was for sure, she was going to speak with her brother first thing in the morning. The very next person in line would be Pete. That man also had some explaining to do.

Talking to Pete would also solve her problem about going to the homicide guys. She'd tell Pete everything she knew. Now that protecting Will's identity was no longer a consideration, it was the most sensible course of action. The police would know where to direct their investigation into Malee's death and could then make plans to rescue the girls, like she'd promised Angel.

Savannah turned onto her side and tugged the bedclothes up around her shoulders. She was exhausted, emotionally drained and sore. Her feeble attempts on the stainless steel pole had rubbed skin off the inside of her thighs and she hadn't yet done anything about treating it. She needed to dab antiseptic ointment on the wounds and she needed to get some sleep.

She closed her eyes and as it did so often, an image of Will filled her mind. She bit her lip against the surge of emotion that burned behind her eyelids. It was a good thing to discover he was on her side—it *was*. She just had to come to terms with the not-so-good fact that he'd lied to her about it for so long. Delaying the truth was as good as a lie.

Or could be just as bad…

CHAPTER 16

Wednesday morning

The *Daily Mirror* office buzzed with the usual morning activity of ringing phones and coworkers who hammered away on keyboards. Low-grade anger and an ever-present anxiety stirred in Savannah's belly.

She'd woken that morning intending to have it out with Dylan, but by the time she'd showered and dressed, the couch in the living room was empty and her brother was nowhere to be seen. She'd called his cell phone a number of times, but each time, the call had rung out to voicemail. She'd lost count of the number of messages she'd left, each one more terse than its predecessor.

What was adding to her tension was that she also hadn't spoken to Pete. She'd called him an hour ago, but had only been able to leave him a message. Waiting for both men was eating away at her peace of mind.

The jarring ring of the telephone on her desk made her flinch, reminding her how edgy she was. Snatching up the receiver, she took a deep breath and answered.

"*Daily Mirror.*"

"Savannah, it's Pete. Before you say anything, I want you to know I've spoken to Will. He told me everything."

And just like that, her anger resurfaced.

"How *could* you, Pete? How could you keep the fact that

he was a detective from me? I've been investigating the Black Opal. I was knee-deep in it. I thought he was working with Vince Maranoa. I nearly printed a story in the paper about the illustrious Will Rutledge and his double life. I-I could have *destroyed* him."

"I'm sorry, Savannah. I had no idea. The night of the ball, Will gave me some lame excuse about not wanting you to know about his occupation because you didn't like coppers. He told me he liked you and he wanted you to get a chance to know him before you judged him by his job. I didn't know until later that he thought you were a prostitute with an active role in Maranoa's activities."

Heat stole up Savannah's neck and spread across her cheeks. She bit her lip and tried to think of a suitable reply. Before she could do so, Pete spoke again, his voice as dry as the Sahara.

"Don't worry, I know all about your forays into the Black Opal, including your attempts to participate in the live entertainment." He swore succinctly. "I can't believe you'd be that stupid. Savannah. Who the hell knows what might have happened if your cover had been blown? I think I aged ten years when Will told me."

Savannah was flooded with remorse. "I'm sorry, Pete. I didn't think. The first time I went in there, I didn't know anything about Maranoa or his reputation. Once I discovered what was happening... I-I had to go back."

"Why didn't you call the police? It would have been a hell-of-a-lot-safer option."

"Well, I'm calling you now. I need your help."

"Is this about the illegal immigrants?"

"*Yes!* I'm so glad Will told you. Oh Pete, it's just *awful!* You have to do something about it. I promised Malee and Angel I'd help them. I promised you'd get them out of there."

"Tell me everything."

Savannah relayed what she'd seen and learned. After she'd finished, Pete was silent. Eventually, he spoke again.

"You're sure about this?"

"*Yes!* I spoke to those girls, Pete. They're so young and

scared stiff of Maranoa. They didn't want me to go to the police. I did my best to convince them it's their only hope."

"Leave it with me, Savannah. I assure you, there's a taskforce already on it. Immigration has been watching the brothel for months. I'm sure it will only be a matter of time before arrests are made and the girls released."

"Oh, thank God!" she breathed in relief. "I've been so worried! Ever since I saw that photo in the paper..."

Pete's tone sharpened. "What photo?"

"The one of the girl they dragged out of the harbor. I'm sure it was Malee."

"Are you telling me we're not only dealing with kidnapping and the supply of prohibited drugs, we're also talking *murder?*"

Savannah's heart was heavy. "I-I think so."

Pete cursed. "Why the hell didn't you tell me this before? I need you to meet with the homicide guys who are working that investigation as soon as possible."

"Yes, of course. Let me know where and when. I'll do anything I can to help."

"I'll get a number for you. In the meantime, stay out of that goddamned brothel before you get yourself killed."

Savannah flushed again, but sighed softly. "Thanks, Pete. And thanks for listening. I really appreciate it."

"Anytime."

CHAPTER 17

Wednesday afternoon

Vince drew deeply on his cigarette and crushed it out against the overflowing ashtray that sat on his desk. Dylan watched him in silence and wondered with more than a little nervousness why he'd been summoned. Eventually, his boss spoke.

"William Rutledge was here last night."

Dylan frowned. *Of all the luck...* He'd only been gone an hour, two at the most. The asshole must have turned up while Dylan had been at Savannah's. Watching Vince's narrow-eyed gaze, he latched onto the first excuse he could find.

"I-I wasn't feeling so well last night. I went out for a while to get some fresh air. I-I must have passed out. I woke up this morning in some girl's bed on the other side of town."

It sounded believable and it was mostly true. After failing in his mission to rid himself of his sister and then being sick all over her carpet, he'd hightailed it back to the brothel in time to complete his shift. He'd kept an eye out for her, but he hadn't seen her and was relieved that perhaps his guess that she'd returned there was off the mark. It was sheer luck he'd made it back to her condo before she'd arrived home again.

To Dylan's relief, Vince appeared to buy his excuse. "I

hope you showed her a good time beforehand?" he smirked.

Dylan allowed a knowing grin. "Oh, yeah. I know how to show them a good time, all right. Everything I know, I learned from you."

Vince grinned back and then straightened in his chair. "Well, anyway, what I was sayin' was I spoke to Robert Rutledge and his young whelp last night. I wanted to get a take on him. You know, see if he was legit."

"What did you find out?"

"It's just as I thought. He's a rich, spoiled brat who likes to party. He asked me again for some shit and took one of the girls out the back, although I gotta give it to him, he's got manners."

"Manners?" Dylan smirked. "Who the fuck cares about manners?"

"Hey, Kid, that's no way to talk to your superiors," Vince admonished with another grin. "You could learn a lesson or two off young Rutledge. He even bought me a drink."

Dylan shook his head, his grin widening. "He bought *you* a drink? What the hell?"

"As I said, he's got good manners. He knows how to show respect. It was good. I got a kick out of it."

Dylan nodded, pleased his absence hadn't caused a problem. "Do you still want me to watch him?"

Vince shook his head. "Nah, I think he's good. If he finds out we've been keepin' an eye on him, there'll be hell to pay. No sense in antagonizin' a potential long-term customer, especially one as well-heeled as young Rutledge."

Savannah glanced at her watch. It was lunchtime and she was starving. Although she still hadn't heard from Dylan, now that she'd spoken to Pete, she felt much better about most of what had been tearing her up inside and was well on the way to feeling normal again.

Bending low, she collected her handbag from beneath her desk and headed toward the elevator. Minutes later, she strode out of the lobby and into the bright sunshine. Being outdoors always lifted her spirits. The sky was a brilliant blue with only wispy strips of cloud scattered across its vastness. The hot summer air was offset by a faint breeze that blew up from Circular Quay, bringing with it the salty scent of the ocean.

She crossed the street and entered Hyde Park and the outdoor café on the corner. Pigeons wandered with brazen confidence amongst the tables, pausing occasionally to snatch pieces of fallen bread and other crumbs from beneath the feet of the lunchtime diners.

Her stomach growled. She moved over to the counter and ordered a chicken and mayo roll and a latte´. A short time later, her lunch was handed to her in a paper bag. With the story she still hadn't written looming in her mind, she headed back to the office.

Rounding the corner of Castlereagh Street, she clattered up the flight of steps in front of her building and entered the foyer that housed the bank of elevators. From the corner of her eye, she noticed the security guard who stood watch near the entrance. It was Carlo, the man she'd seen speaking with the bouncer at the brothel.

No crime in that. They were living in a free country. The man was entitled to work wherever he pleased. She probably wouldn't have thought anything of it if she hadn't been aware of the illegal activities going on at the Black Opal.

The elevator chimed its arrival and she stepped in and hit her number. Moments later, it reached her floor. Stowing her handbag beneath her desk, she seated herself and stared at the computer screen in front of her, mentally deciding what angle she'd take for the story that was due the next day.

Vince Maranoa deserved to be exposed. Despite Max's opposition, she was sure he'd support her once he read her story. Even without the celebrity slant, it was dynamite and hopefully would yield another sellout.

She drew her keyboard toward her and hammered out the first line and then the next. A paragraph quickly followed. She thought about how she'd seen Maranoa and Will deep in friendly conversation and marveled again how much she'd misread the scene. It just went to show how deceiving appearances could be. She was beyond relieved she hadn't included him in her earlier story. She couldn't imagine how terrible she'd feel knowing she'd gotten it so wrong.

Relieved she no longer had to contemplate that possibility, she once again turned her thoughts to the story unfolding on her screen…

Will, as he'd been the last time she'd seen him, staring at her with concern and uncertainty right before she'd left the brothel, filled her mind. Her fingers slowed and then halted.

She realized she'd never been in love before. She'd thought she was with Jonathan, but it wasn't until she met Will that she realized what she'd felt for her ex fiancé hadn't come anywhere close. Every time she thought of Will, her belly tied in knots. She could barely string two words together when he was near. She didn't know if it was love, but she was old enough to know what she felt seemed very much like the real thing.

Did she dare tell him how she felt?

She sighed. It was times like this she missed her parents most—as a sounding board for her problems with Dylan; the distressing things she'd discovered at the brothel; her feelings for Will. The familiar tightening in her chest made breathing difficult and a wave of longing washed over her. What she wouldn't give to be able to call them.

As busy as her parents' lives had been, she'd always known they would offer a shoulder to cry on or an ear to listen to her problems. But, suddenly they were gone and she'd been left to pick up the pieces. And what a mess she'd made of it. She thought of Dylan and the guilt of her failure weighed her down.

With an impatient sound in the back of her throat, she continued typing. She'd never been the kind of person to sit around feeling sorry for herself and she wasn't about to start now. There were plenty of other people in the world worse off than she was—she only had to look at Angel and the rest of the girls. They had everything to feel sorry about.

Determination surged through her. As soon as Pete provided her with the contact details for the homicide guys, she'd call them. It was way past time she did something constructive to help. Then, when she was finished writing her story, she'd think about finding the courage to call Will.

CHAPTER 18

"Savannah, how are you going with the article for Friday's paper?" Max's unkempt gray hair bobbed wildly above the partition as he neared her desk. A second later, he peered down at her.

"I-I'm not quite finished. Give me another hour or so and it should be good to go."

"Good. In the meantime, I've come to tell you I need you to cover a movie premiere tonight. It's the new Hugh Jackman movie. *Prisoners*, I think it's called. It's playing tonight at the Greater Union in George Street."

"You want *me* to go? What about Roz?" she replied, referring to the flamboyant journalist who usually covered the social pages.

"Roz's son broke his arm on some playground equipment at school. She's gone to the hospital. Who knows what time she'll get out of the emergency department? It's nearly four o'clock. Even if she manages to leave before five or six, I can't imagine she'll be in the mood to frock up and attend a movie premiere."

"But, Max, I don't know the first thing about premieres. I've never been to one. I assume it's a red carpet thing?"

"Yeah, black tie, so wear something smart. Rex will take the photos. He'll meet you there. Starts at seven, but you'd better get there well before that if you want to get a good spot. Hugh Jackman will draw the crowds. If you can't get an interview with him, you'd better make sure you at least get an interview with some of the co-stars."

Her belly fluttered with a mixture of excitement and nerves. She'd never covered stories on celebrities before or attended big opening nights. That was Roz's department. Not that she wasn't confident she could do it, she just didn't know what the deal was.

"What happens when they all go inside? I mean, do I go in with them?"

Laughter burst out of him. "Of course, you ninny! What do you think? That you wait outside with all the screaming fans? You'll have a Press Pass for the event and will go in there and talk to them, try and get some quotes from people our readers will actually recognize. Then, you go and watch the movie."

"Oh, so I actually get to watch the movie?" She hoped she didn't sound as naïve as she felt.

Max chuckled and shook his head. "You really haven't been to one of these things before, have you?"

Heat suffused her cheeks. She looked away. His condescending tone irritated her. Refusing to let him get the better of her, she raised her chin and looked him straight in the eye. "No, Max, I really haven't been to one of these things. I've been here six months. I've never been asked to cover one. When I worked in Canberra, I covered breaking political stories, not movie premieres."

She drew in a breath and made an effort to calm down. "I'm happy to help you out, even on such short notice, but I would appreciate it if you didn't have any more fun at my expense."

The smile slowly slid off his face. "Savannah, lighten up. I'm not making fun of you. I'm just having a little amusement at your expense. There is a difference."

Anger smoldered in the pit of her belly. Her gaze narrowed. Max raised his arms in mock surrender.

"Okay, okay... I'm sorry." His lips tugged upwards into a placating smile. "Listen, just stick with Rex. He knows what to do. He's attended hundreds of these things. He'll even be able to tell you which celebrities are worth approaching.

Don't worry; it'll be fun. Think of it as a reward for the great story you did earlier this week and the even better one I'm sure you're putting together for Friday."

Nerves jangled in her stomach. "I hope so. I haven't had a chance to tell you about the developments there."

His gaze was suddenly sharp. "What do you mean?"

She swallowed. "I mean, I went back to the Black Opal last night and—"

Fury turned his cheeks scarlet. "You went *back?* After I specifically told you to leave the place alone? What the hell's the matter with you?"

Savannah's face was on fire, but she refused to back down. "There wasn't time to do a story on one of the other brothels. Besides, we still haven't told the whole story about the Black Opal. There's more going on there than what you could even imagine."

As he opened his mouth to interrupt again, she continued quickly. "I spoke to another one of the girls. She verified everything I was told the first time. It's *true*, Max. Those girls are being held there illegally, forced to prostitute themselves—Max, one of the girls was only *fourteen!* We can't turn our backs on this!"

He stared at her. His eyes glittered with anger. "If you really think it's happening, why haven't you called the police?"

She held his gaze defiantly. "I have. They're looking into it."

"When? When did you call them?" The intensity in his eyes alarmed her.

"T-today." She blinked, uncomfortable under his close scrutiny. Without warning, he spun on his heel and strode away as fast as his bulk would allow.

"Max! There's more. I haven't finished telling you about—"

"Save it!" he yelled back at her and continued a rapid path to his office. "I have to make some calls. Don't go anywhere. You disobeyed a direct order, Savannah. I haven't finished with you."

The threat was clear. She slumped low in her seat. She'd probably just lost her job.

Great. Now who was going to pay the bills?

With a heavy sigh, she turned back to her computer. Until Max had actually issued her with termination papers, she'd assume she was still employed. And that meant she needed to do some research on the premiere he'd told her to attend. With her employment status now rather precarious, it was even more important that she was as prepared as she could be for the job ahead. The last thing she needed was to give her editor another excuse to chastise her. Hell, apart from Hugh Jackman, she didn't even know who was starring in it.

Clicking open the Google search page, she typed in the name *Hugh Jackman + Prisoners* and waited for the results. From the number of hits that came up, it was clearly a popular movie. Then again, anything with Hugh Jackman starring in it was sure to do well. There was something about that smile and those sexy eyes...

Unbidden, another pair of sexy eyes flashed into her mind, along with thick dark hair and a movie-star smile. She groaned. She could almost feel the hard muscles of his chest as they'd pressed against her breasts. It wasn't fair that he could turn her on with such little effort. The slightest grin tossed in her direction sent her insides to jelly.

With a sigh of impatience, she clicked on the Google image of Hugh Jackman looking gorgeous in an Armani suit and dark Aviator sunglasses. Scrolling down quickly, she read the movie blurb and was pleasantly surprised to discover it was an American thriller. Just the kind of movie she loved.

Scrolling down further, she discovered Jake Gyllenhaal, Viola Davis and Maria Bello were co-starring. She wondered, a little nervously, how many of them would show up.

She glanced at her watch. It was nearly five o'clock. Max was yet to reappear. She'd have to hurry if she wanted to get home, shower and change and get back to the city in time.

Shutting down her computer, she bent down and collected her handbag and headed toward the elevator.

Max and his termination speech would have to wait. She had work to do.

"Hugh, Hugh, over here!"

The noise was something Savannah hadn't anticipated. Crowds of people, young and not so young lined the street, pressing against the barricades that had been erected between the road and the cinema complex.

A red carpet stretched from the footpath to the glass-fronted doors of the Greater Union and uniformed doormen stood guarding the entrance.

A few of the lesser-known stars had already gone inside. The main attraction had just stepped out of his limousine with his smiling wife by his side. Waving to the crowd and acknowledging them with a brief smile, the couple walked along the carpet toward the entry.

Rex stepped out in front of them, dragging Savannah with him. Caught off guard and frantic for something to say, she brought the microphone up to her mouth while he snapped off a few photos with an impressive-looking camera.

"Hugh, welcome to Australia." She gave him what she hoped was a confident, friendly smile.

He turned to face her. His brown eyes sparkled with amusement. "Thanks, it's good to be back. This is home, you know." And with that, the couple walked past them and disappeared through the opened doors.

Rex turned to her, aghast, an incredulous look on his face. "Welcome to Australia? *That's* what you ask the star of the movie? You had a chance to ask him anything at all, and that's what you say to him?" Shaking his head in disgust, he stalked off, muttering under his breath about the trials of having to work with inept and inexperienced journalists.

Several more limousines pulled up to the curb and a group of people Savannah vaguely recognized as young actors from *Home and Away* alighted. Judging from the screams coming from the younger section of the crowd, she assumed they were some of the show's more popular stars.

As Rex's camera snapped away again, she looked up. Her heart leaped into her throat. Will strode along the red carpet, a beautiful blond woman on his arm. Savannah froze. Shards of jealousy pierced her heart. He came closer. Unable to avoid him, she prayed with quiet desperation that he wouldn't stop.

———————

Will spied Savannah where she stood just inside the roped barricade which ran along both sides of the red carpet and his eyes widened in surprise. He almost stumbled into his date. Savannah held a microphone awkwardly in her hand while a photographer snapped off pictures beside her.

Candi tugged impatiently on his arm, drawing his attention to the fact he'd come to a halt. Offering Savannah a polite nod of recognition, he forced himself to continue, heading toward the open glass doors which led inside.

Damn! Of all the people to run into. If he'd had the slightest inkling she'd be here, he'd never have come. He hadn't wanted to attend this function in the first place. In fact, he'd completely forgotten about it until Candi had called him to ask what time he'd be by to collect her.

Truth be told, he'd even forgotten about Candi.

A model he'd dated a couple of times, she was easy going and easy on the eye. The fact she didn't have an original thought in her head had never worried him. At least, it hadn't until he'd met Savannah. Now, it seemed he couldn't help but compare all of his girlfriends to her and it was irritating him no end that none of them seemed to measure up.

Even though he'd forgotten all about her, Candi's call had come as somewhat of a relief and he'd seized upon the chance to put Savannah and her fine green eyes out of his mind. If he didn't know any better, he'd think he was beginning to fall for her.

Which was beyond ridiculous.

"Would you like a glass of champagne, sir?" A tuxedo-clad waiter materialized beside him, brandishing a tray laden with crystal glasses filled with pale sparkling champagne. He lifted two glasses off the tray and handed one to Candi.

"Ooh, I just *love* these events!" She took a sip from her glass and pressed herself against him. "Hugh Jackman, he's so *gorgeous!*" She grabbed Will's free hand and squeezed it lightly.

He forced a polite smile and tried to extricate his hand without causing a scene. The room was crowded and he couldn't tell whether Savannah had come in from outside. He cast around, hoping to spy her trademark red hair.

He hadn't failed to notice how spectacular she looked in a short black, sleeveless cocktail dress that complemented her tanned skin. The low-cut neckline allowed a generous glimpse of her impressive cleavage and had given him flashbacks to the way her soft breasts had felt in his hands.

His cock stirred. As if on cue, Sandi's hand stole around the front of his trousers. Her eyes widened in surprised delight. He cursed under his breath.

"Oh, darling, if I'd known you were that eager to see me, I would have suggested you come over a little earlier. I could have taken care of that for you before we left."

Will tensed and removed her hand. "Candi, please. We're in public." He frowned inwardly, knowing what a hypocrite he was. If it had been Savannah's hand on his cock, he would have enjoyed every minute of it, public be damned. In fact, he'd done just that at the ball.

Oblivious to his annoyance, Candi laughed, deep and throaty. The sound of it normally turned him on. Tonight, it grated.

"Will, darling. I didn't know you were such a prude. You certainly didn't seem to have any inhibitions a few of weeks ago down at the beach. Don't tell me you've gone all shy?"

Much to his relief, a voice toward the front of the crowd directed them to take their seats, saving him from replying. He swiped another glass of champagne and gulped it down in a few quick swallows. It was going to be a long couple of hours.

———————

Savannah watched as Will took a glass of champagne off a tray and drained it. The blonde with legs up to her armpits and boobs only money could buy draped herself all over Will. Savannah quietly seethed.

He looked good enough to eat in his black-on-black Armani and her heart had thumped crazily from the time she realized he stood less than three feet away from her on the red carpet. He was now halfway across the room with his Barbie look alike plastered to his side. Savannah strained her neck around a large man in order to keep them in sight. Rex shot her an odd look.

"What the hell's the matter with you?"

She blushed and forced her gaze away from them. She flashed Rex a smile. "Nothing. Why do you ask?"

"You've been staring at someone over there and it's becoming quite obvious. The thing is..." He sighed with weary resignation. "I know you've never been to one of these celebrity dos before, but you're supposed to stay cool, you know, act like they're just ordinary people, not freaks from another planet."

Her face turned to fire. She could have spontaneously combusted from embarrassment. A part of her hoped desperately that she would. "I-I'm not! I know they're not freaks!"

Gathering what little pride she had left, she tilted her chin defiantly. "And I was not staring. I was just... I thought I saw someone I knew," she finished lamely, refusing to meet his eyes.

"Just as long as you have a story, that's all Max wants. I

got some great shots of Hugh and Jake. Too bad that other young babe... What's her name? Maria Bello... That's right. Too bad she couldn't make it. She's hot."

Savannah looked at him. He had to be pushing sixty. "Isn't she a little young for you?"

"Young? No way," he scoffed. "She's just how I like 'em. Young, fresh and sexy. And all that blond hair. It does it for me."

She turned away in disgust, grateful that the announcement for the audience to take their seats saved her from responding. Praying silently she wouldn't run into Will and his date, her hopes were dashed when she saw them coming toward her. They were less than ten feet away; she had no choice but to acknowledge them.

"Savannah." Will's voice, low and husky, sent shivers of awareness down her spine. "It's good to see you again." He held her gaze and lifted her hand to his lips. She stiffened in surprise. Barbie threw daggers with her eyes.

Will turned to the woman beside him. "Candi, I'd like you to meet a...*friend* of mine, Savannah O'Neill. Savannah, this is Candi."

Savannah blushed furiously. Nobody used the word friend like that, unless they meant *lover*. Everybody knew that. Even Barbie, if the fierce jealousy flashing from her heavily made-up eyes was anything to go by.

A fresh wave of embarrassment washed over Savannah's cheeks. She mumbled something incoherent and pushed her way through the crowd, determined to leave. There was no way in the world she'd be able to sit through nearly two hours of movie knowing Will was in the room with another woman.

She looked around for the exit. Her thoughts tumbled wildly. Why would he introduce her to his date and then make it clear to her that he and Savannah had been lovers? Why would he insult the woman like that? It didn't make sense. Unless he wanted Savannah to know he had no interest in the blond bombshell. Could he have been trying to send her a message?

"Savannah!"

She stopped and turned. Rex jogged toward her, his camera swinging from the strap over his shoulder.

"Where the hell are you going? The movie's about to start."

She improvised quickly. "Rex, I'm sorry. I'm not feeling well. I think I have a migraine coming on. Do you mind if I leave you here? I'm really sorry."

"But what about the party afterwards? It's the best time to get quotes off these people. Their tongues get a lot freer after a few glasses of bubbly, especially when it's on the house."

"I'm sure you're right, but I really can't stay. Besides, I'm certain I have enough already to keep Max happy. You stay, enjoy the movie. It looks like it's going to be a good one."

Not waiting for his response, she turned away and headed toward the exit.

———————

Climbing into bed a couple of hours later after hurriedly putting together an article on the movie, Savannah couldn't prevent the flashbacks to her evening and in particular, the ones of Will and his date.

His date.

According to Pete, Will had said he really liked Savannah. *Had* he meant it? She just didn't know what to believe.

Sighing deeply, she switched off the lamp on her nightstand and snuggled beneath the sheets. The familiar sound of a train rattling along the tracks outside her window calmed her scattered thoughts.

She had to talk to him. She had to lay it all on the line and tell him how she felt. The thought of doing so sent equal tremors of fear and excitement coursing through her veins, but she'd made the decision. It was done. She'd call him.

Tomorrow.

CHAPTER 19

Thursday afternoon

Will stood before the plate glass window that ran from floor to ceiling in his office at Rutledge Advertising and tried to quell his nerves. The ocean glittered invitingly in the distance. Despite his career in law enforcement, he hadn't been lying to Savannah when he told her his father kept an office for him on the top floor of the building. He could only guess his old man remained hopeful his son would see the error of his ways and return to the fold. Either that, or Robert Rutledge was doing his best to keep up the façade.

Will was no longer certain about anything. The father he thought he knew had managed to shock him to the core. Not that he was blind to the possibility that his father enjoyed intimate benefits with the bevy of socialites Robert escorted to various functions around the city, but it had never occurred to Will that he might frequent a brothel.

Will had been stunned to discover him at the Black Opal. The only thing he was thankful for was that his father hadn't blown his cover. When he'd turned his back on his father's world and had embraced the life of a law enforcement officer, relations between them had hit an all-time low.

It wasn't as if Will had anything against advertising, or even working for his father, despite their lack of closeness. It was more a case of a total lack of interest in what went on in his father's world. Advertising could never measure up to his passion for police work. He'd always dreamed of making a difference. Police officers routinely faced life and death situations. They were an integral piece of the fabric of society. Without laws and law enforcers, he believed it was a fast road to anarchy.

His training at the Police Academy in Goulburn had left him with some of the best memories of his life. Finally, he'd found a purpose. Finally, he was making a difference. The Academy was also where he'd met his best mate, Andy Warwick.

They'd graduated together and had then gone their separate ways, being stationed as probationary officers in busy police stations in Sydney suburbs which couldn't be any further apart, but they'd kept in touch and now, with both of them living and working in the inner city, they often socialized together on their days off. Will recalled his promise to Andy to take the yacht out and made a mental note to call and confirm.

The telephone on Will's desk rang, interrupting his musings. He turned away from the window to answer it. "Yes?"

"Will, it's Carol. Your father's ready for you now."

The nerves he'd almost managed to suppress immediately rushed back to crowd his belly. He swallowed the lump in his throat and licked his dry lips. Now that the moment was upon him, he didn't have a clue what he was going to say, but to delay the confrontation would achieve nothing. He drew in a deep breath then released it slowly and strode determinably across the room and opened the door.

A few minutes later, he stood before his father.

"Will, come in. Carol told me you wanted to see me."

"Yeah, I did. The other night, at the Black Opal, I—"

"I get it. You were on a job. I'm not stupid and I'm not surprised. You think I don't give a damn about your police career, but the truth is, I knew within a few days of the paperwork being approved that you'd transferred to the DEA and I knew why."

His father's familiar, steely eyed gaze bored into him, alight with challenge. Will did his best to conceal his surprise. "I-I had no idea."

"Of course you didn't. That's exactly how I wanted it. All these years, you thought I didn't care, but I've always cared. I'm not denying the death of your mother hit me hard, but you're my son. How could you think I didn't love you?"

Pain tore through Will at his father's words. A second later, rage surfaced. "That's total bullshit! You didn't love me! You didn't give a damn about me. From the very day he was born, it was all about Cole. You brought him home and I ceased to exist."

"No." The cold certainty in his father's voice gave him pause, but Will quickly recovered.

"Yes, Dad. That's exactly how it was. I was thirteen. I'd lost my mother and I might as well have lost my father, too. There was no one else for you, but Cole."

"You were jealous."

"You bet I was! I was a kid! I stood by and watched while you lavished him with love and praise. He was the golden child who could do no wrong. I was the third wheel. It was always that way." Will's breath came fast. His chest heaved like he'd sprinted up every single one of the ten flights of stairs that led to his father's office.

Pain and regret flooded his father's face. "It was never meant to be like that, Will. I swear. I-I pushed you away, I know that, but I never... Your mother died giving birth to Cole. She gave her life for him. I had to honor her sacrifice. Above all else, I owed her that much."

His voice cracked with emotion. Will steeled himself against the sympathy that rushed to the surface. He wouldn't feel sorry for his father. *He wouldn't.*

"It's too late, Dad. I don't care." The lie tasted bitter on his lips.

Deep sadness and grief slackened his father's features. With his head bowed, he spoke quietly. "Although I've tried to justify it, there's no excuse for my actions. I can see that now. I don't expect you to forgive me. I ask only that you think of me a little less unkindly, every now and then."

Guilt tore through him. He thought of Savannah and the burgeoning feelings he had for her. He barely knew her and yet every time he thought of her, he was filled with a fierce need to protect her and keep her safe from harm. He couldn't imagine what it would be like to be married to her for thirteen years, to be beyond besotted with her, only to lose her in tragic circumstances...

His shoulders slumped on a heavy sigh. Without conscious thought, he drew closer to where his father sat hunched over his desk.

"I'm sorry, too, Dad. I've been mad as hell at you all these years. I never took the time to look past my pain. I can't imagine what you went through when Mom died and now Cole..." Will's voice cracked. It was too soon... Every time he thought of his little brother—the smile that lit up his face like sunshine, the cheeky glint in his eyes—he ached all over again.

"I miss both of them so much," his father said quietly.

Will's breath hitched. "Me, too."

"I'm sorry, Will. I'm sorry for all of us. I should have been there for you when your mother died, I should have been strong for you. I was the adult, the one you should have been able to rely on for help. I let you down and I let Cole down."

His father stared at him. "You tried to tell me Cole was struggling. I didn't want to listen. He was my beautiful boy, my flawless child. I couldn't bear to think of him as anything other than perfect... It was only right before the end that I realized you were right. I pulled some strings... I got him into rehab...but he wouldn't go. And then it was too late." He shook his head in disbelief. "Cole, of all people, knew how much I grieved over the loss of your mother. I couldn't believe he would... I still can't believe it."

Emotion tightened Will's chest. He cleared his throat and opened his mouth to speak. His father beat him to it.

"I've always been proud of you, Will. I'll admit I was

disappointed when you weren't interested in working alongside of me in the advertising business, but I couldn't help but admire your career choice. Being a copper is a tough gig, in anyone's book. There are plenty not cut out for it. But you were determined to succeed and you've worked hard to get where you are. Apart from all of that, you love it, don't you?" Robert turned back to face him.

Will nodded, his throat tight. "Yeah, I do."

"I've followed your career from day one. At first, I thought it was a simple act of rebellion on your part. You knew how much I wanted you to be part of my business world—but the longer I watched you, the more I realized you were doing it for no other reason than because it was what you wanted to devote your life to—serving and protecting others. I was humbled by your dedication to the cause. I-I still am."

Will shook his head, flooded with uncertainty. "But what about the arguments we had, when you refused to accept my career in law enforcement? You even kept an office here with my name on it."

Robert grimaced. "It was stupid, wasn't it? I guess I wanted you to know you'd always have a place at Rutledge Advertising, if you ever felt the need for it. Cole was always going to follow in my footsteps. I-I wanted you to know you were just as welcome."

"So you didn't do it in the hope I'd come to my senses and forget all about my policing efforts?"

His father looked at him in surprise. "Of course not. Like I said, I've always been proud of your selfless commitment to others. I-I guess I'd begun to see how I'd lavished Cole with perhaps more than his fair share of attention. I wanted to somehow make it up to you; to let you know you were an equally important part of our family."

Will closed his eyes at the enormity of his misunderstanding. All these years, he'd thought his father had been ashamed of Will's career choice, ashamed of *him*. A torrent of emotion surged through him.

"I wish you'd told me, Dad. I wish—"

"So do I, son. So do I." He breathed a heavy sigh. "When I

saw you at the Black Opal and realized you were there undercover, my heart nearly stopped. Vince Maranoa's not a man to be messing with. He's a dangerous criminal who cares nothing for the law."

Will frowned. "I don't understand. Why do you go there, then?"

Robert shrugged and looked away, a faint blush staining his cheeks. "What can I say? Your mother's been gone a long time. I get lonely. All of those establishments ride the edges of legality. I don't need to tell you that. The fact is, Vince runs a good shop. He's picky on who he allows through the door. His girls are clean and disease-free. The surroundings are more than comfortable. I can relax with a drink or two and know that my presence will go no further than the walls of the Black Opal. Whatever else Vince is, he's the epitome of discretion. You can't say that about any of the others. A man in my position can't be too careful."

Will blinked and tried to come to terms with all that he'd learned. There had been one revelation after another and it was a lot to take in. First and foremost was the need to let go of the pain from his youth and to accept that his father was just as fallible as the next man. Will was absolutely certain that until he'd made peace with his past, he'd never be able to give his all to the future. A future he hoped included Savannah...

―――――――――

Will stared at the blotter on his desk in Rutledge Advertising, his thoughts still in turmoil. It had been more than an hour since he'd left his father's office and he still hadn't reconciled himself to all that his father had revealed. Among the chaos that churned inside him, relief slowly trickled into his veins, followed quietly by hope. It blossomed and grew and little by little brought him peace.

The years of anger and hurt and disappointment were over. He'd managed to put them behind him. He'd even found the strength to forgive his father...and Cole.

His thoughts centered on Savannah and another surge of hope rushed through him. Was it possible she might come to care for him, like he cared for her? The way she'd left him at the brothel, he had his doubts, but he was nothing if not determined and he wasn't a man who gave up without a fight.

The phone at his elbow pealed in the stillness of his office. Rousing himself, he leaned over and answered it.

"Oh, Will. It's Carol. I have Andy Warwick waiting to see you. He doesn't have an appointment but—"

"Thanks, Carol. Send him in."

Will wondered briefly at the presence of his friend at Rutledge Advertising, but strode toward the door and opened it.

"Andy! What a surprise. How did you know I was here?"

Andy walked past him. "Hey, Will."

Will frowned at Andy's somber tone. "Are you okay, mate?"

Andy sighed and threw himself down in the chair opposite Will's desk. "Failing that negotiator's course has knocked the wind out of me. I wanted it so much I could taste it...and yet, I failed."

Will remained silent. There wasn't anything he could say that would help.

"At least I'm allowed to have another crack at it," Andy murmured.

Will returned to his seat and nodded. "That's good news. When are you going to reapply?"

"As soon as possible. There's no waiting period. It's just a matter of getting my head in the right space again and going for it a second time."

In an effort to cheer Andy up, Will changed the subject. "You missed a good time at the ball the other night. Too bad you couldn't make it."

Andy sighed. "Yeah, I'm sorry, but I didn't feel up to socializing."

"I understand, mate. Maybe next time. How's Nikki?" Will asked, referring to Andy's girlfriend.

"Yeah, she's good. It's still early days. She doesn't know about..."

"Your father."

"Yeah."

Silence fell between them. Andy's expression closed. Will could only guess at the terrible memories that bombarded his friend. Andy's father had battled with demons that eventually took his life. It was the reason Andy was so determined to become a negotiator.

Will cleared his throat and spoke again. "I checked the roster. I'm off on Friday. How about we take the boat out?"

Andy lifted his gaze and attempted a smile. "Yeah, that sounds great. I'm working a late shift, but I'm good for the morning."

"Great. I'll meet you at the marina at ten."

Andy nodded. "Thanks, mate. For everything. I really appreciate it."

Will nodded solemnly. "You know I'm here for you."

"Yeah. I do."

"You'll be fine, Andy. You'll sit that test and pass with flying colors. In a couple of weeks, you'll be bouncing in here bragging about how you nailed it."

Andy gave him a grateful smile. "Yeah. Absolutely. It's not going to get the better of me." Andy pushed back his chair and stood. He held out his hand.

"Thanks, Will. Thanks for..."

Will nodded in understanding. "Anytime, mate. Anytime."

After seeing Andy out, Will returned to his seat, stacked his hands behind his head and sighed. Less than a minute later, the phone rang again.

"I'm sorry, Will. It's Carol again. I have Savannah O'Neill on line two. She says she's from the *Daily Mirror*."

His heart leaped into his throat and his pulse beat double time. His focus changed and his concerns about Andy dissipated. Ever since he'd seen Savannah at the movie premiere, he'd been unable to get her off his mind.

No, scrap that. Ever since he'd first seen her, he hadn't been able to get her off his mind.

When he'd noticed her at the premiere, it was like he'd been kicked in the gut by a longhorn. He'd cursed silently when he realized the conclusion she'd draw when she saw Candi by his side.

He only hoped she'd understood his none-too-subtle message that Candi meant nothing to him. Savannah had left so abruptly, he hadn't had the chance to speak with her and clarify. As soon as the movie had ended he'd dropped Candi off at her condo. She asked him inside, but he'd let her know he wouldn't be seeing her again.

He regretted the brief look of hurt that had flashed in her eyes, but she'd recover from his rejection soon enough. It was part of what had appealed to him about girls like Candi—girls who were after a good time, not a long time. He couldn't believe how one redheaded woman had changed him so much.

Aware that he hadn't responded, he cleared his throat. "Thanks, Carol. I'll take it." Giving himself a few seconds to grapple with his racing heart, he drew in a couple of deep, calming breaths.

This was crazy. It was like he was sixteen again and about to talk to a girl he'd had a crush on all year. He pressed the flashing line.

"Savannah, nice to hear from you." He hoped like hell she bought the calm routine he'd managed to steal from some reservoir deep inside him.

"Will, thanks for taking my call." She hesitated. "I wasn't sure if I should."

"Should what?"

"Call."

The quiet, uncertain voice on the other end of the line tore pieces out of the calm facade he'd managed to fabricate. Where was the feisty, take-no-prisoners girl he'd come to admire and perhaps...even love?

Love? Did he really put Savannah O'Neill and *love* in the same thought? Was he *mad?* Before he could give it any further thought, she spoke again.

"Well, you know…you and Candi last night. And before that, at the brothel…"

He bit his lip. "I'm sorry about that. Candi—she's just a girl I know. We've been out a few times, but never anything serious."

Savannah sighed. "I'm glad to hear that."

He heard the relief in her voice and was pleased. She might care more for him than she was prepared to admit.

"About my job," he added. "I-I should have told you earlier. I'm sorry. I didn't mean to deceive you. I wasn't sure what was going on with you and…"

"It's okay. I-I'm not exactly without fault. I was a little too quick to jump to conclusions. I-I was hoping we could call a truce and maybe… I-I thought we might… That is, if you would like, um… I was wondering—"

"What is it, Savannah?" He was suddenly inordinately pleased she was having as much difficulty with their conversation as he was. She sounded…nervous. Her next words came out in a rush.

"What I meant to say was… I mean, to *ask* is whether you would like to meet me somewhere for a drink?"

Will's heart leaped with excitement. "Sounds good. When would you like to hook up?"

Savannah's heart skipped a beat at Will's quick response. With an effort, she controlled the sudden galloping sensation in her chest and answered. "H-how about after work today?"

She groaned inwardly as soon as the words were out of her mouth. She didn't want to sound too eager. He might think she was actually keen to see him again. Which of course, she was.

"This afternoon? Yeah, sure. I can probably get away by five. "Where would you like to get together?"

"Um... How about the Marble Bar at the Hilton?"

His voice was low and intimate in her ear. "The Hilton it is."

"Okay, good." She was anxious now to get him off the phone so that she could drag some oxygen into her deprived lungs.

"G-great."

"How will I know it's you? I mean, are you coming as an escort? A journalist? Or someone who's just looking for a fuck?"

She gasped in outrage. "How *dare* you? You are crude and rude and *utterly* without manners. I don't know why I even bothered."

"That'a go, girl! Glad to have you back. For a while there, I wasn't sure who I was talking to. See you at five."

The line went dead in her hand.

Savannah replaced the handset slowly, still in shock over his language and then his abrupt change of tack. She replayed the conversation and thought about it. Until he'd drawn attention to it, she hadn't noticed how subdued she'd been. She guessed it had stemmed from her concern that he wouldn't want to meet with her—that after walking away from him at the brothel, she'd worried he'd wiped his hands clean of her.

When she'd seen him with Candi, she was sure whatever might have sparked between them was well and truly over.

She couldn't deny how relieved she was that he seemed happy about their upcoming meeting. Surely, if he had no interest in her at all, he wouldn't bother? A man like Will was certain to have an endless choice of ways to spend an evening.

Glancing at her watch, she noticed it was just past four. In a little less than an hour, she'd meet him face to face. Her heart rate accelerated. A frisson of nervous excitement zigzagged down her spine like an electric charge. Her request that he meet her at the Marble Bar hadn't been a random choice. Apart from the fact she loved the intimate ambience of the gorgeous room that housed the bar, she was sure he'd remember the last time they'd been at the Hilton.

Did she intend to have passionate sex with him again?

She mulled the thought over. He'd told her Candi meant nothing to him. If she were honest, she'd have to admit, a repeat of their night at the hotel was far too appealing to ignore. Memories of their performance on the king-sized bed flashed through her mind. Heat immediately pooled low in her belly. She suddenly yearned to be naked and close to him.

She forced the desire from her mind and focused on the words on her computer screen. She tried to concentrate on the final aspects of the story she'd put together. She'd expected to submit it to Max the day before, but had lost some time preparing for the movie premiere and hadn't had a chance to finish it. She still hadn't caught up with him and only hoped that if she pretended his outburst hadn't happened, it might be forgotten so she wouldn't have to deal with his refusal to consider her follow-up story or worse, the unemployment line.

As if on cue, she looked up and saw Max lumbering toward her. Her stomach clenched with dread.

"Savannah? I'm glad I caught you. I meant to get back to you yesterday about this Black Opal thing."

"Ah, yes, Max. I'm almost finished. You're not going to believe—"

"*Enough!* I don't want to hear about it. I told you already. I'm not printing any more stories about that brothel. Not now, not ever. Unless you have something else in the pipeline, it looks like you won't have a story in tomorrow's paper."

"Max, I assure you, it's every bit as sensational as the first one."

He took a deep breath and exhaled slowly, as if trying to bring his temper under control. "Savannah, your last story was great. It was shocking; it was sensational—it was everything I like to see in a front page story. But there are plenty of other brothels out there. I'm sure it's not the only one pushing the boundaries of the law. Go and do a story on one of those, like I *told* you to." He turned away and retreated toward his office.

With a sigh, Savannah stared at the words on the screen in front of her. It was a good story, just like she'd told Max. It wasn't fair that he wouldn't even look at it. She refused to accept the time and effort she'd put into it had been wasted.

With a determined set to her jaw, she quickly composed the final paragraphs and emailed it to her boss. Her brief burst of satisfaction was quickly replaced with fear that she'd just ended her short but illustrious career at the *Daily Mirror*.

She glanced at her watch again and saw that it was now a few minutes to five. She'd have to hurry if she didn't want to be late. Shutting down her computer, she grabbed her handbag and walked quickly into the bathroom.

Pulling out a hairbrush, she ran it briskly through her hair, brushing it until it fell in soft, loose waves around her face. She riffled in her handbag for her purse-size bottle of perfume and sprayed her neck and wrists. A quick slash of bronze lip gloss and she was almost done.

Smoothing out the wrinkles in her short, black tailored skirt, she gave herself a once-over. Her crisp, white blouse now looked more than a little tired, but it would have to do; she didn't have anything to change into.

Besides, one of the advantages of the Marble Bar was the discreet lighting throughout the room. It barely allowed for you to make out someone else's face, let alone the state of their clothing.

It made it the perfect meeting place. At the end of a hot, sticky day, she never looked her best. She didn't need to draw attention to it by meeting Will in a room with all the lights on.

With a final glance in the mirror, she picked up her handbag and left the room. As she waited for the elevator, she prayed silently she wouldn't run into Max. Making her way out of her building without incident, her breathing picked up its pace. Excitement and nervousness vied for attention. She was only a couple of blocks from where the hotel was located in George Street. In a matter of minutes, she'd be there.

With Will.

In the Hilton.

Again.

Chapter 20

Will took a sip of cold beer from the glass in his hand and glanced at his watch. The beautiful bar, with its subtle lighting and elegant, but very masculine décor slowly filled with suits. It was five-ten.

She was late.

Her building was only a five-minute walk from the hotel. If she'd left at five, she should have been there by now. He couldn't help the unwelcome thought that perhaps she'd changed her mind.

A shaft of disappointment went through him and he frowned in annoyance. He shouldn't be having such a strong reaction to a woman he barely knew. He wasn't used to feeling so possessive, so primeval—like he wanted to claim her for his own. He didn't know if he was ready to deal with the emotions she stirred up in him. It had been a long six months since he'd allowed himself to feel anything other than icy determination to see those he held responsible for his brother's death, behind bars.

He didn't know what it was about this particular woman that had him agitated, nervous and excited all at once, but he couldn't deny it was true. Every time he saw her, he wanted to take her home, take her to bed and then take care of her for the rest of his life.

He sighed in disgust. He was a goner. He couldn't deny it any longer. He'd fallen for her. She was smart, feisty and beautiful. She did it for him. He only hoped the physical attraction she felt for him went deeper. He owed it to himself to find out and he wasn't above exploiting her attraction for him if it meant she'd come around to his way of thinking. He'd learned the hard way that life was too damn short to waste time.

A whiff of exotic perfume drifted past his nose. A second later, he spotted her reflection in the mirrored glass on the wall behind the bar. She stood less than four feet away. Her gaze meshed with his for a long indefinable moment. His heart stuttered.

He swiveled around on the bar stool and shot her a slow, sexy smile. His gaze paused very deliberately on her chest which, he noted with satisfaction, rose and fell in rapid succession. Yes, he knew where her Achilles heel was. It had everything to do with the sudden hardness between his thighs.

"Sorry I'm late." Her voice was soft and breathy. She moved closer and took a seat beside him at the bar.

"No problem. I hope you don't mind me starting without you?" He indicated the beer in his hand.

"Be my guest. It's not your fault I'm late." She smiled, her beautiful eyes wide and guileless. His heart tripped over.

Oh yeah, he was a goner.

"What are you drinking?" he asked. "My treat."

"Well, in that case, it's top shelf all night."

Will laughed. Warmth spread through him. The iceberg in his chest cracked under the pressure.

"So, what'll it be?"

"*Mm*, I'll have a Kahlua and milk, thanks. Plenty of ice."

"Kahlua and milk?" He smiled teasingly. "That's such a girlie drink."

"Excuse me!" Her tone was indignant, but her eyes sparkled with amusement. "I *am* a girl, in case you hadn't noticed."

"Oh, I noticed all right." His voice dropped to a husky growl. "From the very first moment I saw you, I noticed." He held her gaze. She blushed and lowered her gaze to her lap.

Patches of crimson stole across her face. He was filled

with tender delight. "I love it when your cheeks go all rosy. It reminds me of how you look when you climax."

"Oh!" Her cheeks turned even brighter, like a blowtorch had been applied to them. "Will, please, don't."

"Please, don't what?" he murmured. "Please don't remind you about the mind-blowing sex we shared? Please don't remind you of the sighs you made when I kissed you behind the ear or licked your nipple or when I sucked—"

"Will, please!" She grabbed his arm. "I didn't ask you to meet me to talk about this. I—"

"That's bullshit, and you know it. Come on, Savannah, it doesn't take a genius to work out why you suggested we meet here. Of course you wanted to discuss this attraction between us, or you would have asked me to meet you at a bar downtown. There are only about a hundred others you could have chosen."

He pitched his voice lower. "Now, are we going to be adult about this, or am I going to have to take you upstairs again and fuck you silly before you see sense? I'm beginning to think that's the only language you understand."

He turned back to the bar. "A Kahlua and milk, thanks—with plenty of ice." He gave the order to the barman without drawing breath.

Belatedly, Savannah noticed the barman hovering nearby and realized he'd overheard everything. Her eyes widened in embarrassment and she turned her face away. When the barman took his leave, she reluctantly turned back to Will and flashed him a sheepish grin.

"Okay, okay." She raised her hands in mock surrender. "I admit it, you're right. I was hoping if we met at the Hilton, you'd remember when we were here last." Her voice dropped to a husky murmur. "To be honest, I haven't been able to get it out of my mind. I even hoped—"

She stopped, as if unsure whether to continue. Will held her gaze. His heart thumped hard. He silently urged her to continue. She stared up at him, her eyes dark with emotion. Need uncoiled inside him.

"You were hoping...?" he prompted.

"Uh, um… I…" She stumbled over her words as if overcome with shyness and her gaze fell to the scrunched-up fists in her lap.

"Savannah, look at me."

After a moment, she met his gaze.

"Let's give the Hilton a miss and go to my place. It's right over the Bridge at Kirribilli. We'll be able to…talk without interruption."

Her face turned crimson, but her gaze didn't stray from his. Desire turned her green eyes to emerald. His cock immediately reacted.

All of a sudden, his condominium seemed too far away. He lifted her hands to his lips and pressed kisses across her knuckles. It wasn't enough. Leaning forward, he kissed her on the lips.

Sparks of heat and fire ignited inside him. He increased the pressure and slanted his mouth, taking all that she offered, loving the feel of her mouth against his.

She kissed him back. Her hand came to rest on his chest and caressed him through his shirt. A pulse fluttered rapidly against the soft skin of her neck. The sweetness of her lips nearly undid him. His cock strained against his pants. He wanted to take her there and then and slake his incredible need for her. Winding his arms around her, he tugged her off the barstool and pulled her in tightly against him. His lips found hers again.

"*Ah hm.*" The barman had returned. He placed Savannah's drink in front of them. "That'll be eight dollars fifty, when you're ready," he grinned.

Will reluctantly dropped his arms to his sides and moved slightly away, pleased to see Savannah's breath came as fast as his. He tugged a twenty from his wallet and handed it over. "Keep the change."

The barman accepted the money and nodded his thanks. "By the way," he said. "I'm not sure if you noticed, but this *is* a hotel. We have rooms upstairs—pretty good ones too…so I've heard."

Savannah ducked her head in embarrassment, but Will

only laughed. "Thanks, mate. We might take you up on that."

The bartender winked. "You two have a good night."

"Oh, you can bet on it." Will threw Savannah a cheeky grin. She smiled back at him and picked up her drink. Her eyes sparkled with mischief. Batting her eyes at him seductively, she took a sip of the creamy concoction.

He burst out laughing. "Lucky I already know how good you are in bed, Red, or you might have found yourself on your own tonight. I'm sorry to be the one to tell you this, but your seduction routine needs a bit of work."

"Really? It sure as hell worked on you the first time."

A fresh rush of hormones centered themselves in his groin. "You'd better hurry up and finish that drink. It's time we got out of here." In a couple of quick gulps, he emptied his glass and set it down. She finished hers just as quickly.

Will put his arm around her shoulders and drew her close. "Let's go home," he smiled. Together, they walked up the stairs and outside into the still, warm evening.

"Wow, this is some view you have here." Savannah took in the one hundred and eighty degree view of Sydney Harbour from inside Will's condominium. The view wasn't the only thing that was impressive.

Her entire unit could have fit inside his open-plan kitchen/dining/living room. A sixty-inch flat screen TV was mounted on the far wall and sophisticated stereo equipment stood discreetly in one corner. A fully stocked wet bar was situated in another corner, adjacent to the kitchen. A dark cedar, rectangular dining table that seated twelve stood near the double sliding glass doors that led onto a wide balcony.

Will had already given her a tour of the three spacious bedrooms, each with their own bathroom and gorgeous view of the harbor. A separate laundry completed the space. The color scheme in the condominium was a neutral pale gray with glossy white trims. Bold splashes of color had been added in the form of several original Pro Hart paintings which hung on the walls of the dining room. A burnt-orange modular leather sofa, big enough to seat a football team, complemented the artwork. The sofa curved seductively in front of the plate glass, floor-to-ceiling windows, taking maximum advantage of the view.

Savannah collected the glass of wine Will had poured for her earlier and headed out to join him on the balcony. He glanced up at her almost shyly from his position in one of the white cane deck chairs. "What do you think?"

She slid the glass door closed behind her and took the adjoining chair. His opened bottle of beer rested on the ceramic-tiled top of the matching cane table that stood between them.

"What do I think?" She shook her head, almost lost for words. "It's totally and utterly amazing. It's *huge!* I've never been in a condominium this big before. And the view is spectacular. How do you drag yourself away from all this every day and go to work?"

He gazed out over the balcony at the lights which twinkled around the shoreline. "Yeah, it's a great spot, for sure."

She sat her glass on the table and leaned forward. "How long have you lived here?"

"Nearly six months." He hesitated. "I bought it right after my brother died."

She remained silent, remembering the conversation they'd had about his brother—among other things—a couple of nights before.

"It's okay, Savannah. Really. Cole did what he had to do. I might still be angry at myself for not seeing how close to the edge he was, but the saner part of me knows he made the decision all on his own. Dad and I both tried to get him help. Short of an actual intervention, there wasn't anything we could have done." His lips compressed. "Of course, knowing how it ended, we should have done just that."

"We're all geniuses with the aid of hindsight," she murmured, wanting to remove the shadows from his eyes.

"Yeah. That's what I told Dad. At least, I tried to. He took it hard."

"What about your mother?"

His eyes turned cobalt with emotion. "Mom died during childbirth. They couldn't stop the bleeding."

Savannah bit back a gasp of surprise, unable to believe the pain Will had experienced over the course of his life. With nothing more to offer than meaningless platitudes, she remained silent.

Will drew in a deep breath and exhaled. "Dad has always lived in the eastern suburbs. After Cole's death, I had to get away from that side of town." He lifted a shoulder in a slight shrug. "So, I bought here, in Kirribilli. Every time I leave work and I'm heading for home, I turn north. It's kind of like turning my back on it all and moving forward." He averted his gaze, appearing a little embarrassed. "At least, I hope I'm moving forward. It sounds silly, I know."

Tenderness surged through her. "It doesn't sound silly at all and I know exactly what you mean." She moved her chair closer and stroked him gently on his stubble-roughened cheek.

He caught her hand and brought it to his lips, pressing a soft kiss against her fingers. "I think you really do."

He moved his head until his lips were inches from hers. Moments later, there was no distance between them at all. His lips moved hungrily over the lush softness of her mouth and he groaned.

Her arms went around his neck and he deepened the kiss. She opened her mouth to his probing tongue. It swept inside and tasted her, loving her. He took her hand and pressed it against his erection.

"Let's go inside," he said huskily.

––––––––––––––

Will lifted Savannah into his arms and strode across the balcony. Her heart pounded in anticipation of what was to come. Opening the sliding glass door with his foot, he closed it behind them and carried her down the dimly lit hall. In what seemed like only a few seconds, he placed her gently on a king-sized bed with a carved headboard made of some kind of rich, dark wood. He lay down beside her and gathered her into his arms.

Kissing her with renewed passion, he rolled her onto her back without breaking contact with her lips. His arousal pressed against her stomach. She burned with need. Every part of her body reacted to his touch. She wanted him. She needed him. She couldn't wait another second.

With urgent hands, she undid his shirt, the small buttons playing havoc with her clumsy fingers. With a groan of frustration, she threw caution to the wind. Grasping both sides of his partially opened shirt front, she pulled them apart with an almighty heave. The buttons popped off and flew across the bed. She gasped in satisfaction. Smoothing the fabric open, her fingers at last found his bare, tanned skin. She sighed in relief.

"Lucky I didn't wear my favorite shirt this morning." His murmur was just below her ear. He dropped another kiss along the side of her neck.

"To hell with the shirt." She grinned. "I'm sure you can afford another."

"Cheeky girl." He grinned back at her. "Now, it's my turn."

Before she realized what he was up to, Will pulled the ends of her blouse out of her skirt and tore it open with a single, sharp tug. More buttons went flying. She couldn't help but lament the loss.

"Hey, that *was* one of my favorite shirts." She slapped at his hands playfully.

He shrugged. "So, I'll buy you another one. Or ten. Or fifty." He grinned unashamedly.

She punched him lightly on the shoulder. "Now who's being cheeky?"

"Enough, woman," he growled. "You still have way too many clothes on."

"I could say the same thing about you." Reaching down, she undid the button on his suit pants and eased the zipper down. Running her hand over the satin of his boxer shorts, she squeezed his cock. She heard his sharp intake of breath and smiled with satisfaction.

"Easy, sweetheart. We're going to take this much slower than last time. Tonight, I want to taste every inch of you. I haven't been able to think of anything else since we were together at the hotel."

Savannah felt a rush of warmth at the endearment. Her heart was going to explode. She lifted her butt and he slid her skirt down over her hips. She rolled over onto her side so he could tend to the clasps on her white, lacy bra.

Tossing the underwear to the floor, he stood and dropped his trousers. Her gaze drank in his body, from the impossibly broad shoulders that tapered into narrow hips, to the taut, flat planes of his stomach. Desire swept through her, leaving her tingling.

Stepping out of his boxers, he stood before her, proud and erect and again let her look her fill. She sat up on the bed and wriggled over to the edge.

"You're so beautiful," she breathed. She ran her hand lightly over his chest. Scraping his flat nipples with her fingernails, her hand wandered lower until she got to his cock.

Will steeled himself, knowing he'd die if she didn't touch him soon. The blood pounded in his ears and even more insistently in his groin. When her hand finally encircled him, he gasped. She stroked and flexed in a rhythm that drove him crazy.

And then her hand was gone. It moved lower to wander lightly over his balls, lifting and squeezing until he didn't think he could bear it any longer.

"Savannah." His voice was half plea, half groan.

"*Shh*." She opened her lips and took his cock into her mouth. Sucking and licking, her hand mimicked the movements of her mouth along the lower end of his shaft. It was excruciating. It was unbearable. He couldn't get enough.

Grasping the back of her head, he lifted long red strands of hair away from her face so he could watch. Her small pink tongue darted out and licked the head of his cock, dipping into his slit and sliding out again.

He didn't know how much more he could take. Gently pulling away from her, he stepped back. She looked up at him, her eyes fathomless, green pools of desire. He eased her down across the bed until she lay on her back. Climbing onto the bed beside her, he kneeled in front of her and worked the white lace panties down her slim hips before tossing them onto the floor to join the growing pile of discarded clothing.

Then he lowered his head and tasted her. Slowly at first, his tongue moved in lazy circles around her clit. She raised her arms and took hold of the intricately carved cedar headboard as he did his best to drive her crazy with his mouth.

The stubble on his chin scraped along her aroused flesh and she gasped. His tongue stroked longer and deeper. Parting her with his fingers, he slid his tongue inside her moist center and laved her. He continued the rhythmic movement until she squirmed against him. She let go of the headboard and reached for him.

"Please." Her voice was a shivery whimper of need. "I'm going to come. I want to come with your cock deep inside me. Please, Will. Fuck me."

Listening to her words, Will knew he ought to be shocked. But he wasn't. Somehow, with her, the raunchy way they spoke to each other wasn't vulgar or disgusting. It was right.

If anything, his cock grew larger, harder, thicker. She half-sat and reached down to encircle him with her fingers.

He moaned and pushed her back down onto the bed.

Reaching for a condom in his nightstand, he quickly rolled it over his cock and positioned himself in front of her. Spreading her legs wide with his knees, he eased into her warmth an inch at a time. She thrust her hips upwards, encouraging him to move faster.

"Easy does it, sweetheart. Don't be in such a hurry. We have all night."

She groaned in frustration. "I want you. I want to feel your cock inside me. *Now*."

He plunged into her fiercely, forcing a gasp from her. "Yes," she breathed. Clinging tightly to his shoulders, she met his strong, rhythmic thrusts. "Yes, that's it. Don't stop, please don't stop."

"There's no way in hell I'm going to stop, Red. You don't have to worry about that." His smile was strained as he fought for control.

With great deliberation, he slowed his pace and changed position, lifting her legs above his head. She moaned. He continued to thrust his cock into her slippery center.

Her eyes were shut. Little whimpering noises of need escaped her compressed lips. Her head turned from side to side with increasing urgency. She was close.

"That's it, babe." He gritted his teeth and continued his rhythmic stroking. "That's it. Come for me, sweetheart. I want to see you come."

As if his words tipped her over the edge, Savannah cried out, clutching at him as the first pulses of her orgasm caught up with her. Her inner muscles convulsed around him and it was all he could do not to bury his cock deep inside her and seek his own release.

Instead, he slowed his rhythm once again and waited until her orgasm was over. She gave a long, satisfied sigh and opened her eyes.

"*Mm*, not bad." A cheeky grin spread across her face. "Now, it's your turn."

With a low growl, Will surged into her, needing no further encouragement. Within minutes, he shuddered deep inside her.

Collapsing upon her, he breathed deeply and tried to regain his breath.

"You feel so good," he murmured, shifting his weight and pulling her in close beside him.

"You feel pretty good, too." Savannah smiled shyly up at him.

Will pressed a kiss against the softness of her hair and then moved over to once again tug open the drawer of his nightstand.

A slight frown creased Savannah's forehead. "What are you doing?"

Will flashed her a grin. "I'm checking the supply of condoms. I'd like to repeat our performance in the near future and I want to know if I'm going to have to duck out now and find a drug store."

She blushed and hit him playfully on the arm. "You're pretty confident, aren't you?"

He grabbed her and pulled her on top of him, wriggling her bottom until she was straddling his hips.

"Yep, I am." He grinned cheekily. "With reason, I might add."

"Oh, yeah?"

Her soft wetness came into contact with his cock, stirring it to life once more. "Oh, yeah!" He moaned.

A look of surprise crossed her face. "You can't be ready again? I thought when guys got older, you know, it got harder to um—" She broke off abruptly. Her blush deepened.

Will laughed unrestrained. "Hey, I'm not that old. Thirty-two is not exactly ancient. Besides, it seems where you're concerned, parts of my body have a youthful mind of their own."

Her face bloomed even rosier. She ducked her head so that he couldn't see. He held her chin with gentle fingers and turned her face toward him.

"You're so beautiful when you're embarrassed. I can't believe a woman of your advanced years is capable of such shyness." He grinned cheekily.

"Oh!" She gaped, grabbing the pillow and whacking him in the head. "How rude."

Leaning back to give him another swipe, she gulped when he snatched the pillow out of her hands and threw it toward her. Laughing, she managed to dodge the feathered missile and fell to her side next to him.

"Just how old do you think I am?" she asked, her eyes sparkling.

"*Mm*, now this is a question fraught with danger." He smiled back at her. "It's a question no man can truly answer and come up tops. Why don't you just tell me?"

"*Mm*, you're right. If you say I'm, like, nineteen or something, I won't believe you and I'll know you're saying it because you think it's what I want to hear and I'll never know from then on whether you're telling me the truth about something, or whether you're telling me what you think I want to hear.

"If you say I'm like, thirty-eight or something, I'll never speak to you again. So, I know what you mean. It's a lose/lose situation. Even if you guess correctly, I won't be pleased because every woman likes to think she looks younger than she is; every woman over twenty-five, anyway."

His eyes widened in mock surprise. "Do you mean to tell me you're over twenty-five?"

She shook her head at him and rolled her eyes toward the ceiling. "You're perilously close to getting another whack from the pillow."

"You think?" With one quick movement, he rolled her underneath him again, pinning her helplessly to the bed with the weight of his body.

"You were saying?" he teased.

Instead of struggling, Savannah brought her hand up between their bodies and flicked her fingernail lightly across his flat nipple. Next, she wet her finger inside her mouth and drew lazy circles around the now-hardened nub.

Will groaned, enjoying the sensations she induced. When her tongue snuck out and licked him, his cock stirred once again and he pressed the hardening flesh into her softness. She peeked up at him from beneath her lashes.

"Do you like it when I do that?"

"I like it very much, Red." He brought his head down to hers. Pressing soft, feather-light kisses against her lips, he sampled her slowly, savoring the fruity tang of wine he could still taste in her mouth.

Her arms came around his neck and pulled him down hard against her chest. Her breasts strained against him, eager for attention. He deepened the kiss and his fingers sought and found one of her breasts, kneading it with his hand. He pinched her nipple and listened to the soft gasps and moans that came from the woman beneath him.

His woman.

His cock jutted impatiently against her center. She was still wet from their earlier lovemaking and he reached down and ran his hardness up and down her opening until he was slick with her juices.

She moaned again and thrust her hips up against him. Needing no further encouragement, he sheathed himself once again and pushed his cock inside her, groaning when he was once again deep within her warmth.

"God, I can't get enough of you." He groaned against her neck. "You're so warm, so tight, so wet."

He strained to hear her shy whisper. "I love the feel of you inside me. It feels so right."

Growling low in his throat, he tightened his hold on her and increased the pace of his thrusts. "You feel right. Too damn right," he muttered close to her ear.

Savannah brought her legs up and tightened them around his hips. His strokes became deeper and longer. She tensed underneath him. Her muscles once again tightened and flexed around his cock until she found her release. He surged into her, burying himself deep into her warmth. He groaned his relief.

Slowly, he became aware of his weight on top of her. He shifted slightly until he lay on his side, and gathered her close against him, spoon fashion. Kissing her softly on the back of her neck, he inhaled the exotic, musky scent of her hair.

Within minutes, he was asleep.

<h1 style="text-align:center">CHAPTER 21</h1>

Friday morning

The blast of a ferry horn right outside the window awoke Savannah with a start. The room was dim, but the faint illumination of the morning sun reached for her through the double glass sliding doors adjacent to the bed.

The heavy damask curtains that covered the windows were open and the sight of Sydney Harbour spread before her in all its sparkling glory, looking close enough to touch, disorientated her. She moved slightly on the bed. Will stirred beside her. His arm tightened around her and he pulled her back into the curve of his body.

"Where do you think you're going?" His voice was clouded with sleep.

She smiled. "I was getting up to have a better look at the view." She turned in his arms to face him.

His eyes lingered on her nakedness. "I think the view's pretty damn good right here."

"*Mm*, that may be so," she agreed, stroking her fingers along his cheek, "but I also have to use the bathroom."

She extricated herself from his arms and scooted across the bed, tugging the sheet with her. He groaned in protest. Wrapping it around her securely, she padded into the bathroom and closed the door. After using the toilet, she hefted the sheet back around her and walked into the bedroom. Will was propped up on his elbow, an amused expression on his face.

"You mean to tell me after all we've done, you're still shy about me seeing you naked?"

She ducked her head, thankful for the dimness which concealed her embarrassment.

"Come here." His voice was a velvet command.

Her pulse leaped. She made her way back to the bed. He lay sprawled across it, bared to her gaze.

"Sit down."

She sat.

He leaned over and gently tugged at the sheet still clutched in her hands, exposing her nakedness.

"You're so beautiful." His response was husky with emotion. "I love looking at you. Don't be embarrassed."

"Okay." She smiled, feeling beautiful under his tender regard. His arm snaked out and drew her close into his side. She snuggled into him.

He glanced at the clock on his nightstand and groaned. "It can't be that time already. It feels like I only just closed my eyes."

Savannah blushed at the memory of their night of lovemaking. "Don't tell me you're complaining?"

Will's arm tightened around her. "Not on your life. I'd happily repeat it every night—and every day," he added, his eyes twinkling.

"Too bad we have to work for a living."

"Yeah." He hesitated and then grinned. "Except, I'm on a day off. How lucky is that?"

Savannah faked a pout. "It's all right for some. What about me?"

Will raised an eyebrow. "You could call in sick."

Savannah contemplated the idea for a total of two seconds and then grinned, feeling deliciously naughty. "You're right. In fact, the more I think about it, the more I feel like I'm coming down with something." She coughed. "There it is. Definitely a sore throat and I'm feeling...achy all over."

Will's eyes darkened with emotion. He leaned over and kissed her, taking the time to linger over her mouth. His hand came up to cup her breast. He rubbed her nipple with the pad of his thumb.

Desire kindled low in her belly. She couldn't believe how quickly he could arouse her.

"Tell me where it hurts." His mouth moved down to nuzzle her neck. Her head fell back.

"*Mm*, that feels good."

His hand moved to her other breast. His fingers kneaded and squeezed. "How about here?"

"Yes, I think that needs some attention."

His mouth replaced his hand. He drew her nipple into his mouth and suckled. She gasped and moved restlessly beside him.

"Don't move. It's not good to tax yourself while you're feeling unwell. Let me fix it. I've been told I'm good with my hands."

His hand skimmed across her taut belly. Moments later, his finger slid along her wet slit and slipped inside. She moaned.

"Yes, Dr Will. You certainly are good with your hands."

His cock lay thick and hard against her belly. She widened her legs in silent encouragement. Releasing her nipple, he positioned himself between her thighs.

He stared down at her. "I can't get enough of you," he muttered, his voice hoarse. He reached quickly for a condom. His cock pressed at her entrance. She lifted her hips to meet his savage thrust. She cried out and clung to him, riding the waves of desire until they both found fulfillment.

A few moments later, Will shot her a look full of mischief. "How are you feeling? Still achy?"

She grinned and turned on her side to face him. "You may have helped a little. I'm not sure I'm up for a day at the office, though."

His expression sobered. "No, you're right. Your color's high. You need take it easy today. Bed rest would be preferable."

She laughed and gave him a playful punch to his

shoulder. "I'm sure that can be arranged. I'll call Max and let him know. I submitted a story to him before I left yesterday. It's now up to him what he does with it."

"Is it about the Black Opal?"

Savannah nodded. "Yes. I kept you out of it, but as for the rest of it, the public has a right to know, despite what Max says. Anyway, Pete told me the immigration department and the homicide guys are all over it. I assume they'll be making arrests any day, which makes it even more important we get the scoop."

"I know it shouldn't matter who locks Maranoa up, but I wanted to be the one to nail the asshole for drug dealing. He could do fifteen to twenty years if we found out where he stores the gear."

"I understand where you're coming from, especially after hearing about Cole."

"Ever since I transferred to the DEA, I've dreamed of being the one to snap the cuffs against that asshole's wrists. I'll never know if he was Cole's supplier, but he and his ilk are all the same. They don't give a damn about the lives they ruin. It's all about the dollars."

"Unfortunately, you're right." She reached for his hand and threaded her fingers through his. "I'm sorry about your brother. My brother's the only family I have left."

Will squeezed her hand. "What happened to your parents?"

She sighed. "They died in a freak accident a little over six years ago."

"How did it happen?"

"They were camping." A wry smile turned up her lips. "They'd never been camping in their lives, but they both decided it was on their bucket list. They wanted to go and explore the great outdoors. They bought one of those tent trailer things—you know, the ones that fold out from a box trailer?" He nodded and she continued.

"Mom and Dad were both academics and not at all practical." She smiled wistfully. "They raised me to be an independent thinker, encouraging me to ask questions and not be content just to accept someone else's explanation. They gave me a sense of appreciation and awareness of those around me—people who were less fortunate than me, the ones most of us try to forget. They led by example and gave me a social conscience."

"I guess that explains your dogged determination to get to the bottom of the brothel story," he murmured, a rueful smile tugging at his lips. "Even if your research approach was incredibly stupid."

She frowned and pushed against his chest. He tried to pull her back into his arms, but she moved away.

"I'll have you know, I had everything under control in there. You were the one who decided to take me to one of the bedrooms. I'd planned to finish my dance and disappear the way I'd come, with no one the wiser." She stared at him defiantly.

"And what would you have done if some other bloke, infinitely less desirable and understanding than me, had requested your services? Maranoa told me he was interested in having you for a plaything. I bet you didn't even consider that possibility?"

Savannah scowled. "Of course I considered it, but I decided the risk didn't outweigh my need to go there and find out what was happening."

"Why didn't you just call the police? That's what we're here for."

"You're right and I thought about it. But by that time I'd met you and I didn't know where you fit into the whole scene. I thought you were in advertising, remember?" she said, giving him a pointed look and then continued.

"Once the police were involved, innocent or not, any chance of you staying out of the spotlight would have vanished. I-I didn't want that on my conscience."

The annoyance on his face dissolved. He pulled her unresisting form into the warmth of his chest. "Even then you were looking out for me," he murmured, nuzzling her hair. "I think you might be a little bit in love with me, Savannah O'Neill."

She stared at him. Her heart thudded. It wasn't the first time she'd thought about her feelings for him. Surely, she didn't know him well enough to be in love with him? She certainly *liked* him a good deal. How far she wanted to take that, she had no idea.

"Hey, don't look so serious," Will smiled. "I was joking. Now, tell me what happened with your parents' camping trip?"

Shelving the idea of analyzing her feelings for a later time, she continued the story.

"Right, the camping trip. They were so looking forward to it," she said. "They'd taken long service leave from their jobs and planned to travel around Australia for a couple of months, stopping at camping grounds along the way. Dylan, my brother, was at boarding school and I was old enough to take care of myself. There was nothing holding them back."

She smiled in memory. "I laughed at them when they told me. They didn't know the first thing about camping. But they didn't care. They were sure there'd be plenty of people along the way who could help them if they needed it and that was true. They'd call me or send me an email from the middle of nowhere and tell me all about the adventures they were having and all the friendly people they'd met. I was happy for them. They'd worked hard for many years and they deserved to have a break."

She sighed. "Everything was fine until they pulled into a camping ground near Alice Springs. They'd been away about three weeks." Memories came flooding back to her. She paused.

"It's okay." Will rubbed her arm soothingly with the pad of his thumb. "You don't have to say any more."

Savannah blinked back tears and looked up at him. "No, I think I need to. I haven't spoken about it to anyone since the funeral. Not even to Dylan." She took a deep breath and continued.

"The police told me my parents had parked the trailer under a stand of huge gum trees—looking for shade, I guess. Even though it was spring, it was already hot up there. They don't call it the Red Centre for nothing."

She paused and drew in another breath. "A limb fell off one of the trees through the night and hit their trailer. Just like that, they were gone. There'd been no wind, no rain…nothing. A freak accident. That's what the police said. I've since learned you should never park anything under a gum tree. They're notorious for dropping branches." They lay in companionable silence. Will was the first one to break it.

"Tell me about your brother."

Savannah sagged against him. Burying her head against the reassuring solidness of his chest, she took comfort from his strength.

"Dylan's nineteen. He's the reason I moved back from Canberra. He-he's found it hard since Mom and Dad died."

"How do you mean?"

Savannah's lips compressed and she was flooded with emotion. At last, in halting sentences, she talked to him about her brother and the difficulties he'd faced after their parents' deaths and the toll it was taking on her.

"Does he still live with you?"

"No. He's been in rehab since we arrived. At least, he was. He—" Her voice hitched. Will tightened his arms around her. She shot him a grateful look.

"He came by my condo a couple of nights ago and told me he was done with it. He's checked himself out a month early. The judge spared him a custodial sentence on the proviso he spend a minimum of six months in rehab. I'm so scared he'll be brought before the courts again and resentenced."

Will pulled her closer, his eyes insistent. "It's not your fault, Savannah. You're not responsible for him, sweetheart. He's an adult, now. I know exactly where you're coming from. I've been there, too. As much as both of us might want it to be different, things move beyond our control."

"You're right, but it doesn't make it any easier. I just hope he hasn't fallen back in with the men who got him into trouble in the first place."

His hand stroked along her arm, providing comfort. "Are there any signs that he has?"

She thought of the man she'd glimpsed at the Black Opal. She was almost certain it had been Dylan, but something held her back from telling Will. He was a police officer, after all. Her brother was the only blood relative she had left. He deserved a level of loyalty. Will contemplated her, waiting for her to answer.

"He turned up wearing expensive new clothes and a pair of boots that must have cost five hundred dollars." She shrugged. "He has no money. I've been supporting him his entire life. Besides, he's been living at Dexter House. Where would he come up with the funds for things like that?"

"Did you talk to him about it?"

"No. He would have thought I was accusing him of returning to his old ways. It would have caused an ugly scene and, to tell you the truth, I was pleased to see him. It's been awhile since I visited him. I-I missed him."

"You're too kind to him."

"Maybe I am. Maybe I should have been harder on him when he didn't behave the way he ought. I don't understand why he seems so intent on destroying himself and causing pain for the one person who loves him. I-I don't know how to help him." Her voice broke on the last words. All of a sudden, she felt overwhelmed. Hot tears spilled from the corners of her eyes.

Will hugged her tightly and pressed his lips to the top of her head, murmuring words of comfort against her hair. A long while later, he spoke.

"The night you saw me getting cozy with Maranoa, I'd just discovered my father was a regular patron of his brothel. In fact, he was there that night, sitting right beside me at the bar."

Savannah frowned in thought. "I recall seeing an older man in the vicinity. I don't know why I didn't recognize him. I guess my attention was focused elsewhere."

Will smiled briefly and then sighed. "I'd never thought about what his life must have been like after Mom died. At the time of her death, I was a self absorbed teenager with troubles of my own. Dad and I have been estranged for years. The other night, he had the opportunity to blow my cover in front of Maranoa and I would have been in a world of hurt, but he didn't. He played along and Vince was no more the wiser. I went and saw Dad at his office yesterday."

Savannah looked up at him in surprise. "How did it go?"

Will drew in a deep breath, his chest expanding beneath Savannah's ear.

"It went surprisingly well. We talked about Mom and Cole and about our relationship—stuff we'd never ever discussed. He told me he was proud of the fact I was a copper. After all these years, it was good to hear it."

"Did you talk to him about the Black Opal?"

"A little. He goes there for the same reasons most men go there—to relax and enjoy the companionship of a woman. I never thought about it before, but he's right. Mom's been gone a long time. He hasn't remarried and apart from the odd eye candy on his arm at social events, he's never had a girlfriend. He told me he gets lonely."

Savannah caressed his cheek tenderly with her fingers. "We all deal with life's hurdles in our own way. He's not doing anything illegal. He's dealing with it the best way he can."

"Yeah, I just wish he'd chosen someone else's brothel to relax in. Why did it have to be Maranoa's?"

She had no answer for that and Will didn't expect one. The rumble from her belly brought a smile to his lips.

"Is that your subtle way of telling me you're hungry?" He grinned when she blushed.

"I haven't eaten since lunchtime yesterday. I must admit, I'm a bit famished. What time is it anyway?"

He glanced over at the clock. "Eight-thirty."

Savannah sighed. "I'd better call Max and plead illness."

"Damn! I nearly forgot!" Will reached for his cell phone on the nightstand.

"What is it?"

"I promised a mate of mine we'd go sailing this morning. He's been doing it tough lately. I thought a day out on the water would take his mind off things."

A pang of warmth surged through her at his thoughtfulness. "Please don't change your plans on my behalf. It sounds like your friend needs you."

Will smiled at her tenderly. "Thanks, that's nice of you. Perhaps we could all go together? There's plenty of room on the yacht. I'll call Andy and see if he's okay with it."

Will punched in a number and Savannah reached for the discarded sheet. Tugging it around her, she padded down the hall to the kitchen. She found her handbag on the countertop and quickly left a message with Max's secretary that she wouldn't be in.

Feeling like a naughty schoolgirl playing truant from class, she headed back to the bedroom. Will stood gloriously naked in the doorway which led to the shower. He turned when he saw her. "All good?"

She nodded.

He grinned. "Excellent. I spoke to Andy, but he's come down with a stomach bug. He's going to give today a miss, so it's back to just you and me. What do you feel like for breakfast?"

Savannah deliberately let her gaze drift over his naked form, taking in his smooth, tanned chest, flat stomach and the impressive male length of him which now rested innocently on a thick bed of dark, springy hair.

Her eyes stayed steadily focused on his cock. "What did you have in mind?"

"I thought *I* was insatiable," he teased and reached out to her. "Wanna join me?"

"I thought you'd never ask."

CHAPTER 22

Friday afternoon

Savannah and Will spent most of the day getting to know each other. He took her to the marina at Rushcutters Bay and wowed her with his sailing prowess. He told her stories of times before his brother had been born when his father and mother had taken him out on their yacht to while away the hours swimming, fishing and enjoying each other's company.

He told her about one occasion when a toddler had stumbled and fallen over the side of a neighboring yacht and how he'd dived into the water to rescue the baby without thought or hesitation. He'd been all of eleven and had been totally embarrassed by the attention his heroic actions had caused.

She finally clued him in about her age. She could tell he was pleased to discover there were only four years between them. They dropped anchor near Watsons Bay and over a picnic lunch on the deck, he shared stories about his sixteen cousins and their myriad children. The light in his eyes when he spoke about his extended family touched her heart and a pang of sadness surged through her. With the death of his only sibling, it was possible he'd never know the joy of being an uncle to nieces and nephews.

Just like her. The thought sobered her. If anything ever

happened to Dylan, she'd be as alone as Will was. Even more so. At least he still had his father.

With a determined effort, she pushed away the sad thoughts and vowed to make a bigger effort to set aside her differences with her brother and accept him, warts and all. If he had gotten himself caught up with the likes of Vince Maranoa, she'd do all she could to help him. Surely, he hadn't been out of rehab long enough to become too involved? She'd prevail upon him to see sense, like she had the last time he'd gone off course and hopefully, he'd return to the hospital.

She'd accepted that it wasn't her place to try and change him. He had to walk his own path. All she could do was to be there for him, to help him through the good and the bad, and to love him without reservation.

Now, as the sun sank in the west, casting a rainbow of red and orange and pink across the water, Savannah closed her eyes and tilted her head back against the headrest of the cane chair on Will's balcony. Inhaling the scent of the salt water, she listened as it lapped at the shore below.

"It's so beautiful here," she murmured. "I can't believe I'm only fifteen minutes from the city. It feels like a world away."

"You're right," Will smiled from his spot in the matching chair opposite. "It does."

"I thought my little unit in Waverton was great, but it has nothing on this." She smiled.

"Waverton? Do you mean all this time you've been living right around the corner?"

"Yep, at the bottom of Carr Street, near the train line. It's funny, after awhile, you don't even hear them as they rattle past. And I do have a great view of the water from my living room window. Not as good as yours," she grinned wryly, "but it's pretty nice."

"I'd love to see it."

She winked at him. "And so you shall."

He smiled back at her. She took a sip from the glass of chilled white wine he'd handed her only minutes earlier and sighed.

"Today's been so perfect." A moment later, she giggled. "I can't believe I took a sickie."

Will shot her a teasing grin. "Yes, it was very naughty of you, Red, but I'm eternally grateful. Who knows? You might even do it for me again."

She nodded and then frowned as if giving the idea serious consideration. "I think I could get used to it, especially if you go out of your way to pamper me like you have today, but I doubt Pete will go for it. Or Max, for that matter. I wonder if he ran with my story?" she mused.

"I remember you said something about Max's opposition. Was there a possibility that he wouldn't use it?"

"Oh, yeah. He and I didn't exactly see eye to eye on the whole Black Opal thing."

Will leaned forward in his seat. "How so?"

Savannah frowned. "It's really quite weird." She took another sip from her glass and proceeded to tell him about Max's odd reactions.

"At one stage, he even implied I'd be doing *you* a favor if I left the Black Opal alone," she added.

Will frowned. "Me? What did I have to do with it?"

"Something about Rutledge advertising dollars," she replied, embarrassed to admit she'd told Max about her suspicions. To prevent him from questioning her further, she hurriedly continued.

"It's not like him to care about whose toes he might tread on. All he used to care about was selling newspapers, but he's made it more than clear he isn't going to print any more stories on the Black Opal."

Renewed feelings of anger and frustration surged through her. Unable to sit still any longer, she pushed away from her chair and paced the confines of the balcony. After awhile, her shoulders slumped in defeat. "Is it just me? What do *you* think about his behavior?"

"I think it sounds a little strange, too. Did he say anything about your job still being on the line?"

"No, it was almost as if he'd forgotten about it and I certainly wasn't going to raise it."

Will stood and drew close. Bending low, he pressed a soft kiss on her lips. "Let's not worry about it right now. Finish your drink so we can go inside. I think it's well past time I ravished your body again."

CHAPTER 23

Saturday morning

Vince Maranoa's lip curled upwards in a feral snarl. Anger coursed through him. His fist clenched around the newspaper in his hand. It infuriated him when his orders were ignored. He snatched up his cell and punched in a number.

"What the fuck, Max? You told me you'd deal with the bitch. You've fuckin' let her write another story. What the fuck is this shit? She'll have every copper in Sydney on my tail if she keeps this up."

"I'm sorry, Vince," came the sniveling reply. "I couldn't help it. She went against my express instructions to leave the Black Opal alone. When she told me she'd been back, I ripped her head off."

"She's on your fuckin' payroll, Max. You're the boss. She does what you say. She writes what you tell her to write and at the end of the day, if it doesn't fuckin' work like that, then what the fuck are you doin' there?"

"I'm sorry, Vince. I truly am. But the girl's right. It's a hot story. I took a call from Reid Marchant late Thursday, after I'd spoken to you. Reid owns the paper. He called me personally to make sure I was going to do a follow-up. I sure as hell couldn't argue with him. He would have asked too many questions if I hadn't run it. You'll have to keep your head down until it blows over."

"Don't fuckin' tell me what to do, Max. There's no way in the world this is goin' to blow over. You've already told me this bitch has gone to the cops. We'll be crawlin' with pigs and it'll be all your fault. We got lucky the last time they raided us. They didn't find the cellar. But there's no way I'm riskin' it a second time. You can bet your ass they're not gonna go away empty handed a second time. I'm gonna have to move the shit. Find somewhere safer to store it. This is gonna fuckin' cost you, Max. You mark my word."

"I have an idea," Max exclaimed. "Take it to the warehouse in Surry Hills. The place is virtually empty. It's been a dumping ground for dinosaur printing presses and other junk for years. You might have to clean it up a bit, but it's yours if you want to use it. No one will guess you're storing gear at a newspaper warehouse."

Vince went silent. His brain ticked frantically in time with his pulse.

It could work. Fuck, yeah, it was brilliant. He curbed his enthusiasm before he spoke again. No sense having Max feel like all was forgiven.

"The *Daily Mirror* warehouse, you say? Who has access to it?"

"I do, of course and I assume Reid does. I'm not sure if there's anyone else, but the place hasn't been used for years. You'll wade through a foot of dust just to get in there."

Excitement leaped in Vince's veins. He knew the warehouse Max referred to. It sounded perfect. Situated in an area surrounded by a lot of similar warehouses, the comings and goings of delivery trucks wouldn't necessarily arouse suspicion. Max was fuckin' brilliant. Not that he'd tell him that.

"It sounds like it might work out, at least in the short term. It has to be better than leavin' it here. I expect I'll be served with another fuckin' search warrant any day."

"I'm sorry, Vince, I really am. It won't happen again. I promise."

"That's what you fuckin' said last time," Vince growled. "What's the bitch's name, anyway?"

"S-Savannah O'Neill. She's only been here six months."

"Six months too long from the sound of it. Leave her to me, Max. I'll deal with her."

"W-what are you going to do?" Max sounded fearful.

Vince grinned. "Don't you worry your fuckin' little head over it, Max. I'm all over it."

Vince ended the call and swore long and loudly, excitement warring with relief. He'd found a solution to his problem. Who'd have thought Fat Max would come to his rescue? It had never been that way before.

Not wishing to waste another second, he spun on his heel and strode into the main room of the brothel. Georgie stood behind the bar, polishing glasses. He worked a cloth into the narrow openings, his thick biceps bulging from the effort.

"Where the fuck is the Kid?" Vince growled.

Georgie looked up and shrugged. "I don't know, boss. Last I saw him, he was with the new girl. She might only be fifteen, but she has the sweetest ass—"

Vince swung around and headed through the staff door that led to the bedrooms. The first two rooms were empty. Most of the girls took time to shower and rest or launder their clothes prior to another night on the job. He opened the third door. Two girls were sprawled across the bed, asleep. Vince nodded his approval; they'd be ready to face another busy Saturday night.

The fourth door was locked. He tugged out a set of keys from his pocket and fitted the right key to the lock. The door knob opened easily under his hand.

The room was dimly lit by a pair of lamps that stood on nightstands either side of the king-sized bed. Billy's bare ass moved up and down in rhythm with his cock as he plunged it in and out of the new girl. She stared at the ceiling, almost oblivious to the man between her legs.

Vince's cock grew hard. He hadn't had a fuck all week. He'd been too wound up about the fuckin' journalist who'd had the balls to infiltrate his domain. The thought of the little bitch—Savannah O'Neill, Max had said—sent a rush of blood straight to his groin. His cock swelled even further and pressed against his jeans.

Billy groaned and collapsed on top of the girl beneath him. Vince popped open the button on his jeans and slid down his zipper.

"I hope she was fuckin' worth it, Kid. You know you're only allowed to fuck 'em on your own time."

Billy leaped off the girl like he'd been shot. His eyes were wide with fear until he spied Vince with his cock in his hand.

"Sorry, boss. She has such a sweet pussy, I couldn't resist." His gaze rested on the engorged shaft in Vince's hand. "I'm-I'm happy to share."

A bark of laughter exploded from Vince's chest. "*Share?* You're a fuckin' cheeky bastard. I fuckin' *own* that pussy. Now fuck off out of here so I can have a go at her. Don't go too far away. I'm not through with you, yet," he growled.

Billy tugged up his pants and slipped through the doorway. Vince strode over to the bed and picked up a whip from the nightstand. His chat with Billy could wait. Right now, there was a more important matter to attend to.

———————

Dylan tossed the raw scotch down his throat and grimaced. The fiery liquid burned all the way down to his stomach and still didn't go far enough to ease the dread that had cemented itself in his gut.

"Take it easy, Kid," Georgie muttered. "You'll be passed out on the floor by the time Vince gets back. Then he *will* be pissed."

Dylan glanced at the barman and shook his head. "Fuck, he scared the shit out of me when he barged into that room. I still had my cock in her. I thought I was a dead man. Do you know why he wants to see me?"

Georgie shook his head. "Nope, only that he tore in here yelling for you, looking fit to be tied. When I told him you were out the back, he stormed off. That was the last I seen of him."

Dylan lowered his head and stared at the polished timber bar. Vince would be out any minute and he was still no closer to knowing what had fired the man up. The door swung inward. Vince stepped into the bar area, still adjusting his jeans. He spied Dylan at the bar and a feral gleam glinted in his eyes. Dylan's belly took a nosedive.

"Kid, come over here."

Refusing to show his fear, Dylan emptied the rest of his glass in a single swallow and stood. Pushing away from the barstool, he met Vince at the end of the bar.

"What's up, boss?"

A meaty fist flew toward him. Pain exploded in his mouth. Blood poured from a gash on his lip where his teeth had cut through. His hand pressed to the wound in an effort to stem the blood.

"Shit, Vince. What did you go and do that for?"

"That's for bein' caught fuckin' on the job. You were told when you first started here it was against the rules."

Dylan held his hands up in surrender. "Okay, I'm sorry. The little slut kept coming on to me, rubbing herself against me like a bitch in heat. In the end, I had to fuck her just to get her away from me. It won't happen again, I promise."

Vince gave him a hard look. "It better not. Now, I have another job for you. There's a little bitch who works for the *Daily Mirror*—Savannah O'Neill's her name. She's causing trouble, big time."

Shock immobilized him, even though he'd been expecting it. His heart thudded. His mouth fell open. He closed it in a hurry and his teeth clicked from the effort. Fresh pain surged through his jaw. He blinked back the sting of tears and did his best to concentrate on Vince's words.

"Her stories are stirrin' up a fuckin' hornet's nest. The coppers will be all over us. I want you to help me move the gear. Then you're goin' to find this bitch and get rid of her." Vince's gaze narrowed on his face. "Understand?"

Dylan nodded. He had to tell him. Blood pulsed in his ears. "Vince, the girl—Savannah—she's—she's my sister," he blurted out.

Surprise flared in Vince's eyes and then it was replaced with laughter. "Your sister, eh? That's fuckin' fantastic! I guess you'll have no problem findin' her then."

Dylan dropped his gaze.

"Will you, Kid?" The threat in Vince's voice was unmistakable.

Nausea churned in Dylan's gut and dread weighed down his limbs, but he knew what he had to do. In the end, he had no choice. He'd known that all along. He raised his gaze to Vince.

"Oh yeah, I know where to find her."

———

Savannah awoke to the sound of Will in the shower and the smell of percolated coffee wafting through the air. A glance at the clock told her it was almost nine. She stretched in the luxurious bed. It was the weekend and she was with the man of her dreams. Apart from her niggling doubt about Dylan, life couldn't get any better.

The water stopped running. She scooted out of bed and wrapped the sheet around her. Will, naked and steaming, stepped out of the bathroom toweling himself dry. Her eyes drank him in.

"Good morning."

"Morning, gorgeous." He smiled and leaned over to give her a quick kiss. "How'd you sleep?"

"Great." She couldn't wipe the goofy grin off her face. She couldn't help it. If it hadn't been for her concerns about Dylan and the fact she still hadn't heard from him, she'd be on top of the world.

He grinned back at her. "Glad to hear it. You ready for a shower?"

"Yes, that'd be great."

"Help yourself to a clean towel. Unless of course, you'd rather use mine," he teased.

"A clean one would be great."

"And here I thought you couldn't get enough of me."

Sauntering closer, she planted a kiss on his mouth. "You're right, of course. It's true. I can't get enough of you. But your towel is looking decidedly damp and you need to know this about me—I can't stand soggy towels."

Will laughed. "Use as many as you like. I have a lady who comes in and does the laundry." His eyes glinted wickedly. "She'll know right away I've had someone stay over."

Savannah blushed and dropped her gaze. "I've never been that kind of girl."

He grinned. "Then lucky for me you're a fast learner." He leaned in close and kissed her. "You'd better get into that shower before we get distracted."

Having worn her work clothes on Will's yacht the day before, they were now stiff with salt spray. Reluctant to drag them on again, Savannah opened a drawer in his bedroom and stared at the neat array of folded T-shirts and shorts that greeted her. She selected a pair of drawstring board shorts and a plain white T-shirt.

With no other choice, she put her bra on, but decided to go commando under the shorts. There was no way she was going to wear twice-used panties, despite the fact there was a very real chance that the oversized shorts would fall off.

She'd have to go back to her condo after breakfast and get a change of clothes, or three. No doubt there would be more sleepovers in the weeks to come. Excitement and happiness bubbled up inside her.

She padded barefoot into the kitchen where Will was pouring coffee. He turned and caught sight of her. Taking in her ensemble, he gave her an approving wink. "How does fresh coffee sound?"

"*Mm* it sounds heavenly."

He picked up the pot of coffee and filled another mug. "Milk? Sugar?"

"Milk, one sugar, thanks." She watched while he fixed the coffee. Noting that he added nothing to his, she smiled. "You take it black, I gather?"

He nodded, handing her one of the mugs. "What would you like to do for breakfast? We can go up to North Sydney, if you like, or there's a nice little café in Kirribilli. It's not far from here. They do a great eggs Benedict."

"I love eggs benedict. I bet we can even walk from here."

"Ah, so you know Bobbi's then?"

"Of course."

He laughed. "That's right, you live nearby. You must show me your condo."

"I was thinking the same thing a moment ago." Looking down at her clothes, she grinned. "I think I need to get a change of clothes before I have a wardrobe malfunction."

He gave her a slow once-over, lingering on her breasts which were clearly outlined beneath the T-shirt. His eyes darkened to cobalt.

"You look just fine to me and you definitely won't hear any complaints if your shorts just happen to fall off."

"Ah, but you don't realize I'm not wearing any panties. It could be very embarrassing if the shorts were to come down while we were out at breakfast."

"No panties?" His eyes sparkled with mischief. "Really?"

Coming up close beside her, he slipped his hand down the waistband which was still loose around her middle, despite the drawstring.

Inching his hand lower, his fingers tangled in the curls between her legs. He groaned with appreciation.

"*Mm*." He stroked her soft folds. "How hungry did you say you were?"

She laughed, the sound of it low and husky. "I didn't, actually. But now you mention it, I'm feeling rather *famished*." She reached up and wrapped her arms around his neck and pulled his head down for a kiss. She pressed herself against him, making her meaning perfectly clear.

Removing his hand, Will pulled her into his hard embrace. He thrust his tongue inside her mouth, deepening the kiss.

Savannah kissed him back, loving the feel of his lips on hers. She slipped her hands under his shirt and tugged him closer and then caressed the bare skin of his back.

He lifted her onto the countertop and spread her legs until he stood between them, his lips still fused to hers. When at last they broke apart, they fought to catch their breath.

"God, what are you doing to me, woman?" His words were growled low in his throat. He grabbed her T-shirt and pulled it over her head.

A few seconds later, his shirt joined hers on the floor. He unclasped her bra. Her breasts jiggled and bounced.

"I don't think I'm ever going to get tired of looking at you."

Savannah's breath hitched. Her heart thumped at the need in his eyes. She reached out to him. He lowered his head and his lips captured hers in a searing kiss of possession. She returned it with fiery passion, moaning when his hand cupped her bare breast and tweaked her nipple.

"Lift your butt," he urged and took hold of the board shorts and tugged them off. Working the button and zip on his denim shorts, he shucked them, along with his boxers, until he stood naked before her.

With a groan he spun on his heel and headed down the hall. "Stay right where you are," he threw over his shoulder.

Within moments, he returned brandishing a condom. His cock strained, thick and hard. After sheathing himself, he grabbed her hips and drew her forward until the tip of his erection touched her wetness. Wrapping her legs around his waist, she took hold of his arms and braced herself as he plunged into her.

Again and again, his cock stroked her, his rhythm alternating between short and hard to achingly long and deep. Staring into his eyes, her climax gathered momentum. She reached the summit and toppled over, crying out from the sheer relief of it.

Will's thrusts came faster and harder. His eyes were almost black with desire. Savannah clung to him, reveling in the tension in his face. Passion finally overtook him and he collapsed against her.

A few moments later, he pulled back and grinned down at her where she lay sprawled over the countertop.

"You are so bad, Red. This is all your fault; I can't keep my hands off you."

"It's not all *my* fault. You're the one who keeps pulling my clothes off."

His eyes widened innocently. "Only because you told me you weren't wearing any panties."

She grinned, drawing herself up until she sat with her legs dangling over the side of the countertop, unable to believe how comfortable she felt with him. "So...what was that about breakfast?"

CHAPTER 24

Will was pleased to discover Bobbi's was almost empty when they finally made their way to the café. Most of the breakfast crowd had gone and only a few late risers filled the tables. Taking a seat at one of the outdoor tables, he handed Savannah a menu.

"What are you having?" he asked after a few minutes.

"I'm trying to decide between the bacon and eggs with sausages and hash browns or the pancakes with strawberries and cream."

His eyebrows flew up in surprise. "Way to go. I like a girl with a healthy appetite."

"You won't get any argument from me." She grinned. "Unfortunately, I've never been one of those lucky girls who could get by on the whiff of a lettuce leaf. I need to eat *real* food."

"You look just right to me." He gave her a thorough once-over. "Curvy in all the right places."

"Thanks." She looked away. A faint blush stained her cheeks. His heart melted. He felt a level of satisfaction he'd never known. This gorgeous, kind hearted, sexy girl was his. As his gaze lingered on her, he vowed silently never to let secrets or misunderstandings come between them again.

A waitress approached their table. "Are you ready to order?"

"I'll have the eggs Benedict and a cappuccino, thanks." He gave her a polite smile.

"And I'll have the pancakes and a latté," Savannah said and handed the menu back to the girl.

"Shouldn't be too long." The waitress smiled briefly and headed back inside.

"So, the pancakes won out?" Will teased.

"Yep." She grinned back at him, a cheeky glint in her eye. "I feel like something soft, sweet and juicy."

He groaned. "You're going to be the death of me. Everything about you reminds me of sex. It's even in every word coming out of your mouth, now."

She blushed again and lowered her gaze to the table cloth. "Keep your voice down. Someone might hear you."

He shrugged, grinning. "Who cares?"

She heaved a sigh and rolled her eyes, but he could tell from the look on her face she didn't really mind. Which was good, because he found it incredibly liberating to talk freely, like they were, about their feelings. Maybe women were onto something when they talked about anything and everything with each other?

"So," Savannah said, interrupting his thoughts. She took his hand and threaded her fingers through his. "What are we going to do for the rest of the day?"

"Well, much as I like seeing you in my clothes, I guess we'd better swing by your place so you can pick up some things."

She grinned. "How many nights am I sleeping over?"

Will hesitated and his heart began to pound. "Oh, probably another twenty thousand or so," he replied and waited for her reaction.

A wide smile broke across her face. "Are you asking me to move in with you?"

"Um, yeah. I think I am. If-if you want to," he stammered and then cursed the heat that spread across his cheeks. *When had he become so tongue tied?*

Savannah's smile grew even wider. She stood and moved around the table and threw her arms around his neck.

"Yes, I'd love to move in with you."

A warm glow of contentment seeped through his bones

and left them smoldering. The ice that had formed around his heart long years ago snapped and broke and melted under the heat of her excitement. He didn't know how he'd managed to find her, but he'd be grateful forevermore that she'd stumbled into his life.

Savannah returned to her seat. The waitress appeared with their order and they both tucked in ravenously. She washed down a bite of pancake with her coffee.

"Would you like me to cook dinner for you tonight?" she asked. "I'm actually a pretty decent cook."

Will thought of the phone call he'd taken from Pete while she'd been in the shower and his jovial mood disintegrated. The surveillance team had gathered intelligence to the effect that it appeared Maranoa was doing a drug run that night. Whether the information panned out or not, one thing was certain, he wouldn't be "eating in" with Savannah.

Frowning, he took a bite of his eggs and chewed slowly, using the time to come up with a reasonable response to her invitation. While he considered what to say, her face fell and confusion clouded her eyes.

"Will, I'm sorry, did I say something wrong? If we're going to have any chance of making this work between us, we have to be honest with each other. Otherwise, we might as well end it right now."

He took her hand across the table and squeezed it reassuringly and then sighed.

"You're right and I'm sorry, too. I don't want anything to end. It's just that, I'm not used to having to explain myself to anyone, and especially not about work."

"Has something happened with the investigation?"

He nodded. "As much as I'd like to, I can't talk to you about the investigation. It's highly confidential. People's lives are on the line."

Her frown deepened. She pulled her hand out of his. "I understand all about confidentiality. It's not as if I'm going to tell anyone."

"The less you know, the better. It's an operation fraught with peril. Maranoa's a dangerous man. If he gets even the slightest inkling we're onto him, we're all in big trouble. And then there's this guy, Billy. We don't know who he is or where he fits in."

"What are you going to do?"

He pursed his lips and looked across at her, his blue eyes intent on her face. "I'm going back there tonight. I have to. I'd much rather be home with you and your delectable body, but unfortunately, I'm going to have to take a pass on dinner. When it's all over I'll tell you everything. I promise."

She smiled reassuringly and leaned over to pat his hand. "Don't worry about it. I *completely* understand."

"You do?" Suspicion warred with relief over her sudden capitulation. Relief finally won out.

"Of course, I do." She smiled sweetly at him. "I've been there, remember? I know what those poor girls are being subjected to. I want to see Maranoa rotting in a jail cell just as much as you do. You have to do what you have to do."

He smiled hesitantly and reached over to once again enfold her hand in his. "Thank you, Savannah. It makes it a hell of a lot easier when I know I have your support."

"Oh, you have more than that. I'm coming with you."

"No way in the world!" His voice was louder than he'd meant it to be. He pushed away from the table.

"Will, I'm going with you!"

He growled, shaking his head, unable to believe what he was hearing.

When was she ever going to learn?

"We're not having this conversation, Savannah. It's too dangerous. You are *not* going back there and that's final."

Her face flushed with anger. "You can't tell me what to do! I've been there *twice* before, remember? I know how to get in *and* I know how to get out."

"As if I could ever forget." His own voice tightened with emotion. "I'm not having you put yourself in danger like that again. You were damned lucky you ran into me those times and not some over-amorous sicko."

Her eyes flashed fire. Folding his arms across his chest, he returned glare for glare.

"You're *not* going, Savannah. I refuse to discuss it with you again."

———

Savannah fumed in silence. She was twenty-eight years old and had been living on her own for nearly a decade. She knew how to take care of herself, even if Vince Maranoa had proved himself capable of murder. If it wasn't so important to find out if her brother was involved, she wouldn't even consider it, but that didn't mean she wanted or needed Will to turn all macho and think he had to protect her.

Although, she conceded grudgingly, it was kind of cute that he wanted to. He looked so sexy doing his macho-boy thing. Even now, she could see the tension in his chest as he stared in the distance, his foot tapping an impatient rhythm on the sidewalk. It would be convenient to have him close by, but she didn't need his help to get back into the brothel to get the answers she needed. She'd managed it without him twice already.

Besides, she couldn't tell him about her suspicions about Dylan. If her brother was mixed up with Maranoa and the police found out about it, she'd be fast-tracking her brother's journey to jail. She couldn't bear the thought of having that added to her already overburdened conscience.

Smiling seductively, she changed tack because there was more than one way to skin a cat. Let him think he'd won and she'd be fine.

"I think it's really hot when you do that." She gazed up at him from beneath her lashes.

"Do what?" He sounded suspicious, distrustful, wary of her sudden change in demeanor.

"You know, act all manly and protective. I'm not used to having anyone react like that around me. It's kind of cute. Maybe it will grow on me."

"*Grow* on you? Like mold?" His eyebrow lifted sardonically.

She laughed. "If you like, but I was thinking of something a little more flattering." Stretching her arms above her head, she tried to suppress a yawn.

"Sorry if I'm keeping you up," he growled irritably.

She poked her tongue out at him. "It didn't seem to worry you last night."

"Nor you, I might add."

"Touché. So, what else is on the agenda for today?" She kept her voice purposefully light. "Your night's obviously booked out. Am I going to be able to spend any time with you today outside the bedroom?"

"You forgot about the shower and the kitchen." His eyes smoldered.

She smiled and pushed back her chair and stood. "Come on, let's go to my place so I can change out of these clothes." She took hold of his arm and tugged him from his chair. "We could always go shopping in the city."

Will shuddered in mock horror. "Shopping? I think you've mistaken me for Lucy."

"*Lucy!* Oh my God! I haven't called her since the ball! She must be going crazy not hearing from me." Pulling her cell phone out of her handbag, Savannah glanced back at Will. "Do you mind?" She pointed to the phone in her hand.

"Of course not; go ahead. While you're doing that, I'll touch base with Pete and confirm our plan of attack." He strolled a few feet away and tugged his cell out of his pocket.

Savannah dialed Lucy's number and waited a little nervously for her to answer.

"Hi, Luce, it's Savannah."

"Hey, I've been wondering how things went with you and Will. You've been holding out on me."

"I'm sorry, I-I've been busy." She was suddenly tongue-tied.

"Yeah, yeah, yeah. I've heard it all before. So? How did it go?"

"Um, it went pretty well."

"Okay," Lucy said slowly. "What does that mean?"

"Well, it means that we talked things out and you know, one thing led to another and...we've spent the last two nights together."

Lucy's screams on the other end of the phone nearly deafened her. Holding the phone away from her ear, Savannah waited until it had died down before bringing it back to her ear.

"Oh, my God! I don't believe it! After your terrible run with Jonathan, I didn't know if you'd ever commit to someone again. I take it you're prepared to commit? It's not like you to sleep with someone *two nights in a row* and not have it mean something."

Savannah laughed. "Of course it means something. I-I really like him."

"Wow, that's pretty sudden."

"Not really. Sometimes, I think you just know, don't you?"

"I guess you do," Lucy agreed slowly. "It was like that for Pete and me."

"Yes, and you were only twenty-two."

"Indeed, I was." She paused. "I still don't believe it. You and Will Rutledge. I think it's fantastic news. Wait until I tell Pete."

"Lucy, hang on. I think you'd better—"

"That's him now... He's just arrived home. Gotta go! Talk to you soon." The call was disconnected.

Glancing up in time to see Will stride out of the café tucking his wallet back into his pocket, Savannah smiled.

"Thanks for breakfast."

"How was Lucy?"

"Loud. Shocked. Excited. Pete apparently just arrived home. She was in such a hurry to tell him, she hung up on me. I hope you don't mind?" She watched him a little anxiously.

"Of course not. I told you, I'm happy for the whole world to know. I would have told him myself if we hadn't been discussing other serious matters."

"Maybe we can meet them both somewhere for coffee this afternoon?"

He shook his head. "I'd love to, sweetheart, I really would. But Pete and I are going over a few things before the operation tonight. There's surveillance reports, telephone intercepts and a heap of other last-minute stuff—you do understand, don't you?"

Savannah forced a smile. "Of course. I should have thought."

"I promise I'll make it up to you." Pulling her close, he gave her a quick kiss on the lips. "Are you ready to go?"

She nodded and collected her handbag from underneath the table. "Sure, let's go."

———

Dylan let himself into his sister's condominium with the spare key she always kept on the ledge above the door. The place was spotless, as usual. Even the smell of vomit had disappeared. She'd always had a thing for neatness. It was one of the things she'd been forever on his back about.

'Pick up your clothes, Dylan.' 'Wash up your dinner plate.' 'Leave your dirty boots outside.' The list went on and on.

Even so, his heart thudded at the thought of silencing her forever. It wasn't like he wanted to. Vince had ordered the hit. It was kill or be killed. Not that he thought Vince would actually kill him—"Billy the Kid" was Vince's current favorite— but Dylan had witnessed the savagery of Vince's anger toward those who fell out of favor. It hadn't been pretty.

Dylan had been furious when Savannah announced they were moving back to Sydney so he could go to rehab. He had a nice life in Canberra, hanging out with mates, doing drugs, making a tidy sideline profit.

It had all changed when he'd been caught by the cops, but a court appearance and little slap on the wrist by the judge wasn't anything to get your panties in a twist over—at least, that's the way he saw it.

It was unfortunate Savannah hadn't felt the same way. But now, after living back in Sydney for six months, the infectious vibe of the city had gotten into his blood. He'd done the obligatory time in rehab—well, all but the last month—and it hadn't been too bad. He'd said all the right things and promised them what they wanted to hear. Besides, if he'd never gone to rehab, he wouldn't have met Tony and through him, his Uncle Vince.

Okay, so he hadn't exactly signed on for murder, but what the hell—it was a small price to pay and the few people he'd killed so far had deserved it. Someone had to do Vince's dirty work and if that someone happened to be him, then so be it.

Dylan had the big picture in his sights. Vince wouldn't live forever. He wasn't married and had no kids. The money had to go somewhere and even if a portion of it went to Tony, there was still plenty left over for a favored go-to man.

It was unfortunate Savannah had come to Vince's attention, but then again, the silly bitch had put herself directly in the line of fire. How stupid was she to sneak into Vince's domain and not only obtain secret information, but then go and publicize it? She only had herself to blame.

Dylan thought back to the last time he'd been at his sister's place. She'd told him she was going out for a night on the town with her girlfriends. He wondered again if she'd returned to the Black Opal. He hadn't seen her there, but that didn't mean shit.

Anger coursed through him. He should have strangled her when he'd had the chance. Forget that she was his sister. She'd been stupid and stupid people paid a price. It was just the way it was. It would have been kinder than what Vince planned now.

Voices outside the front door halted his movement. He could make out his sister's voice, but there was someone else with her, a man with a deep, unfamiliar tone. Were they merely passing in the stairwell or had she brought someone back with her? It wasn't like her to entertain male guests in her condominium. In all the years he'd lived with her, he couldn't ever remember that happening. He didn't know where she went to fuck, but it certainly hadn't been in her own bed.

The sound of the key turning in the lock threw him into action. Whether she was alone or not, he wanted the element of surprise. He needed to get the job over and done with, but he wasn't going to be stupid about it. No sense leaving a witness behind.

He ducked inside the broom closet and managed to pull the door closed just as the front door swung open. Dylan watched through the tiny crack between the door and the wall. Savannah tossed her head and laughed. She entered the room, followed closely by a hulk of a man. His shoulders barely fit through the narrow opening.

Fuck. There was no way he could take them both out. He cursed under his breath, knowing he was now stuck in the broom closet until he found the way clear to escape. It could be hours. He swore again and damned his sister to hell.

"You have a great view from here." Will looked out the living room window of Savannah's condominium. The dark blue of the ocean sparkled in the distance.

"Yes, almost as good as yours," she joked, coming to stand beside him. Milo prowled around her ankles, mewling hungrily. She hurried into the kitchen to fill his bowl. From the doorway, she saw Will bend down and hold out his hand, encouraging the cat to come closer. Milo stood his ground, staring at him balefully, his eyes wide with suspicion.

"He's beautiful," he called out to her. "What's his name?"

"Milo. Purebred long-haired Siamese." She walked back into the living room. Her voice softened. "He belonged to my mother."

"Wow." His eyes held hers. "It was good of you to keep him. Especially given how unexpectedly she died."

Distracted, he stood and gazed out the window. "I'm not sure I could have taken on a pet of my brother's... Too many memories."

"I know what you mean. Milo brings back memories, too, but that's okay..." She smiled gently. "They're usually good ones. My parents left him with me when they went traveling."

Will put his arm around her shoulders and pulled her in close against his side. They stood in silence for a while, each lost in their thoughts.

"You're in a great spot here, not far from the city. With the train station so close, I bet you get into work even quicker than I do," Will murmured.

She grinned. "Seven minutes from Waverton to Town Hall. It's great. I love it."

"I hope you won't mind too much leaving it behind?"

For a moment, she pretended to consider his question and then answered. "*Mm,* let me see. You know what? I think I'm prepared to rough it in your little shack by the water." She shrugged. "It's kind of grown on me."

"Are we back to that mold thing again?" Will teased.

Smiling, she stepped away from him and walked the short distance to her bedroom.

Savannah strolled past the broom closet and Dylan gritted his teeth. He was still in shock that his sister had brought a man home. And not just any man—she'd brought home William Rutledge, the son of the advertising mogul.

Dylan had recognized him straight away. He looked just like he had in the photos. And here he was, following Savannah into her bedroom.

What the fuck? He shook his head in confusion and swallowed a sigh. The door to Savannah's bedroom stood open. The broom closet was diagonally opposite. There was no way he could sneak out without being seen. With his jaw clenched tight, he settled in to wait.

Will followed Savannah into her bedroom. By the time he got there, she'd stripped off the borrowed T-shirt and board shorts and wore nothing but her bra. His heart thumped.

Seemingly oblivious to his presence, she strolled across the room to a chest of drawers and bent low to pull out the bottom one. He was treated to a view of her naked rear end. She bent over and he caught a hint of the soft pink lips of her sex.

He sucked in his breath. Blood thundered through his veins and centered in his cock. He was amazed he could get hard so quickly after the marathon sessions of sex they'd enjoyed over the past couple of days.

"I beg to differ about the view. It's every bit as good as the view I have from my condominium." His voice was thick with need. He stepped forward and ran a finger along her exposed slit, feeling her liquid warmth envelop it. "In fact, I think it's even better."

He probed her deeper with his fingers. Savannah gasped and stood slowly upright.

"Mm, that feels very nice." She leaned back against him. His free hand came around to play with her breasts. Fiddling one-handed with the clasp of her bra, he eventually gave up and pulled the garment over her head. It dropped to the floor.

Within moments, his cock was thick and hard and throbbing. He pressed it up against the soft cheek of her ass. His fingers continued working rhythmically inside her. He now knew just how she liked it. A thrum of satisfaction surged through him when she pressed down onto his hand and breathlessly pleaded for more.

Standing on tip toes, she drove herself up and down on his fingers. Within minutes, her movements became frantic.

Mewling noises of need escaped her tightly compressed lips.

Kneading her breasts with one hand, he murmured soft words of encouragement and did his best to ignore the painful throbbing between his legs. "That's it, sweetheart. Come for me, babe."

Moments later, she fell over the edge and collapsed against him. He eased his fingers out of her. Turning her around to face him, he kissed her before picking her up in his arms and laying her down on the four-poster bed that dominated the room.

Dylan listened to the sound of them fucking and curled up his lip. Of all the times to be caught hiding in Savannah's condo, it had to be the one and only time she brought a man home. From the sounds coming from the bedroom, the pair of them were well and truly occupied.

He could do it now. He could whack both of them. They wouldn't even know what had happened. Unless something went wrong. Unless Rutledge saw him before he had a chance to kill him.

Dylan suddenly remembered he hadn't brought a weapon and cursed under his breath. He hadn't thought he'd need one because he towered over his sister and weighed nearly double. Once he had his hands around her throat, it would only be a matter of minutes before she was dead.

He hadn't counted on her having company—and definitely not company who looked like he could handle himself. Muscles bulged across the man's arms and shoulders. He was taller than Dylan and easily outweighed him. Rutledge would be no soft target.

With a sigh of resignation, Dylan cracked open the door to the broom closet and slipped into the hall. The sounds from the bedroom continued, camouflaging the slight noise the front door made when he swung it open.

Closing it behind him, he jogged down the short flight of stairs and into the yard below. His sister lived to see another day. Determination surged through him. The third time, she wouldn't be so lucky. He'd make sure of it.

Savannah lay spread-eagled across the bed, her legs opened wide. Sheathing his cock with a condom from his wallet, Will positioned himself between her legs and plunged into her slick center. He groaned in ecstasy when her tight walls hugged him close. He thrust hard once, twice. The third time he spurted his release and collapsed on top of her, spent.

"We have to stop doing this," he mumbled when he'd recovered the power of speech. He rolled onto his side and grinned at her. "It's not normal. I'm sure it's not. I know I've never done it this much before. Do you think we might do ourselves an injury?"

A blush crept across her cheeks. She lowered her gaze. "I am beginning to feel a little sore down there. It's probably just as well you're going out this afternoon."

He was immediately concerned. "Did I hurt you? Why didn't you say something?"

She shrugged and looked away. "I'm okay. I'm not used to all the friction, I think. And it was worth it."

He grinned again. "Okay, I'll try and leave you alone for the rest of the day. Good thing I have work to do. At least the job will take my mind off trying to get you naked."

"Yes, good thing." She smiled back at him.

Will frowned, remembering her earlier resistance. "You're sure you're all right with me leaving you?" His eyes probed hers.

Her gaze slid away, but she smiled with reassurance. "Of course, I am. You're just doing your job. I understand."

"Is it okay if I drop you off at my place about two? That'll give me a few hours to meet with Pete and get the lowdown before I have to be at the brothel."

"Actually, I might stay here tonight, if that's okay with you? I presume you're going to be home late?"

He nodded reluctantly. "Yeah, it's gonna be another late one. But you don't have to stay here. I'd be more than happy to come home in the wee hours and find you warming my bed." He grinned at her.

"As tempting as that sounds, I think I might spend the night here and get a head start on the packing. You're still happy for me to move in, aren't you?"

He pulled her close. "You bet. The sooner, the better. Tomorrow wouldn't be too early."

Savannah leaned over and kissed him lightly on the mouth. Will held her head with one hand and deepened the kiss, slanting his lips over her mouth. Fierce emotion scorched his soul.

"I-I love you, Savannah."

Her eyes widened in shock. "You do? Are you sure? I-I mean, just because we've had fantastic sex and I've agreed to move in with you doesn't mean—"

Will made an impatient sound in the back of his throat. "Would you be quiet? I just told you I love you. Can't you simply accept it and tell me you love me back?"

Savannah blushed and dropped her gaze. "I-I'm sorry, I didn't mean to make you think—"

Will cut her off again, suddenly needing her confirmation.

"Savannah, I'm dying here. Do you love me, or not?"

"Of course I do. I never imagined loving anyone like I love you. I'm still trying to get my head around it all. It feels so...so..." She shrugged helplessly, unable to find the words.

"I know exactly what you mean. I feel it, too." He took her hand and placed it against the bare skin of his chest, right over his heart. "You're in here. Way deep inside. I'm not sure how it happened, but just so you know, I'm never gonna let you go."

Chapter 25

Saturday evening

It was a little after eight-thirty when Will arrived outside the Black Opal. It was too early for many of the club's regular patrons, but the surveillance guys had reported the place was abuzz with extra security. Something was definitely going down.

A Tactical Response Group, or TRG taskforce, had been hastily assembled earlier in the day and now waited in cars strategically parked along the street outside the brothel. As soon as Will gave the signal, armed law enforcement officers would raid the building.

Striding to the entrance, he cast a casual glance around him. The usual bouncers were outside the closed front door, but three more guards stood off in the shadows to his left. A quick glance to his right identified two others who leaned against the end of the building, smoking and talking quietly.

Will gave the doormen a brief nod and greeted them with a smile. "Evening, fellas."

"Good evening, sir," the taller of the two responded, stepping forward to open the door.

"Busy night?" Will asked, keeping his voice conversational.

"Not so far," the other one replied. "But it's a bit early, yet. You wait until midnight; the place will be pumping."

"Sounds good." Will stepped through the doorway and

into the foyer. He waited for his eyes to adjust to the dimness and then made his way over to the bar. He took a seat on one of the barstools and ordered a scotch. From his vantage point, he surveyed the room.

The crowd was comprised of a few small groups of men at separate tables. Another man sat on his own near the stage, talking into a cell phone and taking intermittent sips from a glass of dark liquid that had been placed in front of him.

The stage was silent and empty, but a couple of scantily clad Asian girls worked the room, carrying trays of drinks from the bar and occasionally stopping to engage the men in conversation. As far as he could tell, nothing seemed out of the ordinary.

In fact, given the meager scattering of patrons, the increased security presence seemed way out of place. His curiosity was aroused. Their intelligence appeared to be spot-on, but the action sure as hell wasn't happening in here. It was time to take a closer look outside. A lot of old houses had bunkers built beneath them during the war. It was possible Maranoa had access to one of them. It was the only thing that made sense. The inside of the building sure as hell wasn't large enough to store the quantity of drugs it appeared they were talking about. It would also explain why drugs weren't found in the last raid.

An unfamiliar barman sat a drink before him. Will fished out his wallet and handed over a few bills. "Listen, mate. I've left my phone out in the car. Do you mind keeping an eye on my drink for a minute?"

The man eyed him in silence and then gave him a brief nod.

"Thanks. Won't be long."

Will returned the way he'd come, stepping outside and straight into one of the bouncers.

"Oomph!" The full force of Will's shoulder jabbed into the bouncer's back. He grunted and fell forward. The ploy worked as Will had hoped. Within seconds, a second bouncer strode up to see what the fuss was about.

Will held up his hands in a sign of surrender. "Sorry, mate, just coming out to get my phone from the car. I didn't see him behind the door."

Successfully setting up a valid reason for him to be once again outside, Will sauntered from the brothel and headed toward his parked car. As soon as he was out of sight, he crossed to the other side of the road. Keeping to the shadows, he made his way past the brothel again and sought out a path to the rear of the building.

The sliver of moon provided little assistance as he picked his way over the rough ground, but it also made it easier for him to stay hidden. Ducking behind some shrubbery overhanging the fence that adjoined the brothel, he discovered a narrow pathway that ran between the two buildings.

He trod carefully and did his best to minimize the crunching sound of the gravel and rocks beneath his boots. He halted and listened for the guards. He heard nothing but the sound of his own intermittent breathing and the adrenaline-charged pumping of his heart.

Rounding the end of the building, he found himself in a medium-sized backyard. Apart from a single tiny patch of dirt directly beneath the solitary tree, the ground had been concreted right up to the high wooden fence that completely surrounded the property.

One way to save on mowing.

In the meager moonlight, and with assistance from a light that glowed above the back door, he made out an old rotary clothesline that stood in the cracked concrete about thirty feet from the back door.

A large blue dumpster sat in the far corner, deep in the shadows. He took a quick look around to make sure the way was clear and then jogged over to it.

At first, he thought it was empty, but when the moon came out from behind a cloud, he noticed a bundle of old newspapers caught on the bottom. Leaning over the rusted metal side of the dumpster, he grabbed hold of the thin nylon rope that tied them together and hauled them out.

The first thing he noticed was the rectangular-shaped piece that was missing from the middle. The lines of the cut were clean and had been made with a sharp instrument—more than likely a box cutter. The rectangular hole measured about the size of a tissue box and had been cut right through the entire bundle of papers.

Holding them up to the faint moonlight, he saw it was the *Daily Mirror*. The date on the top page was January twentieth—a few days ago. He flicked through the bundle, pulling pages randomly from the thin nylon that bound them.

Same thing. Each one was a copy of the *Daily Mirror*. Each one was dated January twentieth.

Having nowhere to stow the bundle, he carefully tore off the front page from one of the papers and folded it until it fit inside his shirt pocket and then scanned the back fence for an opening. The rocky path he'd traversed between the buildings was far too narrow to allow for a garbage truck, or any vehicle for that matter. There had to be a gate in the fence somewhere.

Voices coming from the direction of the brothel caught his attention. He cast around for somewhere to hide. With nothing but the dumpster to conceal him, he scooted back to it and crouched low in the shadows.

He raised himself until he could see above the heavy rusted metal. A pair of security guards rounded the building. With flashlights in their hands, it was obvious they were doing a routine patrol.

Will waited until they'd disappeared and then stepped out from behind the dumpster and walked stealthily behind them. It was risky, but as long as he was quiet, it wasn't likely they would turn and retrace their steps. More likely was the chance that another patrol was close behind the first. Tonight, for whatever reason, Vince wanted the building secure.

The investigation was on the verge of a breakthrough. The last thing Will needed was to be discovered and forced to answer awkward questions about why he was loitering at the back of the building. The search for a gate in the back fence would have to wait, along with his search for the cellar.

Making it safely back onto the street and knowing he'd been away longer than anyone would expect his supposed errand to take, he quickly formulated an excuse. Pulling out the cell phone that had been in his pants pocket all along, he dialed Savannah's number just as he came within earshot of the bouncers. He couldn't help the genuine smile that tugged at his lips when she answered.

"Hi, babe. How are you? I'm at the Club. I'll be home in an hour or two."

She reassured him she was fine. When she added that she missed him, he wanted nothing more than to head over to her condominium and leave Maranoa and the investigation far behind him.

Instead, he told her he loved her and ended the call. The bouncer grinned and opened the front door for him, a knowing glint in his eye.

"Got to keep the missus happy," Will quipped. He dropped the phone back into his pocket and made his way inside.

Savannah ended the call, relieved that she'd had the foresight to turn her phone to vibrate before she'd left home. She strained to make out the uneven path ahead of her. It was almost ten o'clock. Will was already inside. He thought she was home, packing boxes.

A shard of guilt sliced through her. She hated to deceive him, but he hadn't given her a choice. She simply had to know if her brother was involved. And if so, she had to help him get out of this scrape before he totally ruined his life.

Deep down, she knew it had been Dylan she'd seen and heard during her previous visit. What was more, she had a sinking feeling he was the man Malee and Angel had referred to as "Billy."

Despite her earlier confidence, she didn't really have a plan on how to get into the brothel if the back door was locked, other than to once again prevail upon the stupidity of the security guards and hope like hell they weren't the same two she'd spoken to during her last attempt.

Fear at the possibility she might come face to face with Maranoa again threatened to choke her. Will said Maranoa wanted to have sex with her. He was a dangerous criminal, a murderer—or at the very least, a man who condoned it. Her discovery at the brothel could result in consequences too awful to contemplate, but she could hardly walk away without knowing the truth. If Dylan was involved with Maranoa, she had to get him away from the place and talk sense into him, before he was discovered by the police. There would be no leniency from the judge this time around.

She thought about Will and bit her lip. He'd be furious when he discovered she was here—and rightly so. The dangers were indisputable and he'd made it clear he didn't want her anywhere near the place.

The sound of the back door opening interrupted her thoughts. A security guard strode through the doorway and down the steps. She stifled a gasp of alarm and plastered herself against the wall, silently cursing the light that spilled across the concrete, reaching out for her.

The man walked across the backyard and disappeared into the shadows. A moment later, she heard him sigh and seconds after that, the unmistakable sound of him urinating.

Her heart pounded. The guard hadn't stopped to close the door. If she hurried, she could sneak inside before he noticed. It was a stroke of luck she wasn't about to let pass her by.

As quickly as she could, she dashed across the last few feet that separated her from the back door of the brothel. Stepping through the opening, she breathed a sigh of relief.

She was in. Again.

She'd taken the time to dress in dark clothing, hoping to remain as inconspicuous as possible. She'd teamed the short, black leather skirt she'd worn the last time with a tight, black T-shirt. The fishnet stockings were also back, as were the five-inch heels.

Her black wig looked a little worse for wear, but she'd done her best to smooth it down. Even so, it was more of a "just climbed out of bed" look which she supposed would fit in just fine. She had no intention of ending up out on the stage again, but she didn't want to look conspicuous to the casual observer and that meant dressing the part.

Malee had told Savannah during her first visit that it wasn't unusual for the girls to wander around the main part of the club before a show, offering drinks and engaging in small talk with the patrons. It was all part of the service and a way to entice the men to spend more intimate time with them behind closed doors, where the real money was made.

Her plan was to pretend to be one of the girls working the floor. She'd do her best to use her time to seek out any place her brother might be. She'd seen him in the main room the last time. It was possible, if he worked for Maranoa, he might be there again.

She only hoped she wouldn't run into the boss. According to Will's intelligence, something big was going down. The last thing she wanted was to get caught up in the middle of it, but knowing arrests might be imminent only increased the pressure to find her brother—before the police did.

————————

Will's drink sat untouched on the bar. Regaining his seat, he thought of Savannah and frowned. She'd sounded strained, but he guessed she was still a little annoyed that he'd refused to allow her to accompany him.

As if he would ever willingly put her in danger like that again? It was ludicrous to even suggest it, but he'd have to tread carefully. She was used to making her own decisions and her stubborn independence was one of the things he admired about her. She would also have to realize there were certain things he was not prepared to negotiate. Hanging out in a brothel owned by a dangerous criminal while pretending to be a prostitute the drug lord had already expressed an interest in was definitely number one on his list.

Will picked up his glass of scotch and took a healthy swallow. The room was still a long way from crowded, although there were a few more girls circulating and another small group of men had taken up a position at a table in the far corner of the room. His gaze swept over them again and he tensed when he realized one of the men was Vince Maranoa.

In an effort to catch a glimpse of Maranoa's companions, Will slid off the stool and leaned back against the bar. He caught a flash of wild gray hair and suddenly knew the identity of at least one of them.

Max O'Connor. An interesting coincidence. Too bad for Max, Will didn't believe in coincidences. He turned back toward the bar to avoid being recognized by the editor and noticed the bartender standing uncomfortably close. Knowing that the man had probably caught him staring at Maranoa and his companions, he decided to play it straight.

"That's Vince Maranoa over there, isn't it?" He flicked his head nonchalantly in the direction of their table. The barman nodded.

"I've heard so much about him. What's he like to work for?"

The man shrugged noncommittally. Using a cloth he'd slung over his shoulder, he picked up glasses from a rack nearby and began to dry them. Will took another sip from his drink and tried again.

"Been working here long?"

"Three years, give or take a month or two. Every day's the same after awhile."

Will grinned with forced camaraderie. "Yeah. I know what you mean. Same shit, different day, right?"

The barman offered the tiniest of smiles and continued drying.

"You must see a fair number of people pass through here?"

"Yeah, I guess."

"What about the blokes talking to Vince? You ever see them here before?"

The barman moved slightly away until he had a better view of the men at the back of the room. He gave Will a slight nod.

"Yeah, they're both regulars. The young one's Billy—Billy the Kid, Vince calls him. He's Vince's right hand man—or so the brat brags to anyone who'll listen. I don't know how he got so thick with Vince in such a short time. He's only been here five minutes. Georgie reckons the Kid reminds Vince of himself when he was younger."

"And the other man?"

"Yeah, the older bloke's a mate of Vince's. He's known him forever."

Will's heart pounded. *Could the barman's information be right? Could Max O'Connor and Vince Maranoa have a history?* If that was true, it was another coincidence in a string of them that were making Will very uneasy. And what of Billy?

Out of the corner of his eye, Will saw Max stand and shake Vince's hand. The editor would have to pass right by the bar to reach the exit. Will muttered a curse under his breath, thinking fast. Standing abruptly, he headed for the men's restroom in the opposite direction. Despite Max's knowledge of Will's tendency to frequent the Black Opal, he had no desire to remind the man of his connection to it.

Shouldering open the door to the bathroom, he went into a stall and shut the door behind him. As he closed the lid on the toilet and sat down, a tumult of thoughts raced through in his head.

O'Connor was living beyond his means. Will had found recent, strangely altered copies of the editor's newspaper in the brothel's dumpster. If the bartender could be believed, Maranoa and O'Connor had known each other for years and O'Connor was a regular patron of Maranoa's brothel.

The editor had warned Savannah away from the Black Opal.

The pieces fell into place. Will cursed aloud.

Max was involved. There was no other explanation. He was the common denominator. Everywhere Will turned, there was a link to the man.

He glanced at his watch. It was a little after ten. He thought wistfully of Savannah who was probably getting ready for bed after their marathon sex sessions the night before. He was exhausted too and suddenly yearned to have the night over with, so he could join her.

Opening the door of the stall, he rinsed his hands in the sink, threw some water over his face and dried off with paper towel. He looked at himself in the mirror. His hair was decidedly disheveled. It looked like he'd been involved in a scuffle. It must have happened while he'd been ducking for cover outside. Running his hands through his hair, he smoothed the strands in an attempt to tidy up.

He pulled open the door to leave the men's room and glanced around the main bar. O'Connor was nowhere to be seen. The man named Billy had also vanished. Two other men had now joined Maranoa at his table.

Will turned back toward the bar, intent on finishing his drink. He was halfway across the room when the staff door swung open. Seconds later, Savannah breezed inside and sauntered over to the bar, barely decent in a tight, revealing outfit.

Will gaped in disbelief. Shock was quickly followed by blinding anger…

CHAPTER 26

Moving toward the bar, Savannah's hips swayed with a confidence she was far from feeling, but it was all about appearances. She pulled her shoulders back and thrust out her breasts. If she *looked* like she was meant to be there, people would assume she was. At least, she hoped they would.

Her gaze wandered around the room, searching for Dylan. The place hadn't yet filled up. She recalled how it had been the last time when she'd danced before the men. They'd stared at her with hungry, desire-filled eyes. Nerves jumped in her belly at the memory.

"You, there!"

The shout came from the direction of the bar and cut through the murmur of the crowd. She tensed. It was the bartender. Turning to face him, she kept her eyes lowered and closed the distance between them.

"Take these drinks over to Vince's table, would you? The boss is having his usual. The beers are for his friends. Got it?"

Savannah's heart thumped so loudly, she was surprised he couldn't hear it. She risked a quick glance at the barman and then jerked her head in a sign of acquiescence.

Maranoa was here. She'd been asked to serve him a drink. Panic threatened to overwhelm her.

What was she going to do? She couldn't risk him recognizing her. Sooner or later he would realize she wasn't one of his girls and then she'd be in all sorts of trouble.

"Hurry up, girl. I haven't got all night."

Fear kept her rooted to the spot. She kept her gaze lowered to the floor and tried to buy time. "Where's he sitting?"

"He's over there at the table in the far corner." She glanced up to see the barman pointing with his chin in the direction of the stage. Her chest tightened until she couldn't breathe. Her head spun.

She couldn't do it.

She had to do it. She had no choice.

Already the barman was looking at her strangely. She couldn't afford to draw any more attention to herself. She had to hope Maranoa wouldn't look at her. After all, she was just another one of the girls—or so he thought.

With a steadying breath, she lifted the tray and picked her way through the scattered patrons. Lingering gazes from some of the men she passed pressed in upon her. Her nerves ratcheted up another notch.

She did her best to stay focused on Vince's table. He sat with his back to her. A couple of men in designer suits were seated opposite him. They huddled together, talking intently over the general thrum of conversation and the quiet background music, oblivious to her presence.

Holding the tray with one hand, Savannah distributed the drinks, doing her best to remain aloof from the men. She felt Maranoa's gaze on her while she set his drink before him.

Despite her desperate, silent pleas that he ignore her, Maranoa gave her a slow and thorough once-over. Conversation at the table ground to a halt.

"Sally, ain't it?" His tone was rough and uneducated, in sharp contrast to his five thousand dollar suit.

She nodded and kept her gaze lowered.

"How are you doin' tonight, Sally?" His hand snaked out and moved slowly up her bare thigh. "Been busy?"

Savannah froze in shock, but she forced her brain into action. "Yes. Busy. I go now."

Without warning, he grabbed her roughly by the chin and forced her to look at him. She winced and swallowed a cry of alarm. Dark malice lit his coal-black eyes. She fought to suppress a shiver.

He indicated the men across from him who watched the exchange in bemused silence. "Show 'em your tits."

Savannah gasped. Vince's smile was pure evil.

"B-but, Vince—"

His narrowed gaze glinted with menace. "I *said, show my friends your fuckin' tits."

Fear like she'd never known paralyzed Savannah's limbs. She tried to lift her arms, but they refused to move. In panic, she glanced at the men seated with Maranoa, desperately searching for an ally, but was met with half-grins and eyes that were glazed with avid anticipation.

Knowing she couldn't blow her cover, she forced her hands into action. Grabbing the bottom of her T-shirt, she began to inch it up over her head.

"Vince, it's good to see you again."

Savannah froze, the deep, familiar voice halting her actions. Will strode toward them. A tight smile tugged at his lips, but his eyes were chips of jagged blue ice.

"Mind if I join you?" He indicated the empty chair on Maranoa's left.

"Well, well, well. If it isn't the Rutledge pup." Vince's face broke into a smile. "I've never seen you here before this week and now, you're here all the time." His gaze slid slyly over toward Savannah. "I wonder what keeps bringin' you back?"

"Vince, it's all you." Will's grin was quick and easy. Only Savannah noticed the angry tic at the side of his mouth. "And maybe the girls." He flicked her a cursory glance.

"I think you've already met Sally?" Vince nodded in her direction.

"Yeah." He gave her another quick once-over. "Sally and I have...met."

Savannah saw the tension in the hard line of his jaw and knew he was barely containing his fury. She eased away from them and discreetly straightened her T-shirt.

"Going somewhere, Sally?" Will's mouth twisted into a

semblance of a smile. His eyes glinted steel.

She halted, not sure what he wanted of her. She met his gaze bravely, almost wincing at the fury in their depths. She wanted to throw herself into his arms and beg his forgiveness, but both of them were on very dangerous ground. If Maranoa caught even a hint that something was amiss, they'd be in a world of danger.

Pasting a flirtatious smile on her lips, she stepped closer and leaned against Will, rubbing herself against him, while her hand caressed the hard muscles of his chest.

He was casually dressed in a short-sleeved, red polo shirt and a pair of designer jeans. Shiny, black RM Williams boots were on his feet. His dark hair was slightly mussed, as if he'd run his hands through it more than once and he looked for all the world like a man who'd sought out a few hours of relaxation in his club on a Saturday night.

His muscles bunched beneath her fingers. Ignoring his tension, she slid her hand inside the opening of his shirt.

"How about me and you get to know each other again, mister?" Her tone was seductive, as was the look she threw him from underneath her lashes.

Vince watched them, idle curiosity playing over his face. Pressing even closer, she licked the soft lobe of Will's ear. "I promise I'll make it worth your while."

Will's arm came around her and slapped her on the bottom. She jumped and let out a little yelp, quite sure the amount of force he'd used was no accident.

"Yeah, why not?" His gaze burned into hers a moment or two before he turned back to Maranoa. "Thanks for the freebie last time, Vince. I'm more than happy to pay for it tonight. She wasn't a bad fuck, after all."

Vince chuckled, showing vast amounts of perfect, white teeth. "I'm glad I could help you out. We aim to please."

"That's why I like to come here, Vince. Your hospitality is second to none." Leaning in closer, Will lowered his voice to a conspiratorial whisper and tapped his nose. "Any chance of a bit of nose candy? It'll really get the party rocking." He winked.

"I'd love to help you out, but I'm afraid we're out of that shit. I can probably rustle up a few pills."

Will answered with a casual shrug. "Nah, I'm good. Pills don't do it for me. Not like the powder does."

"Next week, mate. Come back next week and I'll see to it that you get whatever you need."

"You're on." Will shot him an easy grin. "In the meantime, if you don't mind, I might take Sally out the back and work up a bit of sweat."

Vince grinned back at him. "Go your hardest, mate. I'm sure she'll make it worth your while."

"Oh, I know she will." Will's gaze hardened. He reached for her hand and determinedly dragged her toward the door that led to the bedrooms.

———————

Will seethed with fury. He couldn't remember ever feeling so angry. He strode along the dim carpeted corridor, dragging Savannah along behind him. Her sky-high heels and tight leather skirt made it difficult for her to keep up, but right at that moment, he didn't give a damn. She could twist her ankle, for all he cared. It was probably better than having her neck wrung, which was what he felt like doing.

She'd lied to him. Rage at her deceit washed over him, fueled by the memory of his terror when he'd seen her with Maranoa and his sense of helplessness that he could do nothing that might blow their cover. The intensity of his anger scared him.

His heart pounded so hard it felt like it was going to thump right out of his chest. He forced air into his constricted lungs and fought to regain control over the emotions that threatened to undo him.

When he'd seen Maranoa manhandle her, he'd moved without conscious thought. One moment he was frozen to the spot and the next he was exchanging pleasantries with the brothel owner with his fists clenched at his sides and doing all he could not to drive them into the asshole's face.

And it was all *her* fault.

———————

Savannah's breath hitched. "Will, *please!* Slow down, or I'll twist my ankle."

"Shut up." He didn't even spare her a glance, but continued to drag her along the darkened hall, past a flurry of closed doors until they got to one that stood ajar. Taking care to check that the room was empty, he pulled Savannah in quickly behind him. With a flick of his wrist, he locked the door.

Savannah's heart pounded. It was déjà vu. Her palms went damp. Will strode to the bed and switched on a lamp. Spinning around, his gaze pinned her where she stood.

"Will, let me explain—"

"*Explain?*" His voice was a fierce whisper. His cobalt eyes sparked with fury. "Where would you like to begin, Savannah? At the part where you smiled sweetly and told me you'd be staying home tonight? What about where you told me how supportive you were of my job—how much you *understood* my need to come here tonight, to finish what I'd started. Would that be a better place to start?"

He paced in front of her, his fury rolling off him in almost tangible waves. "I can't believe I *fell* for that crap!" He came to an abrupt halt and turned to her. He stared at her with hard eyes. "You had absolutely no intention of staying home tonight, did you?"

"Will, please. I didn't—"

"Didn't what?" He interrupted her, his voice harsh. "Didn't lie to me? Didn't purposefully deceive me into believing you actually *agreed* when I explained why I didn't want you here? Yes or no, Savannah? Did you purposefully set out to deceive me into thinking you were going to do as I'd asked?"

"It wasn't like that!" she pleaded. "Will, please, you have to understand—"

"Yes or no, Savannah. It's that simple." His voice was deadly calm.

She shivered under his icy facade. She'd had no idea he'd be so upset. After all, it wasn't as if she hadn't been to the brothel before. She knew the risks she was taking and so far, she'd been able to take care of herself. She didn't need him to make the unilateral decision that he was now responsible for her welfare. When had she become incompetent?

Anger smoldered inside her. She could remind him how, as nice as it was to have someone looking out for her, she'd been doing an absolutely fine job on her own, thank you very much. She could tell him she didn't appreciate him macho-ing in on her life just because they'd shared great sex and she'd agreed to move in with him. It didn't mean he owned her.

But after taking another look at his face, as impenetrable as granite, she refrained from saying any of those things. Drawing in a deep breath, she met and held his angry gaze.

"I'm not talking about this with you right now. You're not in the mood to listen to a thing I have to say and I refuse to compete with your anger. I apologize for deceiving you. I feel awful about doing it, but you—you left me with no choice."

She paused and then forced herself to continue while her courage held out. "When you've calmed down a little and you're ready to talk about this rationally, give me a call."

With that, she walked across the room, unlocked the door and stepped into the corridor. Pulling the door closed behind her, she walked to the back door as quickly as her tight leather skirt and five-inch heels would allow. Relieved to find it unlocked, she let herself out into the quiet night.

———————

"Hurry the fuck up, Kid. We ain't got all night."

Dylan gritted his teeth and did his best to ignore Vince's

chiding. He glanced at the dark shadows of the security guards who stood above him and cursed under his breath. At least one or two of the fuckers could have given him a hand. He hauled another carton of powder out of the cellar and tossed it up to Vince, who missed the catch. The carton tumbled to the ground and split open on impact.

"For fuck's sake, Kid. Be careful. That shit's worth a fortune."

Dylan drew in a deep breath and set his mind to the task. The quicker he emptied the brothel's cellar of drugs, the quicker he could take his leave. It couldn't come a minute too soon. He'd had about enough of Vince and the Black Opal for tonight.

The man had become a veritable ogre of late. His demands were becoming increasingly annoying. It was only because of Vince that Dylan was contemplating killing his sister.

As if the man could read his mind, Vince stared at Dylan with a narrow-eyed gaze and leaned over the hole which led to the cellar. "You found that sister of yours, yet?"

Dylan dropped his gaze and shook his head. "Nope."

"You can't tell me you don't know where she lives. She's your fuckin' sister."

"I know where she lives," he mumbled. "I've been busy."

Vince laughed without humor. "Busy, my ass. Busy fuckin' *my* girls. Listen to me, Kid and listen well. You've got two days. *Two days*, or I find her myself."

CHAPTER 27

Will watched Savannah depart through the rear door of the brothel. Relief that she'd escaped unharmed warred with his anger and disappointment. Knowing there was nothing more he could do about it now, he made his way back into the main bar.

The crowd had increased tenfold. Men hovered close to the stage where another live show was about to commence. He looked around, but Maranoa had disappeared.

He cursed Savannah again. Thanks to her, he didn't know whether the asshole had left the building or was somewhere inside it dealing with whatever was purportedly going down. Will suspected a shipment of drugs was being unloaded, but where?

He had yet to find a cellar, but that didn't mean one didn't exist. The most logical explanation was that it was accessed from the back of the house. It would be an easy operation to have the shipments delivered through a rear gate and unloaded. He thought of the TRG officers waiting outside, concealed in the darkness—waiting for his signal to charge. If he gave the order too soon and they came up empty handed, Maranoa would make damn sure there was nothing to find the next time around.

Obtaining another search warrant would be next to impossible. They'd already had one failed attempt. He sure as hell wasn't going to contribute to another. There was nothing else for it: He had to find concrete evidence of Maranoa's criminal activities; something solid enough to ensure a conviction.

Heading toward the exit, he opened the front door. Five of the bouncers he'd seen earlier now lounged along the side of the building. Another one stood to the side, smoking a cigarette. All of them looked bored and disinterested.

Will's gut clenched with disappointment. Whatever had been planned had either already happened or hadn't come off.

With a polite smile plastered across his lips, Will nodded goodnight to the guards and made his way along the sidewalk in the direction of his car. His thoughts turned to Max O'Connor and the near certainty that the editor was connected to Maranoa.

He recalled Savannah telling him about Max's strange behavior. It was possible the editor had already warned Vince the police had been notified. If that was the case, they had little chance of finding him with incriminating evidence. The drug lord was way too smart for that.

Will's shoulders slumped at the thought that yet again, the asshole had gotten away with it. Just as quickly, steely determination surged through him. He thought of Cole and his spine straightened. There was no way he was giving up.

The night was still. It was late and traffic was light. Unlocking his black BMW, Will pulled open the door and slid behind the wheel. He pulled out onto the road and took the first left and drove slowly along the darkened street that ran parallel to the brothel's street frontage. Within moments, he spotted it. A narrow, unmarked gravel laneway ran right along the brothel's rear boundary.

"Bingo." He turned into the laneway and crept forward. Within moments, he spied the gate. He pulled out his cell phone and called Pete.

"Will, what have you got?" Despite the late hour, Pete's voice was sharp.

"Not what we were hoping for. If there was going to be a haul tonight, we're either too late or it's been called off, but

I've found the gate that gives the brothel access to a back lane. Now we know how they're getting the shit into the place. I haven't found a cellar yet, but it must be there. It's the only thing that makes sense.

"We need to relocate the surveillance team around the back and tell them to be on the lookout for a reasonable-sized truck. Maranoa assured me tonight he'd be fully stocked with drugs again next week."

"Good work, Will, although it's a shame our intelligence was off about tonight. I guess the TRG boys can go home."

"Yeah, for now, at least."

"You go home, too. Get some rest. You'll need to be fresh again for tomorrow. We'll keep everybody on call until we nail these pricks. If Maranoa said he'd be back in business next week, it won't be long." Pete paused and then added, "Oh, by the way, I hear congratulations are in order."

"Yeah, thanks."

"You could sound a little more enthusiastic. Don't tell me you're having second thoughts already?"

Will sighed. "No, but I can't say the same thing about Savannah. After tonight, who knows what she's thinking?"

"What do you mean, after tonight? Did you two have an argument?"

"No, well, yes, I guess. Pete, she was here again tonight, after I specifically told her not to come. She left me thinking she was going to spend a nice quiet evening packing her things at her condominium and what happens? I'm in the Black Opal, doing my best to work out what Maranoa's up to, when Savannah strolls through the door dressed to kill. Next minute she's serving at Maranoa's table."

"Shit, are you kidding me?" Pete was incredulous. "I warned her off that place, too. Damn, I'm going to kill her!"

"You'll have to wait in line." Will's voice was drier than sandpaper.

"What the hell does she think she's *doing*? Is she trying to get herself *killed*? This guy is serious. The body count around him keeps piling up. He's not going to let a journalist come in and sabotage everything. How could she be so *stupid*?"

"Exactly. And now that I'm almost certain her editor is in the thick of it, her actions were even more reckless. For all we know, Max might have already identified Savannah to Maranoa."

Pete's voice sharpened. "What's this about O'Connor?"

Will went on to tell his boss about the altered newspapers and discovering the *Daily Mirror's* editor was a friend of Maranoa's.

"Were you able to find anything on him?" Will asked.

"Well, he doesn't have a record. Apart from a few minor traffic offences, he's as clean as a whistle. I did a background check on his finances. Both parents died years ago. Interestingly, they were murdered during an armed robbery."

Pete went on. "They owned a corner store in Marrickville, but didn't leave anything very substantial as far as assets went. There was the family home in Marrickville. It was sold, but even that wouldn't account for the way O'Connor's living now. We're talking fifteen, twenty years ago. He's got a penthouse suite overlooking the harbor at Vaucluse and there are at least three luxury sports cars registered under his name. Not to mention—"

"Hang on a minute," Will interrupted. "Where did you say his parents lived?"

"Marrickville, I think. Just give me a second and I'll go and get the file."

A few minutes later, Pete was back on the phone. "Here it is. Yeah, O'Connor sold a house in Marrickville seventeen years ago. Must have hung onto it for a while after his parents died. Far as I can tell, there are no siblings."

Adrenaline pumped through Will's veins. "Pete, I'm sure Maranoa went to school in Marrickville. I remember reading it in his file. Surely, that has to be more than a coincidence?"

"Leave it with me. I'll have someone go back a bit further, find out where O'Connor went to school. Maybe the two of them go back that far?"

"One of the bartender's at the Black Opal said Maranoa and Max having a long history. Maybe that's the link? They could have been friends since high school."

"Okay, first things first. Let me contact the surveillance team and tell them to get their asses around the back. I'll go into the station early tomorrow and run a few more searches on O'Connor, see what I come up with. In the meantime, I think we need to assume our friend has talked to Maranoa about Savannah. If Max is involved, it would be stupid to assume Savannah's articles haven't been discussed. I can only imagine how Vince has reacted to them."

Fear tightened Will's gut. "I need to warn her. Tell her to keep a look out. Any chance of posting an officer outside her place?"

Pete sighed. "You know the system as well as I do. There's no way we're going to get approval for a protection detail without any evidence of a threat, but it wouldn't hurt to tell Savannah to be a little more aware of who's around her. Just do it as diplomatically as you can," he added dryly. "I don't want her too scared to step out of her living room. After all, we don't know anything for sure, yet."

"You're right. No sense in alarming her unnecessarily. If I wasn't so mad at her, I'd pull security detail myself," Will growled.

"It might be best if I—"

"It's fine, Pete. I'll call her when I get home." Will paused. "We're getting close, Pete. I can *feel* it."

"Yeah, let's hope so. It's time we nailed these assholes."

"You have that right. Oh, I almost forgot—Savannah told me earlier that she'd seen one of the security guards from the paper at the brothel. Apparently, he works there as a bouncer: just another coincidence."

"One too many, if you ask me."

"I agree. O'Connor and the paper are the link, Pete. Get back to me as soon as you can."

"Yeah, will do."

"Oh, by the way, do you know anything about a young bloke who goes by the name of Billy the Kid? He was here tonight with Maranoa. The barman said he was Vince's right hand man."

"What's he look like?"

"Can't really tell you. I only saw him from a distance and he was seated. Dark hair, young, well built. About all I could see."

"Doesn't ring any bells, but I'll run his name through the system. See if we get a hit."

"Sounds good." Ending the call with a sigh, Will switched on the ignition and turned his car in the direction of home.

───────────

Tired and drained from his long night and the thoughts of Savannah that continued to whirl around in his head, Will arrived at his condo, stepped out of his clothes and straight into the shower. Moments later, he collapsed into bed. The dials on his alarm clock read three fifty-five. His head throbbed from a lack of sleep and his eyes were full of grit.

He still had to call Savannah. Not that she'd be likely to listen to him. Hadn't she castigated him only hours earlier about his overprotectiveness?

Just like that, his anger resurfaced. He recalled the look she'd tossed him as she'd told him to call her when he was ready to talk to her rationally. Hell, the way he felt at the moment, rational might never be part of his vocabulary again.

He couldn't believe how helpless he'd felt when he'd been forced to stand halfway across the room and watch her being mauled by the head of Sydney's underworld. Her reckless stupidity ignited a fury that even now, continued to smolder.

And for what? She knew damn well there was an extremely dangerous covert police operation going on and yet she'd blithely ignored all of that, including both his and her editor's order to stay away from the place.

Savannah didn't know Max was probably mixed up with Maranoa. Whether she agreed with her editor's reasons for vetoing any stories about the Black Opal or not, the fact was, she'd been told to stay away and she'd waltzed on into the brothel as if she'd had every right to be there.

Groaning aloud in frustration, he threw himself out of bed, unable to stay still a minute longer. Pacing up and down his bedroom, naked but for a pair of satin boxer shorts, he struggled to get control of his temper so that he could think *rationally*. He drew in a couple of deep breaths and flung himself back on his bed.

He scrubbed at his hair and grimaced. His fists clenched and he groaned again. A moment later, he sighed heavily and the anger seeped out of him. If they were ever going to make a life together they'd have to learn to work through their differences. Besides, he'd told Pete he'd call her.

He reached over to the nightstand for his cell phone and composed a text message.

Hi there. Bed feels v lonely without u. I'm sorry 4 things I said. R u ready 2 talk?

Pressing "send" on his phone, he stretched back out on the bed and stacked his hands under his head. Now that he'd had time to calm down, he could see why she'd been upset about the way he'd handled the situation. Or, more importantly, the way he'd handled *her*. Until yesterday, she'd been living her life on her own terms without having to consider anyone else—apart from her brother. She'd been looking out for herself and Dylan for a long time and had obviously managed it successfully.

He could almost understand how his order for her to stay at home might be unwelcome—even be perceived as arrogant. Who was he, after all, to tell her what to do? He sure as hell wouldn't be pleased if she suddenly started giving him orders about what he could and couldn't do.

His phone beeped to indicate a new text message. He sat up in a hurry and reached for it. It was from Savannah. His heart leaped into his throat.

Thx 4 that. In bed wide awake. Thinking of u. Can I come over?

His heart accelerated. He quickly sent off a reply.

Sooner the better.

Dylan paced up and down the largely deserted platform of the train station and tried to curb his impatience. The train was late. He wanted to do it now, before his cocaine high wore off and the sun was up. With a bit of luck, Savannah would be home in bed. He already knew she was alone.

He'd spied her boyfriend at the Black Opal. The asshole had been drinking at the bar and hadn't seen him. Dylan took it as a good sign: Tonight was the night.

The bright lights of the approaching train cut through the blackness of the tunnel. Relief surged through him. Savannah's condo was less than ten minutes away. With a bit of luck, he'd be in and out before her neighbors began to stir after their Saturday night revelries.

The train screeched to a halt. The smell of engine oil and grease infiltrated his nostrils, turning his gut. The doors slid open. He stepped onto the train. Less than a handful of bleary-eyed passengers filled the compartment. Not one of them looked up.

He took a seat furthest away from the other passengers and turned to stare out the window into the darkness. His body pressed against the bulge in his jacket pocket. He took comfort from the presence of the gun.

It was the same one he'd used on the bum. He'd pocketed it straight after they'd finished emptying the cellar. After the debacle of his last attempt, he wasn't taking any chances. Savannah and anyone who was with her, would be dead before daybreak.

Savannah read the text message from Will a second time and smiled. Her heart did a flip flop. She was still mad at the way he'd spoken to her, but now that she'd had time to think about it and had calmed down a little, she could see he'd only had the best of intentions when he'd told her to stay at home. He'd said it because he'd wanted to protect her and it made her feel warm inside that he cared enough to look out for her.

It had been a long time since anyone had wanted to do that. Even Jonathan had encouraged her to maintain her independence. When she looked back at it, she realized they'd lived almost completely separate lives, with the occasional sleepover thrown in. They'd been little more than friends with benefits. Now that she'd met Will, she couldn't believe she'd been willing to settle for so little. It was just a matter of teaching the new man in her life how to be a little more diplomatic.

After exiting the brothel through the back door, she'd breathed a sigh of relief when she'd reached her car without incident. She'd seen no sign of Angel and she worried now, wondering if the girl was all right—not that she could anything about it.

Sliding out of bed, she padded across the carpet to the bathroom. Thanks to the wig, her real hair was a mess. She sighed with resignation. She wanted to get over to Will's place as soon as possible, but with hair like that, she'd have to wash it before she went anywhere.

With a sigh, she pulled off her bathrobe and stepped into the shower. Closing her eyes, she lathered her hair with a generous amount of shampoo. She scrubbed quickly and then ducked her head under the steaming water. The door to the shower squeaked. She opened her eyes in surprise.

And screamed...

———————

Dylan kept the gun trained on his sister. He should have just shot her in the shower. The job would have been over and done with and he'd have been out of there. Instead, he'd hesitated. The thought of the neighbors and later the cops staring at her naked, wet body had turned his stomach. Instead, he'd ordered her out of the shower and told her to dress.

Anxiety gnawed at him. She was taking way too long. Even now, she had barely pulled on underwear and a shirt. Damn it, he'd just do it. He'd aim the gun and pull the trigger. Half-clothed, unclothed—what did it really matter? Dead was dead.

He let off the safety and cocked the gun. The sound of it was amplified in the silent room. Savannah spun around from where she stood at the door to her open closet and stared at him. Her mouth gaped open. It looked like she was trying to form words, but she made no sound.

"Hurry the fuck up, Savannah and get dressed. I swear to God, I'll kill you now if you don't get a move on."

Tears formed in her eyes. "Why, Dylan? *Why?* What have I ever done to you? I *love* you. I did my best to take care of you. It wasn't my fault Mom and Dad—"

"Shut the fuck up!" he yelled and waved the gun around. He refused to be moved by her tears. Okay, maybe it wasn't her fault their parents had favored her or that they'd had the stupidity to die too soon, but it was her fault she'd pissed off Vince. No one had forced her into the Black Opal. No one had forced her to write those stupid stories.

After Vince had told him, he'd gone onto the Internet and had Googled the articles. He couldn't believe what she'd written—or how accurate they were. He could see why Vince wanted her dealt with. She was trouble. Killing her would send a clear message to anyone else with the audacity to interfere with his affairs. There was no other way. It was as simple as that.

She'd tugged on a pair of jeans and now sat gingerly on the edge of her bed. Every now and then, she threw a cautious look in his direction. Shock and fear shadowed her eyes. She shook her head, as if unable to believe what was happening.

Dylan grinned to himself. *Oh yeah, it was happening, all right.*

In sudden decision, he strode over to the bed and put the gun to her temple. She flinched and cried out. He laughed.

"Not so brave now, are you sis?" Too bad you didn't think about the consequences before you meddled in Vince's business."

She stared at him in shock. "Vince Maranoa? This is about *Vince Maranoa?*"

He smiled and nodded. "Of course. What did you think it was about?"

Savannah shook her head. "I-I don't know. I had no idea why you'd break into my condominium and threaten to shoot me. What kind of brother does that?"

He should have been overwhelmed with guilt, but the truth was, what little guilt he felt was fleeting. So what if he was her brother? Vince had ordered him to get rid of her. He was only doing his job. It wasn't his fault Savannah had stuck her nose into Vince's business and it sure as hell wasn't his fault Vince wanted her dead.

It's just the way it was. Surely Savannah could see that? He thrust his bottom lip out.

"You fucked with the wrong guy, sis. Vince wants you dead and what Vince wants, Vince gets."

Her lip curled up in disgust. "And you're the eager executioner, is that it?"

He squirmed under her regard. "Vince relies on me to get the job done. I haven't failed him yet," he boasted.

Savannah's eyes narrowed. "Don't tell me you had anything to do with Malee's death?"

He frowned in concentration. "Which one was Malee?"

Her eyes widened in horror. "You mean there's been more than one?"

Dylan shrugged, trying hard not to let her reaction matter. "Maybe."

"Dylan! How *could* you? You're a hired killer. At least, I assume you get paid."

"Oh yeah. Vince pays well. That's one thing he does."

Savannah shook her head, disgust clouding her eyes.

"Look at yourself. You're higher than the Centrepoint Tower, talking about murder like it was a Sunday School picnic. Where is the brother I know and love? Where is the brother who brought me flowers from the garden when I was sick in bed with the flu? Where is the brother who was there when I picked up food poisoning and who wiped my forehead when I vomited for the hundredth time? Where is—?"

"Enough!" Dylan spun on his heel and paced the length of her bedroom. He couldn't stand to listen to her a minute longer. The more she spoke about their past, the more the voice inside his head urged him not to do it.

But Vince wanted her dead. There was nothing else to it.

Vince wanted her dead.

The words reverberated in his head. He put his hands up over his ears to block them out, but still they echoed inside him until they slowed like a gramophone record winding down. A sudden thought illuminated his mind. Vince wanted her dead and he would have her dead. But it would be Vince who would be doing the killing.

It wouldn't be as quick or as painless as it would if Dylan did it, but it was better this way. This way, Dylan's conscience could rest easy, knowing it hadn't been him, her own flesh and blood, who'd pulled the trigger. He could text Vince and find out where he was. The asshole would be pleased Dylan was bringing his sister in.

He swung around to face her. The color had leached out of her face. Apart from her wide-eyed fear, she looked like she was already dead.

"Get up. You're coming with me."

He strode over and seized her by the arm. He hauled her to her feet and marched her out of the bedroom.

"W-where are you taking me?"

"I'm taking you to Vince."

Dylan prodded her forward with the gun and kept it trained on her while he sent a text to Vince. A moment later, Vince replied. Dylan read the message and smiled. He dug into the pocket of his jeans and felt for the key Vince had given him when they'd moved the gear to the warehouse hours earlier. His fingers closed around it and he nodded to himself, pleased with his decision. Vince could kill her. A brother shouldn't be forced to kill his sister. It just wasn't right.

CHAPTER 28

Will stared at the front door of his condominium and waited for the doorbell to ring. What the hell was taking Savannah so long? She should have been there an hour ago.

She couldn't have been caught in traffic. There was hardly a car on the street. Perhaps she'd changed her mind? She'd sounded willing enough, but maybe she'd had second thoughts? But, why hadn't she contacted him?

He cursed under his breath and picked up his cell phone from the kitchen counter. No new messages. With an impatient sigh, he gave in and sent her a text.

Where r u?

Twenty minutes later, he still hadn't heard from her. With gritted teeth, he dialed her number. The phone rang out for what seemed like forever. It eventually went through to her voicemail. Will bit down on a curse and left a brief message.

"Hi, it's me. Um…call me."

He ended the call and stared at the phone in his hand. With another curse, he tossed it onto the couch.

Why wasn't she answering her phone?

He spun on his heel and paced the length of his living room, oblivious to the new day that would shortly break over the horizon. Anxiety nipped at the edges of his consciousness, but he refused to pay it heed. Any second, she'd be knocking on his door with a smile and a load of excuses. He was sure of it.

His phone rang and his heart leaped with relief. What had he told himself? She'd been held up, that was all. He grabbed for the phone and checked the screen.

It was Pete.

Tapping down on his disappointment, he answered the call.

"Will, sorry to call you so early. I hope I didn't wake you, but I've been following one lead after another all night. You won't believe what I've discovered."

Will's pulse skipped a beat. Excitement coursed through him. "Tell me."

"You were right about O'Connor. I pulled his school records. He finished alongside Maranoa in 1970 at Marrickville High."

"Shit, Pete, that's fantastic. It was only a hunch I had after you mentioned his parents used to live there. I can't believe the two of them have known each other for so long. Another piece of the puzzle has fallen into place."

"There's more. The surveillance team caught sight of a truck bearing the *Daily Mirror* insignia in the back lane behind the brothel last night. It appeared like they were loading newspapers, but apparently they took an awful long time at it and after what you told me about the papers you found in the dumpster, I have my own theory about what was happening."

"We're onto them, Pete. The noose is slowly tightening."

"Yeah, let's hope so. I also ran a search on the *Daily Mirror*'s security guards. Turns out a guard by the name of Carlo Tilocca has Romano Enterprises listed as one of his employers on his last tax return."

"Who's Romano Enterprises?"

Pete's reply was dry. "Guess."

"Vincent Maranoa."

"One and the same. He's sole director of the company."

"This is it, Pete. The only thing left to do is to find out where they're keeping the gear. They're using the paper's trucks to get it in and out, but where are they storing it?"

"I think I might be able to shed some light on that. While I was searching the Land and Property Information database under Max O'Connor, I ran a search under Reid Marchant."

Will frowned and searched his memory. "Reid Marchant? Isn't he the owner of the *Daily Mirror*?"

"That he is."

"I can imagine he has a substantial property portfolio."

"You're right. His listings ran for three pages, but I found mention of a warehouse in Surry Hills. I'm not familiar with the building, but I wonder if it's being used by the paper? There are a lot of industrial factories in that area. I think *The Sun* also has a warehouse somewhere in Surry Hills."

Adrenaline flooded through Will's veins. He recalled the conversation with Declan Munro at the ball when he'd mentioned something about finding a dealer's stash of drugs hidden inside rolls of warehoused carpet.

"It's definitely worth a look," he said. "I say we call in the other members of the TRG and pay a surprise visit to whoever's occupying the warehouse."

"Exactly what I had in mind." Pete paused. "It would be nice to know who this Billy the Kid is."

"I take it he wasn't in the database?"

"No, not under that name, anyway. I got a couple of hits on that nickname, but the ages didn't pan out. One of them was forty-five and the other one was in his sixties. From what you said, they couldn't be our guy."

"Don't worry about it, Pete. He'll surface. They always do and when he does, we'll be waiting."

Silence fell between them. A moment later, Pete spoke again. "By the way, how did things go with Savannah? Did you kiss and make up?"

Will's disquiet returned. "Not yet. In fact, she was supposed to be on her way over here more than ninety minutes ago, but she hasn't shown up."

"That's a bit odd."

"Yeah, that's what I thought. Now she's not answering her phone."

"I assume she made it home all right?"

"Yes, she texted me earlier and told me she was there."

"I wonder where she is?"

Will pressed his lips together to stem the dread that was growing steadily in his gut. "You and me both."

"Let me know when she turns up. In the meantime, I'm calling the duty judge to apply for a search warrant and then I'll call the boys in for a pre-raid briefing. Provided we get the warrant, we'll aim on hitting the warehouse sometime today. It's a Sunday and that will work in our favor. If anyone is on site today, they're probably not there legitimately."

"I'll make sure I'm ready. Where are we meeting?"

"Give me a couple of hours. Even after I speak with the judge, I'll still have to attend his chambers. We'll meet at headquarters and make sure everyone knows what they're doing."

Anticipation surged through Will. "Let's do it."

———————

Savannah trudged up the steep hill and did her best to keep up the brisk pace set by her brother. He'd fastened her hands in front of her with a length of cord he'd torn from the curtain in her bedroom. A jacket cleverly draped over her shoulders concealed the arrangement from the casual observer.

She'd ridden the train to Central Station with the gun pressed against her side. There was a brief moment when Dylan tugged out his phone and had started texting that she'd thought she might be able to get away from him, but as if he'd read her mind, he'd jammed the gun in harder and had warned her not to try anything.

The minute they'd arrived at the station, he'd dragged her up several flights of stairs until they'd reached the outside. The faint glow of dawn colored the horizon. Savannah thought of Will and wondered if he assumed she'd changed her mind.

Dylan turned toward Surry Hills and hauled her along

beside him. His fingers dug into her arm. He seemed oblivious to her cries of discomfort.

The steep climb continued. Her heart thumped with the effort. A cramp sent a stab of pain radiating through her side. With her hands out of action, she had no way of assuaging the agony.

"Please, Dylan, slow down. I-I need to stop."

"Shut up. We'll be there soon. Enjoy every breath you take. Who knows how many you have left?"

Tears blurred Savannah's eyes. She was still at a complete loss to explain her brother's total lack of conscience. How he could blithely hand her over to a man who wanted her dead was beyond her comprehension.

Had she been too hard on him? Foisted too many expectations on him? Shown him enough attention? Enough love? Too much? The questions swirled around her head until she was dizzy and she still came up empty-handed. She had no answers and the harsh reality of it was, she probably never would.

At last, they reached the top of the hill and he dragged her across the road. Another hill loomed in front of them and Savannah couldn't stifle a groan. Her chest hurt. Her feet ached. Every loose stone penetrated the flimsy shoes that covered them.

When Dylan had ordered her to dress, she'd been dazed with shock. With no idea what he had in store for her, she'd grabbed for the nearest thing at hand. Now, she longed for her comfortable, supportive Nikes.

"Hurry up," Dylan growled and tightened his hold on her arm. "Vince is waiting."

Fear renewed its grip on her heart. Blood pounded in her ears. She couldn't believe her life might soon be over. She refused to believe it. Determination surged through her. She wouldn't go down without a fight.

———

Will spied Pete and a handful of TRG officers outfitted in battle fatigues and Kevlar vests standing around the corner from the warehouse owned by Reid Marchant. The street was quiet, with only the occasional car passing by. Daylight had broken, bathing the sky in an array of orange and gold and pink. On another day, Will might have appreciated the colorful display. Today wasn't that day.

He'd phoned Savannah again before he'd left and yet again, the call had gone through to her voicemail. He'd left another message begging her to contact him and let him know she was all right, but he still hadn't heard from her. Now, with his recent knowledge of Max's definite connection to Maranoa, his gut ached with uncertainty. He couldn't shake the dreadful feeling that something terrible had happened to her.

In anticipation of the upcoming search, he'd turned his cell phone to silent. He now slipped it out of his pocket and checked again for messages.

Nothing.

With a grimace, he returned it to his jacket and tried to force his mind away from wondering about what the hell could have happened to her.

He clung to the possibility that she'd had second thoughts about reconciling and resolutely pushed other, more ominous, thoughts away. Now wasn't the time to lose focus on the job at hand. He halted a few feet away from the group of officers. Pete stepped toward him.

"You all good?"

Will nodded. "Yeah. How'd you go with the warrant?"

"Good. It's extensive, so we shouldn't have a problem with the admissibility of any evidence we find."

"That's what we like to hear."

"A couple of the others have done a reconnoiter of the building. There doesn't appear to be too much going on. There's a pickup truck parked ten yards or so up the road. We're running a check on the plate right now to see if it belongs to one of our players."

"Do we have any idea of the layout of the place?"

Pete nodded. "I found some old building plans online. The owner lodged a development application in the mid-nineties with the local council for extensions. There's a small door next to a couple of big roller doors. You walk in on the main floor. It's a large open space where I presume they used to house the printing press. There are a couple of smaller rooms at the back."

"That's where we hit first."

"That's the plan."

"When do we go in?" Will asked.

Pete glanced at his watch. "We'll start the countdown in five."

———————

The blister on Savannah's heel had become unbearable. Blood squelched beneath her foot and made walking even more difficult. She limped and wheezed and panted against the pain. Dylan remained unmoved.

He dragged her the final few feet to an unpainted door that provided entry to a large brick building. The brick had faded over the years to a brownish-red and the sidewalk that surrounded it was thick with pigeon droppings. She tilted her head and spied hundreds of the birds roosting along the eaves.

"W-where are we?"

"You don't know?" Dylan asked, his eyes widening in surprise.

Savannah frowned in confusion. "Should I?"

A smile tugged at his lips. "It's a warehouse owned by the *Daily Mirror*. I'm surprised you weren't given a tour."

Savannah shook her head in disbelief. *Why would Vince Maranoa meet Dylan in a warehouse owned by her newspaper?* Nothing about that scenario made sense.

"I can see you don't believe me," Dylan said and then shrugged. "It doesn't matter. You'll find out soon enough."

He dug into the pocket of his jeans and withdrew a key.

Fitting it into the lock on the front door, he turned it. The door opened with a click. He shoved her through the opening.

Meager amounts of early morning sunlight barely penetrated the darkness of the warehouse. Savannah blinked her eyes in an effort to adjust to the dimness. The place smelled old and damp. The stale odors mixed with the familiar smell of ink.

Dylan produced a flashlight and with a less-than-gentle push to her back, guided her toward the rear of the building. A few moments later, he halted outside the door of what appeared to be a small office. The murmur of voices sounded from within. Savannah was suddenly paralyzed with fear.

Ignoring her sharp intake of breath and the small cry of alarm she was unable to contain, Dylan pushed open the door and dragged her in behind him.

––––––––––––––

"It looks like the place is empty." Pete squinted in the dimness and then pulled down his night-vision goggles. The rest of the team followed suit. They'd come through the side door after one of the TRG officers had cut the lock.

Will made out darker shadows of what he assumed to be part of the heavy equipment used in the printing process. They now sat still and silent, like figures in an elephant graveyard. The smell of ink was sharp and caustic. The warehouse was quiet, apart from the sound of his breathing and the occasional scrape of a boot on the concrete floor made by one of the taskforce officers who waited for instructions behind him.

Pete lowered his voice to a murmur. "I want you to take a few of the others and check out the back storage rooms. It's the most logical place to start. Once we've cleared the building, I'll look around for some lights so that we can give the place a thorough sweep."

Will nodded his assent and gave Pete a thumbs-up

before turning on his heel. He pointed to three of the officers and communicated with hand signals that they were to follow him. Once he was satisfied they understood his instructions, he turned toward the rear of the building and picked his way through the derelict machinery.

The further back they went, the stronger the smell of ink and machinery oil. Will guessed it was because even less fresh air filtered its way all the way to the back. How anyone managed to work in the dark, dank space, he didn't know. It wasn't a place he'd want to turn up to every day. Then again, the warehouse didn't exactly look like it had been occupied of late.

Dust lay thick on every surface. To his left, he spied a wall of newspapers. They were tied in bundles and were stacked to a height well above his head. He continued forward and came upon a partition wall that housed the small rooms Pete had mentioned.

The murmur of voices sounded from the other side of the wall. He put up his hand to halt the men behind him and strained hard to listen. There were at least two men and maybe a third. The sound of a woman's cry of anguish broke the silence and stopped him cold.

———————

Savannah stumbled into the room and gasped. An exposed light bulb hung from the ceiling and illuminated Vince Maranoa and Max O'Connor where they stood in one corner, holding bricks of white powder. The room was piled high with bundles of newspapers. They spun around as one and stared at her. Maranoa was the first to recover.

"Well, well, well. Who have we here?" His smile was as friendly as a barracuda's. His eyes gleamed with feral anticipation.

Savannah backed up a step and collided with the solid wall of Dylan's chest. He elbowed her in the back, propelling her toward Vince. Shock and confusion at her discovery that

Max was in cahoots with the drug lord left her frozen.

"This is my sister. Savannah O'Neill."

Vince closed the distance between them. His gaze traveled over her and his smile widened. "You're a pretty little thing, aren't you?" He reached out and tilted her chin upwards with his fingers. Savannah flinched.

He frowned. "You look a little familiar, Savannah. Why is that?"

Fear congealed, cold and heavy, in the pit of her stomach. Her limbs were as limp as boiled spinach, but she refused to allow him the satisfaction of seeing her terror. She clenched her jaw and stared at him in defiance.

"Oh, we've met before. I've been in your brothel on more than one occasion. I've spoken to your girls. I've heard their terrible stories. How do you think I was able to write about it?"

The back-handed slap came from nowhere. She caught the flash of a ring on one of Maranoa's fleshy fingers before it connected with her mouth. She cried out and went to clutch at her face, forgetting for an instant that her hands were bound.

Her lip throbbed from the impact. Within moments, it was double its size. Blood trickled from a cut and ran into her mouth. Her eyes watered from the pain, but she refused to allow the tears to fall.

Maranoa's eyes blazed with fury. "That's the least you deserve, you little bitch."

Max stepped forward, his hands held out in a placating manner. "Vince, I'm not sure she needs to be treated like—"

"Shut the fuck up, Max. If you'd done what I'd told you and kept her away from the place, none of this would have fuckin' happened. I wouldn't have the fuckin' cops breathin' down my neck. I wouldn't have had to move the shit and I wouldn't have this sneaky little slut pokin' her nose in where it isn't wanted."

Max wrung his hands in consternation, fear edging the shadows in his eyes. "Of course, Vince, I understand. She disobeyed my order. She must be punished. But... Do you have to be so violent about it?"

Vince scoffed. "You call that violent? That was nothin'. The little slut will be beggin' me to kill her after I've finished with her. Right, Billy?"

Recalling her brother's presence behind her, Savannah tensed and tried to edge away. Dylan's laughing reply chilled her to the marrow.

"Oh, yeah. I was gonna kill her myself, but the more I thought about it, the more I knew I had to leave her to you. It was the right thing to do."

"I like the way you think, Kid," Vince chuckled. He moved closer until he stood inches away from her. He reached out and slid a hand down her face and then let it fall to her breast. He sneered at her and then gave her nipple a vicious pinch.

Savannah gasped from the pain and humiliation, but there was nothing she could do. With her hands still bound, the only thing she could resort to was her mouth.

"Get away from me, you vile piece of filth. I won't rest until I see you punished for your crimes. You disgust me. You—"

His fist barreled toward her and connected with her cheek, right below her eye. The ring she'd noticed earlier split the skin above her cheekbone. She cried out again, wishing she could reach up and stem the burning pain that radiated across her face. Blood trickled down her cheek. She silently damned her inability to keep her mouth shut and vowed not to antagonize the evil brute again.

Vince turned to Dylan, his lip curling up in disgust. "You need to teach your sister some fuckin' manners, Kid."

Dylan stepped forward and grabbed Savannah by the arm. With the nails of his fingers digging into her, he dragged her toward the back of the room. She stumbled into a stack of newspapers and stubbed her toe, gasping involuntarily from the pain.

"What the fuck do you think you're doing, you stupid bitch?" Dylan spat at her. "Do you *want* it to be slow and painful?"

Savannah stared up at her brother. Shock and

overwhelming confusion rendered her speechless.

How could this maniac be her brother? How could he have changed from the bright young boy with a few troubles as he struggled to adjust to the unexpected death of his parents to this—this...monster?

Dylan dragged her further back into the shadows. Her mind and body were weighted with concrete. Tears of anguish burned just below the surface. Her lip throbbed, her cheek ached, the blister on her heel flamed. Exhaustion weakened her determination to withstand Maranoa's onslaught. Knowing her brother, her flesh and blood, was aiding and abetting her demise, crippled her resolve.

Will's heart thumped hard. Blood pounded in his ears. He gulped in oxygen in an effort to ease the adrenaline that surged through him. Someone was on the other side of the wall. A few someones, from the sound of it.

He turned and motioned to the men behind him. With as few whispered words as he could manage and plenty of hand signals, he explained how they were going to deal with the presence behind the wall. The men nodded in understanding. Will counted them down with the fingers of one hand.

He eased himself forward and located a closed door. He looked down and noticed a faint gleam of light filtering through underneath. Straining to listen above the pounding of his heart, he eased his hand under his shirt and undid the clip on his holster. Another startled cry came from the other side of the door.

A sense of urgency flooded through him. He pulled out his gun and held it up in readiness. Checking that his men were with him, he leaned his shoulder into the door. To his relief, it opened without a sound.

Light flooded the room. He squinted through the brightness and hauled off his night vision goggles, leaving them dangling around his neck. The three TRG officers barged into the room behind him, their guns drawn.

The outline of two men materialized in front of him with their mouths gaping in shock. There was no sign of a woman. *Perhaps he'd been mistaken?*

"Freeze! Police!" Will's voice echoed loudly in the confined room. He trained his gun on Vince Maranoa and Max O'Connor.

Will's mouth compressed into a thin line. "Well, well, well. What do we have here?"

Maranoa's hand snaked down toward his belt. Will cocked his gun and aimed it directly at the drug lord. "Arms up above your head!"

The other TRG members, looking menacing in their combat gear, kept their guns trained on the men. Max trembled violently, shock and fear evident in his eyes.

"It's n-not what it l-looks like. I-I didn't even know w-what was going on. I-I just came across Vince here. I-I came in to ask him w-what he was doing." Tears formed in the editor's eyes.

"That's fuckin' bullshit, and you know it," Vince exploded. "Don't go rattin' me out now, mate. We're fuckin' in this together. That's how it's fuckin' always been." His voice dropped low and threatening. "Don't you go forgettin' what I fuckin' did for you, Max. I stabbed that fucker for you, Max. The fucker who killed your parents. I did that for you. The cops had fuckin' nothin'. That fucker would have got away with it if it hadn't been for me."

Max's eyes bulged. "B-but Vince, I c-can't go to *jail!*"

"Who says we're goin' to jail?" Vince scoffed. "I know this bloke. He and his father are fuckin' regulars at the club. This asshole probably heard me talkin' one night and now he wants a cut. He's been at me for some fuckin' shit all week." Vince eyed Will disdainfully. "Ain't that right, big fella?"

Will smiled grimly. "I'm afraid you're out of luck this time, Vince. There are at least half a dozen more police officers waiting outside this door. They'll be happy to take you quietly, but they'll be just as happy to take you screaming. It's your pick."

Max blubbered. "I-I told you to watch out for him! I-I knew something wasn't right! Now look what's happened!"

Vince turned to him, irritation etched on his face. "Just shut the fuck up, would you! You always were such a fuckin' cry baby. I should never have fuckin' let you in on it!"

"D-don't yell at me, Vince," Max wailed. "You k-kept telling me how the c-cops were all over you. If it w-weren't for me, you w-wouldn't have had anywhere to store—"

Max stopped. Comprehension dawned. He turned wide eyes to Will, his mouth gaping.

Will shook his head, amazed Max had managed to scale the upper echelons of management. With his gun still trained on Vince, he pulled cuffs out of his belt and immobilized the editor.

"Righto, Vince. It's your turn. Don't go trying to be a hero. Get your arms behind your back and turn around. You're not going to get out of this one."

He breathed a silent sigh of relief when Vince submitted without a struggle. As one of the other officers secured handcuffs over Vince's thick wrists, Will gestured with his chin.

"Okay, boys, let's take it out of here. Max, you take the lead and walk real slow. Don't try anything stupid, or you'll end up with a bullet in your hide."

Max whimpered. His hefty body appeared to shrivel. Two of the officers grabbed him by the arms and herded him toward the door. Max shuffled past Will, his gaze averted.

Vince moved forward with the assistance of the other member of Will's team. When Vince drew alongside Will, he shot him a look that was full of confusion and surprise.

"What the fuck did I ever do to you? I would have been happy to cut you in on a bit. All you had to do was ask."

The lifeless face of Will's younger brother flashed before him. For long moments after he'd found Cole, he'd held him to his chest, asking the same desperate question over and over. *Why?* Guilt had overwhelmed him. It had been a long while later that he'd rung for emergency services.

Making no effort to stem the anger and pain that flooded through him, he stared at Vince with narrowed eyes and replied in a voice that was as cold as ice. "You're the reason my brother's dead."

Vince's forehead creased in confusion. "What the fuck are you talkin' about? Your brother? I didn't even know you had a fuckin' brother."

Will's gaze burned into Maranoa's. "Yeah, that's right. Just like the other hundreds of nameless people who die of drug overdoses every year in this city. If it weren't for you, they wouldn't be able to get the stuff."

Vince cackled. "You really fuckin' think if I'm not around, there'll be no more drugs in this town? You've got to be fuckin' kiddin'? You shut me down, another fuckin' three will have set up in my place by the mornin'. You aren't gonna fuckin' get rid of this. Too many people are hooked on it. Rich, poor, it don't make no fuckin' difference. You've got no idea how it can fuckin' get ahold of you."

Cold determination flooded through Will. "And I'll shut them down too, one outfit at a time." He prodded Vince forward with his gun. Vince flicked his gaze over Will's shoulder.

"Now, Billy. *Now!*" Vince yelled.

Will whirled around. In the same instant, a third man, who until then had remained concealed behind the stack of newspapers, stepped out and revealed himself. He dragged a woman with him. Red hair spilled across the man's arm where he held it clenched around her neck. Light glinted off the gun in his other hand.

Will froze. Savannah stared up at him from her awkward position twisted against Billy's chest. Her green eyes were ravaged with fear and pain. Her hands were bound in front of her. Blood trickled from her mouth and a cut had opened up beneath her eye. Fury like Will had never known boiled through his veins.

"Let her go." His cold command was met with a sneer of laughter from the man who held her.

"Like hell. Let's do it this way. I'll let her go when you let Vince go. *Quid pro quo* as they say."

Will struggled to breathe through his anger. Helplessness and fear surged through him. He glanced behind him and was relieved to discover the remaining TRG officer had his gun trained on Vince.

Will looked at Savannah again and a fresh wave of helplessness washed through him. How she'd come to be there, he had no clue and now wasn't the time to become distracted by questions. There would be time enough for her explanations later. At least, he prayed there would be.

His mind spun furiously. The officers who had left with O'Connor should have made it out of the building by now. They'd notify Pete of their discovery. Pete was sure to head straight to the back room. Will could only pray he wouldn't be too late.

Buying time, he attempted to engage the man Vince had called Billy, in conversation.

"So, Billy, you must be pretty friendly with Vince to want to risk holding a woman hostage over his release?"

Billy's expression softened. "Yeah, we're friendly, all right. Vince knows how to treat me right."

Savannah struggled against the man and Will's blood ran cold. Didn't she know her best chance of surviving this was to remain as inconspicuous as possible? He clenched his fists and gritted his teeth. His gun remained steady on the man who held her.

"For fuck's sake, would you be still?" Billy jerked her harder against him. Savannah's head snapped back. She cried out in pain and then sunk her teeth into the man's forearm.

"You bitch!" Billy pulled his arm back and slammed the gun across her face. The sound of her nose breaking was loud in the quiet room. She screamed. Blood spurted from her nose.

"Dylan! H-how could you? You're…you're my *brother*."

Shock ricocheted through Will. Moments later, he was engulfed by rage. His vision turned red—as red as Savannah's blood. He shook from the impact of it. He pointed his gun at Billy's head.

He saw the flash of orange seconds before the force of the bullet's impact in his chest hurled him backwards. He slammed into the concrete floor. Pain exploded through him. His body was on fire. Like a man drowning, he struggled to breathe. Savannah's brother stood over him. In slow motion, he watched as the man raised the gun a second time.

CHAPTER 29

Savannah screamed again and hurled herself at her brother. Aiming for his gun hand, she braced herself for the impact. Her shoulder connected with the solid plane of his chest. Pain shot up her arm. Dylan cursed and flung her aside. Without the use of her hands to break her fall, she landed hard on the concrete floor and grunted in pain. Will lay still and silent a few feet away.

Fear clogged her throat and threatened to choke her. *Please, God, please God, please, God. Please don't let him be dead.*

Her attention was drawn by the clatter of boots on the concrete. The sound of men shouting frantic orders to each other slowly infiltrated her daze.

"Freeze! Police! Put the gun down! Put the goddamn gun down. *Now.*"

It was Pete. He stood in front of her, his arm extended. The dim light glinted off the barrel of his gun.

"Pete, you have to help Will. Please, you have to help him!"

"Savannah?" Pete's voice cracked through the silence, taut with surprise. His gun remained trained on her brother. Pete glanced in her direction. "You have to get out of here."

She turned her frantic gaze in his direction. "Pete, can't you see? Will's hurt. I have to do something."

"Get out of here." Each word was bitten off. Even in the dim light, his lips were white with anger.

She flicked uncertain eyes toward Dylan. His gun was still pointed at Will's head.

"Dylan, what are you *doing*? Are you out of your *mind*?"

Dylan glanced at her, his eyes wild with fear and excitement. "Shut up, Savannah. Do as he says and get the hell out of here."

She pinned him with her gaze. "I'm not leaving until you hand that over." She nodded toward the gun.

"It's never gonna happen, sis." His face was suffused with anger. His gaze swung crazily between her and Pete. Her stomach tightened in fear.

She took a deep breath and forced herself to remain calm. "Dylan, please. Just hand the gun over. We can talk about this. Let's go outside. I'm sure we can sort this out."

"No one's going anywhere, Sav. Not you. Not me. And especially not *him*." His head flicked in Will's direction. "This is it for me. The end of the line." He gave a snort of humorless laughter. "They don't call me Billy the Kid for nothing."

His eyes were insane. She barely recognized him. Her heart leaped into her throat. Sweat trickled between her breasts. Fear froze her to the floor.

"Stand back, Billy. Drop the gun, or I'll shoot." Pete's voice cracked in the stillness.

"Go your hardest, copper. I'm going out swinging."

In the end, it took only a matter of seconds. Shots rang out, deafening in the enclosed space. The blinding flashes of gunfire burned into her retinas. Savannah screamed and turned her face away. Awkwardly throwing herself over Will's prone form, she buried her face in his shirt. The sound of bullets behind her thudding into flesh sickened her.

And then, it was over…

The silence terrified her. She didn't dare move. A hand fell on her shoulder and she cried out in fear.

"It's okay, Savannah. It's over."

As Pete's words sunk in, she collapsed in relief. Peering up through the dimness, her gaze strayed sideways.

She made out Dylan's still form where he lay in a crumpled

heap on the floor. His shirtfront was stained dark with blood. "Oh, my God!"

"I'm sorry, Savannah. I had no choice."

She stared in horror at her brother. Blood trickled from his nose. His chest remained motionless. She knew she should go to him, but her legs refused to move.

Pete reached for the bindings around her wrists and severed them with a knife. A few moments later, she was in agony as the blood rushed to her fingers. A groan from Will snatched her attention.

"Oh, thank God, you're alive!" Now oblivious to the fire in her fingers, she bent over him and clasped his head In her hands. "Please, please, Will, wake up. Please, wake up. You need to wake up now."

"Savannah, you'll have to move away," Pete murmured. "The paramedics are here. They need to get in and see him."

Savannah pulled away and looked dazedly around her. Two paramedics hovered behind Pete. One of them carried a large medical bag.

"Excuse me, ma'am. We need to get through."

With her eyes fixed on Will, she stood slowly and backed away. One of the paramedics knelt beside him and checked his injuries. The other one went to where Dylan lay. Savannah looked away, unable to watch.

"We need to get a couple of stretchers back here. Can someone make a bit more room for us?"

Savannah's attention returned to the paramedic who had spoken. She indicated Will with her hand. "Is he okay? He's going to be all right, isn't he?" Her voice shook.

"He's going to be fine. He's got a fair lump on the back of his head, though. Probably knocked himself out when he hit the concrete. He'll be a bit sore in the stomach for a few weeks. Took a bullet by the look of it. Lucky for the vest. It saved his life."

"Oh, thank God!" Her legs weakened in relief. She reached out blindly toward Pete for support.

"We'll take him to hospital, just to be sure. He needs to be checked over by a doctor, maybe kept overnight for observation." He turned to look in Dylan's direction. "I'm afraid it's too late for this one."

Her legs moved of their own accord. She knelt by her brother's side in a pool of sticky, wet blood. Her hand reached out and brushed a dark lock of unruly hair from his forehead. Hot, quiet tears ran down her cheeks.

"Oh, Dylan. I'm so sorry. Where did I go wrong? How could I have been so blind to what you were going through? Why didn't you say something?" Her voice broke in anguish. Hot tears fell in earnest. She bit her lip to stem the sobs that threatened to overwhelm her and then cried out when the pain of her split lip made itself known.

"Savannah, we need you to come away. This is a crime scene. It has to be preserved." Pete's voice was gentle, but insistent. He gripped her elbow with firm pressure and pulled her to her feet.

"Come on. Let's go outside. They'll bring Will out shortly. Besides, someone needs to see to your injuries."

Savannah was met by a contingent of red and blue flashing lights upon her exit from the warehouse. The sun had climbed higher and now shone as bright as diamonds. Feeling had finally returned to her fingers and she held up a hand to shield her eyes against its intensity.

Uniformed policemen swarmed everywhere. TRG officers, still in their combat gear, milled around, talking to each other in muted tones. A few moments later, the paramedics strode out wheeling a stretcher.

Recognizing Will's dark head, she hurried over. His pain-hazed eyes squinted at the daylight and connected with hers. Relief flooded through her.

"Oh, Will, you're awake! I'm so glad you're all right!" Her legs almost collapsed beneath her. She reached for his hand where it lay limply on the white sheet and squeezed it tightly.

"How the hell did you get here? I thought you were coming over to my place?" he muttered, his voice weak and unsteady.

She closed her eyes briefly at the memory. It seemed like a lifetime ago. "I was. I really was. But Dylan..." She shook her head, unable to continue.

He nodded feebly, his head barely moving on the pillow. She had to lean low to hear him when he spoke again. "You look like hell, but it sure is good to see you."

"Ditto," she whispered and squeezed his hand again.

The wheels of a second stretcher crunched on the pavement. Savannah turned her head toward it. Her brother's body had been covered with a sheet.

Her legs trembled. She tightened her grip on Will's hand.

"Who?" he rasped, watching as the paramedics wheeled the stretcher toward another waiting vehicle. The words *Glebe Morgue* were painted in stark lettering across its back doors.

She forced her gaze back to his. "It's Dylan. My-my brother."

He frowned. "I remember you saying something about your brother." He shook his head. "How...?"

"I don't know all the details. He-he turned up at my condominium and held me at gunpoint. He brought me here so Vince could...kill me."

Will closed his eyes. "Billy the Kid. He was Maranoa's offsider."

Savannah nodded sadly in agreement. Will's hand tightened on hers and she was filled with gratitude. She didn't know how long it would take for her to come to terms with her brother's horrific double life and his tragic death. She'd tried to look out for him for so long and still things had gone terribly wrong.

"Hey, beautiful. Don't look so sad. Have I told you lately how much I love you?"

His voice was still weak, but the pressure against her hand reassured her. Tears pricked her eyes. She gave him a wobbly smile. "I can't believe how close I came to losing you."

"You're not going to get rid of me that easily. I have at least another fifty or sixty years in me." He grinned up at her, but it was strained at the edges. Pain shadowed his eyes.

"Will, you need to get to the hospital. Let them take a proper look at you. They can give you something for the pain."

"Yeah, that's probably not a bad idea. It feels like a buffalo sat on my chest."

Pete strode up to the stretcher. "Better than a bullet," he said with a dry smile. "Lucky for you, I was already on my way through the doorway when the first shot rang out. I arrived just as O'Connor stumbled out, looking petrified. You flew backwards and I realized you'd been hit. Savannah came from nowhere and attacked the shooter. She deflected his arm and he was unable to get off the other shot."

Will turned his head to face her, his eyes wide. "You saved my life."

She looked away, pleased but embarrassed.

"I'm sorry about your brother, Savannah," Pete murmured. "If I'd had any choice..." His eyes clouded over with regret.

Her smile disintegrated. "You did what you had to do. Dylan made his own choices. I was there, remember? If it wasn't for you, Will would be the one on his way to the morgue."

He shrugged uncomfortably. "The paramedics said Dylan died instantly."

"I guess that's a good thing." Savannah came around the side of the stretcher and hugged Pete tightly. "Please don't beat yourself up about it. Even I accept Dylan was an adult. Only he was responsible for his actions and their consequences."

Her gaze returned to Will's pale face. "I can't tell you enough how thankful I am that you saved Will's life. I don't know how I'm ever going to repay you."

Pete looked away, embarrassed. His voice was gruff with emotion. "Don't be silly. Will would have done the same thing for me."

"Too right," Will readily agreed. "But that doesn't mean I won't be eternally grateful." He reached for Pete's hand. "Thanks, mate. I owe you one."

Pete colored, but returned the handshake. "Just get yourself better so you can get back on the job. We're short staffed as it is."

Will smiled and closed his eyes. A few moments later, he opened them again, his expression fierce. "We scored one for the good guys today." He looked past both of them toward the clear, blue sky above him. "And one for you, too, baby brother."

The waiting paramedic cleared his throat. "Come on, let's get you to Prince Alfred Hospital. You need to get those ribs checked out to make sure none of them are broken. Taking a bullet like that can still cause damage, even though it's not lethal." He wheeled the stretcher over to the waiting ambulance.

Savannah watched until the doors closed behind Will. She turned back to Pete. "What happened to Max and Maranoa?"

"They've been taken back to the station. We'll interview them and then lay charges. They're going to be spending quite some time looking at four square walls."

She shuddered, still trying to come to terms with the knowledge her boss and her brother were tied up in such despicable activities. A sudden thought occurred to her.

"Pete, what about the girls? What's going to happen to them?"

"It's okay. "I've spoken to the guys in immigration. They've had their eye on Maranoa for a while. They knew we were investigating him for drug importation. They decided to let us have first go at him." He shrugged. "Everyone felt for those girls, but the drug operation had far more implications for the wider community."

She bit off a protest, knowing he was right. At least now they'd be safe."What's going to happen to them?"

He shrugged again. "I guess it depends on immigration. They'll probably be sent back to Thailand." He turned back to her. "You need to get yourself to the hospital, too. That nose looks broken and the gash under your eye could probably do with some stitches."

Savannah touched a tentative finger to her injuries. "Yes, doctor."

"If we go now, we should be there by the time Will's seen by the medical staff."

Savannah sighed gratefully. Now that the drama was over, the pain in her face had become more pronounced. Her nose and lip felt twice their normal size. Her cheek throbbed. "Thanks, Pete." She frowned down at her ankle ravaged by the blister. "That would be great."

Thankfully, Pete's unmarked vehicle was close by. She climbed in and sighed with relief. Her head dropped backward on the head rest. She drew in deep breaths of air and did her best to come to terms with all that had happened.

She was inordinately grateful Will had survived the ordeal relatively unscathed and the whole sordid brothel business had been resolved, but she couldn't help the heavy pit of sadness that had lodged deep in her belly when she thought of Dylan.

Her head knew what she'd told Pete was right, but it wasn't that easy for her heart to accept and believe it. The guilt of failure still weighed heavily. Perhaps it always would.

She thought of her parents and knew they would have been devastated over the loss of their son, but proud of the part she'd played in seeing justice done. No matter what happened, she was going to have one hell of a story.

She thought of Will and the all-encompassing love she felt for him. Despite the pain in her face, a gentle smile curved her lips and calmed her racing pulse. She clung to the feeling, recognizing it as hope. She pictured their future together and let the healing joy of that scene trickle into her heart.

CHAPTER 30

Three weeks later

Will strode into the living room where Savannah was unpacking the last of her things.

"That was Andy on the phone. He's passed the course! He's now a fully certified police negotiator." The grin on Will's face couldn't get any wider. Savannah returned it. Will had already told her about Andy's past and why becoming a negotiator was so important to him. She couldn't wait to meet a man she'd already heard so much about and couldn't help but admire.

"That's fantastic, Will. He must be thrilled."

"Yep, about as thrilled as I am to be out of that hospital and to have you here with me for good. And not only that, Pete's extended my leave for another week. We have all the time in the world to get to know each other better." He pulled her into his arms and bent his head and nuzzled the side of her neck.

Savannah pulled away, looking up at him dryly. "Don't think you're getting away with it that easily. I'm happy for Andy, but we need to talk about this—us—before you make me forget we still haven't dealt with it. I didn't want to say anything while you were recovering, but now..."

He sighed and set her away from him. "You're right. We need to talk."

"Okay. Are we going to be mature about this?"

"Yeah, I think we can be adult about it, don't you?" His gaze remained steady on hers.

"I'd like to think so." She moved to sit on the leather couch in the living room. Curling her feet underneath her, she looked up at him. "Are you going to sit down?"

He grinned slowly and moved toward her. He took a seat in the opposite corner of the modular couch.

She rolled her eyes. "You could come a little closer, you know."

"I'm still a little mad at you, remember? And I'm still waiting for *your* apology."

"Okay, then. I'm sorry for deceiving you about where I was going that night. From the moment you told me you were going to the Black Opal, I'd made up my mind to come along, despite your objections. It was wrong and I shouldn't have done it."

His gaze challenged at her. "Why can I hear a "but" coming?"

A wry grin tugged at her lips. "Probably because there *is* one coming."

He sighed. "Okay, let's hear it." He leaned back and stretched his legs out in front of him.

"The reason I didn't say anything at the time was because you wouldn't have let me go. You'd already flatly refused to discuss it when I'd tried to tell you I was going. I didn't want to go behind your back, but you didn't leave me any choice."

His eyes narrowed. The glint of earlier humor evaporated. "Oh, so it's *my* fault, is it?" He stood and paced the floor in front of her.

"You could have gotten yourself killed that night, Savannah. Do you realize that? You had no *idea* who you were dealing with. Vince Maranoa had been in and out of jail since he was a teenager. He was a career criminal with a record as long as your arm. Do you even know what that means?" He and threw his hands up in the air.

Despite her best intentions, Savannah's anger ignited.

Pushing herself off the couch, she came to stand next to him, throwing her head back so she could look him in the eyes.

"Of course I do. What do you think I am? I knew he'd had a troubled past—"

"Ha! Troubled past! Talk about understatement. The man did twelve years for murder when he was twenty-five. He's risen to become the Mr Big of Sydney's underworld and is a suspect in at least four other homicides. And there you were, dressed as a prostitute, flirting with him—all for some goddamned front page *story!*"

Savannah did her best to control her temper. "Okay, so, you're a little upset about that. I guess I understand your perspective. I'll admit it was a bit reckless of me to return and take the risk Maranoa might realize I wasn't one of his girls. I didn't actually think too much about what I was doing at the time and I certainly didn't plan on coming to Maranoa's notice again." She folded her arms across her chest and stared back at him. "But it wasn't just for some 'goddamned front page story.'"

She held his gaze a moment longer and then looked away from the anger in his eyes. Her own temper dissolved. She lowered herself onto the couch again and drew in a deep breath.

"I went back to find out what Dylan was up to, what he was involved in. I-I'd seen him at the brothel the time before and I needed to find out why he was there."

Will's eyes narrowed in disbelief. "You mean to tell me you saw your brother there that Tuesday night and you didn't *tell* me?"

She looked away. "I-I wasn't absolutely certain it was him. I didn't want to say anything until I knew. And..." She raised her eyes and gazed at him defiantly. "And I wanted to get him away from the place before the police—"

"You were going to *warn* him?" Will shouted, his eyes now wide with incredulity.

"*No!* Yes. I don't know." Savannah shook her head in confusion. "I didn't know what, if any, part he played in the whole thing. I thought he might have been there buying drugs…or something. Please, Will," she said, begging him to understand. "He was my brother. He's all I *had*."

Her voice cracked with emotion. Tears burned her eyes. The stress of the past few weeks caught up with her again. Leaning forward, she buried her face in her hands and sobbed.

Will sighed heavily. He walked the few steps to the couch and sat beside her. He drew her in close against his side and pressed his lips to her hair.

"*Shh*, sweetheart. It's okay. Please don't cry. I hate it when you cry."

Savannah drew in a deep breath and made an effort to stem the flow of her tears. Will handed her his handkerchief and she accepted it with a grateful smile. They sat in silence for a few moments. When he spoke again, his voice shook with emotion.

"When I saw you with Maranoa, I couldn't breathe. Until that moment when you were with Dylan in the warehouse, I don't think I'd ever been so terrified in all of my life. I wanted to run over there and drag you away from him. When he put his hands all over you, I had to force myself not to leap over the tables and throw my fist in his face." He shook his head, his expression fierce.

"I couldn't do any of those things. That was the problem: I couldn't do *anything*. I had to stand there and watch while one of the city's most notorious criminals manhandled the woman I loved!" He stared unseeingly at the wall of glass that framed the perfect harbor backdrop.

"The worst part of it was that the woman I loved had *invited* the attention! You stood there, dressed like a prostitute, playing the part like you'd been born doing it and I had to stand back and watch, all the while praying like hell Maranoa wouldn't see through your act."

He drew in a deep breath and blew the air out on another heavy sigh. His gaze burned with a fierce protectiveness. "You didn't know who you were dealing with, Savannah. You thought he was just a guy who made a few wrong decisions and ended up in jail. You now have some idea about the evil Maranoa was capable of. He turned your brother into a killer. Some people are born without a soul, without a conscience. He's one of them. You can't imagine my terror when I saw you there with him, or how helpless I felt not able to do a damned thing about it."

She leaned over and squeezed his hand. Her voice was just above a whisper.

"I'm sorry. I really am." She cleared her throat. "I didn't think he was a good guy, but I admit I didn't know what you did about him. The worst thing is, I don't even think if I had known, it would've made any difference. All I wanted to do was to find out about my brother. Will," she pleaded, "tell me you understand? All I wanted to do was find out about my brother." Her voice was raspy with emotion. "I didn't mean to make you feel so scared."

With a groan of capitulation, he pulled her into his arms and held her tight. As he drew in a deep breath and inhaled the scent of her freshly washed hair the tension eased out of him.

He pulled slightly away, but kept his arms around her. "I'm sorry for telling you what to do. I should have given you a chance to explain. I would still have told you to stay home, but at least you would've known *why* I didn't want you to go instead of assuming I'd decided I could order you around because we'd slept together. It wasn't meant to come out like that. I guess I reacted instinctively, knowing what I did about Maranoa." When she turned her face up to his, he looked steadily into her eyes.

"I love you, Savannah O'Neill, more than I've loved anyone in my life. I hope you understand that's the only reason I ordered you to stay away from the place. I wanted to protect you, to keep you safe. Do you have any inkling what I'm talking about?"

She reached up and kissed him softly on the lips. "Yes, and I'm sorry for the grief I put you through." She smiled. "Next time, I'll ask a few more questions when you order me to do something."

Will returned her smile. "Next time, I'll explain myself a little bit better rather than coming across all macho and autocratic."

"Deal." She threw him a cheeky look and tugged his T-shirt out of his shorts. His eyes darkened with emotion. She slid her hands under the shirt and worked her fingers up over the smooth expanse of taut muscle. Careful to avoid his bruised chest, her nails scraped across his nipples. He drew in a sharp breath and tensed.

"Don't start something you can't finish, Red."

She glanced up at him. "Oh, I have every intention of finishing." Her tongue replaced her fingernails and flicked across the hard nubs.

He moaned and leaned back into the couch until he lay flat with his back against the leather cushions. She followed him down and continued her sensual attack, pressing herself against the length of him while her tongue worked its magic over his skin.

Awareness surged through her. Within moments, his erection pushed insistently against the softness of her belly. She moved her body higher until his hardness pressed against her clit. Grinding her hips against him, she couldn't contain her moan of pleasure.

She pulled his wallet out of the back pocket of his shorts and tossed it to the floor before tugging at his waistband. Freeing his cock from the constraints of his underwear, she took him in her mouth. Sucking and licking, she stroked her hand along his shaft, feeling him grow even harder under her ministrations.

Her own need grew. She was hot and wet and pulsed with excitement.

"You make me so hard."

She barely heard him over her pounding heart. He massaged her scalp with his fingers, holding her head while she continued to suck his cock.

"I like making you hard." She swirled her tongue around the tip before dipping into his slit. She tasted pre-come on her lips. She pulled away and slid her shorts down her hips.

Lifting her arms high, she tugged her T-shirt over her head, leaving on her black lace panties and matching bra.

Straddling his hips, she pressed her lace-covered wet center against his hard cock, rubbing the moist tip over her aching clit. The pressure was almost unbearable. Waves of pleasure built inside her.

Will reached up and squeezed her breasts, kneading them through her bra. His thumbs flicked over her nipples, turning them into solid nubs of need. Unable to bear the torment a moment longer, Savannah reached down and pulled aside the lacy fabric of her panties just enough so that his cock rested against her opening. Taking it in her hand, she rubbed it up and down her wet slit, moaning at the erotic sensations it created.

"I want you," she moaned.

Needing no further encouragement, Will reached down and fumbled for his wallet. Removing a condom, he rolled it swiftly over his cock. He shifted his hips and thrust into her, sinking into her warmth. She cried out and moved her hips. Rising and falling, she lifted herself up and down his shaft. As she climbed ever closer to orgasm, her rhythm picked up its pace.

Will tugged at her bra, freeing her breasts so that they bounced wildly above him as she continued to bump and grind on his cock. Pulling at her nipples, he lifted his head and suckled one of them. Her moan of need drew a smile. Switching his attention to the other one, he continued the sweet torture with his mouth.

Savannah ground her pelvis against his. "I'm going to come. Will, I'm going to come." He nipped at her nipple. She gasped and fell over the edge. Waves of orgasm pulsed inside her. She collapsed on top of him, panting.

Seconds later, he flipped her onto her back. He spread her legs wide, edged her panties to the side and plunged into her slickness. Thrusting hard, he pounded into her, pulling her legs around his waist and tightening his hold on her hips.

"Look at me." His voice was a soft command. "I want you to watch me when I come."

Opening her eyes, she held his gaze and tightened her legs around his waist.

Thrusting harder and faster, his body took over. With a yelp of exhilaration, he tensed and spent himself inside her. Gasping for breath, he fell on top of her.

After a few moments, she squirmed underneath him. Will shifted his weight off her and lay on his side, drawing her close.

Savannah chuckled. "If that was what they call make-up sex, I'm all for a few disagreements now and then."

He gave her a light swat on her butt which was still encased in the lacy underwear.

"Cheeky girl."

She sobered and stared up at him. "I can't believe how close I came to losing you."

His eyes darkened. "I'm not going anywhere." He kissed her hard on the mouth. "And neither are you."

Contentment and an overwhelming love rushed through her. He was hers and she was his. It was exactly how it was meant to be.

"What's the latest with Max and Maranoa?" she asked quietly a few moments later.

"The DPP told me Max was trying to do a deal: a reduced sentence in return for full and frank disclosure in the witness box. Max has a clean record. The judge will go easier on him. I can't say the same for Maranoa."

Anger and sadness warred inside Savannah. She compressed her lips against the surge of emotion. "Max's capitulation doesn't come as a surprise. I never saw him as a man with a lot of courage."

"Yeah, well, I'm glad he's decided to give evidence for the prosecution. He may be guilty of making less than ideal decisions, but Vince was the mastermind. We found proof amongst the papers in his office that his involvement in the illegal drug industry goes back decades. We also found traces of cocaine and heroin all over the floor of an old bunker built beneath the brothel. It was obviously his hidey-hole before the warehouse."

Savannah closed her eyes against the memories. She drew in a deep breath and let it out on a heartfelt sigh. "I'm so glad you walked out of there."

Will smiled and tightened his hold on her. "Well, not exactly *walked*, but I know what you mean."

"I love you so much. I don't ever want to have to imagine life without you."

His eyes darkened with emotion. He bent his head and pressed another kiss against her lips. "Just so you know, I intend to live a long, long time. You're not going to get rid of me that easily."

Epilogue

One month later

The cool ocean breeze tasted of salt and sunshine. It swept over Will and Savannah where they stood on the rugged cliff-top that overlooked Bondi. They each held an urn in their hands.

The light wind ruffled Savannah's loose hair and tossed it into her eyes. She reached up and swept the errant strands behind her ears. Will held out his free hand and she took it in hers.

They stared out across the pristine blue of the Pacific Ocean. The sun glinted off the wide expanse of golden sand below.

"Dylan loved to come here when he was younger. We'd go swimming in the surf and exploring in the rock pools. Mom and Dad would buy us ice cream before we left. We had some good times."

Will tightened his hold on her hand. "Cole loved Bondi, too. Most weekends, he'd take his board out and ride the waves. He could spend hours out there."

Savannah filled her lungs with the salty air. Exhaling on a sigh, she braced herself for the final step. In mutual, unspoken agreement, they opened their urns.

The wind immediately teased at the ashes. Small wisps of dust swirled and caught in the air. Her throat tightened.

Tears of sadness and regret burned behind her eyes.

She turned to Will. A myriad of emotions chased their way across his face. Sorrow. Regret. Acceptance. Peace. He lifted his urn and swung it in a wide arc. Ash flew across the cliff-top. It was picked up by the wind and scattered on the sand below.

"Good-bye, Cole. I hope you're in a better place."

A lump caught in her throat at the raw emotion in his voice. She took another deep breath and scattered Dylan's ashes. A seagull rose from the water below, its plaintive cry a fitting background.

She thought of Dylan and the choices he'd made—and the ones he hadn't. He was on his own now, just like he'd wanted.

Hot tears spilled over and ran down her cheeks, tasting even saltier than the air. She'd done all she could. Will had helped her understand and believe that.

His arm tightened around her shoulders and he pulled her in close against his side. Her arm came around his waist. She leaned into him and breathed in his solid strength.

"Pete called a little while ago," he said quietly. "Lucy gave birth a couple of hours ago. A healthy baby girl. They've named her after their respective mothers: Margaret Joan. They're calling her "Maggie" for short. Mother and baby are doing fine."

Happiness burst inside her at the news. She smiled. "How fantastic! I'm so glad everything is okay. Wow, a little girl! Lucy will be thrilled."

"I think Pete's every bit the proud daddy, too. I know I would be."

His gaze captured hers, dark with emotion. Love and hope and anticipation surged through her. They'd laid their past to rest. It was now time to look toward the future.

Together.

Note to Readers

I do hope you have enjoyed reading Will and Savannah's story. Please feel free to leave a review for The Deception. Every review is appreciated and really helps a new author like me.

The Negotiator is Book Six of the Munro Family Series and is Andy and Cally's story. You met Andy in The Deception as Will's friend and fellow detective. Cally is also familiar to those of you who have read The Investigator. She appears briefly in that story as Kate Collins' high school friend. Both Andy and Cally have had difficult childhoods and I'm sure once you've read their story, you'll agree with me that both of them more than deserve their happy ending.

Here's a sneak peek:

*When ten-year-old **Andy Warwick** witnesses the murder/suicide of his sister and father, his world is torn apart. Twenty years later, despite his tragic childhood, Andy's a highly respected police negotiator based in North Sydney. He's living a comfortable life, but still suffers from guilt-ridden nightmares from his past and yearns for a family to replace the one he lost.*

*Sixteen, pregnant and abandoned by those she loved, **Cally Savage** learned early to fend for herself, but raising a son on her own hasn't come without a price. It's a decade after Jack's birth, but she's struggling to make ends meet,* *despite her part time job as a cleaner at the North Sydney Police Station. On top of her financial woes, her house has recently been burgled and she's terrified the perpetrator might return…*

In desperation Cally turns to the hot looking detective at the station and seeks Andy's permission to place a "roommate wanted" advertisement on the noticeboard in the squad room. Attracted to Cally's innocent beauty and intrigued by the vulnerability in her eyes, Andy offers to move in with her. The more he gets to know her, the more he wants to be part of her life. But first, he has to break through the barriers she's erected around her heart…

Just when things appear to be on track, the man who believed for more than ten years that his child had been aborted, discovers Cally's deceit. Enraged, he vows not to give up until he's found his son and punished the woman who lied to him…

The Negotiator will be released on 13 October, 2014. If you would like to subscribe to my newsletter to receive news on upcoming Munro Family stories, release dates, book launches and other snippets, please go to my website at www.christaylorauthor.com.au and follow the link. I love to hear from my readers. Please feel free to contact me at christaylor@antmail.com.au Let me know who your favorite Munro family member is.

About The Author

Chris Taylor grew up on a farm in north-west New South Wales, Australia. She always had a thirst for stories and recalls writing her first book at the ripe old age of eight. Always a lover of romance and happily-ever-afters, a career in criminal law sparked her interest in intrigue and suspense. For Chris to be able to combine romance with suspense in her books is a dream come true.

Chris is married to Linden and is the mother of five children. If not behind her computer, you can find her doing the school run, taxiing children to swimming lessons, football, ballet and cricket. In her spare time, Chris loves to read her favorite authors who include Richard North Patterson, Sandra Brown, Kathleen E Woodiwiss and Jude Devereaux.

You can find out more about Chris and sign up for her newsletter at her website:

http://www.christaylorauthor.com.au